Chaz Brenchley has made a living as a writer since he was eighteen; this year marks his twenty-first anniversary. He is the author of a dozen novels for adults, and one book of short stories; he has also published three books for children and some poetry. He lives in Newcastle on Tyne, with two cats and a famous teddy bear.

Tower of the King's Daughter

THE FIRST BOOK OF OUTREMER

Chaz Brenchley

ORBIT

An *Orbit* book

First published in Great Britain by Orbit 1998

Copyright © Chaz Brenchley 1998

The moral right of the author has been asserted.

Visit Chaz Brenchley's web-site at
http://www.geocities.com/SoHo/Museum/3558

A CIP catalogue record for this book is
available from the British Library.

ISBN 1 85723 692 0

Typeset in Adobe Garamond by M Rules
Printed and bound in Great Britain
by Mackays of Chatham PLC

Orbit
A Division of
Little, Brown and Company (UK)
Brettenham House
Lancaster Place
London WC2E 7EN

Best things come in big packages.
The start of something this big,
it has to be for Ian.

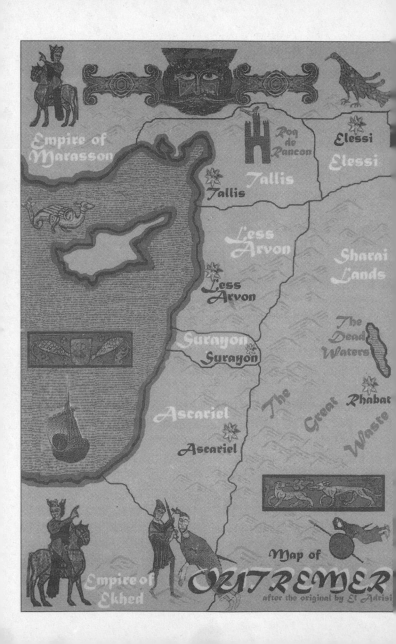

Empire of
Marasson

Roq
de
Rancon

Elessi
Elessi

Tallis
Tallis

Less
Arvon

Sharai
Lands

Less
Arvon

The
Dead
Waters

Surayon
Surayon

Ascariel

The

Great

Rhabat

Waste

Ascariel

Map of
OUTREMER
after the original by El Adrisi

Empire of
Ekhed

Cher a tort unt ses fieuz saiziz;
Bien en devums aveir dolur,
Cher la fud Deu primes servi
E reconnu pur segnuur.

— CRUSADER SONG,
ANON, *c.* 1143

PART ONE

The Road to the Roq

Despite what the church claimed and the people believed, this was still a Kingdom born of younger sons, the land-hungry and the dispossessed.

And those sons were fathers now, they had sons of their own; and their landless younger sons were looking north and east and south themselves, finding this realm of Outremer too tight a glove, seeing no border – internal or outward-facing – invulnerable to change.

The Kingdom of the Hammer they called it, drinking late and talking, always talking in the halls of their fathers: from its shape and from their own aggressive yearnings to see that hammer fall and crush, beat out new territories for the needy.

But the church preached contentment, as ever, *we have what we came for*; and their fathers preached security and caution, *we have all that we can hold*.

And the wisest among them, churchman or father or younger son – or daughter – looked at the land unblinkered, and saw that in truth this was not even one Kingdom, for all that it had one King and many public oaths. Too quarrelsome, these exiles, these families far from kin; they were four states – four and one, but that one closed, that one Folded and never now to be named, torn from maps and memory both – and always in contention, always wrangling each with the others. And of course always, always at war with the world around.

No, the wisest said, this cannot last. It cannot live. A hundred years, perhaps, they gave Outremer; no more than that. Certainly, no more . . .

1

The Bright Dead of the Day

Not the first, Marron knelt in the Chamber of the King's Eye and thought, *What need Ascariel?* Why had his father, had so many fathers fought and died to win possession of that golden city, that dream of priests and kings, when it seemed that they had it all already? When the dream and the deaths and the very Mount itself could be contained within a bare room rock-hewn and chilly, where the walls sweated sour-tasting water and it needed only a single plaited candle and the words of a fat and sour-sweating brother to bring forth miracles?

The thought, of course, was heresy. It should be confessed, and due reparation made. But Marron was fresh come from far away, gentler country where he'd seen no more true magic than the seasons' changes, the hand of blessing laid upon the land; his mind was dizzy with wonder, and it was from that unaccustomed whirling strangeness in his head that the words and the idea had been flung up, all unintended. He thought both souls of the God would understand him.

Besides, his troop had burned a village for heresy only the day before, and he was afraid of his confessor.

It had seemed like a celebration, he remembered thinking even at the time, in the heat and the hard light and the *hurry, hurry* urgency of it all. Not the human arm of the God's justice wielded, but only something done in madness to mark the end of a long march and their new home almost in sight now, very much on their minds. They'd been too many days in the saddle, a storm had forced them ashore too soon; days and days of eating tack and sleeping on dusty earth and riding, riding: the sun savage above the alien hills, their bodies baked as dry as the road they followed, vows resurgent in their minds and untried steel impatient at their backs, seeming as hot and as thirsty as they were themselves.

And Fra' Piet had led them away from the road one morning, promising them the castle by tomorrow sunset and the God's work now; and they had followed a track high into the hills till they came at the bright dead of the day to close-shuttered huts with domed roofs and ragged mud-mortared walls, two dozen such and a well, and a temple of dressed stone at the heart of the village. And the heresy was there, clear to be seen on a weathered board above the temple's door: the Blinded Eyes, the double loop that was the sign of the God Divided but with the hollow spaces filled as though to say His unremittingly watchful eyes were closed, now and always. Fra' Piet had warned them of worse in these hills, of the sign painted with a fringe of lashes below, to say that the God slept; but that was deliberate defiance, a sign of Catari revolt. This, these blank circles were something entirely other.

The Heresy of Korash: that the God moved indeed on His doubled path but that He gave no heed to mortal men, that He cared not a whit for their deeds on the earth. Though Korash had been redeemed by fire and his bones crushed to powder two hundred years ago, he still had his adherents, here particularly, in these hills long lost to the voice of the true church. So they had been told, Marron and his new-sworn brothers, and so it had proved.

They had ridden into that hilltop village, three dozen men with the ache of their weary road still on them, hungry for more than food. Fra' Piet's disfigured hands had swung the axe that smashed that sacrilegious sign, it had been his hoarse voice that called down fire and steel and his own weapon again that hacked the black-robed priest on the temple steps. After that, though, he had only sat his horse and watched. It had been a test, Marron thought later, or a challenge; perhaps a baptism.

One half of a baptism, he thought now, the opening rite. This was the completion, here under the castle, a gift of marvel from the King's Eye.

They had been mad that day, young men crazed by the sun, drawn and deadly. They had screamed, he remembered, louder than the women and the children both; now they were mute, transfixed. In themselves emblems of the God, turning and turning, each one a traveller on two paths: to the savage, to the serene. Looping always to the centre, to the Godhead, and always passing through . . .

Not an hour had passed since their arrival. They'd ridden up the precipitous hill and through the gate of the awesome castle, up the broad shallow steps and the long covered ramp that followed, as weary as their horses and stained with more than travel now. In the courtyard by the inner moat their packs and mounts had been taken from them by thin black-haired boys, Sharai slaves, someone had said; and without even the chance to change their habits or rinse the caked dust from their skins they had been ordered to silence although they were silent already, and led up another ramp too narrow for horses and so into the castle proper. Then down: down and down they had come, soon confused by the winding stairs and the ill-lit passages, shivering in the sudden chill and the uncertainty.

At last a door, cedarwood bound with iron; and beyond that, this. Nothing like the great halls and pillared spaces they'd heard of and not yet seen, caught like bubbles of air in the mass of rock and stone above their heads; a troop of men made this chamber crowded. Where they knelt in a rough circle, each brother's legs and shoulders brushed his neighbours' on either side, but the touch of another human was nothing but relief here. Even the smell of his brothers' bodies and his own too long unwashed, the rank heavy odour of woollen habits damp with sweat, gave Marron something to cling to, something to root him to the known world in a place of wonder and terror strangely mixed.

What is this? was the question they must all have been asking silently as they had filed in behind the brother with the torch. None had spoken it aloud, but Marron had seen it in their eyes as they'd glanced at each other and at the crudely rounded walls and the uneven floor, as some few of

them had reached to touch damp rock and carry the wetness on their fingers to dusty lips. He had done that himself,
and then had wanted to spit, had swallowed instead though
his mouth had twisted at the rancid taste of it.

The brother with the torch, Fra' Tumis had gestured
them into a circle and then onto their knees, his heavy-
jowled face frowning with suspicion as his narrow eyes had
flickered around watching for disobedience, for someone to
speak against his order. Denied that, he had at last spoken
himself, though only to say, 'This is the Chamber of the
King's Eye,' which had told them nothing. Then he had
gone to the only furniture in the chamber, an iron tripod
holding a four-wicked candle, two white and two black
tapers plaited and twisted into a single column.

He had lit the wicks from his torch before handing that
across the kneeling circle to Fra' Piet, who had carried it
outside and closed the door behind him.

Somehow the click of the latch had set a shiver to run
down Marron's spine, nothing to do with cold or rank wet
air. Fra' Piet scared him, to be sure; but it was a fear born of
knowledge and witness, many weeks in the man's company
and one frantic hour caught in his madness, or else brought
by him into the pitiless possession of the God. That fear
Marron could understand and deal with; it was good sense,
to be afraid of Fra' Piet.

This was different. Here he was ignorant and bewildered and his brothers the same, strangers both to the land
and to the life. Only a few short months since, they had
been yeomen or artisans or peasants in another world. Fra'
Piet was their bridge from that to this; he was their mentor,
albeit harsh in his demands and obsessive in his duties; he

was a rock in an ocean, craggy and dangerous and dependable. And he had left them suddenly in the hands of an unknown, in this bare hand-hewn cave of a chamber, and Fra' Tumis had seemed bored or contemptuous or both but not at all fearful and yet Marron was fearful of him, or of what he meant to do.

What Fra' Tumis meant was a mystery; what he did had been hard enough to see, in the moving shadows of the candle's light. Harder still after he had glared around the circle and then stabbed one hand sharply downward, redirecting their nervous, curious stares to laps or folded hands or the dark damp stone they knelt on.

Marron had lowered his head obediently, but no will of his or any other's could have stopped his eyes from spying, as best they could. It had seemed to him, in what bare glimpses he dared risk, that Fra' Tumis held his hands above the bending flames of the candle, to cup the light within his fingers; it had seemed as if that pudgy flesh went too close, there should have been a smell of singeing and a yelp of pain.

But Tumis had chanted softly, and his voice at least was sweet. The words, the language Marron didn't know. Nor did he know how there could have been more light suddenly in the chamber and not less, when Tumis' hands guarded the candle so nearly. Light there was, though, fierce white light that had made him squint, that had drawn hisses of breath from all around the circle, that had made his neighbour – *Aldo, for the love of your skin, be still!* – grunt and draw his hood up over his head, to shade dazzled eyes within it.

*

Light, they had been taught, *is the chief token of the God's even-handedness, that we walk half our time in the sun and half in darkness. It is His gift to us, that we may see our way to virtue; it is also an instrument of His justice, that others may see our sin.*

This was light as Marron had never known it, though, light they had made no space for in his theology. This light drew lines of gold and fire in the air, and not only Aldo was moving now. Men were making the sign of the God against their brows, more in superstition than in prayer, Marron thought; but he gave them only a glance, only a moment before his eyes and his mind were gripped again.

This hard light came, it seemed, from the candle: flames rose above it like glass, like white-hot rods of glass, so rigid and so still. The walls of the chamber were in shadow, though Tumis had snatched his hands away now; Tumis also stood in shadow, though he stood only a pace back from the candle. Fragile and strong as skeins of silk drawn taut, all the light there was struck down to the heart of the brothers' circle, and there it showed them wonders.

You will see miracles, they had been told before ever they set out for the Sanctuary Land, *you will see miracles and monsters; be prepared.*

But how could they ever have prepared their minds for this?

'This is the King's Eye,' Fra' Tumis intoned, against their staring, straining silence. 'It is the God's benediction upon the King, that he may watch over all this land in the God's name, to guard the borders from the God's enemies and the heartlands from heresy. It is the King's kindness to

his subjects, that he gives this blessing also to the Church
Militant, that we may serve the better.'

Was this kindness? Marron was unsure. He sweated cold
in that cold place, his fingers trembled with the beat of his
blood; this was the second time in two days that he had
been stricken to the core of him and the blade in his heart
was not more than half of wonder. The rest was sheer terror.

The light drew lines like golden wires, and planes like
sheets of gold; it drew walls and domes and minarets; it
built a palace or a temple in miniature, like a princess's
golden toy only that this toy burned their eyes, its making
burned their minds like a brand, and it lay still in the air a
hand's span above the floor.

'This is the Dir'al Shahan in Ascariel,' said Tumis, 'that
was their greatest temple when the Ekhed governed the
city. It would have been destroyed,' *it should have been
destroyed* his voice seemed to say, 'when the God gave us
victory there; but the King decreed otherwise, and took it
for his own. Now it is his palace, and the seat of his power.'

And it turned in the air and seemed to move further off,
from all sides at once; and as it moved so other buildings
flowed into the light, and streets, and vast gardens on steep
slopes and a river below, and . . .

'This is Ascariel,' said Tumis, when all the city on its
high hill was before them, gleaming golden in that foetid
air; and Marron thought, *What need the real world, then,
what needed all those deaths?*

Marron had seen maps, in the library of the great abbey
where he had made his profession. He had even seen a map
of these lands, though that had been Sharai work looted at

the fall of Ascariel and sent back as a gift to the abbot, and he could not read it. He had been shown the holy city by an elder brother there, who understood the strange writing; only a mark of coloured ink on parchment, but still he had felt a thrill to lay his finger on it and murmur the name, *Ascariel!*

This, though – this was more than a map, more even than a map of light and magic. This was the blessed land itself, brought forth in glory. It seemed to him that he had seen guards around the King's palace, figures in the streets, horses and wagons and a busy marketplace. Even now there was a shimmer of gold, like a string of beads being drawn slowly through a tiny gate in the outer wall, and he thought that was a merchant's caravan come to trade in the city.

Fra' Tumis brought his hands close to those glassy pillars of light rising from the candle, and chanted words that Marron could distinguish but not comprehend. White faded to yellow, pillars shrank to normal flame and Ascariel was gone.

Like men waking from a dream, Marron and his brothers stirred and shifted, worked their shoulders against a dying tension, gazed at each other's awestruck faces and knew they saw there reflections of their own.

Looking at Tumis, Marron saw him pale and sweating, trembling, rubbing wet hands on his habit. No shell of supercilious boredom on him now, and no contempt.

'Go,' he said, his voice also drained of its strength and self-content. 'Go out, Fra' Piet will show you where . . .'

They filed out as they had filed in, in silence. Fra' Piet was waiting in the corridor, thin-lipped, grim-lipped as ever, but nodding in satisfaction as he read their faces. There was a man, Marron thought, who would never need to see the miracle twice. A vision once witnessed would live in his sight forever, a burning testament to faith and a private covenant between himself and the God. This might have been how it began for him, Marron thought: that he had come to Outremer like Marron himself, a young man no more than ordinarily devout, impelled as much by family history as by religion; that he like Marron had been shown Ascariel in that dank dungeon, like a sending; and that for Fra' Piet at least the fire had never dimmed since, that he had discovered a true vocation then and had sought only the direct path since, the glory of a golden city blinding him to pleasures of the body or the mind, or any earthly glint of light.

Numbed and dazzled, Marron could see that path threatening for himself also, could feel it almost opening like a pit beneath his feet, waiting only for his mind to lose its hold on anything but wonder . . .

But Fra' Piet brought them no sermons, nor – thank the God! – another miracle; he only led them back the way they'd come, up to the moat and the courtyard and the dry hot dusty wind. There were the stables, where their horses dozed now in wooden stalls in cool stone shadow, groomed and watered and revived; but here blessedly was the bath-house, and here were boys in white tunics fetching water in leather buckets from the moat. Here at last was the time to jerk and wriggle free of the heavy habit, to kick off stiff riding-boots, to leave all in a heap in a corner and fight to be first to a bucket; and then to shudder under the sluice of chill water down his back and through his matted hair, to chase the shudder with a laugh and earn Fra' Piet's scowl for laughing. To turn away, rubbing at wet skin, catch Aldo's eye and share a private grin; and in that moment to feel the spell fade, not leave him but recede into the secret spaces of his mind, where it could be kept safe and treasured but not allowed to rule his thinking beyond reason.

Pushing his fingers through his hair and looking around, impatient for another bucket, Marron saw a boy carrying a wooden box. He took it first to Fra' Piet, who grunted and dipped his twisted fingers in, scooping out a handful of something soft and greyish. Marron watched him massage the paste across his lean, scarred body, raising a froth which he rinsed away with fresh water; then the boy caught Marron's gaze, took it for a summons and came across.

Marron peered uncertainly into the box, and asked, 'What is this?'

'Soap,' the boy said in a light singsong. 'For washing.'

The word meant nothing. The paste felt greasy between Marron's cautious finger and thumb, but Fra' Piet had shown him its use; he took a dollop on his fingers and stroked it onto his arm, rubbing at it till he raised a thin grey lather, as on a horse after hard running. When he wiped it away, a swathe of skin showed startlingly pink, in a place he thought he'd washed already. He gave the boy a grin, received a shy smile in return and took more of the soap, working that across his shoulders and neck and into his hair, feeling it foam more stiffly there.

'Not for the eyes!' the boy said urgently, too late. Marron had already rubbed his face with frothy fingers.

His eyes burned suddenly; he gasped, pressing the heels of his hands against them, barely hearing the boy call out in a liquid, foreign tongue.

Searing pain, and then the cool flow of water over his head again. He reached to cup it in his hands and rinsed his eyes as best he could, blinking hard. Two boys there were now, one with a bucket; Marron scooped out handfuls of water and splashed his face until the burning eased.

'Not for the eyes,' the first boy said again, trying another smile.

'No,' Marron agreed wholeheartedly. And not for the mouth either; he'd had a taste of that lather, and his tongue and lips were burning. He rinsed his mouth and spat; but still took more of the paste – *soap, remember the name of it* – before the boy was called away to another curious brother. It hadn't burned his skin, at least, though it made his fingertips pucker; and he felt scoured clean where he'd used it, cleaner than he could remember.

Discipline seemed temporarily in abeyance, even here, within the Order's walls; unaccustomed time they were given, to wash themselves. Marron soaped Aldo's back for him and Aldo his, and they fetched more water from the moat to rinse each other, as other brothers were doing all around them. They drank also, surreptitiously at first – *obedience is the prime commandment, children: to do what you have not been ordered to do is disobedience* – and then openly, after they'd seen Fra' Piet do the same.

At last the boys brought linen towels and clean fresh habits; and when Marron and all his troop were dry and dressed and once more under the bleak gaze of their confessor, they were taken barefoot back into the castle and up to a chapel for prayers.

This at least was familiar and undisturbing, old words in an old tongue, rhythms and responses ingrained into Marron's mind since he was an infant.

Familiar also was the way his mind wandered from the words, even here in the God's own land, where he had thought he might have been different, more devout. Not even the blinding revelation of a miracle could work magic on his digressing soul, it seemed. He knelt on the bare stone floor of the chapel with Aldo on his left side and another brother, Jubal, on his right; and his voice murmured steadily with theirs, with everyone's; and his thoughts slipped free, slipped back to a day, an hour not far in time or distance but far indeed, very far in strangeness.

Aldo, friend of his childhood and friend of his youth, in many ways a brother long before they were brothers in religion:

Aldo with his long-known, long-loved face twisted beyond knowing as he leaned sideways in his saddle to throw a flaming torch through an open doorway; Aldo with his laugh tuned harsh and knowing at the scream that came back, at the sight of a woman running out with her robe and hair afire; Aldo who must have seen the woman in there before he threw, who already had his sword in his hand and used it not to kill quickly but to drive her back, back and burning into the burning hut . . .

Jubal, an older man and a stranger before this voyage but all his life a monk, sent to Outremer by his abbot as penance for an offence not to be talked of:

Jubal wide-eyed and screaming, no longer containing heavy thoughts behind his heavy brows; Jubal a better soldier maybe than he ever was a monk, swinging a mace with joy, his bare arm blood-spattered as he hacked, as he kicked his horse on and hacked again, as he screamed; and there were words within his screaming, that was the Credo that ran mixed with spittle from his mouth as he declared his belief in the one true God, twin-souled and all-pervading . . .

And between Aldo and Jubal there was Marron, there was himself; and he had a new image of himself also to wonder at, to shudder at, to come between him and his prayers, him and the God's due worship:

himself on his feet now, slid down from his bucking, frantic horse; himself with a child in his hands, a heretic, a babe snatched from its father's arms and too young yet to be clearly boy or girl; himself gripping its ankles and spinning with the frenzy like a mad priest on the temple steps, stumbling over the body of the priest but catching his balance with a hoarse cry, crazed even to his own ears as he dashed the babe against the stones of the wall there, as he saw its skull split and heard its sudden silence even in all that noise, as he tossed it through the open doorway into the fire within and turned away from the stain, so small a stain it had left on the wall there, a thin smear of red that the first rains would wash away if ever it did rain in this barren, sun-bright land . . .

2

The Devil in the Dust

A barbaric habit, her father called it, veiling women as the
Sharai did; no practice for a civilised land, he called it, but
that had of course not stopped him sending Julianne into
the hands of men whose practice it was.

It was the same with the litter she travelled in. She'd
fought against that – why be carried at a slow walk, she'd
demanded, when she could perfectly well ride her own palfrey, they could mount the whole party and be half the
time on the road? – but her future husband had sent a
palanquin and the men to bear it, and her father had
insisted. Perhaps he'd even been thinking a little of her
comfort, she granted grudgingly, though mostly of course it
was politics, not to offend either custom or a powerful
man.

At any rate, this easy swaying ride on soft cushions was
in honesty no burden to her, nor seemingly to the eight
black giants whose shoulders took the weight of it. They
talked between themselves in soft voices as they went,

though she couldn't understand their speech; they laughed often, with a bubbling and mysterious humour. The men-at-arms who walked beside – also sent by her intended husband – found the journey more testing, though they were soldiers and all they had to carry was their own packs. She watched them sweat in the hard sun, heard them curse in hoarse whispers and saw how their shoulders drooped in the late of the day, how their feet dragged in the dust.

That dust was the devil, throat-choking and harsh; even the men veiled themselves against it when the wind lashed it eye-high and stinging. No, she hated to admit it but she was better here in the palanquin than on horseback in such heat, in such a land. Better to conceal her face behind soft silken curtains than behind a veil that would be soon damp and sticking to her face, soon clogged and filthy and stifling with the dust. Better to be shaded, cool and comfortable, though she had stamped and shouted, stamped and wept for one last freedom, not to be confined until she must.

Oddly, she had neither shouted nor wept against the journey itself. It seemed odd to her, at least. She had thought herself shamed by the palanquin, until she'd seen the truths of sun and dust; but being first taken and now sent to marry a man she'd never met, for reasons of politics and power – surely there should be greater shame in that, for her and for her father? And yet she didn't feel shame, only a cold dread and a great weariness that she thought would never lift hereafter.

She was sixteen, and the weight of her life to come exhausted her. When she thought about it, when her clouded vision turned that way. *Not yet,* she reminded herself

once more; there was another reason to be glad of this slow
procession.

There were panels of gauze let into the curtains, allowing
her to see out quite easily, though they were small and clev-
erly offset so that the men would see nothing clearly within.

There was little enough to be seen outside, though she
watched for hours, her mind dulled by the swaying of the
litter and the slow drift of the endless hills, yellow and grey
with dust, studded with dark thorns and what other bushes
were tough enough to grow in this hard hot land. Hateful
land, she thought it: and wondered what Elessi would be
like. So much nearer to the desert, so much worse than this,
she thought, she feared. No land to ride in, even were she
allowed to ride. A land without shade, without compromise; and its people much the same; and her father the
diplomatist, the smooth and subtle compromiser, sending
her alone into such a country and for all the rest of her
life . . .

And no, she was not, was *not* going to allow her anxieties
and resentments to blight these last few days of travelling.
Deal with what comes, when it comes; you leave the future be.
That had been her milk-mother's advice when she was a
child, and it had always seemed nothing more than good
sense to Julianne. Why be miserable, when cheerful was
always a choice?

Now she felt that choice had gone, or was going. But she
determined to keep despair out of her soul, where it had
never had a place before and would not be granted one so
long as she could fight it.

She turned her gaze forward, only looking for something

to distract her suddenly rebellious mind, teetering on the verge of falling into the pit wherein it was forbidden to fall; and *blessed be the God and all His saints and angels*, there actually was something for once that she could look at.

Not that it seemed so very much at first, just barely enough to pique her interest. Not of course what her soul yearned for, a city the like of Marasson to bring colour and life to parched eyes; neither what her father dreaded more than she did, a horde of bandits sweeping down to overmaster this small troop of men and carry her off into slavery or worse. It was only someone else on the road, a local boy to judge by his size and dress. The sergeant of her guard was speaking to him, though, and not simply to order him out of the way; that was sufficiently unusual to make her curious.

When her litter drew alongside the sergeant's horse, she reached to strike the chime that would call her bearers to a halt, but then didn't need to do so because he gestured them himself to stop. Even through the blurring gauze, she could read consternation and uncertainty on his face.

'What is it, sergeant?' His name was Blaise, but he preferred her to use his rank, for the sake of discipline; and she'd grown accustomed to holding conversations like this, through the curtain. If she drew it aside, she'd have to veil her face to spare his blushes. Though he seemed to be blushing in any case, and she didn't understand that at all.

'My lady, this lad . . . Well, he isn't what he seems to be. He speaks like a noble's son, though he won't give his name or family. And he says we'll find trouble up ahead . . .'

The sergeant's horse danced aside then, to give her a clear view of the boy. Julianne looked, stared, did twitch the curtain aside momentarily to be certain; and then she laughed and said, 'Sergeant, that lad isn't a lad either. She's a girl.'

Sergeant Blaise gaped. The girl was dark and crop-haired like a boy, certainly, and the dirt on her face was enough to hide her lack of any coming beard. She was wearing the rough burnous of a peasant lad, though her soft boots didn't suit that disguise; she should have gone barefoot, Julianne thought. Nor did the pack she carried seem likely to be of local workmanship.

The girl scowled, and spat into the dust of the road; then she shrugged, and threw an easy smile towards the litter's concealing curtains. 'Someone has eyes, at least,' she said, in a clear voice that certainly hadn't grown up in these hills, and Julianne could well understand her sergeant's confusion. 'May I know whose they are?'

So Julianne struck her chime after all, for her bearers' attention, and asked them to set the litter down. She lifted the curtain aside – while Sergeant Blaise turned his face away, and cursed at his men for gawping – and said, 'I am Julianne de Rance. Will you join me?'

That invitation agitated the sergeant further, but before he could forbid her the girl had stooped and slipped into the litter, settling comfortably cross-legged on the cushions as Julianne made room.

'My name is Elisande. And I could wish that you hadn't made me say that,' added with a rueful twist of her mouth.

'Elisande of what family?'

Julianne was trying to learn what Blaise could not, but she had no better fortune, only a shake of the head in response, and, 'You wouldn't know my grandfather.'

'I doubt that,' Julianne said dryly. Many of the lords of Outremer had passed through Marasson in the last ten years or so; of those to whom she hadn't actually made her curtsey, she could still recite their lineages for a dozen generations.

'Truly, you wouldn't.' Elisande was smiling, enjoying the mystery, irritating Julianne a little.

'Then why not give me his name?' she demanded. 'If it will mean nothing to me, it can do no harm.'

'Nor any good, either. And he is a very private man,' said solemnly, but with dancing eyes. 'I think I will keep his privities a little longer, if I may.'

'As you wish, then.'

'Thank you, Julianne.' And that at least was said honestly, no teasing in her now; and Julianne's chilly stiffness melted after just the one moment, the one brief touch of her father's daughter. Trained though she was to haughtiness at need, in a court where the ability to freeze with a glance was almost a survival trait, she nevertheless couldn't sustain it here, with her curiosity burning so hotly.

'So what will you tell me, then?'

'What would you like me to tell you?'

'Why you're dressed as a boy, why you're on foot and alone, where you've come from, where you're going . . .' and a whole host of questions more, indicated with a wide, curtain-brushing sweep of her arm.

Elisande chuckled. 'In that order?'

'If you like.'

'Well, I'm dressed as a boy because that makes it easier to travel on foot and alone in the places I'm coming from, though not necessarily where I'm going. I suppose,' she went on, sighing lustily, 'I'll have to go veiled and robed now, if I'm not to scandalise your sergeant?'

'You have already,' Julianne assured her, 'scandalised my sergeant beyond repairing. But you haven't really answered *any* of my questions.'

'No. Well, the first, perhaps. This,' with a brush of her hand over coarse-woven wool, 'makes things possible that wouldn't be, else. Some of the villages hereabouts, they'd stone me for walking shameless so far from my house, with no men to watch me. So I cut my hair and wear a burnous and no one looks twice, except to be sure I don't rob them. I keep to the sheep-tracks mostly, and trouble the villagers not at all. Only I saw something was happening ahead, there are camels and wagons standing for half a mile, and they haven't moved for an hour; so I came down to see, and your sergeant wanted to know where the next water was, and got suspicious when I couldn't tell him.'

Some answers, Julianne thought, were designed to bury the question, not to resolve it. She wasn't going to be distracted; Blaise would find out what the trouble was, holding people up on the road ahead. Meanwhile, 'But why alone, how is this possible? How could your father let you?' And how could she keep the envy out of her voice, given such a difference of fathers?

'Oh, he didn't,' Elisande said, with an odd contempt in her voice. 'I knew he wouldn't, so I just left.'

And had left some time since, by the baked brown of her skin. She was lucky, Julianne thought, to go so dark and look so natural; and to have black hair, like all the Catari peoples; and to have eyes that could pass for black, though this close they were midnight-blue and startling. Not many would be let this close, she supposed . . .

'Left where?'

'My father's house,' obviously, and back to mysteries carried openly and unashamed.

'To go where?'

Elisande gave her a smile, and a true answer to that one. 'Roq de Rançon.'

And so was Julianne on her way there, but she felt entitled not to say so. 'Why, though?'

If anything, she was expecting to be told of a young man too deeply loved to be let go without a chase; but really she expected nothing, and was given no more than she expected. 'I wanted to see the Roq,' said Elisande, 'and my father wouldn't bring me.'

Of course, she wanted to see the Roq and ran away from her family home to do it. What girl would not? Again Julianne felt piqued, almost insulted; again she felt the temptation to draw back from any sign of warmth towards this vagrant tease. Again, though, her impulse failed in the moment of its birth. The ability to make quick and accurate judgements of other people was another necessary gift in the Emperor's palace at Marasson, and very much so for her father's daughter; and all her instincts were saying that she could make a friend here, regardless of secrets kept from her. A friend on the road at least, and oh, she would like to come to the castle with a friend in tow . . .

'You must be thirsty,' she said, thinking of the dust and the dry road and the high hot sun beyond her curtains.

'Parched.'

'I have some grape juice here . . .'

There was only one beaker for the juice, so they shared it; and then Elisande said, 'So what of you, Julianne? There are men to protect you here, but none of your family, I think?'

You are as alone as I am, she was saying, and it was true in its way. 'My father was with us,' Julianne said, 'until just yesterday. But he was called away, he had to leave me.' And then, to show that she at least was prepared to share more than a beaker of juice, 'My father is the King's Shadow.'

'Ah. And when the King moves, so must his Shadow, yes?'

A moment of staring, followed by a rising laugh she couldn't choke down for all her years of training. 'That's what he says. Exactly.'

A shrug from Elisande, and, 'All through Outremer, that's what they say. Where did he go, your father, where did the King send him?'

'He didn't say.' He rarely did, and she'd learned early not to ask. Her father kept the King's counsel, the King famously kept his own; few crumbs of information fell her way, and those she hoarded.

Elisande nodded, unsurprised. 'Did he say where he was sending you?'

'Yes, of course,' though in honesty there could be no certainty about it, for anyone who did not know her father. Many men moved their womenfolk like gamepieces, valuable perhaps but not to be consulted, only summoned or sent wherever their usefulness might dictate. Julianne should, she supposed, feel grateful to have had her future explained to her, with reasons and even an implicit apology. 'We were travelling to Elessi; I am to be married to Baron Imber.'

'Are you?' Elisande's eyebrows twitched, as though she were mentally uprating the worth of a daughter of the King's Shadow. 'Which one?'

That forced a snort of undeserved laughter from Julianne. Again it would have been a reasonable question, but for her father. 'The younger. Count Heinrich's son, not his brother.'

'Lucky, then.'

Seen that way, she supposed she was. She'd not met her husband-to-be, but his uncle, the elder Baron Imber, had come to Marasson three summers back. She remembered a heavy, scarred man with a shaven head and a sun-bleached beard, plain clothes and a temper just as plain, a sour twist seeming permanently sewn into his mouth as he'd watched the court at play around him. At the time, she'd wondered why he stayed so long. Wise she might have been for a thirteen-year-old, but not wise enough to see what was obvious, where it touched herself. That truly was when she had been given away, for all that she hadn't learned the truth of it then. The baron had come to study and assess her, to weigh her potential as a future niece, a countess-apparent for his land; and then – once satisfied, as presumably he must have been – to negotiate with her father. Hard bargaining for sure between two unlike and difficult men before at last there were reciprocal promises made, the terms of their trading: dowry and bride-price in land or gold or favour, some elements to be publicly attested and some to remain private, a few more debts and guarantees stored among the many in the subtle and devious head of the man who was the King's Shadow.

And yes, it could have gone another way, had her father

been another man. This Baron Imber was a widower and no doubt could have been attracted by the offer of another marriage. Not greedy for a young girl in his bed, or she thought not; neither greedy for money; but for influence, for power, for the ear of the King – yes, she thought, that self-denying man would neither have had nor have sought the strength to refuse those.

But her father had had so much care for her at least, not to offer. Instead he had sold her to the uncle for the nephew's benefit, and taken two full years to tell her so; and even since the public announcement the nephew had still not come to Marasson, so that she had no independent picture of him in her mind's eye. All she could do was hope that he would not be a shadow of his uncle namesake; but she was sensible above all and always honest with herself, and it seemed all too likely that he would. The Elessan nobles she had met had been cold men all, cast from the same mould as the baron: battle-hardened, dour and devout, suspicious of comfort or compromise. Suspicious of her, she thought, for being raised in the corruption of the Empire. Presumably the advantages of her blood outweighed the taint of her upbringing; or else they thought that taint could be cleansed soon enough, once she was chastely locked among the women in the count's high castle.

'When my father was – summoned,' she said, choosing to say nothing of the manner of that summoning, 'he had no time to do what he thought proper, to take me back to Tallis until Imber could come himself or send a shadow to escort me. Father sent a messenger to Elessi, saying that I was gone to wait at the Roq, until I could be fetched.' Like a prize animal, or a piece of looted treasure held under guard until its new owner could come to claim his gift. Not safe, her father had decreed, for her to go on to Elessi unescorted. They were two days from the Roq, perhaps two weeks from Elessi; heat and dust and scarce forage made for a slow journey. That her father's absence reduced her protection by no more than one man out of twenty meant nothing; his name, he had said, gave more protection than any twenty men, and that she also bore his name made her the more vulnerable without him. All of which was probably true, and none the less unwelcome to her.

No surprise in Elisande's nod, that they had the same immediate destination; nor should there have been, indeed, for this road led nowhere else. 'We could travel together, then? If you would like that?'

'If my men can take the weight of two in the litter,' Julianne amended. 'You can't *walk*, Elisande. You just can't . . .'

'Well. Perhaps not. But perhaps we needn't worry about it, perhaps neither one of us will be travelling anywhere,' twisting to throw a frowning look forward, trying to see through gauze and hills both. 'Maybe the road has gone, or bandits have blocked it, or . . .'

'There's Blaise,' Julianne interrupted. 'He'll know.' He had ridden on himself, it seemed, to discover the obstruction; now he was cantering back with some urgency. He called something to his resting men even before he reined in, something that had them up and checking their weapons, staring down the road, visibly nervous.

And then he was beside the grounded litter and jumping

down from his horse into the cloud of dust it had kicked up, coughing to clear his throat before he said, 'My lady?'

'Yes, sergeant?'

'They say there is a djinni in the road. I spoke to the master of a caravan, and he says it has been there since dawn . . .'

Her first thought was that neither her all-knowing father nor her new and insouciant friend had predicted this; her second, that she had never seen nor ever expected to see a djinni. Nor would she now, in all likelihood. Blaise would take her back, she thought, to the last village they'd passed; he'd commandeer a house for her, and they would wait until the road was clear. Wait days, if need be . . .

But Elisande was moving, was sitting up straight now, half-reaching to draw the curtains back before she checked herself and called out through them. 'Did you see it?'

'I saw a dust-devil, er, my lady. Only it was very tall, and stationary . . .'

That fitted. Even after years of service on the desert borders of Elessi, the dour sergeant would need to have words with a cloud of dust before he would believe it to be anything more than what he saw.

Perhaps Elisande had already understood that of him; her next question was, 'Did you speak to it?'

'No.'

'Has anyone?'

'I couldn't say, my lady.'

'Well, did they tell you its name?'

'Its *name*, my lady? No . . .'

'Oh, for the God's sake . . .!'

And now Elisande did draw the curtains back, in a rush

of impatience; and stepped out of the litter, and paused only long enough to look back at Julianne and ask, 'Are you coming?'

She didn't, couldn't possibly have more than a moment to decide. Blaise would forbid it, and she couldn't overrule him; her father's voice and his own lord's would weigh far heavier than hers. But Elisande's sudden eruption from the litter had set Blaise's horse skittering backwards, and his hands and attention both were occupied, trying to steady it. And she never had seen a djinni, and Elisande clearly meant to hold a conversation with this one . . .

Not running, no – *dignity, confidence, grace,* one of the lessons her father taught her early – but moving as fast as she could manage without, Julianne set her feet on the road and her heart on a new course: something that was less than total obedience to her father's manipulative will, though it felt like something more. She seized Elisande's hand and tugged her almost into a trot to keep up, realising only then that she stood a good few inches taller than her new friend.

Behind them, Blaise's voice called sharply. 'My lady, no! You may not . . .!'

Julianne didn't check, didn't so much as turn her head to acknowledge that she'd heard. All she did was stare with a cold fury at any of the men who made a move towards her. Already flustered and blushing as they were at this sight of her face unveiled, just that hint of the Marasson court's ice-maiden was enough to have them backing away, jerking their eyes aside and mumbling apologies.

And now there was only the road ahead of her, empty as far as the next bend, and she almost felt free of her cage.

But there were also footsteps coming from behind, running footsteps, and that was undoubtedly Sergeant Blaise, horseless at last and his Elessan eyes seeing nothing but his duty, ready perhaps even to handle her physically, to bundle her back through the decent shrouds of her litter.

'My lady Julianne,' and his voice now was intemperate, angry, barely clinging with an effort to the outward forms of politeness, 'will you please come back to the palanquin? *Now?*'

And yes, when she still paid him no heed he did lay his hands on them both, gripping her shoulder and pushing Elisande away; and then before he could turn her she turned herself, she spun around and her free hand cracked across his cheek, with the palm cupped to amplify the sound so that all his men should hear.

She didn't need to say a word. After the startlement on his face, she saw the gradual dawn of understanding, the certain knowledge of how grossly he had offended, though the offence in his eyes perhaps lay more against his master than against her. If what she had been told of Elessan society was not exaggerated, she could ask Imber for his death. And have twenty male witnesses to support her . . .

'Your, your pardon, lady. I — I forgot myself. I was anxious . . .'

And he was pale now beneath his tan, except where his cheek was red; but his back was stiff and only his voice was trembling, and she thought that if she ordered him to do it, he would cut his own throat there and then.

Dignity, confidence, grace. 'Yes, and rightly,' she said. 'I ask your pardon too, sergeant; I neglected to veil myself. It is a custom still strange to me,' and as she spoke she drew her veil up and let it fall across her face. 'Now, if you will accompany me, with perhaps half a dozen of your men for surety, I think we will go to see this djinni.'

And she held out her hand again and Elisande took it, gripping warmly and smiling silent applause; and the two girls started off down the road again, Julianne urgent only with curiosity now, while the bull sergeant was still bellowing behind them.

These steep-sided hills threw out rocky spurs, twenty or thirty feet of sudden, sharp-edged cliff. Just after the road bent around one such outcrop, they found the tail of the queue. A mule-driver with three bone-bare beasts monstrously overladen; then an ox-wagon, another, a small train of wagons; then the caravan Blaise had spoken of, a string of camels that would stretch half a mile or more when they were moving, but were hobbled in small groups at the roadside now while their drivers crouched over cooking-fires in the shade. All these people, Julianne supposed, must be bound for Roq de Rançon: the trade good for them, essential for the castle. And all of it halted, for fear of a creature all the garrison of the Roq might not be able to destroy or chase away; and who knew how long the djinni would choose to dance in the road?

The caravan, Blaise indicated, was keeping a prudent but not a nervous distance from the djinni, just comfortably out of sight. They would find it around the next bend . . .

So they took the next bend, Blaise leading; he and the other men were visibly on edge now, touching fingers to sword-hilts or axe-hafts and muttering useless advice to each other. Even Julianne found her legs moving more slowly, her fingers sweating in Elisande's grip and her eyes with a tendency to jerk a little at every movement they caught, every sound that reached her.

Around the bend the road narrowed, to squeeze between two of those inconvenient outcroppings of rock; and just there, in the eye of the needle was where the djinni stood.

If that was a djinni. Julianne wouldn't know a djinni from an 'ifrit from a manifestation of the God, and for a moment what she saw was what Blaise had described – only a dust-devil such as they'd seen a couple of times already on the journey, a sudden twist of wind made tangible.

But this dust-devil didn't stir, it stood rock-still between its jutting rocks; and it stood quite as high as those walls of rock, like a pillar balanced on a point; and it spun so fast that at this distance it seemed not to spin at all, but to be an endless coil of silver-grey rope that climbed itself and swallowed itself and began the climb again.

A few paces before the djinni stood a boy, ten or twelve years old and dressed much as Elisande was dressed, only that his burnous was torn and soaked a vivid red. He stood transfixed, staring and sobbing; and what he stared at was not the djinni, but what had been his right arm. It hung loose and dreadful from his shoulder, bare white bones barely joined now, stripped of skin and muscle.

Both girls were briefly still, as still as the djinni, as still as the boy. Elisande it was who moved first, who pulled free of Julianne's hold and ran forward, past Blaise's gesture of denial. She reached the boy and took his other arm, and turned him; and beckoned imperiously to the sergeant, shouted, 'Take him, quickly! Back to the fires, look after him . . .'

Blessedly, Blaise asked no questions. This he could deal with. He hurried to take the boy from Elisande's grasp, picked him up and handed him to one of his men, with quick instructions. That man ran off down the road, the fainting boy slack in his arms; and as they passed Julianne she stirred, shook the numbness of shock from her head and walked slowly on to join Elisande and the sergeant.

'Why . . .?' Her voice came out in a cracked whisper; she swallowed dryly and tried again. 'Why do you want to know its name?'

Elisande smiled thinly. 'It helps.'

'So what will you do, just ask it?'

'*No*,' fiercely. 'Never ask a djinni a question, it isn't safe. If you don't know that, just stand quiet,' though her fingers closing tightly on Julianne's sleeve said that she was glad to have her there, if only standing quiet. For her part, Julianne had no intention of doing anything more. This close, she could see the roiling dust that wove the ever-turning rope of the djinni's body, that must have ripped the boy's flesh from his arm when he stupidly, unthinkingly reached to touch. She was frightened beyond measure; almost she wanted Blaise to grip her again, to drag her back to the litter and leave Elisande to face this monstrous thing alone.

Almost . . .

But the sergeant was rapt, stunned it seemed by this proximity to an alien magic. He wasn't offering rescue, nor truly did she want it. Curiosity had brought her here; a swift loyalty would keep her at her new friend's side, despite her craven soul.

Elisande lifted her head and her voice, though both took a visible effort.

'Peace be upon you, spirit.'

'And upon you also.'

The reply came from the heart of the spinning tower, oddly light, almost female but not in the least human. There was no body behind it, no beat of blood, no hint of mortality. Julianne shuddered, and saw Blaise stir in the corner of her eye as though he too wanted to run and could not.

'My name is Elisande.'

A laugh greeted that, like the chime of cold bells; and then, a gift graciously given in return, 'And mine is Shaban Ra'isse Khaldor.'

'I have heard of you, Djinni Khaldor,' Elisande said, with a deep bow.

Again the laugh. 'And I of you.'

'They speak of you in the Silent Quarter, great one, but not here.'

'That is true.'

'Your purposes must be momentous, to bring you so far.' Her voice strained down at the end of the sentence, lower than was comfortable for her, to make it oh so plain that this was an observation only, and in no sense a question.

Once more the laugh: amusement without humour, Julianne thought. The djinni's voice dropped an octave in imitation, perhaps in mockery, as it said, 'This is not far, little one. No distance is far, to the djinn.'

'I have heard that. But I have heard also that the djinn are seldom interested to concern themselves with the deeds of humankind.'

'That too is true.'

'Well, great one,' and here Elisande let go of Julianne's sleeve and sat cross-legged on the ground, even managed a smile as she tilted her head back, squinnying into the hot sun, 'I am notoriously slow to understand, but I see you here,' with a wave of her hand at the road and the rocks, 'and I see all these people unable to pass you by, and I see nothing to cause you to come from the lands where you choose to dwell, because I am sure it is not in your mind simply to cause obstruction to such little creatures as we are. Therefore I say again, your purposes must be momentous; but they are also mysterious to me.'

'As they should be. But I have waited long enough.' The djinni span faster yet, and the column of its body rose like smoke into the sky; and it said, 'Go back to the Sharai, Lisan of the Dead Waters. They will bring you a gift of questions.'

Julianne saw Elisande's jaw drop open at that, and knew that she too was gaping. Go *back* to the Sharai? To the *Sharai*?

But then the djinni spoke again, and this time not to Elisande. 'And for you, Julianne de Rance: go where you are sent, and marry where you must.'

And once more this day – even here, at the foot of a tower of dust and enchantment – she felt the sting of her pride and position, and her voice was entirely ice as she replied, 'And why do you suppose that I would not, or that I need a djinni to point me to my duty?'

Elisande hissed in alarm, and snatched at her skirts too late to still her.

This time, the djinni's laugh was louder. 'I do not suppose either one, daughter of the Shadow. But your mind is murky now. Trust this, that your duty will come clear. The journey is necessary, and the marrying also. And trust this too, that your father's name is great but yours will be the greater, if you fail not.'

And there was a thunderclap that shook slabs from the walls of rock on either side, and made the ground tremble beneath her; she closed her eyes against a great cloud of dust, and when she opened them again the djinni was gone and the road was clear for as far as she could see ahead.

Elisande was still sitting with her head in her hands, muttering to herself. When Julianne touched her shoulder, she glared up and said, 'I told you! I *told* you, don't ask it questions . . .'

'I didn't mean to,' defensively. 'What harm, in any case?'

'What harm? It gave you *answers*!' And then, in response to Julianne's bewilderment, 'Don't you know *anything*?'

'About the djinn, no.' Nor did she care to learn, if it meant having conversations of elliptical nonsense in a constant state of fascinated terror. 'It told me nothing. Though I'd like to know how it knew my name . . .'

Elisande groaned, and pushed herself cautiously to her feet. Even through her own indignation and uncertainty, Julianne saw how drained the smaller girl seemed. She offered her arm for support, and Elisande clung gratefully.

'It knew your name,' she said carefully, 'because it was waiting for you. Perhaps for me, for us both; but certainly for you. That's why it was here.'

'Don't be ridiculous.'

'It *said* so! "I have waited long enough", remember? It

waited, and we came. It gave us both a message; yours was a trap, and you didn't see it.'

'How am I trapped?' she demanded.

'Julianne, you stand in a djinni's debt. Don't you understand? You asked, not it offered. It gave you service, which must be repaid. They always claim their debts; and they choose the manner of repayment . . .'

No, she didn't understand. What could any djinni want of her, what could she do for a spirit creature that it might think worth the doing?

She shook her head, calling up stubbornness again. *Wouldn't* think about it, wouldn't risk worrying it into truth.

'Have you,' she said instead, 'have you really been among the Sharai?'

'Yes. Once. My grandfather sent me, he said it would be good for my education . . .'

'I suppose it would have been,' Julianne said, trying to sound just as casual. 'Well, it was. No one else here knew how to speak to a djinni.'

Elisande made a wry face. 'I've never done it before. But they tell stories, the Sharai, stories that are lessons, how to live in the world; and a lot of their stories are about the djinn. I don't know what to do, though,' her voice almost breaking suddenly, now that the danger seemed past, 'I don't know how to protect you. None of the stories ever offered a way to evade a debt owed to a djinni. Well, no way that worked . . .'

Again a shake of Julianne's head, and, 'We'll be in the Roq by sunset tomorrow. A thousand men to protect me there, and afterwards all the strength of Elessi for the young baron's wife. And besides, I am my father's daughter. His name will do what any number of men cannot.' *And the djinni said that my name would be greater*, but she wasn't going to think about that. 'It called you Lisan,' she went on, remembering. 'What did it mean? Lisan of the Dead Waters, it said.'

'I don't know what it meant,' said Elisande; but Julianne thought she was lying, at least a little.

Walking back towards the litter, they passed the boy with the ruined arm, lying in dark shadow by one of the camel-drivers' fires. Though he seemed unconscious now, three men knelt beside, to keep him still.

The sergeant's man crouched grim-faced over the small hot fire, holding his dagger in the flame.

Neither girl spoke; both perhaps were counting their steps, counting their breaths, waiting. Blaise grunted something to the man, then said, 'Please, ladies, if you hurry now . . .?'

Before they reached the next turn in the road, they heard the boy at last begin his screaming.

3

No Daughter, No Door

The first time Marron and his troop came together with all
their brethren at the Roq, it was at the tolling of the midnight bell and his eyes were useless to him.

Frater Susurrus the summoning bell was called, *Brother
Whisperer*. Tonight it whispered deep in the bones of him,
as a blade might whisper its own name, cutting through.
Three strokes punched at his gut, the first as he slept and
then two more as he jerked awake and curled protectively,
uselessly against them; and three more again as he sat
dizzily awake on his pallet. Stone and bone, flesh and straw
and floor, everything trembled at the bell's resonance.

'Rise,' Fra' Piet's voice ordered in the darkness, in the
stillness after the sixth stroke. 'Rise and dress, and follow.'

Midnight prayers were second nature now, as normal as
the sunrise and the being awake to see it, and the prayers
then also. Marron's groping fingers found his habit where
he had laid it to hand, pulled it over his head as he stood,
and he was ready. Barefoot and obedient, as the Rule

demanded. But follow who, follow how? At the abbey there had been night-lights burning at every turn, to show the way to brothers new or stupid with sleep; here the open doorway was as black as the room. Only the window afforded any light at all, framing stars that blazed surely more brightly here than they did at home. But the window was little more than a slit in an embrasure, for all that it looked onto an interior courtyard and not out over the walls; it helped the night-blind find nothing but itself. Marron's glancing at it only made him the more blind when he turned his head again, trying to see something, anything of Aldo on the pallet next to his.

Well, if they were to go lightless, he could still listen his way to chapel. There were no voices, of course, no one stupid enough even to hiss a word on a breath, but he could hear his brothers' uncertainty and hesitation in the sounds of their dressing, of their breathing, of their waiting to obey. He could hear Aldo's feet shuffling on the chill stone floor, ready like his to go to prayer but ignorant like his of how to get there.

He listened for one thing more, the sound of Fra' Piet's footsteps. He would know that tread, he thought, in his darkest dreams; he thought perhaps it echoed there already. Fra' Piet had a slight halt in his gait, a great scar on his thigh to explain it. And yes, here it came now, that same broken rhythm which somehow underlay the screaming of an afternoon's mad slaughter, both in Marron's chaotic memory and in his equally unclear dreaming. Fra' Piet had been mounted throughout, but it was still the whisper of his footfalls that Marron heard through all the noises in his head. Surely the babe's wailing couldn't have had that unsteady pulse to it, neither its running blood for those few moments that it had had of running . . .?

There are wicked pictures to be painted in the darkness, true or not. Marron prayed for light, for any light to give his eyes some other thing to look at; and light came, slowly, shufflingly. There was a greying first at the doorway, enough to show its edges and Fra' Piet in silhouette between; the greying became a flickering, a yellow light, a flame that brought sounds with it as well as seeing, the soft tread of unnumbered feet.

The flame was a torch, carried by a brother; as he passed the doorway Fra' Piet reached out an unlit torch of his own. No word was said. The brother didn't even pause in his slow marching, only dipped his brand for a moment, just for long enough to touch and share.

After that silent brother came more, many more, hooded shadows briefly glimpsed. Perhaps one in thirty had a torch.

At last the procession ended. Fra' Piet stepped out into the corridor, holding his light aloft; he made no gesture, but the troop followed him in echo of what they'd seen, going singly with their cowls flung up and their heads bowed down, watching the heels of the man ahead.

They filed through the mass of the castle by narrow and bewildering ways: like maggots in a cheese, Marron thought. Twice they stopped; he saw Aldo's sudden halt and jerked to a stand himself, glad not to have been dreaming as he walked, twice glad to be following his friend's heels and not Fra' Piet's. Stopped and waited – while other brothers streamed across their passage, Marron thought, though he couldn't have seen so far even if he'd lifted his head to look – and then began the march again, moving as their brothers moved, unquestioning as slaves.

At last they walked a wider passage, and another file walked beside them; and so they came, two by two, strangers and brothers, through the great doorway into the great hall at the Roq.

Fra' Piet's torch was a spark suddenly, an impertinent glowfly against the night, its light lost beneath a massive weight of darkness. Torches borne by other brothers seemed already impossibly dim, impossibly far away.

Not courage, but fear that took any of the troop out into that enveloping black: fear of being left behind, of being left alone.

'Follow,' they had been told, and follow they did, pressing close upon each other, some even reaching out to touch. Chill skin or neutral habit didn't matter, only contact with something other than stone underfoot and darkness all around. They breathed the darkness, and loved it not at all. One lucky man, the closest – and that was rare, to be thought lucky to be so close – followed Fra' Piet with his light, and like a chain each man behind followed the man ahead. Following Aldo in his turn, Marron lost all sense of walls on any side, or roof above. There was only the velvet pressure of the night, invading even this sacred place, destroying the natural balance that was the greatest gift of the God to His mortal dominions. That seemed heretical, blasphemous, fundamentally wrong: here if anywhere under the sky, light should be an equal brother with the dark, giving way graciously at sunset but never so crushed as this, never obliterated . . .

More than obedience bowed Marron's head as he shuffled in Aldo's wake. He was afraid still, not even the presence of so many brothers all around could reassure him; he thought he was coming into the presence of something that could outweigh the purposes of the God Himself, unless perhaps it was the absence of the God that filled this hall, or left it so very empty.

Fra' Piet made a gesture with his torch at last, a wide swinging motion to one side: briefly they saw a line of kneeling brothers ahead of them. Slow, cautious shuffling – touching each other as they shuffled, rubbing shoulders – brought them into line behind. Marron felt more than Aldo's shoulder against his, he felt a cold hand too, and gripped it hard. They went down on their knees together, and there was as much comfort in finally being still as there was in the touch. Turning his head, hoping for a glimpse of Aldo's face beneath his hood, Marron saw instead how Fra' Piet at the end of the line turned his torch and crushed it against the stone flags, extinguishing its light. No comfort in that; he squeezed Aldo's fingers tighter.

Shadows leaped briefly, wildly, and were lost; he heard more shuffling behind, more breathing and the rustle of habits as yet more brothers came to kneel at their backs. They were welcome; he felt encompassed, though not safe. It still seemed abnormal, this tremendous darkness, a promise broken.

Then there was no more light and no movement behind them, or none that he could hear. He dared not turn his head, he thought perhaps Fra' Piet could see even in so much dark; he did stretch his back and peer forward in search of one last surviving torch but saw none, saw nothing at all.

Sinking down again, still holding Aldo's hand, he waited as they all were waiting. Soon he heard more footsteps coming from the back of the hall, coming closer. Gradually he saw light, showing him the ranks of hooded backs he knelt behind; now he dared not move at all, sure that Fra' Piet would be watching his troop for any hint of disrespectful curiosity.

Torches in pairs, borne by black-robed brothers processing up the aisle; a dozen pairs, a slow parade, and behind them came the preceptor and other masters of the Order. More torch-bearers, and then rank after rank of men in white robes with black cloaks thrown over; Marron frowned, not understanding their place here.

They marched on, and it was hard to see through all the brothers' bodies ahead, but glimpses of white helped a little. Those men spread themselves in line in front of all the kneeling brothers; beyond, the torchlight was rising, where steps must mount to the altar. Then those torches too were put out, and there was no light at all.

One long, dreadful moment of silence, when it seemed that every man there held his breath together with his brothers; and the great bell struck once more, throbbing through Marron's flesh and bone and Aldo's also, he could feel that in how his friend's fingers trembled in resonance with his own; and the voice of the preceptor cried out, '*Fiat lux!*'

And there was light. Blue light, cool at first, flowing and twisting to make the doubled-loop sign of the God against the far-distant wall above the altar; then it burned more brightly, sun-bright, too fierce to look upon, though it still seemed to be running like liquid fire behind its glare. Marron's eyes watered, and he quickly turned his head away.

There was all the hall to look at now, plenty light enough for that, the holy promise holding and balance dramatically restored. But the first thing Marron saw as his eyes found focus was all his troop doing as he did, twisting and staring around; and the second thing Marron saw was the black shadow beneath Fra' Piet's hood as the confessor's head turned to watch his charges, dark eyes gleaming where no light fell.

Head snapped forward, eyes dropped; no more spying. And all he'd seen was kneeling brothers in their hundreds, and the broad shadows of great pillars at intervals ahead.

Another voice began to call the midnight office, carrying easily through this great space. Marron thought there might be magic in that also, as there was in the flaring light above the altar. But he was afraid no longer, only exultant, one believer among so many come to worship; he joined willingly, eagerly, devoutly in the responses, and the only thing he did that perhaps he should not have done was to keep a grip on Aldo's hand throughout the hour of the service.

Even their silence after seemed to echo and sing in the vast vault above their heads. Quiet and still in his soul now, fearful of nothing with the God's bright assertion before him and not even hearing the faltering beat of a baby's blood fall still, Marron didn't so much as glance upward. Obedience was a virtue as well as a duty, it was something owed which was also a pleasure to perform; there would be opportunities later, surely, to discover this place in daylight. Even with the rim of his hood hanging low across his brow and his eyes cast downward, he could still see movement ahead of him, as brothers all along the aisle stood up and raised their arms, lifting dead torches high. Fra' Piet would be doing the same, no doubt. Marron didn't need to look; nor did he wonder why. There would be an answer.

And there was: two brilliant lines of light speared out from the glory above the altar, touching each torch in turn, bringing them to flaring life. At that signal all the brothers stood, Marron's troop just a moment behind the others. Again the masters paraded between them, torch-bearers before and between, the men in white robes behind. As he reached the doorway, the preceptor must have turned back to face the hall; Marron couldn't see him, but he could see the procession halt in the aisle. And he could hear the preceptor's voice pronounce a final benediction; and he could see how the great bright sign faded, how the flow of light slowed and died, leaving only an image of itself burning like a reminder behind his lids when he blinked. He closed his eyes to cherish it, opened them only when Aldo tugged urgently on his hand and then slipped his fingers free.

Half the hall was empty. The remaining torches burned bravely against the black, making a pale path of light into which Fra' Piet was leading his troop now. The man at his back gave Marron a shove; he stumbled to catch up with Aldo, then dropped into the steady pace of the others and walked peacefully back to the dormitory for the second period of sleep, until Brother Whisperer should call them to prayer again at the rising of the sun.

*

The high-risen sun hung like a brazen disc in the white-hot sky, baking down on the castle's upper courtyard, where Marron sweated.

Not alone: all his troop was with him, and Fra' Piet. There had been fifty other men besides, and for an hour they had drilled together with baton-swords, round-edged and blunt-pointed wooden staves that could bruise but neither cut nor kill. *Unless used by a master*, Marron remembered his uncle saying, years before, *but in the hands of a master an ink-pen can kill. I have seen that . . .*

The men Marron had faced this morning had not been masters; he barely carried a bruise. But they had not had his uncle to teach them, either. Marron carried no false pride about his swordsmanship, and no false modesty: he knew he was good because he had worked to become so, under a diligent instructor, but he knew also that he could be better. He had thought to improve here in Outremer, fighting for the God and training with men who had fought for forty years. He no longer hoped for that. What need sword-skills and clever footwork for the hacking down of women and old men, unarmed boys and babies?

There was a bitterness in him this morning that the dawn service had not been able to dispel, the meal of porridge afterwards to settle nor the grim intensity of exercise to sweat out. His dreaming had not been easy, and he felt more duped than awed, more murderous than justified. Today it was difficult even to blame Fra' Piet's zeal for carrying them all into mayhem; how a thing had happened seemed not to matter, against the overmastering weight of the thing itself.

He was here, though, and he had done what he had

done. He stood with Aldo among the rest of his troop, watching others disperse; and there went Fra' Piet also, leaving them alone for a rare minute as he crossed the court to greet a man with a grizzled beard and a great sword hanging from his belt, a big man not big enough to match his legend. Magister Ricard, weapons-master general, who had come to this land as a boy in the Duc's entourage and played as potent a role as any in establishing Outremer, crowning his lord as King; and Marron's hopes might be sour dust in his mouth and throat now, but still he would fight as well as ever he could under this man's eye.

Magister Ricard gripped Fra' Piet's arm and spoke to him as to an equal, which startled Marron; then the two men fell into step, walking slowly back towards the troop with their heads together. They were followed by half a dozen young men whose cloaks were black, but whose robes showed white beneath.

'Who *are* those men?' Marron murmured, seizing the licence of the moment.

'Knights Ransomers, of course,' a voice from behind him, scornfully. 'Don't you know anything?'

I know how to make you bleed. But of course, he should have known this also. Knights Ransomers, sons of the nobility, not prepared to give over their lives or their property entirely to the God but making a commitment of one or two or five years to the Order. Seen as a duty in Elessi, it was more of a fashion, Marron had heard, in other states of Outremer, the black badge sported afterwards like a trophy and any young man who lacked one subtly disgraded. Or else in some families a year's service was a rite of passage, to mark the change from idle youth to adult.

Whatever brought them, they came – Marron had heard – with pages or squires in their train, they ate separately and slept separately and came to prayers or not as they chose. Apparently they dressed separately also, which Marron had not been told. There were knights and there were brothers, he had been told that, with little touch between them; he knew already which he valued the higher.

Doubly so when these half-dozen knights grouped themselves in a corner and cast aside their cloaks, gazing at the troop and speaking low, smiling with just a hint of contempt: all that such motley brothers were worth, their faces said.

Marron felt that same contempt, hoped they could see it reflected back and understand it. Beneath their cloaks they wore white, yes; they wore swords, yes – and they wore shirts of shimmering chain mail also. *Mail!* He'd heard that Knights Ransomers went armoured into battle like their secular kin, but he'd never credited that rumour with any truth at all. And this was only training with baton-swords, and why under the God would they need mail here? Unless it was to show how strong they were, how heedless of the heat and the weight they carried . . .

Around him, his brothers were whispering his own thoughts: 'Mail shirts! Have they no honour? Have they no *faith*? The Rule forbids us . . .'

'Us,' a harsh voice said behind them all, 'but not such as they. They have their vows, we have ours.'

Muted gasps, and sudden stillness: in their distraction, not one of them had thought to keep an eye on Fra' Piet. But for a wonder there seemed no censure in his voice or in his gaze when they dared to meet it, for all that they'd been talking without cause or permission. Could the gulf between brothers and knights run so deep, Marron wondered, that Fra' Piet would rank himself with his troop in this?

No matter, for now: there was no reprimand, and no hint of punishment to follow. That was enough. Fra' Piet made a gesture, to direct their attention; there stood Magister Ricard, foursquare in the sunlight, with his shadow thrown behind him like a trailing cloak in the dust.

'Brothers,' he said, and his voice was like a bell with a crack in it, loud and dissonant. 'You have come as we all came once, to serve the God with your prayers, with your obedience and with your swords. It is my task to see that the last of these is done as well as it may be. I have been watching your drills, from a window above. Some of you handle your weapons like mattocks,' with a fearsome scowl that had a few of Marron's brothers shuffling their booted feet and grinning shamefaced. 'I hope we will train you to do otherwise. A few obviously have been better taught. You and you, you . . .'

His jabbing finger picked out some six of the troop, Marron among them. Aldo not, but that was just. For all their years of practice together, under his uncle's eye or else in private, Marron had never managed to teach his friend anything more than bare competence with a sword. With a bow the opposite was true: Aldo could take a thrush on the wing, where Marron would miss a roosting bustard.

'Step forward, and we will see just how good you are.'

This, then, was why the knights had come; six of them, Marron thought, against six of us. Noblemen's sons against yeomen's, farmers', peasants': this should be no true contest, although Magister Ricard had undoubtedly picked out the best of the troop. The nobility learned the arts of war before even they learned their letters, he had heard.

Still, he would do what he could for the troop's sake and his uncle's reputation, and for his unknown father whose name he bore, who had died in this far country for this same cause. The knights had arrayed themselves in a half-circle; the brothers walked to meet them, and Marron found himself facing a young man perhaps five years older than he, dark-haired and lean as he was but perhaps a hand's-span taller.

A longer reach he'd have, then; but the mail should slow him down. Marron lifted his baton-sword to the guard position; his opponent laughed.

'Formalities first, boy, don't be so eager,' with a mocking bow. 'My name is Anton d'Escrivey.'

'Sieur Anton.' A low bow, lower than the other man's, truly formal; and thank the God he had remembered the proper form of address. 'I am called Marron.'

'Well then, Fra' Marron. Shall we begin?'

The knight drew his sword; and his was a true sword, no wooden training-baton, and not blunted for practice either, by the way the sun glinted on its edges. Marron couldn't mask a moment's hesitation, which had Sieur Anton laughing again.

'Don't be fearful, boy. I beg your pardon – Brother Boy. I shan't prick you – or not overmuch. Not with Ricard standing by to approve my swordplay. I shall use the flat.'

If you can reach me, Marron thought grimly, coming again to the guard with his teeth set in anger but his eyes doing as they had been trained to do, watching the point and the shoulder both. He'd have watched the man's wrist also, only that a gauntlet obscured it.

Around them already were the sounds of steel on wood, hard breathing and grunts, booted feet sliding over gritty stone. Marron focused, screened out the sounds and the glimpses of movement at the edges of his sight, crouched a little lower and shuffled forward.

Sieur Anton came gracefully to meet him, sunlight running on his blade. 'Never try to second-guess a swordsman,' Marron's uncle used to tell him, time and again. 'Watch the point, the wrist, the shoulder – react to what he does, not what you think he'll do.' But – *he thinks I'm a clodpole. And he thinks I'm afraid of his point. He'll feint a stab, just to make me jump back, and then he'll bruise my ribs for me. He thinks . . .*

Marron tensed on his toes, and yes, here it came – the glittering blade thrusting forward, straight at his chest, and then swinging wide to administer a stinging slap. Except that Marron was no longer there to be slapped; he'd leaped forward against the sword's stab, so nearly mistiming it that the point nicked his habit on its swing away. One brief glimpse of his opponent's widening eyes, only a foot's distance from his own; and then he brought the blunt edge of his baton-sword down hard on Sieur Anton's thumb, *there, let him drop his sword in front of his master, let him be the fool and not me . . .*

But Sieur Anton's sword did not fall. The young knight danced back out of reach, true, and acknowledged Marron's move with a nod of surprised respect; but, *metal links in his gauntlets*, Marron thought, chagrined. *And he's alert now, he'll not be careless again . . .*

Neither was he. They closed again and this time fought as equals, blow and block, feint and thrust and parry. For five hard minutes they circled and sparred, blind to all else in the court. By the end of that time Marron's eyes were stinging with sweat, his breath was laboured and his sword-arm ached cruelly, and every move he made was backwards. Because they were not truly equals: Sieur Anton was the master here, and both knew it.

Marron had fought with a stronger man all his life, though; he'd never matched his uncle for size or speed or skill. Defence had always been his strength, and he called desperately on all that he knew. Block and parry, feint and retreat and block again; Sieur Anton had both hands on his sword-grip now and his face was livid with humiliation. He was using his edge too, despite his promise, striking chips from Marron's wooden blade. Would the bout end if the baton broke, would Magister Ricard call the knight to a halt? And would Sieur Anton hear or heed the call?

Marron wasn't sure, but the thought, the momentary break in his concentration was enough to drag his eyes to the side, to look for the weapons-master. And so he was the fool after all: he knew it as he did it, and snapped his gaze back, too late. Sieur Anton was already thrusting through his vagrant guard – and thrusting with intent, with a razor-sharp point and all his frustration driving the arm that drove it.

In the clarity of that moment, Marron saw the young knight's face change suddenly, even as he thrust. Marron dived and rolled – 'always roll *towards* your enemy, lad, never away. Get inside his reach, knock him off his feet if you can, bite his ankles if you have to. If you roll away he'll only follow, and laugh as he kills you' – and would have died regardless, would have died spitted before he hit the ground, except that Sieur Anton flung his sword away with a great shout.

Not time enough even in that gesture to save Marron's skin, but it saved his life. The blade missed his heart, missed his chest entirely, sheared his habit and the flesh of his left arm before it skittered away across the cobbles of the yard. Marron felt the tearing chill of that touch, and a rushing heat after; but he was rolling, rolling to his opponent's feet, and he looked up at Sieur Anton's pale face and found his baton-blade still in his frantic grip.

And thrust upward, not with any strength, he had none; but with strength enough, wit enough to ignore the man's chest in its mail shirt. He stabbed the dull point at Sieur Anton's throat, and touched hard enough to leave a bruise, he thought. Hard enough to cut, if he'd had a blade with an edge to it. Cut and twist, and *a death to me, I think* . . .

Sieur Anton jumped back out of his sight, coughing and cursing; and then stepped forward again, one hand rubbing his throat but a thin smile on his face regardless.

'Well done. Though the first death was mine, I think,' as though he'd read Marron's thoughts precisely on his face. Perhaps he had.

He reached an arm down; Marron let the baton fall, and reached up to grip it. Sieur Anton drew him easily to his feet and held him so when Marron's legs threatened to buckle, gave him a moment to catch his breath and balance; then, 'Show me,' with a gesture towards the other arm.

They looked together. There was a rent in Marron's sleeve, and a wide wet stain around it. Sieur Anton peeled the sleeve back, to find a long and gaping slash across the forearm.

'Not too deep. It'll scar, I fear, but not badly. Not to damage the use of it. What was your name again?'

'Marron . . .'

'Well, Fra' Marron,' teasing again, but not contemptuously this time, 'have that washed and bound, and then come back here, will you?'

A nod, a slap on the shoulder, and Sieur Anton turned away, picked his sword up and examined its edge, pulled a cloth from his belt to wipe it. Marron gazed after him, dizzy suddenly and confused, feeling the pain in his arm now like a hot brand pressing deep.

Shaking his head and blinking against the giddiness, looking around, he realised at last that there was no other movement in the courtyard: that the other bouts were long finished; that his troop-brothers and the knights were all stood back against the walls; that every eye there was fixed on him, or on Sieur Anton, or else moving between the two of them.

He staggered a little then, and Aldo came running. Stocky shoulder under his, an arm tight around his chest and whispered words stumbling over each other, 'Well *done*, you were wonderful, you'd have had the beating of him with a proper sword in your hand, did he try to *kill* you there . . .?' and Marron just stood and shook his head and watched the blood run down to drip from his fingers until Fra' Piet came to say where they should go to find bandages and water and a fresh habit. And even he had a nod of approval for Marron and a blunt congratulation, that he had fought well and not let his brothers down; but somehow the words that rang most strongly in Marron's mind were Sieur Anton's, his parting words, *come back here, will you?*

Not a question, not an invitation, almost a command; and Marron didn't know why, but he wanted to. He would. If he were allowed to.

That first dizziness passed, and at Aldo's urging Marron blotted his bleeding arm with his blood-soaked sleeve, pressing hard to stifle the flow. He could walk more or less steadily now, he found, but Aldo came with him none the less and without direct permission. *To do what you have not been ordered to do is disobedience*; they trod on the flags as on eggshells, waiting for Fra' Piet's voice to call Aldo back.

No call came, and neither one looked to see if he were watching. Better not to know, perhaps. Aldo had tacit approval or else he did not, and if not he would surely find out later. Sometimes doubt made a more comfortable companion than certainty.

They found the infirmary, by dint of asking directions twice. A brother apothecary stanched the wound with a fiery, stinging application that made Marron yelp as the wound itself had not, then bound it in linen strips and promised him a scar less than his little finger's width, if twice the length. From there to the vestry – Marron expecting to be required to wash and mend the damaged habit himself, as the rule had been at the abbey, but finding it taken from him and another given over without comment – and from the vestry necessarily back to the courtyard. Even without Sieur Anton's order, they would not have known where else to go.

All six of the young Knights Ransomers were there, duelling with each other now; Fra' Piet and the troop had gone, as had Magister Ricard.

After a minute Sieur Anton caught a glimpse of them standing in the doorway, unless he had been deliberately watching for their return. He stepped back from his bout, raising his left hand and lowering his sword; his partner nodded and stood at rest while Sieur Anton came across the court towards them.

'You,' to Aldo, curtly, 'your troop has gone to the armoury; you are to join them there. *That* way,' pointing, against Aldo's clear hesitation. 'And you,' to Marron, 'stand over there, and watch. Oh, don't *worry*. I have begged you from your confessor, for this hour at least. Watch me.'

He went back to his bout; Aldo gave Marron one doubtful glance and then took off, almost running to find the troop again.

And what of me, Marron thought, with an anxious look up at the high sun, *when the bell calls us to pray, must I walk into hall with the knights?* He couldn't envisage that; but neither could he wait outside the door. To keep the four Great Hours was the prime duty of any brother, ranking over all.

Brother Whisperer was silent yet, though, and obedience was owed here too, he thought: if not from brother to knight under the Rule – that he didn't know, or couldn't remember – then at least from yeoman to lord, the habit of his life. Marron stood where he had been told to stand, and watched Sieur Anton fight.

And understood at last why these men wore mail even to drill in, and understood also quite why he'd survived his own bout so long. Until the anger of embarrassment overmastered it, some part at least of Sieur Anton's mind must have been always remembering the edge on his weapon and Marron's lack of armour, tempering every stroke with caution. No such inhibitions now, between men equally armed, trained and protected. Marron wouldn't have survived one minute of such fierce sword-play, let alone five; nor would he have survived many or possibly any of the blows he saw skittering off the mail shirts, striking sparks.

All six of the knights were highly skilled, perhaps the best he'd seen; Sieur Anton, he thought, was the finest of the six. That man's sword was a deceiver, dancing with light, teasing and tempting and then striking true. No bout lasted long; the men changed partners often, sometimes fighting two to one, and even in those engagements Sieur Anton won more often than he lost.

Eventually they called an end to the play. They sheathed their swords, spoke briefly in soft voices; then the other five went off together, while Sieur Anton stood where he was, summoning Marron with a glance.

'How's the arm, well enough?' And at Marron's nod, 'Good. Come with me.'

Marron glanced at the sky, saw the sun so near to noon and wanted to ask where they were going; whatever the answer wanted to say, *later, please, I have to go to prayers now* – and didn't. Said nothing, indeed, only walked silently behind the tall young knight, cradling his sore left arm in his aching right as he followed obediently through a narrow doorway and up a turning flight of stairs, along a corridor to a door that Sieur Anton opened.

These must be his private quarters: a small chamber and not luxurious by noble standards, perhaps, but to a junior brother of the Order it seemed almost shockingly easeful. The walls were hung with bright tapestries and there were woven rugs on the floor and shutters for the window, furs on the bed. A finely carved chest stood in one corner, a bare wooden horse in another.

Sieur Anton unbuckled his sword-belt and tossed it onto the bed, followed that with his battered leather-and-steel gauntlets which had saved him humiliation from Marron's baton and perhaps the loss of a finger from one of his subsequent bouts. He ran one hand through his sweat-matted hair, and then under the collar of his mail shirt.

'Here, help me off with this. If you can . . .?'

Marron's one hand was still cupping his other elbow for support; he released it quickly and stepped forward to grip the shoulders of the mail, wondering at how fine the links were, how supple they made the shirt. Sieur Anton bent and wriggled, backed a step and slipped free. Weight dragged at Marron's hands, making him hiss at the pain rewoken in the muscles of his arm.

'Hang it there,' with a gesture towards the horse.

The mail slid over the wooden frame with a rippling sound; Marron turned back to find Sieur Anton sitting on the bed, lifting one booted foot towards him.

'If you would, please . . .'

*

And so Marron – who had sworn to his uncle never to be any man's servant, only ever the God's – found himself on his knees before this man, hauling off his boots. And was still on his knees, still wondering what he was doing here apart from being subserviently convenient, when the shivering call of the great bell woke his bones to the hour.

He gasped, couldn't help it; and glanced urgently up at Sieur Anton with an unspoken plea on his lips, *I have to go now, though I don't know the way.* And gaped, again couldn't help it, as the knight dropped down off the bed and onto his knees beside him.

'You know the office?'

'Yes, sieur.' Of course he knew the office; but . . .

'Good. We will say it together.'

Marron waited for Sieur Anton to begin, Sieur Anton waited quietly for the seventh stroke that said the service was beginning in the great hall; and then they recited the ancient words, turn and turn about. If it was strange that a secular knight should lead while a professed brother only made the responses as any layman might, it didn't seem so to Marron.

They were quicker through the service, surely, than the massed congregation in the hall, and two murmuring voices were less stirring than hundreds of brothers speaking together, but Marron found it no less devout. Sieur Anton stayed on his knees for a long minute after they had finished, his lips moving in private prayer; and his glance that followed seemed so open, so inviting, that Marron ventured his first question.

'Pardon me, sieur, but – do you always say service here, in your room?'

'I do, yes. I keep all the Hours, as you do – but in private.' And then, with a bitter laugh against Marron's puzzlement, 'What, you think I should parade my virtue with those conceited coxcombs my fellow knights, make a show of myself before your brothers and the God? Exhibit my lineage and my undoubted worth? No, I thank you. No . . .'

He rose abruptly, and paced across to the high slit window that let in only a sombre shadow of the day. Marron stood awkwardly, an apology on his tongue though he didn't understand why he should use it, what offence he had given.

After a moment Sieur Anton turned again, to settle himself in the embrasure with a more natural smile. 'No,' again, 'but that is not your concern, Marron. Now listen to me. We, the knights of the Order, may bring a squire or a servant with us, for the time of our service here. Alas, I have none – not through carelessness, I assure you; I didn't leave his bones in a ditch – and the preceptor has said I may choose one of you new-come brothers to make up the lack. I should like to choose you, but I am told that I may not compel it. I must ask.' His speaking smile turned rueful for a moment, regretting this unaccustomed change in his status. 'So, this one time, I am your supplicant, Marron. Will you act as my squire? The duties are not onerous, I am no demanding master; and I can teach you more than you have learned already, and more than you would learn in twenty years of being a garrison brother in the Roq. At sword, and at other matters also. Will you? I shan't ask twice,' added as a cool warning not to prevaricate or bargain.

That was unnecessary; Marron had nothing to bargain

with, could see nothing to bargain for. Only, 'I, I do not wish to leave my troop, sieur . . .' Mostly, he did not wish to leave Aldo; one friend at least he needed in this vast stern castle, this new and, yes, this vast stern life. But there was also truly a bond between all his brothers in the troop, from which he would not willingly see himself broken.

'Nor will you. I shall need you no more than two or three hours, most days. You will still be a brother here, with all a brother's duties; this is extra labour I would lay on you. Say yes or no, Marron, but say it quickly.'

'Yes, then, sieur. And thank you . . .'

Sieur Anton shook his head mockingly. 'I cut his arm to the bone and then burden him with work, and he thanks me for the privilege. Such is the life of a lordling, Marron; we bless where we touch. Come here. No, *here*,' rising to his feet and reaching, gripping Marron's shoulder and drawing him to the window, pointing out. 'There, do you see?'

'That tower, sieur?'

'Yes, that tower.'

The window looked out on yet another court, smaller than the last: smaller than any in the castle, Marron thought likely. There was one squat tower in the corner, with a lower wall that closed it in on two sides. The Roq proper made a square of the court, but left that tower untouched. It must be standing right on the height, on the very edge of the great upthrust of rock that was the foundation of the castle; that wall must mask a long, long drop.

'This is the oldest part of the citadel,' Sieur Anton said, his hand shifting to Marron's neck and holding firm to keep him looking, 'the first fortress that was raised here by the Sharai. They do not generally build, but they built here and held it until we took it from them. All else we have built ourselves, the outer enceinte is entirely our own. That tower, though, even the Sharai did not build; it was here before. They raised their fortress *around* the tower. To claim it, perhaps? To protect it? If anyone knows, they have not told me. Do you know what that tower is called?'

'No, sieur.'

'If the Sharai had a name for it, I have not heard; but we call it the Tower of the King's Daughter.'

'Sieur?'

'Yes, Marron.'

'The King – the King has no daughter, sieur.'

'Indeed. He named it himself, they tell me. He came here once, according to legend, after the fall of Ascariel but before the Conclave.' Of course, before the Conclave; when else? 'He looked at the tower, and instructed the Order to guard it well. They say that he laughed, as he named it.'

Well he might, it was a thing to be laughed at, if anyone dared. No daughters had the King of Outremer; and no face either, that anyone had seen outside his palace these forty years. He chose to rule in absolute seclusion, without exception or explanation.

Strange though it was, the name it seemed was not the important matter here. Sieur Anton's grip did not weaken.

'*Look . . .*' he whispered; and that was all.

At last, 'Sieur? I see no door . . .' No door and no windows on the two sides that were visible, only blank much-weathered stone; and the wall that framed it was surely built too close to allow a doorway that he couldn't see.

'That's right. There is no door. And that, Marron, that is how some of my confrères think that I should be: alone, isolated. No doors, and no windows. You may find that they have infected their servants also; that may be another blessing you receive from my touch. Do you know how to whet a blade?'

'Sieur?'

'Can you use a grindstone?' And his touch was gone from Marron's neck now, and himself from Marron's back; he was over by the bed when Marron glanced around to find him, hefting his sword on its belt.

'Yes, sieur.' That had been the first lesson his uncle had taught him, before ever he was allowed to use a blade in practice.

'Good.' Sieur Anton flung the sword, sheath and belt and all; Marron caught it awkwardly. 'Her name is Josette. I nicked the edge, I think on Raffel's mail. Take her down to the stables, they will show you the stone. Bring her back when you're done – and treat her with respect, her lineage is superior to yours. Then you can go to find your troop; the service will be finished, and they will be looking for their dinner.'

'Sieur?'

'Well?'

'Should I not fetch yours?' Squire or servant, whichever he was, he knew the duties of a lord's man.

Sieur Anton laughed shortly. 'No. I do not take a meal in the middle of the day. Nor will that be one of your obligations, morning or evening; I mess with some few of my confrères who are – you will be told – not over-particular in the company they keep. Raffel, and his kind. You saw us together at play. Their squires are enough to serve us all. But I thank you for the thought. The sword, Marron, concern yourself with the sword; you may find that I am over-particular about my weapons.'

He swung his stockinged feet up onto the bed, lay back, folded his hands behind his head and closed his eyes.

Marron ran.

As he ran, he thought that there was something else he was reminded of by a tower without doors or windows, no way in. Not Sieur Anton, no – that he didn't understand – but something twitching, tickling in the back of his head.

Running, hurtling along the passages and taking corners at a twisting canter while his mind scratched vainly after a half-formed thought, of course he got lost; probably he'd been lost before he started. Nor were there brothers of whom to ask the way, they must all still be at prayer. And the knights, and their servants too: noon was the highest Hour, for lay folk as well as religious. Peasants would stop work in the fields when they heard the noon bell, to kneel and say a prayer; decent townspeople would flock to church; everyone in a convent would come to chapel. In a convent or a castle, seemingly, at least where that castle was held by the Order.

Everyone but Sieur Anton . . .

Marron had to weave his own path through the courts and the corridors, around unexpected and unwelcome corners, up inconvenient stairs when he needed to go down and there seemed no way. Every window he came to disorientated him further, showing him a view he did not expect. This must have been an extra defence, he thought, in the minds of the castle's builders, to confuse any invader who won so far. Or else it was magic, a spell laid since the builders did their work, to lead any stranger's feet astray . . .

I am no stranger, I am a brother here! He wanted to scream it at the obdurate walls, which allowed him no doors where he needed them, where he thought they ought to be.

No doors, no windows . . . That thought again – or not a thought so much as an idea, an image . . .

At last a doorway yielded a glimpse, a moment of recognition: they had surely climbed that narrow dim-lit ramp yesterday, when Fra' Tumis led them in from sunlight to shadow, before he led them down to the Chamber of the King's Eye?

Marron sprinted down. Yes, here was the open cobbled yard and the inner moat, and here beyond were the stables, finally. And here too were the Sharai stable-lads, slaves and unbelievers, unbaptised, forbidden the service; he asked for the grindstone and one boy took him to it.

As he spun the wheel and pulled Sieur Anton's sword from its sheath, he thought, *Surayon!*

Surayon, of course, that was it. Surayon, the Folded Land: no doors and no windows, no way in or out.

He was glad the thought had not come to him fully formed at Sieur Anton's window, he might have blurted it; and just to say the name of Surayon was disobedience which brought heavy penance, and that was in the abbey at home. Here, he dared not imagine what the punishment might be.

Official punishment, at least. In Sieur Anton's room, he

thought perhaps Sieur Anton's hand would have given him his penance, and that too would have been heavy. If it had seemed that Marron was making a connection between all three, the tower and the knight and the Folded Land of legend, rumour, whispered heretical horror – oh, the God's glory, he thought he might have paid for that in blood . . .

But his blood had been paid out already, and his arm burned to remind him. The God took his penance, it seemed, even for thoughts not spoken where they touched a thing utterly forbidden: a land declared anathema, impossible to travel to, an apostate inaccessible to justice and an enemy intangible, mysteriously gone.

Surayon, the Folded Land. No doors, no windows. And a tower the same, and a knight who claimed the same, or denied it rather, or did both. Marron was making connections despite himself, as he set Sieur Anton's blade against the spinning stone and his teeth against the aching pain of holding it just so against the kick.

He thought he heard a baby's wail in the scream of steel on stone, he thought he saw blood spatter in the sparks; he wanted to bar his doors also, to seal any windows he might own, to be a tower strong and certain, untouchable, alone.

4

How High, How Far Below

At first she'd thought the castle was a cloud, she thought it had to be. A dark, louring, horizon-hugging thunderhead, a rainstorm out of season; what else could mass so broad and heavy against the sky?

Only as the day wore on, as the bearers brought them closer and it moved not and changed not but only loomed the larger, only at last as the sun moved around to dispel its shadows and show it in the light: only then did she believe, when she had to. When she could see that truly behind that obscuring veil of shade were man-raised walls of honeyed stone, pale as fresh-cut comb or dark as the baked crust of a honey pudding, but all cut from the same rock those high walls stood impossibly high upon.

She tried to blame the shadows for her unfaith, and then the eye-bewildering gauze of the litter's curtains; her companion laughed at her.

'Admit it, Julianne, it's just too big, you couldn't see it.'
'Well. It is big . . .'

It was big: it was massive, immense, prodigious. Too big, she thought, in all honesty; and she had lived all her life in Marasson, which was by any measure easily the largest city in the East. Some splendid buildings they had there, too – the palace, the citadel, the great temple with its blue dome, the largest anywhere in the known world, she'd heard – but none that was on the same scale as Roq de Rançon.

The rock the castle stood upon – not the Roq that it was named for, she remembered, no one knew what in the world that meant or used to mean – that rock was no hill like all these other hills, scant of earth and scant of life but normal, natural, only somewhat dry and toothy at their tops. Rather it was a tremendous bare knuckle breaking up from a sudden surprising plain between the hills: a mountain peak from the World Below, her father had called it once, laughingly, from the land of the 'ifrit, a mountain that grew too large for the underworld and had to plunder space above to hold it.

And what the God had made, that remarkable naked vastness of rock, in itself a fortress, man had improved upon. He had built and levelled and built again, so that even at this distance she could see layers to the castle, just as there were layers marked out in cracks and strange dark stripes below it, aslant in the great weight of stone that held it up.

Even full in the sun's light it seemed still sombre, still shadow-draped. Threatening, she thought it. But of course: it was a fortress above all – *indeed, above all*, she thought, having to look up at it even from here, still miles and maybe leagues from the winding way that climbed it – and meant to threaten, though perhaps not to threaten her. A refuge it should seem to her, a place of safety; she was disturbed that it did not.

'How far is it?' she asked, and hated herself both for the question and for the tremulous tone in her voice as she asked it. She sounded like a child to her own ears, neither the sophisticated woman she tried so hard to be, nor the betrothed woman her father had made of her. Rot his bones, this was his fault, twice his fault for bringing her to this forsaken land and then forsaking her within it; perhaps she could be angry, that might help . . .

What helped more was Elisande's practical, cheerful treatment of the question on its own terms, disregarding the nervous quaver that she must have heard. The smaller girl twisted her neck to peer through the gauze panel, then grunted in frustration and tweaked the curtain aside to see clearly. Looking at the land that lay between them and the castle, Julianne guessed, rather than at the Roq itself; its size only confused the eye, making it seem nearer than it could possibly be.

'Half a day?' Elisande said, and even she sounded uncertain for once, which was curious relief to Julianne. 'If the bearers need to rest,' which they must, with two to carry in the palanquin. 'But we should be there by sundown.'

They would need to be. Sergeant Blaise refused to travel after dark, and there was no village to be seen on the road ahead where they might break the journey.

Julianne sighed, trying to think hopefully of an end, or at least a pause in travelling. 'Do you think there will be baths?'

'Cold ones. Perhaps.' Elisande's face screwed comically, and her fingers twitched at the gown she wore, one of Julianne's. Blaise had demanded that at last night's halt: 'She must dress decently, my lady,' *and behave decently too*, unspoken but implicit. The dresses were more of a burden to her, Julianne thought, than the behaviour. Certainly, as a guest of the strict Ransomers she'd have no chance to cast them off in favour of her own rough clothing. There was a chuckling comfort there too, that this girl so deliberately obscure in her intentions should have to make such an obvious and irksome sacrifice to achieve them. Julianne still had no idea why Elisande wanted to come to the Roq; she was glad of her company, more glad with every hour and every word that passed between them, but she resented the mystery of it none the less for that.

The litter swayed and tipped gently beneath them. It was restful, ordinarily, as well as convenient; at least, if her mind were at rest, it could be restful. Alone, she might have drowsed through the heat of the afternoon. With Elisande there, she lay back on her elbows and gazed out, watching the slow passage of the sun-gilded, dusty hills. She preferred not to look ahead. The looming castle dominated her mind too greatly; it spoke of walls, of gates barred behind her, of little air and little light: it spoke of her future, and she would not think of that.

Go where you are sent, and marry where you must. No, she would not think of that either. Of what use was magic, if all it did was underline the dreary world of expediency and intrigue where she was no more than her father's daughter, her life within his gift?

Elisande was dozing, she saw, curled like an animal among the cushions. That girl didn't share Julianne's reticence, not to sleep in the presence of a new friend. Perhaps it was a foolishness; they had after all shared a room and a bed last night, in a crude mud-walled hut above a dry ford. But Julianne was hostess here, and would not be asleep when Elisande woke.

So she watched the land go by, and longed for a little breeze to stir the curtains; and listening in vain for the sough of wind coming down the valley, she heard an entirely different sound. Close at hand were the soft footfalls and occasional hard grunts of the litter-bearers, their voices fallen quiet in this heavy air. To the sides, to the front and behind she could hear booted feet, the men-at-arms who guarded her; behind them the rumbling wheels of the baggage-wagon, obscuring the snorts of the oxen that drew it and the light dancing steps of her palfrey Merissa; ranging forward and back as ever came the thudding hoofbeats of Blaise's horse. All that was normal, a constant. But now there was something more besides, a distant whisper of urgency. She sat up, frowned, wished for the thousandth time to be rid of the muffling curtains that made a drab, disguised thing of the world.

This much was clear, that Blaise had heard it too. He came cantering past the palanquin, calling to his men to be alert. His voice, sounding sharp even despite those curtains, roused Elisande; she blinked, lifted her head and said, 'What is it?'

'I'm not sure. Listen . . .'

They listened both, and briefly Julianne thought the other girl would poke her unveiled face right out to listen better. But it wasn't necessary; the sound resolved itself quickly, becoming familiar and – here at least, on this road, in this country – dangerous.

'Horses,' Elisande said, sitting back on her heels, some-how finding a knife from beneath her skirt.

'Yes.' Many horses, and in a hurry, it seemed. 'Put that away. The men will protect us, if there is a need.' *This close to Roq de Rançon,* she wanted to add, as though that were a protection in itself, as it ought to be; but her tongue rebelled. The castle still seemed as great a threat, or greater.

'And if they don't, or can't?'

'Then your little needle will do us little added good, and likely harm,' she said acidly.

'It could take one life at least, at need. Or two . . .?'

There was an invitation in that, a pact proposed. For a moment, Julianne was tempted. Elisande knew this land, which she did not; Elisande also, it was clear, loved her life, which Julianne no longer did. If time came when the other girl thought fit to leave it sooner than stay, perhaps Julianne should be her guest on that journey . . .

But she shook her head impatiently, *don't be foolish;* and couldn't help but wonder if she might regret that brisk dismissal, and if she did, for how long the regret might last.

A single horse, catching up fast; that was Blaise, return-ing.

'Riders, my lady,' he croaked through a mouthful of dust. Too dry to spit, he sounded.

'Yes, we know. How many?'

'A dozen, two dozen? It's impossible to tell. They ride in a cloud. But they are close . . .'

And getting closer, and the castle was too far to help, even should it have help to offer. Even should these not be men from the castle closing in like floodwaters, dark and turbulent . . . 'Have your men halt, sergeant. Friend or foe, we will wait for them. No sense in seeming fearful.'

No sense in seeming brave either; if the sight of her guard was not enough to deter attack, then the guard's strength was likely not enough to meet it. But she was her father's daughter, and – occasionally – glad of it; she would neither run nor be thought to be running.

Blaise hesitated, before he grunted assent. He gestured to her bearers to be still, which they were already; then he called orders to his men. Quickly there was a double ring of steel around the grounded litter: pikes to the front, swords and crossbows to the rear.

Blaise rode out alone to meet the coming horsemen, and for once Julianne didn't need Elisande's insistence. She hooked one of the curtains back with her own hand so that both girls could see clearly, and never gave a thought to veiling first. Modesty wouldn't save either their lives or their honour, if there were trouble in this.

Trouble there was or might be, but of a slow and insidious sort, not immediately apparent except perhaps to a girl who saw danger where she should have seen shelter's promise.

What Julianne saw that hot afternoon, squinting through the haze and the raised dust, was a troop of twenty men well-mounted; all their horses were as black as their habits, and they rode with their cowls over their faces. She shivered and thought *castle*, thought *Roq de*

Rançon, though she awarded herself no applause for the insight. The Ransomers' style was well-known in Marasson.

Perhaps it was just their garb and their apparent face-lessness, out here on an empty road with the vast rock and its castle louring at her back, but she still couldn't rid herself of that sense of threat. She wanted to cry out to Blaise, *keep away, don't go near them, don't trust.* She wouldn't have done that, though; this was his charge, and his men must see him do it. She was too late, anyway. The men in black had drawn up their mounts, in ordered ranks; one rode forward alone, and after a few words called between them Blaise doffed his steel cap, bowed his head, all but dismounted to kiss the brother's boot.

Which likely made him properly a master, Julianne thought, a senior member within the Order. And someone too whose name or rank was known to Blaise; the sergeant wouldn't accord such respect uncritically.

Now Blaise had turned his horse, to ride head to head beside the other; ranged himself with the newcomers, it seemed to Julianne, taken his stand with the castle. Well, and why not? She should have expected that. Elessans had good cause to be grateful to the Ransomers. There were outposts, small convents of the brothers all around their borders, and she knew that the Order stood high in Count Heinrich's esteem.

The two men talked briefly, and she could have told them all the content of their conversation. *The lady Julianne de Rance, yes, daughter of the King's Shadow; she's due at Elessi, meant to marry the young Baron Imber. I'm charged with bringing her to the Roq, to hold her safe until he*

can send for her. One other girl with her, a companion, Blaise
would be no more indiscreet than that. For his own sake,
not for hers or Elisande's. In strictest terms it was a breach
of his duty to have taken up a stray, an unknown and secretive passenger; senior members of the Ransomers were sure
to judge such matters strictly.

Once they had spoken privily, here they came: the one
to inspect the goods in transit, she thought with irritation,
and approve the other's care . . .

She reached forward quickly, to let the curtain drop.
Elisande gave her a glance, more question than protest.

'Please – do this with propriety? For our reputation?'

'Lady, I have no reputation. But for yours, of course. He
will want to look at us . . .'

And so Elisande searched the cushions until she found
the veil that Julianne had given her that morning, with the
gown. She fussed it neatly into place, then reached across
and did the same with Julianne's; the taller girl didn't know
whether to laugh or hit her.

And then the occasion for either or both had passed,
because the two men were outside the palanquin, and
Blaise was speaking to her through its shrouds.

'My lady, here is Marshal Fulke of the Society of
Ransom, newly appointed provincial commander of the
military arm. Master Fulke, may I name the lady Julianne
de Rance, and her companion the lady Elisande?'

'Indeed. But you will forgive me, my lady; I find it hard
to make my bow to fabric without a human form, however
pleasantly woven the design.' There was some humour
beneath the hood, then. She still couldn't see his face for
shadow but his voice was pleasant enough despite the

ironic crack in it, sharp as a whip. His accent was refined, homeland, she thought, and not any part of Outremer; he must be freshly come, for all his seniority.

'Alas, Master Fulke. In this land, fabric is all you will ever see of my kind; it is the habit of women to go veiled.' Was that too subtle or too barbed, a reminder of his vow of celibacy and just a hint of its opposite, the scurrilous rumours that foolish gossips liked to spread about the Order? Well, let him make of it what he would; no doubt he would shrug it off as the innocent comment of a naïve girl. 'But we can at least reassure you that we do have human form, though we may not show you much of it. Elisande . . .?'

With a mischievous obeisance and an approving laugh in her eyes, Elisande drew back the curtains.

'My lady.' His bow was only a stiff nod; perhaps he was not so thick-skinned after all.

Still, she didn't feel inclined to release him quite so easily. 'Master Fulke, your cowl veils you as darkly as our hangings did us. There is no such custom here for men, nor is it I think the habit of your Order . . .?' Except in a literal sense, but Elisande was biting back a smile already, she could feel it in the girl's fingers where they lay on her arm; Julianne didn't want her bursting with suppressed laughter, or rolling with its release.

'We were advised to shield our heads from the sun's heat, my lady, at least until our skins have grown a little used to it.'

But he lifted his hood back regardless, and regarded her with solemn eyes. Blue eyes, she noted, and fair brows above them, fair also the short-cropped and receding hair.

Yes, he should be careful in the sun; he was not made for this country. But what struck her most, despite that deceptive hairline, was how young he seemed, to be a marshal and a provincial commander. Her father had versed her well in the government of the Order, as in so much else; she knew how much power Fulke's rank would grant him, and she knew how seldom such power was given into a young man's hands. The Ransomers were traditionally a conservative band of men.

'You were well advised,' was all she said, and she made a sweet little gesture with her hand, permission to draw up his hood again. He did so meekly enough, but she warned herself not to be deceived by his complaisance.

'With your permission, my lady,' *with Blaise's permission* he meant, and he undoubtedly had that already, 'we will escort you these last few miles to the castle. Had we but known you were ahead of us, we should have ridden harder; this road may not be safe even here under the castle's eye, for a young woman travelling alone.'

'Hardly alone, Master Fulke.'

He didn't laugh, he didn't gesture; but she felt his dismissal of her men in his stillness as he said, 'Even so. A mounted guard is better; and twice the number is always to be preferred.'

So. Men of Elessi did not match up to Ransomer standards? She felt herself quite heated at the snub, though she was not yet an Elessan and had never wanted to be so. He had much to learn, this young marshal commander . . .

The men ordered themselves briskly under these new and judging eyes; the litter was picked up and the easy, swinging pace resumed.

Elisande let her veil slip around her throat and said, 'Have you made a friend there, Julianne? Or an enemy?'

'I don't know.' Which was poor enough, a confession she would not want her father to hear; but if an enemy, then it was poor work indeed. Ransomer influence was great and would be greater, she thought, in her new home; she thought perhaps this young man had come to make it so. And she could not judge him, could not read him at all.

Not yet, her rational mind did its best to reassure her, without success. *A few brief words, what's that?*

It was time enough to form an early impression, to base a first report on; her father had had her do that often and often, in the court at Marasson. But she could not do it now. Whether this man meant her good or ill or neither one she couldn't tell, though she'd given him some chance to show her; what he might mean to the borders here or to Outremer at large, she had no way of knowing.

The sun was sinking, though its rays still fell full on the massive scarp when they reached its foot. They rested there, at her insistence, for the bearers' sake. Here more than anywhere, she wished she could have Merissa saddled and brought to her; if she had to enter those high forbidding walls above she would far rather do it ahorseback, for what small gesture of independence that could afford.

It wasn't possible, though, she knew that. This break was as much assertion as she could hope for, and even this was begrudged her, granted only on sufferance. The Ransomers had not even dismounted; they walked their horses in tight, impatient circles, glancing ever upward at the road and the overhanging castle. Blaise too, she saw: his men were crouching in what bare shade they could find, but he had ridden some little distance up the slope, seemingly lost in thoughts of his own.

There was only water in her flask today, but Julianne shared that with her friend and said, 'I'm afraid Sergeant Blaise and I have misled these men; they believe you to be my companion.'

'Well, so I am,' said Elisande, smiling. 'What else?' And when Julianne did not reply, 'Does it distress you?'

'Not at all.' She would have been grateful for such companionship all the way to Elessi and after too, though she could not ask for that.

'Besides, it gives me an entry to the castle,' the other girl admitted, 'which might have been difficult else.'

That was true too, and Julianne had already considered it. But that raised the question again of what Elisande was seeking at Roq de Rançon; and she would not ask again, for fear of being rebuffed again. One question, though, she was not shy of asking.

'Do you think Blaise has told the marshal of the djinni?'

'You know him better than I,' Elisande said consideringly. 'But myself, I doubt it. Strongly.'

So did Julianne. Again it was a breach of duty, to let his ward venture so far into risk; and the djinn would surely be anathema to a Ransomer, any contact something close to heresy. No, she didn't think he would talk to anyone about that. His men neither, if his discipline was good, and she believed that it was.

In fact she and Elisande had talked little about the djinni, even last night, in the seclusion of the bed they'd shared. It was too momentous, that meeting, deeply private to each of them despite their having stood together at the time. The creature's words to Julianne had left a bitter tang – what point in its speaking to her, if it only chose to reinforce her father? – and she had sensed that Elisande would not relish questions. Nor answer them, most likely . . .

The bearers rose, to show that they were ready. The men took a minute or two to arrange themselves in the established order of march, and then the caravan set off on the long climb to the Roq.

Long slow climb, no one would hurry on such a path, narrow and twisting with always a wall of jagged rock on the one hand and a terrible fall on the other. How the first force from the homelands had ever taken this place, Julianne couldn't imagine; it should have been invulnerable. Twenty men could hold it, surely, against an army?

Not against an army and the God, that had to be the answer; though the Sharai had their god also, and Julianne's childhood in cosmopolitan Marasson had left her with a secret fascination for other people's beliefs, and some sternly unvoiced doubts about what her own priests told her was immutable truth.

The bearers were doing their best to keep the litter level for its passengers, the men at the front carrying its poles at waist-level while those behind kept them on their shoulders, but it was still a bumping, rocking passage to the top. The girls clung to each other for support, laughing as they swayed from one side to the other. Elisande seemed genuinely to be enjoying herself, but Julianne's laughter, she knew, betrayed her nervousness. She couldn't keep from thinking how there was nothing but the litter's light frame to grab at, if it should tilt too far. The curtains had never seemed so gossamer-thin, especially when they swung wide at the bends to show her the awful drop beneath. And she'd been sulking down at the bottom there, she'd wanted to *ride* up here? She was a good horsewoman, but Merissa was a nervy, excitable mount, used to wide plains and fast running, likely to start and skitter on unfamiliar ground. Julianne found herself once again unexpectedly grateful for the litter. This was an uncomfortable climb, to be sure, and humiliating to her pride; better that, though, than to have Merissa shy suddenly at a falling rock and so to fall herself, to fall and fall . . .

The grunts and cries of the bearers ebbed at last. They set the palanquin down for a moment, then lifted it again, laughing softly. Peering ahead, Julianne saw that they stood before the open gate of the castle. Surprisingly small the gate seemed, for so great a fastness; but that would be defence again, wide high walls and a narrow entry to defy invaders. The horsemen ahead of them were going through in single file, as if there were no room for two abreast; she wondered if there would be width enough for her wagon to follow. Surely, though, if it had climbed the road it could achieve the gate. They must be accustomed to wagons here; how else could the castle be supplied? There had been plenty, she remembered, waiting on the road where the djinni was.

The way was clear now, and her bearers went slowly forward. Once past the gatehouse they climbed a long flight of shallow steps, a chilly passage with only a slit of sky above them; and then none at all, only darkness as they entered a tunnel, it seemed, cold and dank and still sloping upward.

Too much of that; she held tightly to Elisande's hand and all her forebodings came back to her. A broad stable-yard after was nothing but relief. Here the bearers set them down once more, their sighs and murmurings sounding their own relief; and here was Blaise, dismounted now, standing beside the litter and calling her name.

Veil pulled in place with quick, trembling fingers, she pushed the curtains back and stepped out, infinitely glad to feel solid cobbles beneath her feet. One deep breath, a self-conscious stiffening of the spine which Elisande beside her, she noticed grimly, did not need; she gazed about her and saw men standing in groups, horses being led away by white-tunic'd, wiry lads. Marshal Fulke she could not see, though almost all the horsemen had thrown their cowls back now, under this lower, kinder sun. The sky was shot with red above them.

'My lady, if you and, and the lady Elisande,' and there was a mute appeal in Blaise's eyes, that she should maintain this subterfuge, 'if you will come this way, the brother here will show us to guest quarters . . .'

As she followed Blaise and the beckoning, silent brother, she caught a glimpse of her wagon's yoked oxen being coaxed out of the tunnel. And didn't turn her head to watch; she had her dignity, albeit late recovered.

They climbed another ramp, narrower than the last: too narrow for horses, this, let alone wagons. How did they ever bring inside anything larger than a man could carry?

By rope and winch, she decided, over the parapet above the moat; that would be the only way. Here the walls almost brushed Blaise's shoulders, on either side at once. To the left, the inner side, she saw that the worked stone was older, cracked and stained and greying, the exposed mortar gone to dust. That must be the wall of the original fortress, seized by the King in a single night after a siege that had lasted all the summer. Before he was the King, of course, when he was only the Duc de Charelles and a very long way from his family estates. Julianne's father had been one of his company even then, a young squire in the service of his lord; he'd told her much about the great war they'd fought, to drive the infidel out of the Sanctuary Land and recover Ascariel for the God, but little about this battle or that night. She knew that the Society of Ransom had taken the captured fortress and made of it a citadel – this must be all their work on her right and behind her, all that she'd seen so far must be new-built since the war – but not even her other sources, her many friends at Marasson, had been able to tell her how the battle had been waged or how the fortress fell.

Beyond the ramp was a dark and narrow ward between a wall and a low tower, to which the brother led them. Stairs rising into shadow, turning, rising again into light; a lamp-lit doorway, a heavy curtain lifted back, a gesture to enter. Made to Blaise, she noted, not to her. If all the brothers were like this, mute and seemingly disparaging of her rank or person, she thought she might be too angry to feel depressed even in this gloomy place, however long she had to wait.

But no, not all could be, surely? Marshal Fulke had

spoken with her. Crossed swords, indeed, and she thought he'd had the worst of it. There was a thought to cheer her . . .

The room beyond the curtain could cheer her also, if she were in a mood to allow it. There was no view over the outer walls, but at least the window was as wide as her arm was long, it let in air and light through fine-cut wooden screens in the high Catari style. And at least she could see the sky, broad and untrammelled, ever her picture of freedom. She saw a rim of darkness, purple creeping like a bruise into the blue; that must be the east, then. Elessi over there, east and south; all her life behind her, west and north and far behind her now.

She jerked her head away from window, memory, anticipation, dread. Hangings hid the walls and a wonderful carpet the floor, a design to become lost in, so intricate, so many threads and colours. There were two beds, she saw, no need to share tonight; and water and towels laid out ready, to wash and refresh themselves . . .

'You knew we were coming?' she asked, directly of the brother. 'How is that, were we seen on the road? Or did Master Fulke send a messenger ahead?'

The brother shook his head, looking both stubborn and confused; it was Blaise who answered. 'My lady, they always have guest rooms prepared, in any convent of the Order. It is the Rule, to serve pilgrims and travellers . . .'

Actually she'd known that, she'd only wanted to confront the Ransomer, to be sure that he wasn't just shy or tongue-tied or a lad of few words careful not to use up his allotment. Well, she was sure now. She nodded a curt dismissal in lieu of thanks, let him scurry almost to the doorway then called out, 'Wait.'

Saw him check, and turn; and turned herself, turned her back, turned back to Blaise. 'Ask him,' she said coldly, 'if we can have baths. Here. At once.'

The sergeant did glance towards the brother, but only to shake his head briefly. She felt more than heard the young man leave, a sudden touch of air as he let the heavy curtain fall.

'I *said*—'

'Lady,' Blaise interrupted, tight-voiced, his big hands spreading, 'it's near enough sunset now. He can't bring you a bath. No one can.'

Oh. Of course. She'd forgotten the conventual Hours: it was time for evening service. All the brothers would be called to prayer . . .

'I'm sorry,' she said, genuinely regretful, though only for the mistake. She didn't like making mistakes. 'But why couldn't he tell me that himself?' *That or anything, why did he look at me as a Sharai might look at a pig?*

'He's young, my lady,' Blaise said stiffly. 'Young and devout, and determined. The vow is for chastity, but some brothers choose to go further. It is not encouraged, or not officially; there are some confessors, though, who will witness additional vows.'

'Which are?'

'Not to speak to women, begging your pardon, my lady. Sometimes not even to look at women.'

Julianne laughed, with a touch of cruelty. 'Women are not the problem I've heard about, with regard to Ransomer chastity.'

Blaise blushed furiously. 'That is *not* true, Lady Julianne. The brothers keep the Rule, they serve the God, they are not – debauched, in that way.'

'No,' she said, curious and sorry. 'I beg *your* pardon, Blaise, I should not have said such a thing. Ignorant gossip, of course it's not true. But in a community of brothers, what's that young man scared of?'

'Not all serve with their brethren, lady, or in the field. Many have to do with women every day. Some brothers worry. Particularly the young. When you're young, such vows are easy . . .'

That didn't explain why the boy had seemed so contemptuous, the couple of times she'd caught his eye. An attitude learned from his confessor, perhaps?

Never mind. She was suddenly less interested in him, more in the older man before her now. Blaise wasn't so very old, at that. He was Elessan-born, he'd told her, which made him necessarily under forty. Not too much under, though, she thought. His face was lined with more than the journey's weariness. And his eyes were narrowed with more than the journey's stress; he should be relaxing, surely, here on safe ground, all his duties discharged? And yet he wasn't, he seemed more on edge than before, though he'd been edgy enough ever since her father had been called, ever since this enforced change of plan and route. She'd thought that was only the responsibility, her life on his shoulders; now she was wondering if their new destination, this castle had been weighing on him also. *Did you take some vows yourself when you were young, Blaise? And did you maybe break them, or one of them, the one that mattered most?*

She wanted to ask, and couldn't see a way to do it. Easy in Marasson, harder in Tallis, impossible she suspected in Elessi; and the Roq was Elessi in miniature, she thought, hard men with hard secrets, not to be divulged.

A great bell tolled just as the light in the room began to fail, while she was still searching for the words, for the key, for a blade and the strength to crack him open. Again, and again; she thought her own bones were ringing in sympathy, or in response.

Blaise had stiffened further, if that were possible. He seemed pale and strained, under the day's crust of sweat and dust.

'My lady, may I leave you?'

'No,' she said lightly, glancing round for Elisande and finding her watching, head cocked with curiosity.

'My *lady*, I—'

'I know,' she said, interrupting him this time, but with a smile. 'You want to go to service too, yes? Like the brother?'

'I have to go,' he said, fists clenching and unclenching at his sides.

'Of course,' and she kept her voice easy, as if this were no great matter to either one of them. 'We will all go. We are their guests, after all, we should respect the habits of the house. If you will wait one minute, Blaise, while we rinse this dust away – or join us, you will want to go clean before the God – then you can show us the way to chapel. Yes?'

I'm sure you know the way hung in the air between them, unspoken but not unsaid. His nod was an entire conversation.

*

When they had washed, Blaise led them – his own face still glistening wet as he would not use their towels, nor the curtain which Elisande had suggested, smiling wickedly – not to a chapel, but to a gallery overlooking a vast pillared hall lit by flambeaux in sconces on every face of every pillar. Shadows danced in the vaulted roof above; when she looked down, for a moment all she saw was black until her eyes adapted and she realised what lay below. The brothers were here ahead of her, kneeling in rank upon close-packed rank before the raised altar.

There was a narrow aisle between the ranks, running the length of the hall; now a procession came walking slowly, brothers with flambeaux leading a dozen men in habits, their cowls hiding their faces from her. They must be the senior members of the Order, the preceptor and masters; they climbed the three steps to the altar and arrayed themselves in a line before it, bowing low. Behind them were men in white robes beneath black cloaks; again their hoods were raised. Knights Ransomers, she thought, remembering similar dress at services in Marasson.

The knights formed lines below the altar steps, and knelt there. At her side Blaise knelt also, hurriedly, lifting a hand to his head in a gesture of doubt; he wore his steel cap, but still felt the lack of a hood, she thought. A black hood, she was certain, and not from the cloak of a knight . . .

Taking her cue from him, she dropped to her knees and beckoned to Elisande to do the same. The gallery's balustrade restricted her view, but not severely; not so much as the pillars must be blocking the eyeline of the brothers who knelt behind them. Still, they did not need to see. Neither did she, in all honesty, it was only that she wanted to. She straightened her back, to peer over the rail.

The deep-throated bell sang one time more, its weight throbbing through her; a single clear voice began the chant. When the massed voices of the brothers replied, she felt all her skin prickle at once.

There was always a preacher at sundown. She must have heard a hundred sermons for each year of her life, but never in a setting such as this. She was curious, eager almost; when the time came, she rose up again on her heels.

One robed master stepped forward, from the twelve on the altar's dais. She wanted to see his face, and could not – until, shockingly, he lifted his hands to his cowl and cast it back to stand bare-headed before them all. There was a shifting throughout the hall at such a gesture, here in the presence of the God, but she ignored it. A pale head, blond and balding . . .

Marshal Fulke looked deliberately about him, left and right; and looked up too, looked at the gallery, looked directly at her. Then he bent forward, cleared his throat and spat loudly onto the altar steps.

That brought more than a discontented shuffling from the kneeling brothers, it brought a great hissing, hundreds of men catching their breath at once, as she did.

He spread his arms to settle them and said, 'Yes, I will meet my penance for that, and for uncovering at the altar during prayers. But this, this contempt for the God and His church – this is nothing. I say it is *nothing*, to you it is nothing, you mock yourselves and me to pretend otherwise. It matters not a tittle, not a whit. I could lift my habit, bare myself like a babe or an impudent boy and defecate on the altar here; and you, you Ransomers, you soldiers of the God would have no cause and no right to protest it. Neither would the God condemn it. Not in this house.

'You are false, my brothers. You are hypocrites, you deceive the world. You cry the God, you make great show of your virtue and your swords, you stand at all the borders of Outremer and pull faces at the desert to frighten the Sharai; and at your backs the heart of the Kingdom is rank and rotten, and that black heart will poison the whole body, and so Outremer will die and our souls will die with it. And you *know* this, my brothers, and yet you do nothing. You stand with your backs to the most foul corruption that ever touched this land, and you pretend. You pretend that *it is not there . . .*!

'What is my spittle on the altar steps, against the great heresy that is the Folded Land, that place we do not name? Spittle can be washed away, it will not harm the stone, and he who spits can be forgiven. Heresy is more malign, it eats at virtue as a canker eats at good flesh; it needs steel and fire to expunge it. Heretics should seek forgiveness in the flames, they will find it nowhere else.

'But you, my brothers, you who stand and let this canker grow – how are you to be forgiven? You deny the God, by denying your duty to Him. You betray the God, by betraying your duty to His people. You dishonour the God, by dishonouring your duty to this His land.

'You say you cannot find this enemy, this heretic state? I say look within yourselves, find how you have blinded your own eyes, gagged your own voices against telling truth.

You will not even *name* the foe? Then how can you hope to find him out?

'I say let us speak of him – yes, even here, before the altar of the God he so traduces. Surayon! I say Surayon is the enemy, the great betrayer, the canker that will kill us if it is not cut out. Surayon and all its people, from Princip to peasant. How can we face the Sharai when we cannot face what lies within us, our own dark heart . . .?'

It was only as she rose at the close of service that Julianne realised there was another in the gallery besides herself and her companions, one who must have come in silently behind them, some time after the processional entry of the masters; she would surely have noticed, before.

He was a young man, tall and dark and intense: his eyes on the altar still, his hand on his sword, his hair uncropped and wild.

His hair uncovered, though the black cloak that he wore over his white dress had a hood to it.

And Blaise, she saw suddenly – Blaise beside her had taken off his cap and was turning it and turning it between his big hands, looking uncomfortable, looking determined, looking away.

And glancing over the balcony, she could see bared heads among the brothers also as they waited their turn to leave: hoods thrown back and eyes fierce as falcons' gazing about them, seeking out others of their kind.

No bold soul stepped out of his line to walk forward, to go to the altar steps and spit; but she guessed, no, she was sure that some had thought of it.

Not a gesture of disrespect, she thought, nor discontent;

not a momentary swaying by a passionate speaker, though passionate he had been and almost had she been swayed herself. Not a rebellion, even. This was a revolution, or the first seeds of it.

She wished she had a way to tell her father.

Blaise saw them quickly back to their room, and then excused himself: off to the refectory, she thought, not in pursuit of a meal so much as company, like minds talking together, encouraging each other. Boys, working each other up to face a challenge . . .

'The brothers will bring you food, my lady,' were the words he left her with, for fear she should think herself neglected. When next there were footsteps beyond the curtain, though, and a voice calling through, it was not food that was brought to them.

It was a tub and towels, a box of soap, and water.

Hot water . . .

Twenty days their trail measured, at their backs. It was a long shadow over the sands, the salt-pans, the lava plain. The grazing had been bad, the wells bitter and brackish; they had left the bones of ten camels behind them, and two men unburied who would be bones as soon as the foxes found them. *Or the Kauram*, Jazra had whispered that night, *they'll be slipping back now, with their cooking-pots . . .*

Much snorting laughter muffled wetly under blankets, not to disturb those who were sleeping. But there was a truth hidden in the laughter, which was maybe why they'd laughed so hard, and why they'd tried so hard to smother it. Not that the Kauram truly ate men, of other tribes or their own: that was an old joke and only the children believed it, although it was undoubtedly true that the Kauram were a sly and dirty people with no sense of honour, who kept water-secrets hidden to themselves. How else could they live so long with their herds in the *mul'abarta*, the great white sands, if they didn't know of wells they never spoke about, and good grazing that they never shared?

Unless of course they did eat men as the stories said, drink their blood and the liquid in their bellies. No grown man would believe that – though it might of course be true regardless, who could say? – but every man said it, and every man sneered at the Kauram for it, true or not. That was the tradition. The Kauram were cannibals, the Ashti were cowards, the Beni Rus loved only gold and silver, the Saren loved only boys and needed men of other tribes to make their children for them . . .

He was Saren himself, he and Jazra both, and they were bloodsworn to each other and would never marry; but he would still kill any man he heard spreading that lie. Even here, even under all the oaths that he and each man had taken, to ride peaceably together and fight only with the infidel. That was the real truth, he'd thought: that even Hasan could not truly unite the tribes.

That was why the two men had died. There was bad blood between their peoples anyway, and a blood debt long outstanding between their families, a history of raids and deaths and stolen camels told and retold through the generations. And there had been an argument on the march, an argument of nothing, of whose grandfather had been the greater warrior. No one had heeded them; any Sharai could and would argue about anything on a journey, it passed the time and mattered not at all.

But when they'd couched their camels and rested under the sun's most heat, the argument had gone on. Suddenly it was a case of knives, as perhaps had been intended all the time, these men had so much hatred for each other. Steel flashed in the light, steel grated on steel and then a thud and a gasp, and one was down and dying and the red sands drank his blood.

The other had died within the hour, on Hasan's order; the two were left lying by the trail, their weapons taken from them and their flesh open to any dishonour. That night young men might snigger together beneath their blankets – those who had blankets – but there was a doom, he'd thought, written in their laughter. He'd thought perhaps the infidel would win at last, because Sharai knives could not in the end be kept from Sharai throats.

But there had been no killings in this party since, although three hundred men of a dozen warring tribes rode side by side. Hasan's discipline was holding, where the Imam's oaths perhaps were not. Now they were come to Bhitry well, where men of the Rubel were waiting for them as promised. There were no more sands to cross; here they must trade their camels for horses and go on into strange country, guided by strangers.

Bhitry water was sweet and plentiful. The camels had drunk their fill and the men also, for the first time since Rhabat, and still there was enough to wash with before they prayed. And then there was fat and meat to roast over their many fires; the sheikhs of the Rubel had sent fifty goats to welcome them who had eaten nothing but desert bread for days, since the last camel died.

With so much meat there seemed no point in dividing it and drawing lots, to say which share was whose; so he and Jazra fought as they always did, 'You should take more; here, I have too much, this must be yours . . .' until the older men at their fire intervened.

As they ate, his eyes turned to the dark shadows on the horizon, north and west, the hills they must skirt tonight. There would be water and meat there also. Hunger and thirst were no more a worry, a camel's dying no longer meant danger or death to a man; now his thoughts were free to run forward, to the great killing they had come for.

5

These Things Happen

After that whipping sermon, meant to do more than sting, Marshal Fulke raised no more welts; or none with his tongue, though he had not yet done with talking. To the brothers he talked of obedience largely, telling them of the charter he bore from the Grand Chapter of the Order, that commissioned him to use all means within his power to purify and sustain the Kingdom. In obedience, he could do no other than to lead them in holy war against the God-defying apostates of Surayon; in obedience, they could do no other than to follow him.

To the knights, it seemed, he talked of other things: of duty and honour, of courage and the great adventure that lay before them, of the long-delayed completion of what their fathers and grandfathers had begun forty years before.

Marron heard none of that directly, but his day had already assumed a pattern very different from that of his brothers in the troop. By Brother Apothecary's order, he was excused strenuous duty until the gash in his arm had healed; by Sieur Anton's order, he passed the hours this gained him in doing a squire's service, waiting on his knight.

In practice, it meant that he spent much of each day with his hands more idle than they were used to, and his mind more preoccupied. Sieur Anton seemed to have unusual, even unlikely ideas of the proper duties of a squire; Marron saw little of the other knights' attendants.

In the mornings he was required to stand and watch Sieur Anton at exercise with sword and shield. 'I may need you,' Sieur Anton had said, 'to fetch and carry for me. Perhaps to carry me to the infirmary, as your friend did you,' with a twisted smile that said *little enough danger of that.* The smile spoke true; his knight outclassed the others, Marron thought, beyond argument or challenge.

At noon each day they went as before to Sieur Anton's small room, and said the office together when Brother Whisperer struck. Marron could join his brothers in the pillared hall instead, Sieur Anton made that clear; but he found a curious satisfaction in this quiet murmuring of potent words, a new revelation to set against the massed celebrations of the other Great Hours.

Then he was dismissed to eat with his troop while Sieur Anton fasted. After the meal, though, the troop had chores assigned now, kitchen duties that Marron was forbidden. Fra' Piet would send him off with a sneer, and a comment to the others as to how carelessness could sometimes be rewarded; and Marron would run back to the knight's chamber, to ask how he could be used.

Every day brought a different answer. There were broken links in Sieur Anton's mail; it must be taken to the armoury for repair, waited for and then oiled and cleaned with a soft cloth against the dangers of rust and the unacceptability of dirt. Or the knight's fine linens were in need of washing, and again must be watched over in the laundry and on the drying-racks, because those local women were heavy-handed in their work but light-fingered afterward.

Or – once – Marron arrived at the chamber door and scratched on it lightly, and then went in to find Sieur Anton standing by the window with his drawn sword in his hand, frowning as he tipped the blade this way and that in a fugitive beam of sunlight. He didn't so much as glance up to acknowledge Marron's entrance.

'Sieur? Is the sword notched again?'

'What? Oh. No, the edge is good. It wants work, though. I think Sister Josette is thirsty, Brother Marron. Fetch me your sword.'

'Sieur?'

'Your sword, Marron. You do have a sword, other than that cow-beater you thrashed at me?'

'Yes, sieur.' He had a sword, racked in the dormitory with every brother's else until the troop was judged competent to use them in training. Given the choice, he would delay that day until the sword had rotted. He thought it tainted past use, he thought the memory of blood would etch its steel to rags and rust . . .

'Then fetch it.'

Marron fetched his sword, at a canter. Sieur Anton took it, drew it from its worn leather sheath, gazed at it a moment in that same solid-seeming bar of light and tossed it dismissively onto the bed.

'Adequate for practice. Adequate for a peasant, perhaps –

or a yeoman?' shrewdly, watching Marron's face. 'Your father's?'

'My uncle's.' His father's had been lost with his father; never before had he been glad of that, nor ever imagined that he would or could be, but he'd been glad for days and days now.

'Well. It suited him, no doubt. Or he it. Though he has trained you well enough,' touching a finger to his throat, where a faint yellow streak of bruise still showed. 'To begin with, at least. I think we will look a little higher for you now. Here.' He opened the chest in the corner, and lifted out what was lying ready there on a bed of folded clothes, what certainly had not been there when Marron had folded and stowed those clothes yesterday.

It was a sword, in a finely tooled scabbard of white leather reinforced with silver edging. The grip was bound with the same leather; the pommel and hilt were chased steel, much like Sieur Anton's own Josette, expensive work but not gaudy, not ornate. No jewels, such as he had seen on some of the other knights' weapons.

'Take it. Draw it out.'

'Sieur . . .'

'Marron, obedience is the first duty of an esquire, as well as a brother Ransomer. Take the sword.'

Marron took the sword. It nestled into his hand like a warm and living thing, slid from its scabbard as though it very much wanted to. For the length of his forearm the blade also was chased, on both faces, with a fine tracery that finished in a crest of some sort; the room was dim, he couldn't see well enough to make it out without moving to that vagrant beam of sunlight, too close to Sieur Anton.

The sword was a little shorter, he thought, and notice-ably lighter than Josette; and oh, it felt sweet and easy in his grip. He touched the edge and drew blood just from the touch, feather-light and fleeting; and sucked his finger to the sound of laughter, and moved his body and the blade rapidly through the five major and seven minor positions, which a moment before he had been determined not to do; and sheathed it with a flourish, released the hilt with a pang, held his bleeding finger carefully away from the unblemished white of the scabbard as he said, 'Sieur, this is too, too—'

'Too fine a weapon for a cloth-headed, muck-handed oaf like you? Quite so. But you may improve. No, you *will* improve; I shall see to that. I have hopes of you, Marron. The positions again.'

Sword whispered from scabbard, almost before Marron had consciously registered the sharp command. And then it whispered again, whispered differently in the air as he took first position – *elbows so, feet thus and the hand high*, his uncle's voice, as ever in his head when he performed this drill – and slashed the sword sharply down into second, stabbed forward to reach third . . .

'No.'

Sieur Anton's voice checked him, stilled him as he was, in a semi-crouch with the sword thrust out before him; and he expected to feel Sieur Anton's hands on him as his uncle's had been so often, pulling and pressing, only that he couldn't guess what was wrong with his line, so far as he could tell it was perfect all the way from his back foot to the far-thrust tip of this beautiful sword . . .

'Stand up.'

Marron straightened slowly. Sieur Anton had Josette in his hand now, and gestured with it – with *her* – to send him back against the wall.

'Your line is good; but you jerk in your movements, you use too much energy. You should flow from one position to the next. Don't force the blade so, let it rather lead your hand. Learn to trust your sword. Like this . . .'

He demonstrated, and yes, his movements were precise but liquid, like a dancer's. Marron tried to imitate and was stopped, corrected; tried again, and was corrected again. And tried again, and again.

There was sweat on his skin and his lungs were labouring when he finally came from first major to seventh minor position without an interruption. He glanced at Sieur Anton, and saw him smiling.

'Good. Not quite such an oaf after all, are you, Fra' Marron? There is a deal more work to do, but you may yet not disgrace the blade, when you find yourself in battle.'

Hot though he was, a sudden memory chilled him. He had been in battle already, and disgraced himself and his blade both.

'Sieur Anton, I would – forgive me, but I would prefer not . . .' The sword dropped in his hand; he reached blindly for the scabbard.

'Why so?'

The baby's scream was deafening. He shook his head wildly against it, wanted to dissemble, couldn't do it. 'The work they give us is not worthy,' he said bluntly, and the bitterness in his voice all but stained the air.

'The work . . .? Well. Put the sword up, Marron, and

rest. That's right, lay it on the chest and come, sit.' Sieur Anton sat himself, on the furs that covered the bed, and patted the space beside him. 'Here.'

Reluctantly, Marron did as he was bid. He pushed his hands through sweat-damp hair and hid his eyes against his palms, pressing hard to deny the visions in his head.

'Now. Tell me. What work have they had you do?'

Sieur Anton waited out Marron's silence, and then listened without comment to the tale of the heretic village, Fra' Piet's exhortations, madness and slaughter in the sun. Marron spared himself nothing, from the first use of his uncle's sword – an old woman running stumblingly, and the steel sliding into her back – to the last use of his blood-washed hands, snatching the babe from its dead father and swinging it through the air like a father's game with too cruel an ending. And then he told awkwardly how the memory haunted him waking and sleeping; how he saw the taint still on his uncle's sword, how he heard the baby's wail in wind and stillness, in sweet singing and raucous cries, even sometimes behind the chanting of the brothers at prayer.

Sieur Anton was quiet for a measure after, and Marron thought it was disgust that had caught his tongue, and no wonder at that.

But the knight put a hand on his shoulder and gripped hard, touching now where he had not throughout the long lesson that had gone before; and he said, 'Have you told your confessor?'

Had he not been listening, had he not heard? 'He was *there*,' and he was the cause of it all . . .

'I meant— But no. Of course. It was a stupid question,

how could you? Listen to me, then, Marron. Things happen, and you cannot prevent them; sometimes you cannot prevent your own part in them, sometimes they happen to you and through you. Here in Outremer, especially. We walk more closely under the God's eye, and that is not always a blessing. His anger can touch us, as well as His peace; that can make us mad, for a time.'

A pause, a slow breath that was nearly a sigh, and then, 'When I was fourteen, my father had a family hanged. They were Catari, villagers on our estate, infidels who wouldn't convert. There are hundreds such, of course, on every large estate. The amnesty declared at the Conclave protects them, but not their holy places. There was a shrine in the village that my grandfather had let stand, he said it kept them passive; but he died, and my father is a more devout man. He had the shrine destroyed.

'This was an old and honourable family, if there be any honour in poverty; but one of their sons came up to the demesne that night and fired our chapel. For revenge, I suppose, or for justice. He stood in the light of the fire, and cursed us all. One of the guards shot him; Father was angry over that, I think he'd wanted a slower death for the lad, the better to appease the God. But he had the body thrown into the flames, and then in the morning he took us down to the village, my brother and I and a dozen men in case of trouble; and the whole family was hanged. Nine of them, from grandfather to suckling.'

His hand still lay on Marron's shoulder, though its grip was looser now. Marron stirred slightly against that touch, and said, 'Forgive me, sieur, but it is not the same. Your father made you watch; but we, I, I *did* these things . . .'

'Marron, I said he *had* them hanged. By me, by us, my brother and myself, while he watched. There was one tree, and one rope; I put the rope around their necks, one by one, and my brother helped me haul them up. The lightest of them took an age to die, the old man and the children. And I decided the order of their deaths; my father granted me that privilege. I was fourteen, after all. My brother was only twelve. So it was by my choice that the mother was last to die, that she saw all her children dead before her. Neither did I have your excuse, the heat and fury of the moment. I have known battle-rage, and it does blind a man to reason or mercy; but everything I did that day was done coldly and clearly. My father ordered it, but I was not bound to obey. These things happen here, that is all we can say. That they happen to us, that we regret them later – that is the way of our world, or the will of the God, or however we choose to name it.'

This time it was Marron who let the silence hang between them. He felt comforted, and grateful, but could find no words to say so.

'The blade was my brother's,' Sieur Anton said, stirring, standing abruptly. 'It is named Dard. I had best keep it here for you, I think, to save your brothers the sin of envy; you can practise with the other.'

'Yes, sieur.' Reluctance and relief mixed within him. His uncle's sword would never feel the same in his hand now that he had held one so much better, and already he felt the thrill of owning something so fine, so perfectly balanced, so perfect; but he quailed at the thought of having to explain the gift of it to Fra' Piet, or to Aldo.

'Be patient.' Sieur Anton was smiling again, Marron

could hear it though he could not see his face; the knight was standing at his window, gazing out. 'The time will come when you can wear it openly and use it in the service of the God. His true service, with honour. Did you hear Marshal Fulke in the hall, when he spoke of Surayon?'

'Yes, of course. But – were you there, sieur?'

'I was there. In the guests' gallery, not among my confrères. I had heard that he would speak, and that the matter was important. He has also talked to us since . . .'

Which was how Marron learned what had been said to the knights, so different from what had been said to the brothers. He resented that, a little: it was not only obedience that sent the brothers to battle. They fought for honour also, the honour of the God alone, untainted by knights' dreams of personal glory.

Not that Sieur Anton wanted glory for himself. That much was clear; also that he was fired as so many of the brothers were, by the marshal's call to arms. Marron's mind was still clouded. When Marshal Fulke or anyone spoke of heretics, he saw only slaughtered innocents, and his own hands dripping red.

'Sieur? Have you seen Surayon?' *The Folded Land* he still wanted to call it, as he had been trained to; but after the sermon in the hall and Sieur Anton's own casual naming of the place, he assumed permission. Though he still flinched, anticipating a bruise.

No blow, no bruise; only a laugh, short and harsh. 'Seen it? Of course not. No one has seen Surayon for thirty years.'

'No, but – I mean, have you been there? I mean . . .'

'To where it was, or is, or will be? Hard to speak of, is it not? But yes, I have been there. Once. It is – strange. You ride the road that led there, and where the border was you see a twist in the landscape, in the air itself, a shimmer like the desert heat although that land is green. Through that you see the wrong country, the land beyond Surayon, as though twenty miles of mountain and valley were simply gone. And the shadows fall wrongly on the other side, or seem to, because the road you ride runs north but the road you ride towards runs north-west and the place where it turns is missing, so that what you see is impossible, a straight road lit by two separate suns, it seems.

'And you ride into that shimmer that lies across your way, and for a moment you see nothing at all and feel nothing outside yourself, only a great twisting, as though your skin were turned to the inside and all your bones were free.

'But your eyes clear, and – well, I found myself clinging to a frantic horse that galloped wildly off the road and into some thorn-bushes. Luckily, those stopped him; I had to dismount very quickly, to throw my breakfast at their roots. I believe that is quite a common reaction. When I had recovered myself and my horse, I found that we were on that other road, twenty miles from where I had been a minute before. Surayon is – closed; it is not there.'

'But how . . .?'

'How is that possible, or how will we find it? I cannot answer either question, Marron. Maybe Marshal Fulke can, but I am not in his confidence. Yet.'

There was a determination to that last, that quite convinced Marron. Sieur Anton had an aim, an intent, and would not see it denied.

*

Sieur Anton also, it seemed, had private business now, and would not need his squire. 'Take your sword – your *uncle's* sword – back to where you keep it, and seek out your troop. You need not tell them what we have spoken of today,' added as a warning, quite unnecessary.

'Sieur, I never do!'

'No? Not even your little friend, Alden was his name?'

'Aldo. And no, sieur, not even him.' Just as he would not tell Aldo's smallest secrets to the knight.

'Well. My thanks for that. I value my privacy, and your discretion.' Then, as Marron lingered in the doorway, his eyes straying one more time to the white sheath shining in the gloom of the corner, 'Yes? Something more?'

'Sieur, a question. If I may?'

'In view of that valued discretion, you may.' Did he mean as a reward, or simply because he could be sure of Marron's silence? Both, perhaps. Sieur Anton's words were sometimes subtle beyond Marron's ability to weigh them.

'Sieur, you said it was your brother's sword . . .'

'Yes. Made to his measure. He was a year younger than you, perhaps, but much of your height; and I think you will grow no further upwards. A little more flesh we might look for, though not on a brother's diet . . . Yes, it was my brother's sword,' when Marron still hesitated. 'What of it?'

'Sieur, did he outgrow it, then? Or buy a better?' *Why does he not wear it yet?* was the true question, and, *how do you have it in your gift?* was another, and he couldn't ask either one plain.

The answer he was given, though, was plain enough, and dealt with both together.

'No, he did not outgrow it; and no, he did not buy a

better. He could not, there is none better. He was using that
blade, or trying to use it, when I killed him. I took it from
his hand. I will see you in the morning, Brother Marron.'

A *fratricide*?

No, it wasn't possible. It wasn't *possible*! Sieur Anton
played games with words, he liked to talk himself darker
than he was and he loved to shock Marron; this must be
that same black habit, dyed blacker still. No more than
that, it could not possibly be true . . .

And yet, and yet. Sieur Anton did not lie, not ever; or
never had, at least, in Marron's short acquaintance. He had
and kept his secrets, that was sure, and he could be deliberately mysterious at times, but not deceitful. And this,
why would he lie about such a thing as this?

So it wasn't possible, and yet it had to be. Walking slowly
back to the dormitory, his uncle's sword clutched between
his hands, Marron tried desperately to marry those two
thoughts. Not fratricide, not murder – *these things happen*
whispered in his head, in Sieur Anton's voice, but he would
not hear it – so there must have been some legitimate cause
for brother to kill brother. If one had been grievously hurt,
perhaps, hurt past recovery in an accident or a duel, the
other might use his misericorde in grief and pity, to send his
brother on to the God. Or, wait, there was a simpler story:
a bout, a trial of strength between the two of them, *let's test
that sword of yours*; and by cruel chance or a moment's
madness, the mock battle produced a true death. Marron
himself had nearly died, after all, spitted on Sieur Anton's
furious, frustrated blade. Perhaps that had been the second
time. Perhaps his interest in Marron stemmed from that,

perhaps Marron was a new brother-elect given him by guilt, and so the sword . . .

But Sieur Anton should not have the sword. By all custom and honour, a knight was always buried with his arms. If the brother's death had been an honest affair, Sieur Anton should have laid the sword on the body's breast himself, and folded the cold hands over the hilt, and prayed for the God's kinder grace on his brother's soul. Something surely was wrong, that he had taken it and kept it and now sought to give it away.

Perhaps the brother had disgraced himself and the family, lost the name of knight and the sword with it? Perhaps the blade needed to be purified in Sieur Anton's eyes, and hence his gift of it to one who would use it in the God's service and none other?

Perhaps. But perhaps not. Marron felt somewhat reconciled to his uncle's sword: less fine by far and less grand also, having no pretensions to a name, but so much less complicated with it. Marked, damaged, dishonoured only by his own dark acts that he might eventually redeem, at least it carried no questions in its simple lineage, no doubts, no hint of things done that were darker yet, that would paint the midnight black . . .

His wound was aching – no, more than that, his wound was in pain, aflame. Thinking back, Marron could remember a throbbing that began during that difficult, challenging exercise, which he somehow hadn't noticed at the time. Now the throbbing was a burning iron laid across his arm, and when he rolled his sleeve back he found fresh wet stains creeping through the linen bandages.

If he took it to the infirmary in this state, there would be questions asked, perhaps by Master Infirmarer himself; and no more than Sieur Anton – he believed – was Marron a liar. Besides, his skin was sticky and his hair was stiff, he could say, *no, master, I have done nothing against Brother Apothecary's order*, and his own body would deny his words.

He was not a coward; but this had been a war between duty and duty, obedience to the apothecary against obedience to the knight. He surely didn't merit punishment for choosing the one and not the other, nor for trying so hard to please the one he chose. Perhaps if he simply washed the wound and bound it up again, bound it tightly, perhaps it would heal without Brother Apothecary's potions. And if the scar were a little thicker as a result, if it drew his skin a little tight across the arm and restricted his use of it a touch – well, no doubt that would serve well as a reminder, not to find himself caught again between two masters . . .

No blundering through the castle now, mazed by its many heights and angles; running Sieur Anton's errands had taught him quickly to find his way around. The knight was not patient with delay. He took the sword to his dormitory first and racked it with the others, then ran down through the lower courts towards the stables.

Sunlight dazzled him as he came out of the ramp's shadow into the open yard before the moat. Squinting, his eyes found a bucket beside the stone trough where they watered the horses. He filled that, squatted down in the trough's shade and set to work on the bandages with fingers and teeth.

He was still struggling to loosen Brother Apothecary's

ties when a hand touched his shoulder. Startled, he glanced round and saw bare feet, a white woollen tunic, a curious smile, dark eyes and cropped black hair: one of the Sharai boys, a captive slipped away from his work, come to see what a Ransomer brother did down here, alone and private . . .

Blinking against the sun, Marron thought that he knew the face behind the smile. *Soap*, he remembered, after a moment's searching of his memory. This was the lad who had brought the soap to his troop in their first hour at the Roq.

The smile faded; the boy was stooping over him, concerned, saying, 'You have a hurt?'

'Yes.' And then, with a breath of surrender, 'Can you help me? These knots are tight.'

And his one hand was tired and clumsy, but the boy's two not; nimble fingers nudged his aside and picked briefly at the ties that were not only tight but also wet with spittle now where his teeth had tried them.

Then, 'No,' the boy said softly, 'these must be cut. You wait, I will bring.'

He trotted away. Marron sat back, felt the stone of the trough cool against his shoulders, and made a conscious effort not to hunch his head down low, out of sight. He wasn't *hiding* here, no, of course not; simply resting a little while, to be the stronger later . . .

The boy came back, and brought no trouble with him: only a knife and a cloth, and a big clay pot with a lid on it.

The knots yielded to the blade, and Marron yielded to the boy's tending, after a half-hearted gesture of protest.

The bandages were peeled away as carefully as they could be, but still pulled cruelly at the last, making him gasp and his eyes water. Beneath, the long gash was gaping wide and darkly wet again, leaking blood.

The boy hissed softly between his teeth, and murmured something in his own tongue to himself or possibly to Marron, who couldn't understand it either way. Then he moistened the cloth and dabbed the wound clean, holding the arm tight against Marron's flinching; even the lightest touch stung savagely. He looked again, shook his head a little, and reached for the pot.

The lid came off, and Marron saw a greasy salve gleaming in the light.

'What is that?'

The boy was smiling again. '*Haresh*, it is called. We make it for the horses, when they have a hurt.'

He scooped out a fingerful, but Marron jerked his arm away. 'No! I am not a horse . . .'

'It is good for men, too,' the boy assured him, suddenly solemn. His eyes were fixed on Marron's; his unsalved hand closed gently around the wounded arm and drew it back towards him. 'Oil and grasses, good for any hurt. And this,' with a nod down at the slow-welling gash, 'this is not good. It must be—'

A gesture with his greasy fingers finished the sentence. He didn't have the words, but his meaning was clear. *It must be treated*, he meant; and, *you have not gone to the proper place, so you must take my treatment*, perhaps he meant that also.

At any rate, Marron argued no more. The salve was soothing on the open wound, where Brother Apothecary's preparation had been caustic. The bandages were wrapped firmly in place again, and the cut ends tied off; then the kneeling boy sat back on his heels, smiling brightly. 'You must not use it now.'

'I know,' Marron sighed, 'I know.' *Put me in a stable stall, and chain me to my manger.* He wondered how it would heal this time – if Sieur Anton gave it a chance to heal this time – and then thought he was being ungrateful; the boy had done more to help its healing than Marron could, however dubious his medicine.

'What's your name?' he asked.

For a moment, the boy seemed taken aback. Then, 'Mustar. Mustar ib' Sahir.'

'Thank you, Mustar. My name is Marron.'

Their eyes held, in the yard's silence; then the boy made a quick sign with expressive hands, *I must go, before I'm missed.* He rose swiftly and was gone indeed, no more farewell than that. Marron sat where he was for a minute longer, before pushing himself up and turning back towards the shadows that hid the castle's narrow entrance.

When he found his troop they were on their way down to the stables. By the God's grace, he'd been just a few minutes ahead of looking up to find not Mustar but Fra' Piet at his shoulder. With what awful consequences, he dared not wonder . . .

His confessor sent the troop on ahead, to await a camel-train reported on the road; then he turned to Marron.

'I am told,' he said, 'that you have been fetching and carrying for Sieur Anton. A servant's work.'

'Yes, Brother Confessor. In obedience,' added hastily, and in doubt.

'And yet, in obedience, you cannot share the duties of your troop? Well. If you can serve a knight, you can serve your brothers also. Even those who have placed themselves beyond merit of your serving. Go to the kitchen-master, and say you are to take the penitents bread. He will tell you where.'

The way to the penitentiary cells led down from behind the great ovens, a low doorway and a narrow spiral stair. Even fumbling his way down in the dark with a basket under his good arm he could tell that this was old stone down here, the buried heart of the castle. The steps were worn and uneven beneath his feet, making him wish more than once for a light, though he'd have no way to carry it. What did a brother need to do, to be incarcerated here below? Marron didn't know; he hadn't taken the measure yet of this place, so much harsher than where he had come from.

At the foot of the stairs was a small chamber, not built but hollowed from the rock. Here there was light, an oil-lamp burning yellow in a niche; and a barrel and two buckets, one larger than the other; and two brothers with staves in their hands, standing either side of a passageway that ran away into darkness.

One grunted at Marron's arrival, laid his stave aside and moved to lift the lamp from its niche. He walked a few paces into the passage, glanced back impatiently and said, 'Come, then.'

The passage was chill and damp; the warm smell of baking had followed him down the stair, but did not penetrate so far. Instead the air had an acrid tang that took Marron back again to his first hour in the castle, this time to the wonder and terror of the King's Eye, the touch of magic on his soul.

There was no magic here. Only dark wooden doors thrown back against the walls of rock, and a small rough cell behind each open door; inside the first was a man on his knees and wincing from the sudden light, a brother in a penitent's white shift. A brother and a bucket, Marron saw, and a wooden goblet also.

At the warder's gesture, Marron took a loaf from his basket and handed it in. The man took it in silence, and the warder moved on with Marron at his heels.

And so from cell to cell, and only once was it different. That one the warder moved past with just a brief glance inside; when Marron hesitated, seeing the cell not empty, he was told, 'No. Not him. He is for the steps tonight; if he eats, he may defile the stones.'

Marron understood none of that, only that the man's face lifted blindly and there was despair written there, and all his flesh was shuddering with something more than cold.

There was still bread left in the basket and there was still more to the passage, the light hadn't found its end yet, neither an end to its doors; but those further cells were closed and empty. It was a cold touch, Marron thought, not to lock in the penitents, to lay such weight on their obedience.

The brother with the lamp led him back to the chamber, but his duties were not finished yet.

'Fill the bucket, that one,' the smaller, 'and give them all one dip of water. No more.'

The water was in the barrel, under a green scum. Marron scooped that aside to the warder's snicker, plunged the bucket in, lifted it out with his good arm; looking around as the shadows shifted he saw the lamp being held out towards him, and understood that this time he would have no guide to lead the way.

He took the light in his bad hand, praying not to drop it, and made his way along the passage. In each cell, the penitent brother dipped his goblet wordlessly into the bucket; some gave Marron a nod of thanks, some kept their faces turned away.

When he came to the one who had been forbidden bread, Marron was unsure. He took a step into the cell, but the man there shook his head, his eyes wild in the lamplight. Marron whispered a blessing in lieu of water, and passed on.

Back to the chamber once more, and still one further task. This time, Marron had anticipated it; some of the cells smelled of more than rock and bad water.

A glance from him, a nod from the warder; he took the larger bucket down the passage, and collected each man's wastes. And hauled the sloshing, stinking weight carefully up the steps and through the kitchen, along to the latrines; emptied it into a barrel there, rinsed the bucket out and hurried it back to the chamber.

And was done at last, the warder's passive silence told him so. Once more up the stair, then, the basket of bread returned where he had found it, and he went in search of his troop.

*

They had sweated, Aldo told him, under heavy sacks of grain, and a long and winding way to carry them; but that was finished now, and it was time to bathe. For them and for a hundred brothers more, several troops at a time; they ferried water in a long line from the moat – and here at least Marron could take his part, passing full buckets with his good arm, returning empty ones with the other, seize and swing in rhythm, forward and back – and splashed briefly in the bath-house tubs, in and out and make way for the next man, only those who'd had the dirtiest or the hardest labour looking for soap.

Marron stripped, splashed, gasped at the chill of water drawn from deep in the moat where even a day's sun hadn't reached it, jumped out and pulled his habit on over shivering wet skin – and still was not quick enough to deny Aldo's sharp eye. His friend's hand caught at his wrist, drew the sleeve back, and, 'That's blood!'

'Yes.'

Aldo's fingers picked at wet linen, that darkened too slowly to hide what was darker.

'It's been rebound,' he said slowly, tracing the broken pattern of stains, 'but they should have given you a clean bandage . . .'

'I didn't go to the infirmary.'

'How did it happen?' And when Marron didn't reply, 'What have you been *doing*?'

There was an easy answer to that, *carrying bread and water to the penitents*; but he couldn't lie to Aldo. He said nothing.

'You've been with him,' a statement and an accusation both.

'Yes, of course. But only in his room, Aldo. We talked . . .'

'Talking did not do this,' with a hiss and a tight gesture.

'No.' His friend's anger was too much for Marron; and it was only the talk that had been in confidence, so, 'He had me drill for him, with a, with a sword.' No need to say more about the sword.

'Left-handed?'

'No. But the positions, again and again, and the cut opened . . .'

Aldo scowled, turned his back, kicked off his sandals and pulled his habit over his head.

'Aldo . . .'

But Aldo had jumped into a bath and plunged his head beneath the water. Marron groaned with frustration; and then he was jostled, elbowed aside, other men pushed forward and he lost sight of Aldo in the crush.

When the troop gathered together outside the bath-house, wet and cool and fresh, they were under Fra' Piet's critical eye and there could be no more talking. Marron found Aldo and squeezed into line beside him, trying to talk with his eyes; Aldo cast his hood up to deny him.

Brother Whisperer began to strike, and they marched in silence to the great hall. Head held piously low, Marron watched Aldo's heels rise and fall, kicking up the hem of his habit; even that told of his temper.

So did his tense and upright body, kneeling beside Marron's in the hall. Slowly, though, the service seemed to relax him, familiar words and massed sonorous voices; his anger ebbed as surely it must before the peace of the God.

By the hour's close he was sitting easily back on his heels, and it was the edge of Marron's habit and not his own around which his fingers had closed.

Marron sighed softly and sat more easily himself, leaning slightly forward to glance past Aldo to the end of the line. He was watching for Fra' Piet's rising, the signal for them all to rise and go to supper.

But Fra' Piet knelt quite still in his place, as did all the confessors, and thus all the other brothers also. The preceptor had left with the masters and the knights behind him as always; now, though, here came two of the masters back again. Magister Rolf and Magister Sewart, the Masters Confessors, responsible for the morals and obedience, the faith and discipline of all the brethren at the Roq. And in their train two massive brothers, bulking like bulls beneath their habits; and between those two a man in a flimsy white shift, bareheaded, downcast and shuffling, the penitent who had been given neither bread nor water this afternoon and was not allowed even to cover his head tonight, brought in shame before the God.

He is for the steps, the warder had said; and he was led all the way to the front of the hall, to the steps leading up to the altar. He knelt before them, lowering his head to the stone while his guards remained standing on either side. The masters had mounted the steps, and bowed to the altar; now they turned to face the congregation, and spoke turn and turn about.

'Brothers Ransomers, you are all sworn to this Society, and its three redeeming oaths of chastity, poverty and obedience.'

'Here is one of your number, Fra' Collen he is called,

who has paid money to lie privately with a woman in the place below this castle. In doing this he has broken each of the three oaths: he has been unchaste in his body and in his mind; he has kept secret amounts of money to his own use, and enriched his thoughts with privities; he has been disobedient to his oaths, this Order and the God.'

'The God is merciful. Fra' Collen will not be denied the habit, and sent forth naked and without brethren, as he came to us. His penance is less than that; but it must be made before you all, that you may see his sorrow.'

No more talking. The penitent had been condemned and sentenced; the two masters folded their hands in their sleeves and stood motionless.

It was the other two, the big men who lifted Fra' Collen to his feet, holding as much as helping him up, it seemed. They ripped the shift from him and cast it aside; then they laid the naked man spread-eagled across the steps.

Each of them unwrapped a strap from around his waist, wide dark leather of a short man's length perhaps, though these men were not short. The straps glinted strangely in the torchlight; Marron twisted his head and squinted, heard Aldo gasp beside him – always the quicker, Aldo, especially to see pain or danger – and finally understood, as his own eyes found the answer.

Those straps were studded with iron barbs.

There was no count, or none that Marron could hear; neither had any tariff been declared, so many strokes for such an offence. Brothers might be counting in their heads, from either dread or righteousness, but Marron thought that most would lose the count quite quickly. He hoped so.

For himself, he could hold nothing in his head except the moment, the bright image that made this altarpiece: the whirl of one long strap through the air, above the heads of all, easy to see; the soft and distant sound that was the strap biting at the penitent's body; the high wailing sound that came after, cut short only by the hissing drone of the other strap as the man heard it coming and tensed, Marron was sure, clenched his fists and held his breath, had nothing left to scream with. And so the moment began again, in sound and motion, and Marron thought he never would be free of it.

Until a hand nudged against his, and that was Aldo asking for help here, asking for comfort, just a touch, fingers linked to draw each other through the moment and beyond.

Marron's reaction was instinctive, appalled. He snatched his hand away, *not here, not now, by the God's good grace don't be such a fool! Do you want that to be us up there tomorrow? Each man must come before the God alone. And Fra' Piet is sure to be watching. They'll charge us with breaking all the oaths and heresy on top, they'll flog us till our bones show . . .*

Would they? Perhaps not. But Fra' Piet would beat for such an offence, nothing more certain, and he had a heavy stick for it and a heavy hand. Marron tried to say that to Aldo also, with a nudge and a nod and a prayer that his friend should hear his mind's whisper; but the nudge missed its mark, a tip of the elbow was as much as he dared and Aldo had moved away. Not far, only a thumb's-length of shuffle across the floor, and that must have brought him hard up against the brother on his further side; but it was enough. Marron could hear this message, at least: *you fail me, you betray me, I turn to you and find no one where I used to find my friend . . .*

And that made another moment to be trapped and held by, and now he had two. One was a vivid triptych, blood and pain and humiliation, and the other was an alcove of shadow and regret. Both were born of stupidity, nothing new in the ways of man; both sucked at him, and he thought they would tear him from himself. He turned this way and came back, turned that way and came back, blood and shadow, pain and regret. It was the God, he thought, it was always only the God and how could he hope or expect anything else but that looping road, here in the God's place, before His altar?

No count that he could hear even after the screams had died to nothing, no signal that he could see – though he wasn't looking nor trying to look, not now, he only wished he dared to look away – but at last the penance was ended, for them all. All of them who had paid it, at least; Fra' Piet showed nothing but satisfaction as he led them not to the back of the hall but forward, to the altar steps themselves, where they might the better see how their brother had paid.

In full, Marron thought he had paid; there was no movement in that flogged red scarecrow figure, no sign of breath. The head was covered now with the torn linen shift, to show that his sins were expiated and he could again offer his respect to the God; the rest of him, though – from shoulders to calves he was ripped meat on those marble steps, meat fit only for the dogs and it seemed that they'd been at it already.

They left the hall by a different door; and in the ward outside Marron threw back his hood and stared directly at Fra' Piet, crushed down the voice inside his skull that whispered, *stupid, stupid!* and asked the question directly.

'Will he live?'

'Perhaps.' It seemed this was a legitimate thing to ask: not curiosity – which was disobedience disguised – but necessary to their understanding of the Order and their own place within it. 'If the God wills. Sometimes they live.'

'And if not?'

'Why, then he dies shriven and goes to the God. A happy man. I have seen men cast out, denied the habit; they go broken. He will be new-made, however the God chooses for him.'

Marron thought personally he'd have chosen the other he'd have been cast out before he'd have been so brutalise That sounded not so bad: naked in this heat was n penance, and the women in the village below would ha clothing to spare even for a white-skinned beggar. A alone sounded not so bad either, if it meant having brothers who would strip you to the bone, perhaps to death.

He wondered if that were heresy; and on the though turned to find Aldo in the group behind him, and f him just to see him turn away; and thought perhaps h'd been cast out, naked and alone he felt suddenly, anded it not so much after all.

6

Heights of Folly

…umiliated was how Julianne felt, largely. And angry, and
…dish, and stupid, when she should have been laughing
…free; but humiliated largely.

…nd it had seemed such a neat plan, so perfectly manip-
…ve. One for her father to be proud of, on a small scale:
…he'd worked on a small scale all her life, as well as on
…reat canvas that was Outremer. Manipulation was his
…ition of fatherhood.

…ese days in the castle – and mostly in her room, sat-
…g Blaise's notions of propriety while Elisande came
…ent and nosed around with total licence – had made
…t simply restless, they had made her wild. She had
…l to scream and throw things; instead she had quietly
…sted to Blaise that her palfrey Merissa would be suf-
…fer losing condition in a stable stall, much in need of a
…can on the plain below.

'It's true, my lady. My horse, too. I will tell the stablemaster I'm sure he can find men to give them exercise.'

'No,' she'd said immediately, 'Merissa is a difficult beast; she will allow no one but me on her back. We'd best see to it ourselves. If you ask him to have them both saddled and ready after the midday meal . . .?'

Blaise had frowned, as she'd known he would; and then – as she'd known he would – he'd said, 'I'm sorry, my lady, I can't permit you to ride a mettlesome creature down that road. It would be too dangerous.'

'Blaise, that's ridiculous! Do you think I can't control my own horse? I was riding before I could walk.' Well, almost.

'Nevertheless, my lady . . .'

'Then we will lead the horses down. Or you can ride and lead Merissa, and I will walk behind.'

'Not behind, my lady. Not in my dust. Ahead, where I can see you safe . . .'

Very pleased with herself, she'd been. She wanted nothing in the world more than she wanted an hour's hard riding outside these prisoning walls, but she was frankly scared of the long drop that lay between her and that ride. Only she hadn't felt able to admit it; so she'd let Blaise's fears for her, his anxious responsibility do that difficult task on her behalf. Perfect. She would walk – and enjoy that also, her feet were as fretful as her mind – and then at the bottom of the climb she could have speed and wind and freedom for a while . . .

But Elisande had been listening, and she'd wanted to come too.

'You have no horse. My lady.' He always seemed to have difficulty with the honorific, as though he trusted Elisande not at all, and no blame to him for that.

'No matter. I would enjoy the walk; and I can sit on a rock and watch you, while you ride.'

The afternoon was hot as always, though a haze of thin cloud hid the sun that day. Julianne had begged a lump of sugar from the stablemaster, to pamper Merissa with; then Blaise had mounted, hitched the palfrey's reins to his saddlebow and followed the strolling girls down the covered ramp and the steps that followed, to the gate and the road beyond.

In places the road was steep even for feet; Julianne had found hers wanting to scurry, to carry her down at a run. She'd gripped Elisande's arm to restrain them, and discovered that to be no help at all. The shorter girl was skipping beneath her dress, and beaming broadly.

'This is better! Even the air broods, behind those walls. And no one laughs, have you noticed? Even the knights don't laugh. Not around us, at any rate, and the brothers can't find a smile. No wonder they wear black, their souls are in mourning. It makes my bones ache, living in that shadow . . .'

You were the one of us who actually chose to come here, Julianne had thought but not said.

Down to the first corner then, Julianne taking care to stay on the rock side, on the wall side, not to be near the fall. Behind them the steady clopping of Blaise's horse, the lighter skitter of Merissa's hooves – and then a whicker, and the sergeant's voice cursing loudly, heedless of his company.

They'd both turned to see him fighting, tugging at Merissa's reins while she reared and danced at his back, pulling so hard she might overbalance all three. Julianne had gasped; Elisande had gasped and then run.

Had run back, squeezing between the rock wall and

Blaise's unhappy, snorting mount; had run to Merissa and seized hold of her saddle. Had pulled herself up awkwardly, hampered by her skirts and the palfrey's shying; then had lunged forward to grab the ornate bridle, hugged herself to the horse's sweating neck and murmured urgently into the nearest ear, all the time tugging the tossing head downward, turning it away from the drop.

It had seemed to take only a moment, though it must have been longer. Soon, though, Merissa had stood quietly under Elisande's hands and voice.

'Loose the reins, sergeant,' Julianne had heard that clear voice call. 'She needs someone on her back, that's all, she's nervous without.'

Blaise had huffed to himself, looked back, glanced forward at Julianne like a man betrayed – *she will allow no one but me on her back*, she remembered, and blushed for the lie exposed – and then had deliberately undone the reins and let Elisande draw them into her hands.

And so they had gone on down the road, Julianne walking alone and bitterly humiliated with one hand brushing the rock for surety and extra shame while her sergeant and her friend rode behind.

At the foot of the climb Elisande had slipped down without a word, holding Merissa's head for Julianne to mount from a convenient boulder and then, smiling up with no sign of smugness, had perched herself on that same boulder: a gesture, *go on, ride, don't worry about me*.

Julianne was riding still, cantering hard across the dry and dusty plain, aware of Blaise behind her but not looking back, never wanting to see his face again. Nor Elisande's. She was playing the child, she knew; but there was no stomach in her to resist it, unless and until the wind of her passage should blow this sulky resentment out of her head.

She closed her eyes against the dust and sting, trusting her horse to bear her safely – and nearly she lost all trust, all faith and her seat also, all dignity and maybe even her life as well.

Merissa didn't falter, she didn't check or turn or shy aside; she stopped. Stopped suddenly, stopped dead in her tracks. Her hindquarters dropped as she dug her hooves into the ground; Julianne slammed forward against the arched neck, toppled and slid, lost her stirrup, snatched frantically at the long mane and just caught herself in time. She struggled back into the saddle, trembling; found Merissa trembling also beneath her, and looked past the tossing head to see a whirl of dust and sand hanging in the air before them and just beyond it a gulf opened up in the plain, only a pace, a running horse's stride ahead . . .

No, not a gulf, and not newly opened. She looked again, and it was a river bed baked dry under the summer's sun, a fall of perhaps twice her own height before she would have hit the cracked mud and stones at the bottom. Not a gulf, but enough, perhaps. Enough to have broken bones for sure, and possibly every bone they had between them, herself and Merissa both.

A whirl of dust and sand – her eyes jerked back from the drop and saw only a sift of dust and sand falling. She barely had time to think, to wonder *djinni?* before there was another horse drawing up beside her; she stared neutrally ahead, not to see Blaise's anger.

She felt him reach over to Merissa's bridle, felt him seize the reins and draw them from her slack fingers.

'My lady . . .' His voice was tight with fury, and rightly so; like a child, she awaited her scolding. But, 'My lady, we will return to the castle now,' was all he said, perhaps all that he could trust himself to say.

She nodded a mute acquiescence; he tugged Merissa's head around and led back the way they had come, at a slow walk. Humiliation again, but Julianne deserved this. And Merissa needed it. There was still a constant shake beneath her skin, she needed calm and cooling to settle her, to help her forget that moment's terror. Terror of the fall or terror of the djinni, either one.

With nothing to do but sit the horse and feel the shame, Julianne turned her head away from the sergeant's stiff back and gazed around her, as she had not before. The land was brown and barren, growing only thorns. Thorns and dust – she saw a dust-devil and her heart skittered against her ribs, once more she thought *djinni* for a moment before she blinked and stared and saw a shadow within the dust, a horseman coming fast.

Blaise had seen him too. He reined in, gestured to her to be still; his hand went to his sword.

One good thing, he wouldn't want another horse tied to his, if it should come to fighting. He let Merissa's reins drop; Julianne reached forward to retrieve them. She could flee if she had to, if there was cause; if not – and likely not, surely, this close below the castle – at least she could meet this urgent newcomer with her own horse under her own command.

He was slowing now, the man who rode towards them,

kicking up less dust: a young man, she saw, on a massive destrier. He wore white, though a black cloak flowed behind him. One of the knights from the Roq; she released a breath she hadn't realised she was holding.

Blaise had relaxed too, at least to the point of taking his hand away from his weapon.

'Hullo!' the knight called. 'Is all well with you? I saw the lady riding hard, with someone in pursuit, it seemed; and I knew of the river, and thought perhaps she did not . . .?'

'I thank you for your care, sieur,' Julianne said briskly, taking control of more than Merissa. She was pleased to find her voice quite steady. 'We were exercising the horses, that is all. Merissa likes to run.' But that was not quite all; he cocked an eyebrow, and she felt herself obliged to confess. 'You are right, though, I did not know about the river. It's quite hidden, in this drab ground. Luckily, Merissa's eyes are sharp . . .' *Mine were closed*, but she was not going to confess that.

'Indeed. I've never seen a horse halt so suddenly. She's taken no hurt, I hope?'

'None, I thank you, sieur.' Except to her nerve, perhaps, but this was not the time to test it. Neither Julianne's.

'That's good. Are you riding back to the castle now?'

'We are, sieur,' Blaise, grimly.

'You'll permit me to accompany you, I hope.'

'Please.' She'd be grateful for his company.

'Thank you. Ah, your veil has come adrift, my lady . . .'

He was laughing at her, she thought, this young knight. She scowled, swallowed her tongue in preference to thrusting it at him – *not childish, not again* – and reached to draw her dusty and disarrayed veil across her face.

'Too late for discretion, I fear,' she said, as lightly as she could manage.

'My lady, I shall breathe not a word.' He bowed low in the saddle, and yes, he was definitely mocking her now. 'But as I know so much of you already – I know your beauty, and your horse's name, and that you like to ride faster than caution would decree – may I not know your name also?'

'I am called Julianne de Rance. And you, sieur?'

'Anton d'Escrivey. A sworn knight of the Society of Ransom. But I have heard the name of your father, I think, my lady de Rance?'

'And I yours, perhaps.' The Earl d'Escrivey was vassal to the Duke of Ascariel, and held a large estate within that dukedom. So far as she knew, he was childless; the heir-presumptive was a brother. This might be a nephew or a young cousin, though, or else an acknowledged bastard.

'Indeed?' His face was neutral suddenly, a mask; very likely the bastard then, she thought. Sent away to the Ransomers, perhaps, for discretion's sake, with no more than the name to expect from his father. 'Well. If we ride a little to the west, I left my other horse there, and my, ah, my squire. But here they come now, I think . . .'

There was another, lesser cloud of dust approaching, that resolved itself soon into a horse and its rider. Julianne's eyebrows twitched; the horse was another great destrier, but that was no squire on its back. It was a young brother of the Order, barely more than a boy by the look of him, and he was in serious difficulty.

'One moment, my lady, if you will forgive me . . .'

D'Escrivey turned his horse and went to meet the lad;

his voice carried back to Julianne's straining ears, with a bubble of cool amusement in it. 'Marron, the art of couching a lance for battle is very different from the art of conveying a lance home. And no one, no one at all has ever successfully couched two at once, however great an advantage there might be for the knight who first achieved it. Take them further under the arm and grip them so, here, where they will balance . . . Good. Now follow; and as I told you, be firm with Alembert. He will be wilful, if he thinks you weak.'

The lesson learned to the knight's satisfaction, he trotted back to Julianne's side.

'You have an original esquire, Sieur Anton.'

'He is unique,' said solemnly. 'I came close to killing him a few days since, and now he dotes on me.'

Julianne wasn't sure that she believed either part of that; but the young brother was close enough to overhear any challenge, so she held her tongue.

She felt somewhat surprised to find Elisande exactly where they had left her. Now, though, the other girl was standing on the boulder, staring up the slope. There was a party on the climb ahead, above, perhaps halfway to the summit: mounted men Julianne could see, and some on foot also, with what seemed to be a small wagon in their midst.

Elisande turned at their arrival and made a vague bow towards the strangers in the company, then remembered her skirts and made a worse curtsey. It was obvious, though, that her interest was elsewhere; her eyes were already shifting back to find the group on the hill.

Behind Julianne's shoulder, d'Escrivey laughed lightly.

'The wind does play havoc with a lady's veil today, does it not?'

Elisande grunted, and wrenched her veil somewhat across her face.

'Who are those people?' Julianne asked, forgoing the introduction that she should properly have made. She didn't want the insinuating Anton d'Escrivey wondering if perhaps he knew Elisande's father also.

'A baron from the south, with his retinue. They have – they *say* they have a man with them, a prisoner. In a barrel.' Her face twisted, and Julianne thought there was something more, that she was not saying. 'They certainly have a barrel. A wine-tun by its size, sealed and roped to a wheeled platform. Which they have dragged twenty miles, up and down, along this road.'

'To what end?' d'Escrivey demanded, smiling once more.

'To bring their prisoner before the King's justice, they said.'

'The King is in Ascariel.'

'But the King's eye is here, they said.'

Behind her, Julianne just caught an insuck of breath from the brother-squire boy, Marron.

'The King's eye is everywhere,' d'Escrivey observed blandly, 'and it is the duty of any noble, even a petty baron, to dispense his justice. In his, ah, absence. Who is the prisoner?'

'They gave me no name,' Elisande said slowly. 'Only, they told me he was, was Surayonish.'

'Surayonnaise, for preference.' But that was a murmur, and the last for now of his wit; d'Escrivey stared bleakly up the scarp at the distant figures, marked more by their sharp black shadows than themselves. 'I hope it's true . . .'

'Why so?'

She was answered with a shrug. 'He will be tortured in any case; the accusation is enough. The more he denies it, the less he will be believed. At the last, I daresay he will be executed; and why suffer and die for a falsehood, what martyrdom in that?'

It sounded reasonable, for so cool a soul; but once more Julianne did not believe, and this time she had a reason. She had recognised him now, finally. He was the man from the gallery, from her first evening in the castle: the man who had listened so avidly to Marshal Fulke that he had uncovered his own head in the God's presence, as a gesture of an oath unspoken, a bond, a commitment. She thought that he really did hope to open that barrel and find a Surayonnaise within.

Merissa shifted beneath her, bringing her mind back to a more immediate shadow in her life.

Elisande made a sign to her that said, *get down, if you like, I'll ride her up.* Julianne was tempted; but pride could override fear, that was an early lesson from her father, and oh, she was too proud to confess such a weakness in this company.

'Can your – squire take Elisande on his mount?' she asked d'Escrivey instead.

'If he's not too fearful of woman's flesh.' The knight seemed quickly to have recovered his biting humour. 'And if he doesn't lose hold of those lances. Marron?'

'Yes, sieur. I can manage.'

'Then do so.'

D'Escrivey gestured Blaise to ride on and followed immediately after, not bothering to watch. Julianne was less insouciant or more curious; she saw Elisande's slightly graceless scramble up the big horse's flank, Marron's blush as they tried to adjust two slender bodies to one heavy saddle, Elisande's grab that only just saved the lances from clattering to earth. But the knight was getting too far ahead, and she wanted that man's company; she kicked Merissa on at a trot.

The road was already steepening beneath them. D'Escrivey courteously made room for her on the inside, between himself and the rock; she'd been depending on that. Iron manners, the lords of Outremer had, and hammered them into their children too.

Iron manners and a wicked tongue in this one. 'Does your horse dislike the drop, my lady?'

He must have seen the relief on her own face and not Merissa's as they came into the somewhat shelter of his body, the greater shelter of his horse. 'She does,' and that was nothing but true, that was how this afternoon's humiliation had begun. 'I think yours will reassure her, though. And having me on her back, that too . . .'

And so it seemed; Merissa at least was calm enough as the road climbed and turned, climbed and turned again.

It was Julianne who was anxious, who felt a chill sweat on her skin at every corner, where try as she might she couldn't help but see the ground so far below them and nothing to clutch at, only the endless fall just a step, a breath, a moment away . . .

At last her nervousness seemed to reach down and touch her horse; Merissa snorted, sidled, balked suddenly at an outcrop jutting from the rock.

'Lady Julianne,' and d'Escrivey's voice was soft and serious, entirely bereft of humour at her expense or any, 'I think perhaps Merissa would be more settled if I took the reins and led her, by your consent? She would still have you on her back, for reassurance.' The pure diplomat Julianne thought him, just for a moment; until he added, 'If you were to close your eyes, she wouldn't know.'

And neither would Blaise ahead of them, a turn ahead; neither Elisande, mounted with the clumsy brother at least a turn behind . . .

So for the second time that day, Julianne agreed to have her horse led beneath her; and for the second time she rode with her eyes screwed shut.

A murmured word from d'Escrivey warned her of the approaching gate. She took back the reins, and rode collectedly through and on up to the stables. There she gave Merissa over to a boy's care, and stood with d'Escrivey and Blaise as the two laggards of their party came into the yard. Marron, she saw, was blushing still.

Once they'd dismounted, the lad glanced at d'Escrivey, she thought for permission to leave; the knight delayed him, with a casual gesture of his fingers.

'Marron, can you attend me after supper? If I ask it?'

'Yes, sieur.' And there was almost a pleading in his voice, she thought, some reason he'd be glad to.

'Good. Then make it so. My lady Julianne, will you permit me to call on you this evening, in your chamber?

Between your companion and my holy squire, I think we have chaperones enough.'

'Sieur Anton, thank you. I should be delighted.' The evenings hung heaviest; it was a long time, often, between nightfall and sleep.

'Excellent. Marron shall bring me to you, then, after the supper hour. Until then, Lady Julianne, Lady Elisande . . .'

A flourish and he was gone, with Marron following a little flustered, a little uncertain, glancing back to make an ungainly farewell himself.

Elisande chuckled, but Julianne was quiet and thoughtful all the way back to their room in the guests' tower.

Why a barrel?

That was the question that occupied them most through the hour before evening prayers and the hour afterwards, when they ate quietly together in their room. There was something laughable and sinister both, about a man in a barrel. They did laugh, but uncomfortably; and Julianne didn't need d'Escrivey's prediction of torture and inevitable death to sober her.

'The boys in Marasson,' she said slowly, 'they have a game where they will take a dog from the streets, and put it in a barrel. Then they roll the barrel through the city. When they get tired, they put it in the river, and gamble on how far it will float through the falls. They call this game Shaming the Emperor's Brother.'

'Do they?'

'Historically, brothers are notorious. The Imperial throne is no safe place to sit, if you have a brother. The current Emperor had three, when he ascended the throne; now he has one.'

'Are the rest in his cellar, then, does he keep them in barrels?'

'One was poisoned and one died making war, though he was probably not killed by the enemy. But the children's game is older. It is said when the Emperor's great-great-uncle sat the throne, *he* used to have his family put into barrels and rolled through the streets of the city, to keep them submissive. It is also said that his favourite method of execution was to put a man in a barrel and send him down the river to the falls. With all his family floating in line behind him, like as not. I never spoke to anyone old enough to remember if it was true.'

'The children remember,' Elisande said, 'in their games. Believe it. But there's no river here, or none with water in it. Do you think they'll just roll him off the walls?'

'No, I'm being foolish. Of course they'll take him out of the barrel, they must have done it as soon as he arrived. But why put him in it, then? Why not just put chains on the man and let him walk at your horse's heels?'

'I think because it's like a dungeon they can move. It's safe, they have him penned, he can't escape; and also it's dark, it's cramped, I'm sorry but it must stink in there by now. That's punishment, Julianne, as much as the baron dares. He brings the man to face the King's justice, to be sure; but he administers a little of his own along the way, he makes him suffer. Just because he can.'

'Yes. Perhaps. Could the man stand up, in the barrel?'

'Not if he's as tall as I am,' said Elisande, who was not tall at all.

'How do you suppose they gave him food and water?'

'Through the bunghole, if at all. But a journey of twenty miles? I don't suppose they did. Even if they took two days over it. He's from *Surayon*, Julianne. Or they think he is.'

Heretic, blasphemer – of course they wouldn't feed him. He might have been in the barrel a week before they took to the road, and they might not have fed him at all. Twenty slow miles in a barrel under an unrelenting sun, and no food, no water – and she'd been *laughing*? No longer. Julianne had more than one reason to be grateful when there were footsteps and voices, no, one voice rising on the stairway outside, and then the soft sound of a finger scratching at the curtain that overhung their doorway.

She made a hasty sign to Elisande, and they fumbled with their hated veils. Then, 'Yes, come . . .'

There was a moment's hesitation beyond the curtain, sounds of shuffling and confusion; then a short barking laugh that held more impatience than humour in it, and his voice again, 'No, Marron, *you* take the curtain, and you hold it back for *me*. You see?'

'Yes, sieur . . .'

The hanging was pulled back and the knight came in, ducking beneath the lintel. Behind him, Marron had a blazing flambeau in one hand, the curtain gathered in the other; Julianne could see him twisting his head almost frantically from side to side, but couldn't see why until he shrugged and stooped to grind his brand out in the angle between floor and wall, with a shower of sparks.

The curtain slipped from his grip and fell down to mask his antics. Julianne perforce turned her eyes to his master, but still kept an ear cocked towards the doorway. Whatever

they used here in the Roq to give a head to their flambeaux, it was potent but obviously friable; some of those
sparks had been live coals, not dying cinders. She could
hear scuffing sounds, and pictured Marron stamping
urgently on the glows in rope-soled sandals; she heard a
yelp, and grinned pitilessly.

The veil should hide the grin, but alas, she hadn't heard
a word of the florid greeting with which d'Escrivey had
been gracing her. And alas, the veil had not hidden that
from him. With a malicious smile of his own, he called out,
'Marron, leave that heathen dancing and come inside.'

The curtain twitched, and Marron sidled through.
Blushing again, she saw. He hesitated at the carpet's edge,
and shuffled his feet oddly; when he stepped forward, his
sandals remained behind.

D'Escrivey made a soft sound of amusement in his
throat, and gazed around at the room's furnishings. 'It wants
a little elegance, perhaps, compared with what you must be
used to, my lady. I hope you feel comfortable here?'

'Perfectly, thank you.' She sat down on her bed to prove
it, and gestured him towards the settle opposite. He
ignored that, choosing to stroll over to the window, and
talking all the way.

'Good, good. The Order is careful of its guests. We
knights must supply our own poor comforts, while the
brothers are actively forbidden any comfort – is that not so,
Marron?'

'Yes, sieur.'

'Yes. I took the liberty, my lady, of bringing a little wine
with me, for fear that the Order's care did not run quite so
far . . .'

It was Marron, of course, who had actually carried the wine; he fumbled a scrip from his shoulder and delved inside, producing a flask and goblets that gleamed silver in the candlelight. He broke the seal on the wine and poured, brought a goblet to her and blushed once more as their fingers touched. At least his eyes had met hers directly, though, just for a moment. He wasn't one of those who held females in contempt, she thought, only a boy on the threshold of manhood who had probably had little to do with women since he left his mother's teats. They ordered these things differently – better, she thought – in Marasson.

Marron served Elisande, and d'Escrivey; then he returned to the cold hearth where he had left his scrip. He knelt there and folded his hands passively in his lap.

'And the fourth, Marron,' d'Escrivey said quietly.

The young brother lifted his eyes, gazed at the knight and said, 'Sieur, I think wine is a comfort.'

'You are not required to think, lad. That's why you take the vow of obedience, to prevent you from thinking. Pour yourself some wine, and drink it. Oh, and I absolutely forbid you to mention it to your confessor, do you understand me?'

'Yes, sieur.'

D'Escrivey nodded and turned back to the window, folding back a leaf of the screen to see out more clearly.

'Won't you sit down, Sieur Anton?' Julianne insisted.

'In a moment, my lady. I just wanted to see— Ah, yes. There it is.'

Almost, she stood up to go and see what so intrigued him; it was an effort to stay where she was, but she made it determinedly. He was teasing again, and she refused to satisfy him.

Elisande, it seemed, had no such inhibitions. 'There is what, Sieur Anton?'

'A fire, in the stable-yard. I had heard, but I wanted to be sure.' Anything, it seemed, might amuse this man, but this time his voice was cold, and the smile she heard could be nothing but contemptuous.

'What are they burning?' Elisande asked.

'The barrel you saw on the road, my lady. The cautious baron has ordered its destruction, for fear of its being contaminated. I thought perhaps they might keep it to fuel a later fire, assuming that the prisoner burns, but the baron wanted this done in haste. The stablemaster may have felt the same; I imagine it cannot have smelled too sweetly.'

'Sieur Anton – *why* a barrel? It seems so, so foolish a way to transport a man . . .'

'The baron is a cautious man,' he said again, showing her that smile now, that had no hint of generosity in it. 'And a man from Surayon is necessarily a sorcerer. He feared spell-casting on the road, I suppose, a summoning of demons to rescue their benighted brother; so he had the man sealed in a barrel to deny him light and air and earth and fire, which, as is well-known, are all essential to the making of a spell.'

'That is . . . ridiculous.'

'Indeed. You have had the pleasure not to meet the baron; I was less lucky. He is a ridiculous man.'

'What is more ridiculous,' Elisande said, from where she sat decorously on her own bed, 'is the accusation that this prisoner comes from Surayon at all. That land has been closed for thirty years; why would a man leave it now? And how can they tell his country, in any case? Is it branded on his skin?'

'There have always been rumours that some men come and go from Surayon; there have always been an unlucky few wanderers accused and questioned, and I never heard that any were found to be innocent. Confession and death must seem easier in the end, I suppose. When the question is unrelenting.'

Julianne shivered. She had seen exotic deaths in Marasson, they were almost a commonplace in that exotic city; and of course she had always known of the Emperor's inquisitors and their work, invisible but not secret, spoken of in speculative whispers. Indeed she had met some of those men at court, had touched their hands in politeness and been amazed that their skin was not chilled by their duties, that they carried no reek of the dungeons on them.

D'Escrivey noticed her shudder, and smiled. He had been merciful on the hill, but not here, not in company. 'My answers upset you, my lady. I'm sorry.'

'No. You tell the truth, and I am grateful for it. It's the thought of innocents suffering that upsets me.'

'It is always the innocents who suffer,' he replied bleakly. His expression turned inward for a moment; then he shook his head and offered her a brighter smile. 'How long do you expect to remain with us, Lady Julianne?'

'I can't say. My father sent a messenger to Elessi; no doubt an escort will be on its way shortly, if it has not set out already.'

'No doubt. If the messenger arrived safely. There is dangerous ground between here and Elessi.'

That she knew. Sometimes she caught herself hoping

that the message had miscarried, if only to grant her a few days' more grace, even in this dull castle. She was not eager to meet her future husband. But, 'The preceptor has also sent messages, by a man and a bird, for surety.' The preceptor had called on them here, their first morning in the Roq. A kindly man he seemed, with gentle manners and a beautiful voice; she had had to remind herself forcefully that he was master of this stony place and all its men, and that no man who was given guard and command of the Kingdom's northern border could truly be so sweet-natured as she had thought him.

'That is as well, I think. But even so, a bird might meet a hawk and a good man on a good horse will take some days from here; a squad would take longer to return. We have you for a while at least, my lady. Has anyone given thought to your entertainment?'

'Oh, I need none,' said lightly, against her stifled heart. 'I have Elisande for company, and all the castle to explore,' though that was a lie pure and simple. Elisande might explore, and did; Julianne felt the weight of her reputation, and stayed within. She wanted no taint of gossip for Blaise or his men to carry back to their country, that must be hers also. 'So long as I can ride sometimes, and meet congenial company occasionally,' with a little bow in his direction, a feather's-weight of mockery to score against him, though actually she meant it, 'I shall be quite content. Certainly you and your confrères must not trouble about me, you must have burdens enough.'

'My lady Julianne, you are no burden.' *Not even when you gallop near to destruction on the plain, or tremble with terror on the climb home*, his eyes taunted, outscoring her a hundredfold, a thousand. 'I would take you hawking or hunting to ease the time, but alas, it is not only the brothers who take grievous oaths. Such sports are forbidden us, so long as we wear the black. Marron, I think the ladies' goblets are empty; I know mine is.'

'Your pardon, sieur. My lady . . .'

He hurried around with the flask, not staying to see her sympathetic smile; she thanked the back of his head regardless, and sipped. It was good wine, red and warm and spicy; certainly a reason to cultivate d'Escrivey if he had given her no other, so long as he had access to more of this.

'And yours also, Marron.'

The briefest of pauses, then, 'Yes, sieur,' and the sounds of pouring. Julianne didn't turn her head; his face would flush to match the wine, if he felt her gaze on him.

'Sieur Anton,' Elisande demanded, 'are you truthfully telling us that the Knights Ransomers do not *hunt*?'

'No, my lady. I am truthfully telling you that we are forbidden to do so. Many of my confrères hunt regardless; I choose not to imitate them.'

Yes. He was a man who would take his vows seriously. Julianne wondered for how long he had sworn his sword to the Order; and then – *sorry, Father* – forwent all her training, and asked him directly.

'For the period of my life, lady,' he replied just as directly, and his face was set and bitter for a moment. 'Or until my superiors dismiss me, or my King summon me. For no less cause will I leave the Order.'

At her back she could hear Marron choke as he swallowed down a question, and then choke again as he chased it with a gulp of wine. All right, he didn't dare to ask, but she did. Her mood was fey suddenly, or d'Escrivey's honesty provoked her own, or else his mystery her curiosity. 'Then, if your commitment is so great, why do you not take the habit and serve as a brother, be truly a part of the Order?' *And rise as you surely would, be a master, a preceptor, marshal, Grand Master at last?*

He laughed, briefly. 'My lady, I am a trained knight of the Kingdom. My father set me on horseback before I could walk; I have had a mail shirt made to my measure since I was old enough to carry the weight of it; all my swords have had a noble lineage and a name. Saving your presence, Marron, the brothers are a peasant army, farmers and artisans. I will willingly fight with them, but I cannot fight as one of them.'

He was trying to make himself out a proud man, disdainful, protective of his family's honour; once again, she did not believe him.

To her surprise and visibly to his, the voice that challenged him came from behind her. 'We are the God's soldiers, sieur. Not noble-born, no, though some of us too have families that deserve your respect. But we are the finest soldiers in the Kingdom, because we fight for the God alone.'

'And you think that I do not?' The question – if it was a question – snapped back, cold and furious. This time Julianne did turn her head, in time to see Marron flinch. But d'Escrivey crushed his temper in a moment; his voice was soft and teasing and familiar as he went on, 'The Brothers Ransomers are the most feared army in Outremer, it's true. But you fight in your habits, Marron, because the God protects you. I prefer mail for protection, I am so much weaker in faith.'

'No, sieur.' Another surprise, that flat contradiction; Julianne wanted to read the expressions on both their faces, and so saw neither properly.

'Well. Let us not fight about it. It's demeaning, to argue with one's squire. Remind me to beat you later, for contradicting me in front of these ladies.'

'Yes, sieur,' but Marron said it smiling. Julianne thought that probably the reminder would be given, but the beating surely not. Oh, he was complex, this d'Escrivey, his moods and his mind were quicksilver; and his relationship with Marron was only one aspect of his complexity, one small thread in the tangle that she was finding so hard to unravel.

Enough of trying, at least for tonight. Here was a girl with wit and charm and mystery, in Elisande; in d'Escrivey here was a man with wit and charm and mystery and wine, and what more could she need or want?

The wine, she thought, might be having some small effect on her mood. It was very good wine, they were drinking it unwatered, and a second flask had followed the first out of Marron's scrip. Even so, she hadn't taken anywhere near enough to make her foolish or muzzy-headed. Any girl growing up even on the fringes of the Imperial court learned to hold her alcohol well, or else to abstain from it.

She didn't know where Elisande had grown up, but that girl also showed no signs of flagging. As for d'Escrivey – well, it was his wine, after all. And it had always been considered a young nobleman's duty to drink his peers into unconsciousness if he possibly could; it was an art they practised much. D'Escrivey, she thought, could go on like this all night and still be smiling in the morning. Laughing, indeed. Elisande had said that even the knights didn't laugh; here was one who disproved her. Julianne even thought that once or twice this evening she'd heard him laugh from pure merriment, with no other message in it.

What she had forgotten was that they were not the three of them alone. She was so used to being waited on, to having servants watch her every move against a summons – *though not on this journey,* a slightly bitter memory, a problem not resolved – she'd forgotten that d'Escrivey had made Marron more than a servant tonight. And sitting where she was, with her back to the hearth, she saw him only when he came round to replenish her drink and the others'; and if she thought about him at all, what with the wine and the talk and the laughter, she thought that was all that he did, that he watched and served and waited to serve again.

Until she heard him snoring.

Startled, she betrayed him completely, twisting her head to gape. He was still on his knees but slumped now, head and shoulder resting against the wall and his mouth hanging a little open. It hadn't been a loud snore, exactly, but here was another: and if the other two hadn't heard the first they certainly heard the second.

Elisande snorted; just for a moment d'Escrivey looked abashed, embarrassed either by his squire's gaucherie or else by his own, for having attached such a gauche boy to his service.

He recovered quickly, though, rising and making a bow so low and decorated that his sleeve was in danger of brushing the carpet.

'Ladies, my regrets. My squire reminds me, I have stayed too long.'

'Not at all, Sieur Anton. He has no head for wine, that's all.'

'Ah, but I was using him as my timekeeper, his snores my signal. I am inclined to overrun at the mouth, when the company is congenial; I had hopes that he might prove convenient in this way. If you will excuse me,' as Marron snored again, 'I believe he is getting louder. I will remove him.'

He tried a boot, a gentle nudge to the ribs; Marron only stirred, muttered and subsided, snored again. D'Escrivey sighed, stooped and slipped an arm around the boy's shoulders, another beneath his knees. And rose, lifting him smoothly and easily, where Julianne had expected no more than a sharper kick or two.

Marron stirred a little against d'Escrivey's chest, and the left sleeve of his habit fell back to his elbow.

Julianne frowned. 'What's that? On his arm?'

D'Escrivey glanced down. 'Oh. That's where I nearly killed him. He was lucky to come away with so little harm. Fast, and fast-thinking, but lucky also.' Then he frowned slightly. 'It seems to have been bleeding again.'

'That dressing is overdue a change,' Elisande said, reaching to pick at a crusted stain on the bandages. She bent closer to sniff, and an odd expression passed across her face before she added, 'There's no corruption, though, I think it's healing clean.'

'Even so,' Julianne said, pitching her voice low as Marron was astonishingly still sleeping, and he really couldn't have a head for wine, 'someone should look at that wound, Sieur Anton.'

'Someone will, my lady, I assure you. But not tonight,

and certainly not you, if you were thinking of it. He would die of shame.'

Of blushing, perhaps, if that were fatal.

'Better us than a horse-doctor,' Elisande suggested, quite forcefully.

'Perhaps; but better Master Infirmarer than either one, I think. I will send him in the morning.' He turned towards the curtained doorway then, but checked, glanced back at Julianne and said, 'I have been wanting to ask this all evening, but could not find a way to frame it without seeming offensive to your father's care of you. This gives me an opportunity. I might perhaps have handed Marron to your women tonight to be washed and bandaged afresh, if there had seemed an urgent need; but I am told you have no women to attend you?'

'No.' Except for Elisande, who didn't count.

'May I ask why? It seems curious, that a high-born lady should travel to her wedding with only men to serve her.'

'Sieur Anton, in Marasson I had companions to attend me who were also my friends; I had servants; and I had slaves. I could not ask my friends to come to a country such as Elessi. I would not order my slaves to come; and when I asked my servants, none of them chose to do so.' Nor could she blame them for it. She'd been relieved, mostly, not to have that guilt to bear atop her other burdens.

'Ah. Yes, I see. That is — admirable, Lady Julianne, though I have hopes that you will find Elessi less of a cage than you fear. May I suggest, however, that you not say that to others, or not quite so bluntly? The Elessans are a more sensitive people than they may appear . . .'

'And they expect their women to be silent but grateful?

Thank you, Sieur Anton, I am aware of that. You I can trust, I think, but I have been more careful elsewhere.'

D'Escrivey nodded, bade them both goodnight and turned again towards the doorway. Elisande drew the curtain aside, and peered a little uncertainly down the stairs.

'Sieur Anton, I could carry a candle for you, if you wished it. The brothers leave few lights burning after dark.'

'Lady, the brothers leave no lights burning, except outside your door. But there is no need for you to stir yourself. I have the eyes of a hawk.'

Elisande's eyebrows twitched, but she said no more. Julianne joined her in the doorway, to watch while d'Escrivey felt his way cautiously down and out of sight. They both heard his sudden curse a few moments later, and both guessed its cause; there was a raised step from the tower into the court outside, which his eyes had clearly missed.

'Sieur Anton,' Elisande called down, soft and mischievous, 'hawks cannot see in the dark.'

His voice came back to them, echoing oddly in the stairwell. 'Thank you, I *know* that . . .'

Still chuckling, Elisande let the curtain fall and walked over to the hearth.

'He left the wine, Julianne.' She stooped to pick up the flask, and shook it gently; there was a suggestive gurgle.

Julianne nodded. No doubt they should go to bed, but there couldn't be much left. Pity to let it spoil . . .

With her goblet replenished, she returned to sit on her bed; Elisande drifted to the window, twisting her neck to gaze upward at the stars.

'I wish I could come with you, when you leave,' she said slowly.

'No.' There might have been an opportunity there to ask why it was impossible, to try once more to learn why Elisande had come to the Roq; but Julianne would not prevaricate. Not in this. 'I will not take a friend into that seclusion. You would hate it, Elisande, more than I will.'

'Yes, but I should be there none the less. You will need me.'

'For what?'

'For when the djinni comes. You know nothing of them.'

Julianne sighed, sipped, said, 'Elisande, the djinni will not come. Why should it? How can I serve a creature such as that?'

Elisande had no answer, only, 'It will come. You know nothing,' again.

Jemel had blood on his robes and grease on his fingers, meat in his belly and a guest at his fire; and not only Jazra's eyes to see what honour was paid to him this night, though Jazra's were of course the only eyes that counted.

Still, from where he sat he could see the soft red glows of other fires, the shadows of men moving around them; and every one of those men he knew could see who else had come to eat of his kill, to speak with him and with Jazra.

The blood was a boy's, a child's. Hunting in the last of the daylight, hunting hares for their own fire before the night's march, they'd surprised a flock of half a dozen goats, strayed too far in search of grazing. Easy work for their ready bows: they'd made a game of it – and Jemel had been winning, three to two – when the boy had come stumbling from behind a rock, rubbing sleep from his eyes and staring, sobbing . . .

Staring, sobbing and then running, but not back behind his sheltering rock, neither towards his fallen charges: running towards their slaughterers he'd come, and pulling a clumsy knife from his belt as he ran.

There could have been an arrow for him too, and Jemel the victor in the game. But that knife was brave, and deserved a better answer. He'd dropped his bow and pulled his own knife, leaving the last of the goats to Jazra. He'd slipped past the boy's waving blade, gripped the tear-wet chin and drawn his edge swiftly across the exposed throat; and only then had he seen the thong around the child's neck, the blue bead that hung from it, bespeaking his faith and his allegiance.

Well, too late; and it could have made no difference in any case. The boy had seen them, might have seen others, would certainly have carried the tale back to his village. His death had been needful, and as swift as Jemel could have made it.

Even so, they had taken time to build a rough cairn above his body to keep the foxes off, and had said the *khalat* for his spirit's sake; then they'd carried a goat each back to where their tribe was camped, and had told them where to find the rest.

They had not meant to share that meat with others. Each tribe foraged for itself now, and rode apart, not to leave too obvious a sign of many men's passing. But a guest at the fire must be fed, welcome or otherwise; and where Hasan rode, where he walked, where he sat he was always welcome. If he chose to sit this night at Jemel's fire, to eat of his kill, he was more than welcome. He shed honour as a flame sheds light, and all men marked him.

He leaned forward to cut at the blistered, blackened meat, and his face was lit by the fire's glow. Shaven cheeks, a sharp hooked nose above a neat beard, white teeth and glittering, hooded eyes: Jemel wondered what it was about this man, what power he carried in his voice that could make so many listen and believe, and ride together to follow him against all custom.

Hasan chewed and swallowed, asked what was proper of Jazra's family and Jemel's, spoke of Rhabat and of the desert; and at last he tossed a bone through the dull cloak of ashes to send up a shower of sparks from the fire's heart and said, 'I need men. A few men, a small party to lead the attack and open the way for the rest. I do not wish to favour one tribe above the others; will you two come with me, for the Saren?'

Jemel caught his breath; it was Jazra who said, 'You do us too much honour, Hasan. There are older men at every fire here, wiser in their thoughts and with their swords . . .'

'I do not need age, or wisdom. I need men not afraid to climb in the dark. I have spoken with your elders, and they say you two are goats with owls' eyes, vicious as foxes. Will you come?'

It was true, they had been children in caves on a high cliff's face, scorning the long slow paths where hands and bare feet could scramble directly, up or down in sun or starlight.

'Oh, yes,' Jemel said softly. 'Yes, Hasan, we will come.'

7

What They Carried

A hard hand gripping his shoulder, a dizzy exhaustion in his head: Marron struggled against both, mumbled something unclear even to himself around a tongue too thick to shape words, gave it up willingly and rolled back towards the insistent suck of sleep—

—and hit his nose sharply on stone. Stinging pain jerked his eyes open; he found himself trying to outstare a wall. What wall, he couldn't think.

The hand was back on his shoulder, shaking him vigorously. There was a voice too, a voice he knew. 'Marron, wake. Wake *now*, it's midnight. Can't you hear the bell?'

Hear it, no. He could hear the voice, hard by his ear, and he could hear his own thudding heartbeat, and a groaning that he thought was coming from his own dry throat; he couldn't hear Frater Susurrus. Him he could feel, though, thudding into his bones.

He twisted himself away from the wall, fell onto his back and lay staring up at Sieur Anton. The knight was wearing a simple white sleeping-robe, and holding a lit candle.

'Sieur . . .? Where—?'

'You're in my room, Marron. Never mind why. Up you get now, it's time for prayers.'

Midnight prayers. And his brothers, his troop half the castle's width away, perhaps filing out of the dormitory already behind Fra' Piet's torch; and him not there, which Fra' Piet was sure to notice, he noticed everything . . .

Marron struggled to his feet under an overmastering feeling of doom, of calamity. The last he remembered was drinking wine with the Order's lady guests, and arguing with Sieur Anton. He'd been promised a beating for doing so, he remembered that also; but it hadn't seemed to matter then, and really didn't matter now.

'Sieur, I must, I must go . . .'

His feet felt the unfamiliar textures of Sieur Anton's rugs, his toes curled around a rumple; he was barefoot. He cast about for his sandals, and couldn't see them among the furs that had made his bed. Never mind. A pair of sandals lost would no doubt bring its own penance, but that was nothing, nothing . . .

'No.' Sieur Anton's hand was on his shoulder again, holding him fast. 'It's too late for you to join your brothers. We will say the prayers together, here. Tell your confessor that I kept you late; the fault is mine, not yours. Forget that now. Our duty is to the God.'

Perhaps so, but it was not the God's anger that Marron must face in the morning.

Still, he had neither strength nor wit to argue, with Brother Whisperer tolling his final stroke. In the hall the preceptor would be calling light from darkness, in his nightly miracle; here there was only that solitary candle to speak of balance, of two paths and one promise.

They knelt by the bed as they did each noon, and said the words together; but Marron's tongue stumbled and he couldn't concentrate his thoughts, they kept turning from midnight to dawn, from Sieur Anton's shadowed face to Fra' Piet's hooded eyes and his cold, disfigured hands. Rumour said that Fra' Piet had been a prisoner of the Sharai, that they'd broken all his fingers and tattooed their own god's name across his knuckles before they traded him back to whichever lord he'd followed then. That was when he'd come to the Ransomers, rumour said, to take the black habit and the vows; the vow of chastity was not necessary, rumour sniggered, because it wasn't only his fingers that the Sharai had broken . . .

Marron knew only that there were faded blue lines etched into each of Fra' Piet's knuckles, and that his fingers were twisted out of true. But he could still swing a sword or an axe, or a stick with wicked effect; and he had other uses for his hands that could make a defaulting brother feel worse, far worse than any simple beating.

At last they finished the prayers, though Marron took no good from them. He stayed still, his head sunk into his hands where they rested on furs still warm from Sieur Anton's sleeping; the knight's hand touched his neck lightly, and Marron came close to sobbing.

'You had best stay for what remains of the night, I think. Here . . .'

Marron heard Sieur Anton stand and move around the room, heard a flask uncorked, lifted his head and stammered, 'Sieur, I – I want no more wine . . .'

'I agree. Drink. This is water.'

And it was, cool and instantly welcome to a parched, greedy throat. He drained the goblet and held it out, mutely asking for more; Sieur Anton chuckled and refilled it.

'Sip this time, it'll do you the more good. Then back into your corner, boy. And this time see if you can wake me at dawn bell, as a squire ought.'

'Yes, sieur . . .'

He thought that was a test, and he was determined not to fail. He'd stay awake the rest of the night, rather than have Sieur Anton rouse him again. But the knight blew the candle out and darkness drew Marron down into itself, and thence into sluggish, difficult dreams that held him in confusion until a deep thrumming sound shook him free.

This time he knew exactly where he was. Where and when, because that was Frater Susurrus calling again; which meant that the sun was creeping up over the horizon, and there was no time for him to creep for all that his body yearned to . . .

He threw off the furs that covered him so warmly, such rare comfort; *the brothers are actively forbidden any comfort*, he remembered, and wondered if he would have to confess this too. No time for panic either, though. Not now, not yet. He rolled to his feet and ran the width of the chamber, three quick paces to Sieur Anton's bedside.

The knight's eyes were open and clear, he was wide awake. Marron felt a stab of guilt, of failure; but Sieur Anton only smiled, and said, 'Yes, boy?'

'Sieur, the bell, the dawn bell . . .'

'Ah. Thank you,' for all the world as though he hadn't heard or felt it himself. He rose gracefully from his bed, knelt and gestured for Marron to join him. 'This time try to keep your thoughts on what we do, boy.'

'Yes, sieur.'

And he did, he managed that more or less, despite his fears for the day. Sieur Anton's soft voice was a guide this morning, drawing his attention back to the God each time it threatened to wander.

When they rose, he thought he would be dismissed straight away to the morning meal. And to Fra' Piet, to confession and awkward attempts at explanation, to stammering half-truths and disbelief and a hard penance thereafter. But Sieur Anton had not done with him, it seemed; he gestured towards Marron's hidden arm, and said, 'Tell me about that.'

'Sieur?'

'The wound has bled since it was bandaged, Marron; by the look, it's been unwrapped and bandaged again. But not, I think, by any brother apothecary. Am I right?'

'Er, yes, sieur.'

'Why so?'

Confession, awkward attempts at explanation that were ruthlessly cut short.

'You're saying that it was my fault, for overworking you?'

'No, sieur. Not your fault. It, it happened, that's all . . .' *These things happen.*

'Well. Perhaps; but I should have been more careful. I did know of the wound,' with a flickering smile like the flicker of light on his blade that morning, when it happened. 'Who treated it for you?'

'Sieur, one of the boys in the stables.'

'One of the *Sharai*?'

'Yes, sieur.'

'Why?'

'I was washing it, sieur, washing off the blood, and he saw, he fetched me something to put on it.'

'Oh? And what was that?'

'An ointment. He said, he said they used it on the horses; but it was good for people too, he said, sieur.'

'*Horse-liniment?*'

'Yes, sieur.'

For a moment, an odd, thoughtful expression touched the knight's face, as though a curious memory had touched him, or a question had been answered only to raise another question in its stead. But then his eyebrow quirked, and he said, 'No doubt it'll do you no harm. But tell your confessor after the meal, and ask him to excuse you to the infirmary. That's an order, Marron.'

'Yes, sieur . . .'

'Go on, then. And after Brother Apothecary, come to me as usual.'

Marron went. As he went, he anticipated. He would join his troop-brothers at table in the refectory. No one would speak to him as they broke and shared bread, because that was the Rule, that meals were taken in silence. Afterwards, he thought, still no one would speak to him. They would all know his dereliction, they would stand in awe of Fra' Piet's anger, none would dare stand with him for fear of the taint. None except Aldo; and Aldo would not stand with him or speak to him because Aldo had not willingly done either now for days.

He would be one alone among his brothers, as he always was these days, these bitter days; and Fra' Piet would set the others to their daily tasks, but Marron he would beckon, lead aside. He would trace the God's sign on the floor in some quiet, shadowed, stony place. Marron would kneel there, raising his habit so that it was bare skin that settled on the stones; and then Fra' Piet would close his hands around Marron's head, gripping hard. They would gaze into each other's eyes – no shifting, no dissembling: they spoke to each other but they spoke before the God, and nothing could be hidden or secret there – and Marron would confess . . .

In fact, he turned out to be wrong from the start, the very beginning of his tale of woe. Fra' Piet met him at the door to the refectory, standing like an avenging angel, dark and ominous.

'Marron. The dog seeks his dinner, I see. Had you not, the dogs of the castle should have been seeking you within the hour. Come with me.'

He led and Marron followed, much like a cringing dog. Through the castle they went, along ways that were no longer strange but dim and threatening none the less, woven with shadow. At last they passed through a doorway and into the small chapel where the troop had been brought on their first evening in the Roq, though never since. A lamp burned on the altar; Fra' Piet genuflected deeply towards it, and Marron imitated. Then a gesture had him scurrying again at his confessor's heels, over to where the sign of the God was set in brass on the stone flags between two pillars.

This was worse than he had anticipated, that he should make his confession here and hungry. He drew up his habit and knelt, shivering from more than that chill touch; Fra' Piet laid his fingertips on Marron's cheeks, and there was a touch that was more than chill.

'Now. Here, brother, before the God: you have absented yourself from your troop without permission, and you have missed holy service twice. You will tell me where you have been, and why.'

'Brother, Sieur Anton, the knight I must serve . . .'

'Yes?'

It was hard, so hard, with Fra' Piet's eyes boring into him and the God listening, the God who knew already. Marron thought of wine and drowsiness, of dozing off to the sounds of laughter, of waking to muddle and headache and the warmth of furs; he struggled to tell truth but not that truth, to deceive with honesty. Better the anger of the God than Fra' Piet's, he thought . . .

'He did not dismiss me, brother. When we heard the summoning-bell at midnight, there was no time for me to join the troop. We said the service together in his room, as we do at noon; and then he said I should sleep there until the dawn, and again we spoke the prayers together . . .'

Those hard, distorted, icy fingers clamped harder around Marron's skull. 'You passed the night in his room? In *Sieur Anton's* room?'

'Yes, Brother Confessor.' Here was an opportunity to lie by omission again, to distract with a small confession. 'I should have slept on the bare floor, I know, but he gave me furs from his bed, and I did use them . . .'

'What more?'

'Brother?'

'We do not sleep softly, Brother Marron, that is the Rule and you have been tempted from it. Very well. What more have you done, that you ought not?'

'I—' His bare feet were cold against his buttocks; he snatched at that. 'I forgot my sandals,' *and pray he does not ask where*.

'You forgot your sandals. What more?'

'Brother, I do not know how else I have offended.' Those were ritual words, the end of confession, and a lie direct; the wine burned acid in his stomach, Fra' Piet's nostrils flared, and he thought his confessor could smell it on him.

But, 'I cannot fault your absence, as you owe obedience to the knight; it is not my place to fault him for keeping you. But for the furs you slept on, you will not eat this day, brother. Going hungry to your bed will be a restitution. For discarding the sandals which the Rule prescribes, you will go barefoot about your duties until I say otherwise.'

'Yes, brother.' That should have been all, and he felt so lucky with it, and so besmirched; he hadn't lied in confession since he was a child, and he half-thought the God would disown him with thunderbolts. But there was still one thing more, and that was a penance in itself. *After the meal* had been Sieur Anton's command, only there was to be no meal, not for Marron. Better now, then, do it all at once . . .

'Fra' Piet, may I have permission to attend Brother Apothecary?'

'Why, are you ill?'

'No, brother, but my wound has bled again.'

'Show me.'

Reluctantly, Marron bared his arm. Fra' Piet looked at the stained bandage and said, 'This has been opened and rebound. By you?'

'Yes, brother.'

Fra' Piet's fingers gripped his forearm, and probed through the bandage. Marron winced, though there was little pain. Those twisted fingers worked silently against the knots, and peeled back the bandages.

The scar was red and raw still, but the cut was healing. Mustar's salve had left a stain, though, yellow on his skin. Fra' Piet rubbed at it, lifted his finger to his nose and sniffed.

'What did you put on this, boy?'

'A liniment, brother.' And then, still on his knees, still confessing, 'From the stables . . .'

'*Horse*-liniment?'

'Yes, brother.'

Incredibly, Fra' Piet laughed: a single, hoarse cough of a laugh. His hands gripped Marron's head again, and yes, this was still confession; he said, 'Who gave it you?'

The fault was his own; he couldn't name Mustar. He lied again. 'No one, I took it myself. I had . . . overused the arm, in exercise,' he couldn't name or blame Sieur Anton either, not in this, 'against instructions . . .'

'And so you were afraid, and sought to hide it. To do what you are not ordered to do is disobedience, brother. To treat yourself for an injury is rank disobedience; if you had done it badly, if the arm had been poisoned through your stupidity, your service would have been lost to the God.

This body is not yours now, to do with as you will; it is pledged to Him.'

'Yes, brother.'

'You may not go to the infirmary,' Fra' Piet said slowly. 'There is no need for it. Since you have treated yourself as a beast, so will we treat you. The troop will be riding horses on the plain this morning, but one beast does not bear another. Instead you will bear burdens, as a packhorse does. Go to the stablemaster, say that I sent you, and tell him you are to be used so.'

'Yes, brother. Uh—'

'Well, what?'

'The bandages, brother . . .?'

'You managed before,' Fra' Piet said. 'You can manage again.'

Left alone, he could and did, with one hand and his teeth; though he managed badly, and the linen would surely work loose again before his long day was done.

Marron was sweating already by the time his troop came filing down into the stable-yard in Fra' Piet's wake. Defaulting brothers sent to the stablemaster for penitent labour clearly had no more status than a slave. There was a duty he would not set a horse to, he'd said, that might yet be fit work for such a brother; and so Marron had been sent to the far corner of the yard, where the dungpile was. Marron knew the rich smell of horse manure and rotting straw, but the stench from this massive heap spoke of something more. A thin liquid trickled from it, running warm and foul under his bare feet; flies swarmed around his head. This must be where the brothers' latrines were emptied, and the chamber pots used by the knights and masters. Emptying Sieur Anton's pot was one of his daily tasks, but he'd always taken that to the latrines. And still would, he thought, breathing shallowly through his mouth against the miasma rising from the slurry.

Magister Raul was watching him, from a little distance; Marron hefted the spade he'd been given and began to shovel the stinking mass as he'd been told to, into a hand-cart that stood beside the heap.

It was heavy work, but he was used to that. And the courtyard was still in blessed shadow, the sun hadn't climbed above the walls yet to bake the sweat from his skin and leave him panting for water; only the foetid air made this vile, so that he poisoned himself with every snatched gasp of breath.

Another shovel drove into the pile close beside his, making him startle. One quick glance showed him a dark head, a white tunic; the boy even spared him a smile, white teeth flashing against nut-brown skin, before he bent again to the work.

They filled the cart, mounding the dung high. Dribbling liquor oozed out between the planks, to spatter on the cobbles below. At last the boy gestured, *enough*, and tossed his shovel up into the cart. Marron copied him, then said, 'What do we do now?'

'Now we pull,' the boy said slowly, frowning over the words. 'Down,' with a wave of his arm towards the sloping tunnel that led to the castle gate.

A pole ran out from the front of the cart, ending in a crossbar; when the boy trotted over, gripped the bar and lifted, looked back and gave a summoning jerk of his head,

Marron understood. This oozing refuse might be nothing but waste up here; on the plain below it would feed the parched and greedy soil, and be welcome.

He took his place at the pole, put both hands on the crossbar and leaned all his weight against it. Bare feet slipped on slimy cobbles, and for a moment the cart felt impossibly heavy; but Marron heaved, glancing across to time his effort with the boy's, and the wheels jerked forward.

Once the cart was moving, it was easier. They'd only gone a few paces, though, when a voice called, soft and liquid, and another Sharai lad came running over. Marron stopped pulling, necessarily, because his partner had. He looked up, and saw that the newcomer was Mustar.

The two boys had a brief conversation, then the other stepped away from the bar and Mustar took his place.

'We will do this,' he said, smiling across.

Marron glanced around anxiously. No sign of Magister Raul. Even so, he was uncertain; no brother would swap a duty so, after he'd been ordered to it. Mustar seemed to have no doubts, though; he just set his slim weight against the bar and pushed with a will. Nothing Marron could do, then, but match him step for step.

They hauled the cart across the cobbles to the head of the ramp; Mustar checked there and said, 'Now we turn, yes?'

Marron didn't understand until he saw the boy hauling at the pole, dragging it around. Marron ducked under and joined him; they turned the cart until the pole was at the rear, then they gripped the bar again and pushed. As soon as the wheels met the smooth slope of the ramp, the cart began to roll; Marron felt the tug of it and leaned back as Mustar did, pulling against the dragging weight.

After the darkness of the tunnel came the steps in their dim-lit canyon of stone. The cart jolted down from one to the next, veering wildly so that they had to fight to keep it straight. Then the gatehouse, the gate and a little level ground, where they had to push again; and then they were out on the road and hauling back, feeling rough rock bite at their bare soles as they struggled to steady the cart.

The road had never seemed so long, nor so steep. The cart dragged them into a constant, scurrying trot; at every corner it tried to plunge straight on, over the edge; Marron's weight and Mustar's were barely enough to hold it, to bump the wheels around. Halfway down, though, he saw Mustar grinning. Another desperate turn that had their heels flying out over emptiness as they teetered on the very edge, only pulled back to the road by the cart's own rolling weight, and he heard Mustar laugh.

No, it had to have been a sob of fear, surely? But a glance across showed the boy visibly enjoying this hectic progress. He beamed at Marron, and shouted above the noise of the wheels. 'It is like riding a horse, yes? A young horse, not trained yet . . .'

Marron forced a smile in return, thinking his companion mad. But a second thought followed hard on that, and denied it. Not mad, no. Only young himself and enslaved, taken from his people – and, yes, his horses – to be forced into drudgery. Mustar's life must be an endless round of work and sleep and waking to work again. Small wonder if he snatched at any thrill that offered.

Thinking that way, thinking for the first time about the

thrill and not the danger, Marron felt his own spirits ease. He was short on simple excitement himself, and young himself, he remembered; and there was a curious pleasure in running the risk and defying it, another in using his body's strength. Another too in being free for a short time, unwatched by censorious eyes . . .

He heard himself laugh abruptly, and forgot that this was meant to be a penance. Where the road ran straight for a while and Mustar began to run also, he didn't hold back; he just let the cart pull him on in great leaping bounds. Never mind the shock of it as his bare feet slammed to ground, and never mind their shared panic and the crazy skid that barely carried them around the bend that came up all too quickly, this was still the closest he'd ever felt to flying.

The road levelled out all too quickly now, the rock beneath his aching, stinging feet turned to dust and pounded earth and the cart was suddenly heavy again, needing to be forced along. They stopped to turn it, to pull instead of push; and having stopped they did neither, just grinned at each other with sweat-matted hair and glittering eyes, pounding hearts and labouring chests . . .

Marron's legs couldn't hold him suddenly, his knees turned treacherous; he had to grab hold of something or else sit down, and there was only Mustar to grab hold of. Mustar or the cart, and that reeked, so he grabbed at the boy. Hung onto his shoulders, wheezing with laughter, and felt thin arms circle his waist and a hot wet snorting head settle against his neck.

'Where now?' eventually, penance and duty resurgent. 'With the cart?'

Mustar pointed to where a rough track left the road, to wind around the base of the great scarp. That would be hard and weary going, and no trace of pleasure to be found in it; Marron sighed, huffed once then stepped deliberately back to the pole. Mustar shadowed him; they bent to their work, dug their toes through dust to find the baked earth beneath, and heaved the cart away.

The track led them around the southernmost point of the scarp, to a village of mud huts and narrow alleys. These people were believers, or they were said to be, though they had their own rites and prayed in their own tongue; it was their women who came up to the castle each day to wash and cook for the knights, a laughing, jabbering counterpoint to the brothers' grim silence.

No women in the village now, or none visible; only old men sitting in their doorways, smoking their *khola*-pipes and spitting, watching the cart's progress with sunken eyes shadowed by heavy white turbans. Marron couldn't even see any children, nor hear them. *Perhaps the brothers came*, he thought savagely, *perhaps Fra' Piet led his last troop here and beat their brains out for saying the wrong prayers* . . .

No, he was being ridiculous. These were no heretics; there was their temple, the largest building in the village, and the God's sign raised on the wall above the door, eyes properly open. Marron bowed his head as he passed under their implacable gaze. Almost he asked forgiveness for the baby, though that surely would be heresy. *These things happen*, he reminded himself bleakly.

Through the village they went, unhindered, unapproached; and came to fields on the far side, or the best this dry country could supply in the way of cultivated ground.

All the land between the village and the river had been broken into rough plots, where millet and maize was struggling to grow. There was no water to be had from the river, though; only a well where an old blind camel walked an endless circle, harnessed to a beam that turned a wheel that raised a leaking leather bucket from the depths. And here were the children: one leading the camel and another driving it from behind with a long switch, one emptying the bucket into a trough and perhaps a dozen more filling gourds from there and running to water the crops. Some seemed no older than five or six; this must be their life, their childhood.

They came running now, to meet the cart. Boys and girls were almost indistinguishable to Marron's eyes, with their dusty brown curls and pinched faces, big eyes and pale pocked scars. They were thinner even than Mustar and his fellow slaves, bone and skin and nothing more they seemed under their ragged robes. And they were shy or wary, talking to each other in hissing whispers but not to Marron, though they clustered on his side of the cart, purely it seemed to keep that much distance between them and Mustar. The Sharai must be devils to them, murdering devils, even here under the great castle. Even a young boy captured and shamed was a creature to be feared, seemingly.

Mustar clambered up into the cart, gesturing to Marron to follow. He did, reluctantly, his feet sinking to the ankles in the stinking load. This was true penance, pitching the dung out onto the track as fast as possible while the stench rose around him like smoke in the heat and the flies swarmed from nowhere, thick as smoke; after a short time his head was swimming as though he breathed *khola* smoke like those old men in the village . . .

Quickly though they worked, the children were quicker. They snatched up this precious filth in their hands and ran off, laying it carefully above the roots of each thin pale stalk before hurrying back for more.

At last Marron leaned on his spade, breathing hard through his mouth, watching Mustar scrape up the last shovelful from the planks of the cart.

'Now we go back,' Mustar said, smiling at his weariness, 'and then we come again.'

Marron groaned. But at least the empty cart would be a lighter burden for the climb, no danger and no thrill; he'd have breath enough to talk with.

'Mustar, how do they live, these people? Those plants will never feed so many . . .'

Mustar shook his head. 'This is second food,' he said; and scowled, and tried again. 'Second time of growing, yes?'

'Their second crop? Second this year?'

'Yes. Now is hot and dry, and bad crop; but in spring the river is full, and all the hills are flowers, and they grow good crop then. This is extra.'

But that extra was obviously needful, or they wouldn't work so hard for such poor results. Likely a second crop made the difference between having enough and going hungry, Marron thought.

Then, 'We must hurry,' Mustar went on. 'The master watches for us; if we are slow, we are beaten.'

And Marron no different from Mustar in Magister

Raul's eyes, not today, just as liable for a beating. They hurried. Indeed they ran at Mustar's urging, at least while the road was flat, and took the hill at a trot for as long as they were able, and so much for having breath to talk with. Marron was gasping and sweating again long before they came into the stable-yard.

When they did, they found it full of horses. Three or four troops were there, all saddling up at once, taking horses out for exercise and training; and Marron's troop was among them, and as he and Mustar edged their cart between the moat and the sidling mass of horses and men he saw first Fra' Piet, and then Aldo.

Fra' Piet gazed at him, at his companion, at what they drew behind them; and he nodded, satisfied. This was appropriate, obviously, this was what Marron deserved.

Aldo gazed, assessed as their confessor had; and his face moved no more than Fra' Piet's, in the short time before his head turned the other way.

Marron didn't understand Aldo. All their lives they'd been friends, close as brothers; everything that had ever seemed worth doing, they'd done together. Even Marron's decision to join the Order had only been possible because Aldo came too. It was what he'd wanted all his life, but he couldn't have done it alone. 'We'll both go,' Aldo had said. 'You join for your father's sake, and I'll join for your sake, and we'll both be famous warriors for the God's sake. There's nothing for me here anyway. My brother will have the land when our father dies, and I don't want to be beholden to him. I'd rather be with you.'

So they'd taken their public oaths together, and trained

together; they'd taken ship together under Fra' Piet, helped each other in times of trouble and sworn private oaths to outmatch the public; and now, in the space of a few dreadful days, that lifetime of love and trust had all turned sour and unkind.

It was jealousy that had come between them, Marron at least understood that much; what he couldn't understand was why. His service to Sieur Anton brought him many extra duties and few rewards. There was the sword called Dard, he supposed, but that was a secret gift and one that only a part of him wanted to accept, for all its craftsmanship and beauty. It was properly a knight's weapon, not a brother's, and its dark history disturbed him greatly. As everything about Sieur Anton's interest disturbed him. Aldo wouldn't let him explain, though, he wouldn't listen; so Marron had taken to avoiding Aldo's company whenever he could, seizing every opportunity to serve Sieur Anton instead, though he knew that each of those occasions only inflamed Aldo's jealousy more.

The cart full again, down they went again; but this time met a camel-train coming up and had to go slow and careful all the way, fighting against the cart's weight rather than swinging with it, squeezing past each high-laden beast with the outer wheel running on the very edge of the road because the beasts preferred to hug the wall.

Down at last, and on the rough track that led to the village, they walked in fierce light now; Mustar glanced at the sky, and reached across to touch Marron's arm.

'The sun is highest,' he said.

Marron squinted up, guarding his eyes with his fingers.

The boy was right, it was noon or near enough. 'So?' No noon meal for Marron today, and none he thought for the Sharai either; what did they have to stop for?

'You will want to pray,' the boy said simply, 'and here is better.'

Of course he would want to pray; only that he had forgotten, and it had needed an infidel to remind him. Marron couldn't believe it, that a lifelong habit could slip his mind so. Hungry and thirsty though he was, sweating and weary and disturbed, his mind on other men rather than his duty to the God – he still couldn't believe it.

The heavy tones of Frater Susurrus rolled down the hill, a minute too late for Marron. The tinny clanging that echoed them must be coming from the village, the priest there calling the children in from the fields and the old men from their doorways, calling anyone else within earshot to come and worship. Marron could answer that summons, he supposed, even Fra' Piet couldn't fault him for it; but he didn't know the order or the language of their service, and he preferred not to be dumb and stupid before the God. He'd pray alone here, as Sieur Anton would be praying alone up above . . .

Praying alone, but expecting not to: expecting Marron, he remembered suddenly. *After Brother Apothecary, come to me as usual* – and Marron had done neither the one thing nor the other, had gone neither to the infirmary nor to the knight. Not his fault, of course, but another trouble for him all the same. No doubt Sieur Anton would devise his own penance suitable to the occasion.

Well. Nothing he could do about it now, except perhaps to compose an apology and an explanation, though he doubted Sieur Anton would have the patience to listen to either. Brother Whisperer was making the air throb about his ears; it was time to clear his mind, and get down on his knees.

Mustar was ahead of him, gone a few paces off the road and kneeling himself. Picking up stones and making a little heap of them, Marron saw, like a cairn. He watched for a minute, once more forgetful of his own obligations; Mustar laid a flat shear of rock across the pile like an altar-slab in miniature, then reached inside his tunic and produced three small slate-blue pebbles, which he placed in a careful triangle atop his construction.

'What is that, Mustar?' Marron asked, seeing that the work was finished and he still didn't understand it.

Mustar glanced back at him, solemn and scowling. 'You pray when the sun is high. So do we, when we are allowed to. Will you stop me?'

'Oh. No, of course not. I'm sorry, I didn't realise . . .' And he was backing away, he realised, nervous before the challenge of a slave and a heathen. Fra' Piet, Sieur Anton, Aldo – anyone else would have stepped forward, kicked the pile of stones apart, cuffed Mustar and promised him a master's beating later. This was blasphemy, after all, right before his eyes. Praying to the Sharai's devil-god might be tolerated elsewhere in Outremer – all the native population was Catari, half of them were infidel even now, and most landowners would endure the offence of their beliefs in exchange for peace and labour – but never here under the shadow of the Roq, and never from a boy who belonged to the Order . . .

Never until now. Let Mustar pray; Marron wouldn't

disturb him. Neither interrogate him, what those three blue pebbles meant. Even slaves were allowed their secrets, or should be; every religion had its mysteries.

Certainly Marron's religion was becoming a mystery to him. He'd thought his God a kindly one, once; he'd thought magic the work of devils. Then there had been the heretic village, the King's Eye, every night the wonder of light in the great hall, light from nowhere at the preceptor's word. He was no longer sure of who or what he prayed to. He'd thought to be closer to the God, here in His own country; instead he felt himself further and further distant.

But he prayed none the less, from habit and obedience and yearning: he wanted to rediscover the easy faith of his childhood, though he was starting to doubt if he could ever do it in this complex and difficult land. He moved a little way away from Mustar, dropped to his knees, and barely remembered to pull his sleeves down and his hood up before he began his prayers.

Saying the words alone, without even Sieur Anton's firm voice to hold him to a rhythm, he mumbled his way through the office more quickly than due respect demanded. All the time a part of his mind was listening curiously to hear Mustar's prayers, and hearing nothing but himself. Soon he was not mumbling but whispering, and still his was the only sound he could catch. Puzzled and embarrassed both, he tried to force himself to a proper concentration and couldn't do it; instead he hastened, concluding in a hissing gabble that could give no satisfaction to him or to the God.

Then he looked around, to find Mustar still on his knees

before that makeshift altar but paying it no heed now, watching him. Marron wanted to ask questions, *do you pray in silence, then, is that what your god or your priests demand?*, but he was too shy or too cautious of giving offence. He stood up and walked over to the cart, Mustar followed him, and they heaved it slowly on along the track.

This time there were no men to be seen in the streets of the village, no children in the fields to meet them. They must still be at prayer; *as I should be also*, he thought, with a spasm of guilt for that poor devotion.

When Mustar moved to climb into the cart, Marron stopped him.

'No, look, it'll be quicker,' *and less vile*, 'if we just tip it. Like this . . .'

He bent his back beneath the cart's side, and heaved upwards. Felt it lift a little and then drop back, too heavy for him alone. Mustar joined him; they strained together, and the cart tilted, toppled, fell with a crash. Marron winced at the noise it made, hoping that nothing had broken.

Half the manure slithered into a heap beside the track; they picked their spades out of the mess and began to shovel at what remained. Mustar was laughing, throwing it high and far to scatter across the crops; soon Marron was doing the same, they were vying to outdo each other, and again it seemed like no penance at all.

Still he sweated, though, his muscles ached and his throat was so dry his laughter scratched at it. When the cart was clear they righted it with a heave; Marron checked the wheels anxiously, decided they had taken no hurt, and then glanced longingly across to the well, where the old camel stood patiently nosing at a pile of dry forage. Even fasting brothers were allowed water, and surely labouring slaves the same . . .?

There was no one to ask, but equally no one to see. He said, 'I want a drink,' and set off determinedly. Behind him he heard a soft scurry of feet, and then Mustar was at his elbow, smiling and panting like a dog to show his thirst.

There was a thumb's depth of water in the trough, enough. He made a cup of his hands, filled it and drank, gulped rather, and then sucked at his wet fingers. Beside him Mustar dropped down and thrust his head into the trough, slurping at the water and splashing it over his hair.

Splashing Marron, too. Warm though it was, it felt cool on hot skin. He threw his hood back and his head down, and splashed enough to feel the wet trickle down his neck when he straightened. He shook his head hard, spraying water like a dog, spraying Mustar. Who scooped a handful of water at him in return, so Marron scooped a double handful back; Mustar ducked and the water hit the camel, which lifted its head and roared.

Marron lost his grin and stared anxiously from the camel to the distant village, for fear someone should come running. There was no movement in the streets, though, and after another bad-tempered roar and a questing turn of its head that seemed to fix its milky, sightless eyes right on him, the camel belched loudly and stood quite still. Marron gazed in fascination as a lump the size of his doubled fists rose slowly up the beast's neck and into its mouth. It belched again, and then began to chew thoughtfully.

It was too much for Marron. He slid slowly down the trough, laughing so much that his ribs hurt and his eyes watered, so that he had to close them against the spangling sunlight.

After a moment he heard Mustar's shrill laughter join with his, and felt the boy's shaking shoulder settle against his side.

'Mustar?'

'Yes?'

'There's a tower in the castle, very old, that has no doors or windows. We call it the Tower of the King's Daughter. Do you know it?'

'Yes,' but the boy's voice was very quiet now, and had no echo of laughter left in it.

'Do you Sharai have a name for it, do you know what it is?'

'Yes,' again, in a whisper. 'It is, it is called the Tower of the Ghost Walker. But please, I did not tell you this?'

'A secret, between us. I swear it. What is the Ghost Walker, what does that mean?'

But Mustar only muttered, 'It is *teref*, it is forbidden. I cannot say.'

Nor would he, though Marron pressed him hard, repeated his oath not to tell, pleaded and almost begged. Mustar tightened his lips and shook his head hard, looking more scared than stubborn.

At last, 'All right, then. We'd better get back.'

'Yes,' and Mustar scrambled to his feet, eager to be off. 'We must bring the cart once more down, and the master will be watching for us.'

Marron groaned, as he followed the boy back to the cart. His body was stiffening already after that brief rest, but his itch of curiosity was redoubled now, and he knew no one else to ask.

Up the hill at a trot again, back once more to the dungheap, stink and shovel and sweat. Through the buzzing that he thought was only flies, Marron heard voices, hooves, the scream of a hawk; and then suddenly one voice, cold and cutting.

'Marron. There you are. I believe I gave orders that you were to wait on me? I am not accustomed to come searching for my squire; nor to find him preferring, ah, agricultural pursuits in curious company . . .'

Marron dropped his shovel, turned reluctantly, stepped forward out of the constant run-off from the heap and saw the knight step an equal distance back.

'Sieur, I—'

'Did you have your arm treated?'

'No, sieur, but . . .'

Sieur Anton's nostrils flared slightly, against his impassive face; Marron flinched inwardly. But then a wonder, Magister Raul at the knight's shoulder and the first time Marron could remember ever being truly pleased to find a master watching him.

'Is there a difficulty, Sieur Anton?'

'Only that this brother has been assigned to do duty as my squire, Master, and he seems to have chosen other tasks without my authority.'

Magister Raul was not a laughing man, but his lips twitched into some semblance of a smile. 'Not of his own choice, I think. This is a penance, set him by his confessor. For what offence, I have not asked . . .'

Neither did Sieur Anton. His eyes found Marron's again for a moment, and he gave a brief nod of excusal, even a touchy smile of his own. Then, 'Too late today, and I'd be glad if you could spare a boy to saddle one of my horses for me; but perhaps we need to discuss this, Master Raul, to be certain whose orders take precedence where they conflict in the same body . . .'

Tell that to Fra' Piet, Marron thought sourly as the two men walked away; then, *please?* he added, picturing the scene. They were both stubborn, both demanding, both intolerant of neglect; only that Sieur Anton had humour too and all the confidence of his birth and position, where Fra' Piet had the grim certainties of doctrine and the Rule. Marron would like to witness that confrontation, just so long as he was not caught in its midst . . .

Behind him Mustar whistled, barely more than a hiss of breath between his teeth. Marron nodded, turned, picked up his spade again but had to lean on it for a moment against a sudden wash of weakness. The flies' buzz was louder now, dizzying, biting at his mind; his skin prickled with a cold sweat even under the brutal weight of sunlight.

Cart full and spades loaded, he bent his back to the bar and pulled across the cobbles, feeling himself truly fallen to a beast's mentality now, unable to think. He followed Mustar's lead without words, turning the cart at the ramp and using his body as a brake, down through the castle gate and onto the road. No caravan's obstruction this time, they could fly again; his body only mirrored his mind, which was flying already.

Down and down, with a hectic swing at every bend. He

was distantly aware of Mustar's laughter at his side, but couldn't share it; his heart pounded in his chest, each gasping breath brought less air than he needed, his sore feet stumbled even on the straight and his head swam sickeningly.

Almost to the bottom now, where the God grant him rest; but they took another corner, nearly the last, and disaster met them. There was a man in the road, right ahead. At least Marron guessed it to be a man, his dim eyes showed him nothing but a blur of red and yellow. He heard Mustar's shriek, though, and knew at least that it wasn't a phantasm.

They threw themselves against the bar, yanking the cart aside. It veered sharply, and by the God's grace just missed the leaping man; Marron had a close glimpse of him, brown hair and beard framing a startled face as they hurtled by. Too fast and the cart too heavy, they couldn't recover. A wheel slipped over the edge, the cart tilted and plunged, the bar jerked and leaped skyward against their frantic grip; Marron felt something tear deep inside his arm, and screamed with the wrenching pain of it as he was dragged off the road.

He lost his grip, and fell. Hit and rolled, sprawled and slid into the cruel spines of a thorn-bush, and only lay there helpless while his mind went on rolling and spinning, lurching and tumbling far beyond hope of his control.

Faint voices, calling; and then closer, perhaps the same voices speaking a name he thought might be his, only that he forgot it again the moment after.

Hands then, tugging hands under his arms and the drag

of rock against his back. Everything glimmered and hazed; he closed his eyes.

Now he was lying flat and hard fingers were probing his head, his ribs, lifting his arm and turning it. There was nothing that didn't hurt, but that hurt worst; he grunted and tried to pull free, drawing a grunt also from the man who held it.

'Don't panic, boy,' he heard, and this time understood the words and clung to them in his mind, something to root him to the dizzying world. 'He's all right, or he will be. Lack of a little blood won't kill him, he'll be lighter for it.'

Then the hands resumed their rough passage, feeling for the bones inside him, tracing the lines of his legs; he slipped away.

And came back to the sound of a horse's hooves, a muttered oath, a voice he knew. 'What has happened here?'

His eyes opened instantly, his mouth tried to shape a word but there was no breath to sound it; he felt not physical but hollow, eggshell. Broken eggshell.

'An accident. My fault, I should have heard them coming and made way.' It was a stranger's voice that spoke, but the other, the newcomer slid with a jingle of harness from his horse and loomed overhead, blotting out the sky. He knew that silhouette as he knew the voice it came with.

'You mean they were coming down too fast. Is the boy badly hurt?'

'I think not, except that he's opened a wound in his arm here. A sword's cut by the look of it, half-healed before . . .'

'I know, I made it. What, then, has he knocked himself silly?'

'Again, I think not. He went over the side, but his skull is whole and his other bones too, so far as I can find. A Ransomer doing a slave's work, though, barefoot, this must have been a penance; which if I know the Order means that he has had no food today and too much work, under too much sun.'

'Heat-mazed, is he? Well, that we can attend to . . .'

The shadow stooped closer, and he felt the rush of cool liquid over his hair. Dribbles ran down his face, and he tried to lick them; then the mouth of a flask was there, water touched his lips and he swallowed greedily.

'Not too much at once . . .'

'I know.'

The flask was taken away, before he'd had half enough. But the dust had been washed from his throat and his voice was there again, or a whisper of it.

'Sieur . . .'

'Marron. You are becoming much more trouble than you are worth.'

Fingers touched his wet hair, far less stern than the voice; he smiled pure gratitude, for the gift of his name returned. With the name came pain, pain and soreness all over and a burning pain in his arm, but no matter for that. The name was worth it.

'What of the cart?'

'Oh, it's lodged in the bushes there, the boy and I can salvage it. It may have to lose the rest of its load, but no worse than that. This lad needs more than a sip of water, though.'

'And shall have it. I'll take him to the infirmary now. If I mount, can you pass him up to me?'

'He may spew on you, when I lift him.'

'I'll chance that.'

Marron clenched his jaws, his throat and his stomach. Sieur Anton might be prepared to take the chance, but not he.

He was lifted in one pair of capable arms, and passed to another. His stomach did lurch a little against the lurching of his body, but a couple of hard swallows settled it. He closed his eyes again and cradled his bad arm against his chest, feeling blood trickle down to his elbow; then before the great horse began its slow swaying walk uphill, he heard: 'I am Anton d'Escrivey, a knight of the Order. And you, sir?'

'My name is Rudel. A jongleur.'

Sieur Anton laughed shortly. 'A jongleur, come to Roq de Rançon? To entertain the brothers, is it?'

'I had thought perhaps there might be guests, who would not be averse to a little music. And I have heard that the brothers' hospitality extends even to my kind, however they find their own entertainments.'

'Well. As it happens, there are guests in the castle. There are also knights, whose pleasures are a little less circumscribed than the brothers'. You will be welcome, Rudel, if you sing as efficiently as you rescue fallen brethren.'

'My voice has likely been ruined by the dust of the road, Sieur Anton,' in a voice deliberately mellifluent, 'but if there be a little wine to soothe it . . .'

'Oh, there is wine. Good, then. We shall hope to hear you tonight.'

8

The Hidden and the Lost

Julianne was not made to be alone.

That was a decision she came to, quite forcefully, after a deal of pacing and gazing out and working her fingers through the wooden screens of the window like a child or a prisoner, like both. There were some, she knew, who thrived on solitude. Hermits, and the like. Similarly, there were those who needed society; she counted herself emphatically among their number, and never more so than now. She wanted laughter and conversation, she wanted bright wit and challenge; above all she wanted someone to talk to, however mysterious that person or evasive that talk might be.

Specifically – because she was practical above all, a girl of her thrice-damned father's making, and there was no point wishing for the unattainable, her old life back again – specifically she wanted Elisande, and Elisande was not there. Nor had she been for hours, for the best part of the day.

Unfettered by concerns of tact or diplomacy or the need to preserve a future husband's honour, unworried by the brothers' patent distrust of womanhood, Elisande had made herself far more free of the castle than Julianne had dared. Every day she'd gone exploring, nosing out its secrets and its hidden corners; but every day she'd returned within an hour or so, to talk of fine views or dark damp passages. It had been quietly understood between them that all of this was shadow and deception, though Julianne never was deceived. The wandering and the searching had a purpose, but that purpose was not to be spoken of, or not yet.

Today, though, Elisande had slipped away shortly after breakfast, and she hadn't returned by noon. Julianne had made her way alone to the great hall's gallery for prayers, and had returned alone also; had eaten her midday meal alone; and was alone still and snarling at it. She felt unkindly abandoned and worse, she felt her generosity abused. Elisande knew herself as much Julianne's guest as the Order's, had said as much and meant it.

She knew herself friend too, though, and usually took no more than a friend's liberties in her comings and goings. Today was more than unusual, it was unprecedented; and quite unlike Elisande, or so her friend thought. She with her darkling hints about the djinni, she who had an element of watchfulness about her always: she would surely not go off like this, without warning and for so long? Julianne was genuinely anxious beneath her anger, although the anger was genuine also.

Whether it was the anxiety or the anger that drove her, at last she stormed across the floor and through the curtain, down the steps and out into the courtyard below before she could think better of it.

She knew the way from here to the great hall unguided, but that was no use to her. She could find the stables too, though, which perhaps held out better prospects. So down the long narrow ramp, dark with shadow; down to where sunlight glinted on water, and the air smelled of horseflesh and dung. There she discovered the stablemaster, and interrogated him. He was hardly forthcoming, but did at least deign to speak to her, albeit with his head twisted awry and his eyes askance, never meeting hers. No, he had not seen her ladyship's companion this day. No, she had not gone out on horseback, not on anyone's horse. She might have left the castle afoot; he was not aware of it, but he had no time to watch all who came and went through the courtyard, he was a busy man. If her ladyship cared to ask the guards at the gate, they might know more than he . . .

The guards had been on duty only since the noon meal. They had seen no lady leaving, on foot or otherwise; nor had their predecessors reported any such. They were sorry, they said, not to be of any help to her; almost she believed that they were. They couldn't see past her veil, but she put as much of a smile as she could manage into her voice as she thanked them, and hoped it had reached her eyes also.

Back up to the stable-yard; she thought about questioning the Sharai boys, but the master's eye was on her – some time he seemed to have found, to watch at least one who came and went through his dominion – and she was reluctant to feed his animosity further.

Where now, then? Elisande hadn't eaten, or not with her, and must have grown hungry before this; the refectory, then, and the kitchens. Where they lay, Julianne had no notion. But she had a tongue, and the will to use it; she waylaid a brother on an errand.

This was a blushing youngster: nothing more than his age, she decided, that made him duck his head and stammer. Nothing more than a willingness to help that had him scurrying on ahead of her, and pausing awkwardly to wait at every junction. Puppy-enthusiastic and puppy-trained, he was, and she'd always liked puppies. She thought perhaps she'd keep him for a while, to be her guide all through this labyrinth . . .

Which thought implied that she knew already that this particular trail would be cold at best, dead more likely, time wasted either way. Somehow she just couldn't see Elisande sitting down to break bread with the brothers, nor the brothers allowing her to do it. Begging a crust from the kitchens was more likely, perhaps; but what guest would be allowed to eat so poorly of the Order's charity, and what woman would not be conducted gently but firmly back to her quarters and her proper meal?

So no, Julianne didn't really expect to find Elisande in the one place or the other. The refectory didn't disappoint; there was no one there but a few brothers scrubbing tables and benches and floor. She had her escort speak to them, to save embarrassment from whatever cause, but none had seen her friend that day.

She spoke herself to the kitchen-master, and that was tactics too: however he felt about women in his bailiwick, he'd take questioning better from a guest than from a junior brother. So she asked, expecting once more the answer no; and was told yes instead, was told that the lady's companion had indeed been to the kitchens this morning. Soon after breakfast it was, and he wasn't in honesty sure what she had wanted there, she hadn't been at all clear about it. Idle curiosity, he suspected, with a sniff that said Julianne should keep a closer watch over her inferior, keep her hands busy with a needle or other woman's work, not let her roam the castle to interfere with men about their business . . .

How long had she stayed? A while; and only left after the questioners had gone down to the cells – with a nod towards a dark corner, an unremarkable doorway – and the filthy heretic they had imprisoned there had started up with his cries. Not fit hearing for a lady, that, and so she had found it. No, he didn't know where she had gone from here; no, nor would any of his labouring brothers, there was no point in asking them. Not their duty, to keep track of a wandering guest. Nor his to criticise, so never mind that she'd taken a pair of apples with her without asking, which in a brother would be greed and theft and disobedience all three . . .

Julianne apologised graciously for the shortcomings of her woman, sketched a diplomatic curtsey and left the kitchens. As she'd hoped, her young guide followed her unquestioningly, assuming himself attached until dismissed.

'What's your name, brother?'

'Estien, my lady,' he muttered, watching his fingers as they picked dry skin off a raw red knuckle. She suppressed a smile, seeing how he wanted to bite it, and barely knew enough not to do that in front of her.

'Well, Estien, this castle of yours is too big to go straying about at random, we could chase each other all day and never catch up.' *And I'm only a girl and a stranger here*, her voice was saying, *I need a young man like you, I'm depending on you* . . . 'We'll have to try to guess where she might have gone; but my guesses have come to nothing, so . . .'

She expected little use from his guesses either; if Elisande was a mystery to her, how much more to a callow boy like this, how could he hope to guess better? But she did need an escort who knew the castle. Once get him feeling involved, make it his hunt as well as hers, and he'd be far more use to her.

He thought, scowlingly; his hand did stray up to his mouth, where his unconscious teeth nibbled on that flaking skin; at last he said, 'There's the infirmary, my lady, she might have gone there . . .'

Indeed she might: might have gone, might have been taken. Estien clearly had no idea in his head beyond memories of his mother carrying herb tisanes to a poorly neighbour, *women visit the sick*; Julianne had another altogether, *she's been gone all day, she's curious and heedless and a stranger here, anything could have happened* . . .

She'd been hoping to keep her thoughts away from the infirmary, for at least a little longer. Too late now.

'So she might,' she said brightly. 'Can you show me the way, Estien?'

He could; he did. There was a room of benches and bottles and stone jars, barrels and mortars, herbs in hanging bunches and a shelf of books. A dispensary: no one there, but she could hear quiet voices coming from a doorway at the end of the passage. Soft though it was, one voice she thought she knew. Estien's face twitched uncertainly; she gave him a smile against her own doubts and took the lead, walking through into a long chamber lined with cots.

Only one of the cots was occupied, and not by Elisande. That much she took in at a glance, and felt her worst anxieties leave her, on a breath of relief. The next breath fought hard to be a giggle; she had to clamp her throat tight to contain it.

He was little more than a boy who lay pale and still on the mattress, and he was quite naked. Two brothers knelt beside him; one had been sponging his face and chest, while the other swabbed at a bleeding wound on his arm. Both were now staring at her in deep shock, giving rise to that treacherous giggle.

There were two men more, standing at the foot of the cot. The elder she thought must be Master Infirmarer; the other was Sieur Anton d'Escrivey. It was his voice she'd heard and recognised in the passage. It was also he who recovered his wits fastest, stooping to pick up a stained and stinking habit which he tossed neatly over the boy on the cot. The movement carried her eyes with it; his presence made her focus on the boy's face. Yes, that was Marron, the young brother who was also his unusual squire . . .

'My lady Julianne.' The voice as ever held a sardonic twist, as though nothing in this bitter world were worth more than a derisive laugh; the hands wiped themselves fastidiously on a damp cloth. 'Are you in need of Master Scobius' good offices?'

'Not I. I was seeking my companion, but I see she is not here. If your squire needs attention, I beg you, don't let me delay it. I'll withdraw . . .'

And she did; but d'Escrivey came with her. Estien

effaced himself, she noticed, scuttling back down the passage and out of sight.

'It's nothing to be concerned about. Too much sun, and a little foolishness that has opened his arm again. Master Infirmarer will sew the wound; a fresh dressing, an afternoon's rest in the cool and he'll be well enough. Though I really ought to beat him, for giving me so much trouble.'

'You ought to,' she said, this time letting the chuckle come, 'but you won't.' He wasn't the only one who could be amused by the idiocies of life, and allow it to show.

'No. Likely I won't. The boy has charms, which appear to prevent me. And he will be sore enough, I fancy, for the next few days. You have, ah, mislaid the lady Elisande?'

'I suppose I have,' but the frustration of that was all gone suddenly; she could laugh at it now, and at herself. Company, someone to talk to: she sought no more, now that she was reassured. 'She'll be spying out some dark corner of the castle, I imagine, making herself unwelcome among the brothers. She finds our chamber . . . unentrancing.'

'As do you, my lady.' Not even a question, that; he gave her no opportunity to deny it. 'The brothers are endlessly hospitable, but not entertaining. Well, I can at least offer a little respite against your tedium. There is a jongleur come to the Roq. I met him on the road, tending my fool of a boy there; I hope that he will sing and play for us tonight. Will you come and hear him?'

Her heart yearned to – if she'd found Elisande by then, if the setting sun hadn't given her new cause to worry about the wretched girl's disappearance – but, 'Only if I may do so without giving the brothers offence.'

His turn to laugh aloud. 'My lady, the very presence of a jongleur gives the brothers offence. It offends them greatly, that their Rule forbids their turning him away. If he will sing he sings for us, for the knights; for knights and guests, if you will come. Only recover your chaperone, for decency's sake, and you will be welcome.'

'In that case, Sieur Anton, we will come, and gratefully.' *If* Elisande had returned by then . . .

D'Escrivey bowed. 'I shall send my squire to fetch you, and light your way.'

'Your . . .? Oh no, not Marron, he needs—'

'He needs,' severely, 'to learn that duty overrides weakness. He will come for you, after you have eaten tonight.'

D'Escrivey led her out into the sunlight, saying, 'May I see you back to your quarters, my lady?'

Estien was waiting for her in the court, but it would be too ridiculous to go on searching fruitlessly, through all this vast castle. She smiled a grateful dismissal to the brother, and said, 'Thank you, that would be kind,' to the knight. And then, 'Tell me of this jongleur, Sieur Anton, who is he? Is he known?' These wandering minstrels seldom wandered so far as Marasson, but she'd heard that some were celebrated throughout Outremer.

'Not to me,' d'Escrivey murmured. 'His name is Rudel, and all I can say else is that he showed a charitable concern for both my squire and the welfare of a dung-cart. We can hope that he will have washed, I think, before tonight; more than that, we must discover together.'

'Indeed?' There was a story there, obviously, but it was equally obvious that he was disinclined to tell it. Julianne forbore to question further, having already met the man's

infuriating talent for evasion; they walked on in silence, and
he left her with a bow and a promise, 'We will meet later,
my lady, for songs and tales, washed down with a little
wine. Though none, I think, for Marron. I'm not sure I
could tolerate his excitement.'

Julianne had given her travelling-dresses over to the village
women to be washed. Having seen the results, she was glad
to have one chest of gowns still untouched. She felt no
great need to impress an unknown jongleur, but the affi-
anced bride of an Elessan baron – the count's heir-apparent,
no less – should not go into even this poor shadow of society in a stained robe . . .

   With no servants to attend her, she tackled the chest herself, and was busy with the unaccustomed and not-so-easy
task of shaking out creases and the intrusive dust of the
road when she heard soft footsteps mounting the stair outside. She glanced round, the curtain stirred, and Elisande
slipped into the room.

   All Julianne's earlier irritation had returned, under the
effort of her labour; when she gritted her teeth, she felt and
tasted dust and resentment in equal measure.

   'Where have you been?'

   'Everywhere.' There was a ewer of water on the window-
shelf; Elisande poured herself a goblet and drained it in
one long swallow. The light falling through the traceries
made patterns of lace on her skin that did not disguise her
pallor and weariness, nor the streaks of damp and mould
on her dress.

   On *Julianne's* dress, that the ineffective washing here
would certainly not shift . . .

'What have you been *doing*?' with a flat-handed slap at the gown she held, that was meant only to emphasise the question but raised a cloud of acrid dust which had her hacking blindly, like an emphasis to her mood.

'Looking for a way out. Why, was I meant to be dancing attendance on you? Brushing out your hair, maybe, after I'd sponged your gown?'

Did it need sponging? She was momentarily uncertain, and had to make a deliberate snatch at her anger before she lost hold of it again. 'You must do as you please, of course. But: *if* you are here as my companion – and it was my name that brought you in through the gates, Elisande – then it would not have been inappropriate for you to have helped me with my dresses. If you are here as my friend, you should not be all day away from me without a word, because you should know that I would worry. And if you are neither my companion nor my friend, if as it seems you are nothing of mine, then it is very much my business to learn what you are and what you are doing here, because I may have brought an enemy into the castle under my shadow.'

'Actually,' Elisande said heavily, 'I think you have.' She dropped onto the settle, brushed at her skirts with a violence that would only work the stain in deeper, and then asked abruptly, 'Have you ever heard a man screaming? I mean, *really* screaming?'

Julianne didn't answer the question, nor she thought did Elisande expect her to. She said only, 'Was it very bad?' And then, when the other girl offered her no more than a bleak gaze in response, 'I looked for you. In the kitchens, as well as otherwise. The master said that you left when the cries started . . . You've not made a friend there, by the way. He was most aggrieved about his apples.'

'Oh.' Elisande fumbled inside her bodice, and produced two small yellow fruits. 'I took them, didn't I? I forgot. I thought I'd be hungry, I think . . .'

'And so you must be, if you've not eaten since breakfast.' That was an instruction thinly disguised, deliberately so to be easily recognised; but perhaps her voice had lost its snap since Marasson. Elisande smiled, shook her head and laid the apples aside.

Very well. She wouldn't eat, and she wouldn't talk of what she'd heard. 'Where did you go, then?' No accusation in the question now, only concern and true curiosity. She'd left the kitchen and snatched apples on the way, thinking she might be hungry later; wherever she'd been in the castle, she'd gone so far in her head that she'd lost or forgotten her appetite; she'd come back with her dress filthy and her hands too, now that Julianne was sitting beside her and taking those hands in her own, seeing and feeling and smelling the dirt on her, and the green mould caked beneath her nails.

'Down,' Elisande said, with a twist to her face that might have been meant as a smile. 'There are tunnels all under the castle, passages carved from the rock. And rooms, store-rooms, chambers, cells . . .' Her voice broke momentarily, but came back stronger. 'Some were locked, but not all; some were empty. Not all. I searched them all, the best I could with an oil-lamp.'

'Elisande – what *for*?'

'A way out,' she said again.

'What do you mean? I asked at the gate, they said they hadn't seen you.'

'They hadn't. I don't want to ask their permission when I leave; so I was looking for another way. A hidden door, a tunnel, stairs that lead to a cave in the rock . . . There must be one, somewhere. No one builds a fortress this size with only one way out. But I couldn't find it,' her voice and shoulders sinking for a moment, eloquent testimony of that long vain search in the shadows.

'Small wonder, if it's meant to be secret.'

'It's not meant to be secret from me. I'm good at finding things. Supposed to be.' But her dark head lifted, her dark eyes flickered and she sniffed self-mockingly. 'I'm just not very good at being faced down and told to be patient. Not by walls, not by anything. Ask my grandfather.'

'I'd like to.' Julianne grabbed at that, being as obvious as she knew how. 'Where do I find him?'

'Oh, you'll find him. I promise. Or your father will. That would be a meeting I'd like to see, I think . . .' She sniffed again, looked at her hands and grimaced, said, 'Let me just wash and I will help you with that gown. It's beautiful. *And* I'll brush your hair out for you, you've got dust in it.'

'I expect I have. We'll need two gowns, though. You can choose the other. The knights are entertaining us tonight.' Deliberately, she didn't mention the jongleur. Let him be a surprise; a pleasant one, if the man could sing decently. If Elisande were still keeping secrets, then so might she. She only hoped that her friend's were no more sinister than her own. Elisande had been with the Sharai, after all, she could be spying for them. Indeed, the djinni had told her to go back – but no. Ignore the djinni, forget the djinni, she would have nothing of the djinni. She would do her own duty by her own will and in obedience to her father's, and there would be no credit owed for that to any djinni . . .

It took not long at all for them to decide or discover that they were both too dirty for a single ewer of water to improve matters much. It was Elisande who ran down, determinedly playing the dutiful companion, to waylay a passing brother; shortly afterwards a small procession brought them up a tub, steaming buckets and a box of soap.

Once they had bathed, put on clean shifts and dressed each other's hair – an unequal task, Julianne had thought that would be, but Elisande's short curls were so tangled the girl was yelping under her hands before she was satisfied – they turned to the chest, and the half-dozen rich gowns it held. Elisande demurred, Julianne insisted; then they argued cheerfully about this one or that, which colour would suit best. The great bell interrupted them, but Julianne decreed that they had no time to go to prayers tonight, even if they'd been decently attired. The bell reminded her, though, that the light was failing; she lit all the lamps and candles in the room, before going back to urge the crimson once more.

The brothers who brought up their supper an hour later found them gorgeously robed and decorously veiled, still giggling a little when they caught each other's eye. The same brothers carried the tub and the buckets away; as soon as they were gone Julianne tossed her veil aside, served Elisande, served herself. And must have eaten herself because her trencher in the end was as empty as the other, but she had no memory of chewing or how the food had tasted. All her focus had been on Elisande, and she'd felt triumphant with every mouthful she saw swallowed. Clearly her adventures this day had shaken Elisande deeply, surprisingly deep for one so insouciant and worldly. Julianne felt proud – justifiably proud, she thought – to have distracted her so far into clothes and toilet that her appetite came back.

Supper over, they waited; and Elisande it seemed had more than her appetite back, she had her curiosity also. She wanted to know who they waited for and where they were going, how the knights proposed to entertain them and why the invitation tonight when they'd been ignored by all but Sieur Anton hitherto?

Julianne smiled her best mysterious smile, and refused to say.

At last there came a scratching on the curtain; Julianne called permission, and Marron came through.

In his good hand he carried a flambeau, still burning. No sore-footed shuffling this time; but that reminded her. 'Marron, you left your sandals behind last night,' with altogether a different kind of smile. 'Where did we put them, Elisande?'

'In the corner. Over there . . .'

'That's right. I'm afraid one is half-burned through, though.'

'Er, yes, my lady.' He blushed, as she'd been sure that he would. 'It, it doesn't matter. I have a new pair . . .' He even twitched back the hem of his habit, to show her. He had a clean habit too, she was glad to see. But there hadn't really been any doubt of that.

'Good. How are you feeling?'

'Oh, quite well, thank you, my lady.'

'Really?' He didn't look well, nor sound it; his voice was as thin and pale as his body had been in the infirmary, those parts the sun had not toasted. 'Does your arm hurt much?'

He shook his head, but his whole stance betrayed the lie. With the flambeau in the other, he'd used that arm unthinkingly to part the curtain, and to show his sandals; now it was cradled against his chest, and she thought it hurt exceedingly.

'Well. Mind you are careful with it, or it'll bleed again. Have they fed you properly?'

'Oh yes, my lady. Mutton broth . . .'

This time, she did believe him. His artless smile said that was better food than he might have expected in the refectory. It might well have been a meatless day for his brothers, but not for him.

'Come, then. Take us to wherever it is that we are going.'

'The lesser hall, my lady. If you will follow me . . .'

He moved towards the doorway, but she forestalled him, reaching the curtain first and drawing it back to save his arm. He blushed again and ducked through, watchful not to bring his blazing flambeau too near the fabric. Julianne smiled and let him lead down the stairs, reaching back for Elisande's hand as she came out behind her.

Across the court from their little private tower they went, and into the vast darkness of the castle proper. Economy, perhaps, that left no lights burning here, but also it must help discipline, keeping the brothers to their dormitories at night. There were so many stairs and angles, even a man who knew his way would surely hesitate to take it blind. She was lost already, and glad of the squeeze of Elisande's hand in hers as they trailed behind the bright fire of Marron's flambeau and the shifting shadow of his back and his turning head, his face a white blur that came and went and came again as he reassured himself constantly that they were with him still.

At last he brought them to a high double door with one leaf standing open, flickering yellow light and a muted roar of voices and laughter beyond. Here he set his flambeau into a bracket on the wall, and gestured them within.

'No, we'll follow you still, Marron,' Julianne said, chuckling. 'Presumably Sieur Anton is among the throng in there; you find him for us. I have no mind to push my way among men I do not know.'

'My lady would not need to push . . .'

'Meaning that you will?' Elisande put in. 'I doubt it, Marron. The quality of the master's guests reflects upon his squire. Courtesies due the lady Julianne will clear a path for you also, depend upon it.'

Or in other words, Julianne thought wickedly, sharing a glimmering glance with her friend, *the knights will keep their distance as readily as the brothers, albeit for different reasons.* Well-trained gentlemen would bow and step back from sheer force of manners; well-informed gentlemen would be wary of approaching the daughter of the King's Shadow, for fear that some of the rumoured power of that mysterious office might be heritable in the female line; any gentlemen of Elessi – and there were sure to be some here, so close to their own country – would be jealously protective of her honour. Which last might lead d'Escrivey into difficulties, actually, only that she thought that particular gentleman well capable of protecting both her honour and his own.

Marron didn't look convinced; but then, Marron didn't look as though he wanted to go through the door at all, either leading or following behind. Likely he only wanted his bed and a full night's sleep. Well, he was in the wrong dress, the wrong place and the wrong position for that: neither brothers nor squires could sensibly expect the rest their bodies hankered for. She sympathised, but he was young; he'd recover. He'd had mutton broth tonight.

She waited, and after a moment he recognised her implacability, bowed and stepped through the open door.

Here indeed were men she did not know: dozens upon dozens of them, perhaps a hundred white-clad knights and perhaps more. They stood in groups by pillar and wall, they lounged and spread themselves on benches and table-tops, they murmured and talked and shouted and gesticulated to the imminent danger of the squires and servants who wormed between them with jugs full and empty. Following Marron made little difference; he obviously knew no better then she where his master might be found in all this chaos. D'Escrivey ought to be watching for them – but then, d'Escrivey really ought to be waiting for them here, by the door, and he was not.

Ah, well. She'd faced worse than this at court, every year since she was six years old and had first walked into a reception hall alone, in search of her father. Facing down the impertinent curiosity of strangers was second nature to her now. Straighten the shoulders, straighten the spine, walk forward firmly but not stiffly, be graceful and gracious and above all be open; look for whom you seek and don't try to hide it, move the head and not only the eyes, and bow to anyone whose eye catches yours in the process . . .

She wondered how Elisande would cope, beside her. Differently, she guessed, but well enough. Stand on a table and cry d'Escrivey's name, perhaps, though the God grant not . . .

Two paces into the hubbub, and already the silence had begun. A stone dropped into slow and heavy water, she thought their arrival was; the silence spread out from them like unseen ripples washing through the room. Or like a circling knife that cut the strings of tongue and arm, killing every conversation and leaving each knight unmastered for a moment, slack and staring.

D'Escrivey might have told them, Julianne thought irritably. *He might at least have told some of them, and let the whisper spread . . .*

They recovered quickly, though, these young gentlemen. Those nearest to the door, nearest to the girls smiled and bowed, made way, gestured them on; others, too polite to stare, watched none the less with a sidelong eye. Talk picked up again after the wave of silence, though softer and less raucous than before.

Through to the very centre of this hall they passed; and she had given up by then on strangers' faces, all but given up expecting d'Escrivey's. She was looking more at the pillars, gazing up towards the roof that arched so high the light of the flambeaux couldn't reach it, thinking that in any other castle this would not be a lesser hall. Here, though, the name was right: it was little more than a cubby by the standards of the Roq, a place for children to play except that here there were no children and so it had been given over to the young men for their games, of which it seemed that she was the butt tonight . . .

Thinking so, she brought her eyes down from that dark and distant roof to find that she stood before a great chimney breast. The fireplace stood as tall as any door in the castle; its stones were black with soot, but no fire burned there in this hot summer. Instead there was a small table set inside, with chairs around it and a lamp in a niche above; there was wine, there were familiar silver goblets; behind stood Sieur Anton d'Escrivey. He made his bow as her eyes met his, and straightened up smiling.

'Welcome, my lady. My lady Elisande,' with another, slighter bow. 'Will you join me? I thought perhaps you might prefer to sit a little out of the hurly-burly; my confrères can be boisterous at times.'

'Sieur Anton,' as her displeasure melted into laughter, 'I apologise. I had begun to think that you had failed our engagement.'

'Not I, my lady.' He drew back a chair and she settled herself into it; Elisande sat opposite her, d'Escrivey between them. At a sign from him Marron hastened to fill the three goblets, and then stood back against the wall.

'Where is your, ah, promised entertainment, Sieur Anton?' She still didn't want to say the word 'jongleur', to keep the surprise for Elisande.

'I think he comes now, my lady. Listen . . .'

Indeed another silence was settling on the hall, of a different quality; through it she could just hear the soft strumming of a mandora.

There was sudden movement all around, as the knights who had been standing jostled for places at the long tables. She stretched to see over their heads, the same way they were all looking. Yes, there he was: a bearded man in his middle years, dressed in gaudy colours, picking chords from his mandora as he made his slow way between the benches and towards the cleared space before the hearth. Towards her, that was; d'Escrivey had had more than his declared reason, she thought, to seat them here.

Elisande also was peering round, looking for the source of this unexpected music. Julianne watched her, to see the results of her little surprise; and was more puzzled than gratified, was almost startled by the depth of her friend's startlement.

Elisande seemed to go quite rigid for a moment, when her eyes found the jongleur. Then she turned and straightened slowly, sat quite still with her hands in her lap and her gaze fixed on the table before her. Her veil hid her face, but there was no hint of pleasure in her pose. Something else, something private, another mystery; perhaps jongleurs had an unwelcome place in her history? Or perhaps this particular jongleur: perhaps they had met on the road somewhere, and the encounter had not gone well for Elisande . . .?

Well, whatever the truth of that, Julianne could discover it later. She was sorry her surprise had not been a happy one, but people who kept so many secrets had no cause to complain if they were obliged in all innocence to confront one. She sipped her wine, lifting the goblet decorously beneath her veil to save affronting any sensibilities, and tried to turn her mind away from Elisande and her shadows.

In honesty, that was not hard. The jongleur might have no known name, but he had a gift of magic in his fingers and his voice. He struck a martial beat and began a song familiar to all, even to Julianne. Not much in the way of music came from Outremer to Marasson; the Empire had sophisticated tastes, and thought itself the heart's home and birthing-place of all art. This was an old tune, though, and one that every battle-hungry boy could hum, from the homelands to Ascariel itself. The words spoke of the great war that won the Sanctuary Land and established Outremer; the jongleur led in a clear baritone, but he soon had the knights singing along with him in a massed chorus, deep male voices and a pulsing rhythm that set Julianne's skin tingling.

The song ended with a triumphant cry of victory; the applause was loud and long, though she thought they applauded themselves as much as the jongleur. Indeed he applauded them also, turning and clapping, bowing, smiling.

Then he lifted his arms for silence, and had it at the gesture; and, 'Sieurs, my ladies,' with a particular bow towards the chimney breast which had Elisande's hand clenching around the stem of her goblet, and yes, surely these two had met before. 'A song may stir a brave man or a coward to a fight; it may turn a woman's heart to love – yes, or a man's,' to general laughter. 'But music has much to teach us, and not all of that is joyful. If I may, I will sing you a *pastorela* of my own composing: a small thing, a sorry thing, but one you will not have heard before. It is called "La Chanson de Cireille".'

Its name brought a gasp from Elisande. Julianne's attention leaped to her friend but found her still once more, only that her head had moved to face the jongleur. Her eyes glittered, with fury Julianne thought, though that damned veil disguised it.

The jongleur was aware of her; he bowed, low and slow, towards their table.

'It is called "La Chanson de Cireille",' he said again, and his eyes moved no more than Elisande's, 'and I, I am called Rudel, who made it.'

Then his fingers plucked at the strings of the mandora, calling forth strange, sharp chords that rang bitterly in Julianne's ears as he began to sing.

I came to a border, a land of my choosing,
I followed a river through towering mountains,
I passed a great castle, its walls long abandoned,
Its gates gone to dust and its towers in ruins.
Beyond was an orchard with fruit in abundance,
But all of it fallen with no hand to pick it.
I was young, I was foolish, with no hand to stay me;
I stooped for an apple and bit of its sweetness.

Birds sang about me, the water sang softly,
And all the same music, a murmuring rhythm
That drew me on deeper through woods to a
    garden,
Its walls high above me, its gate locked against me.

Through bars in the gate I saw poppies and roses,
A maiden among them who sang as she picked
them.
Her voice gave a voice to the birds and the river,
Her words were a burden of grief and of sorrow:

> *'Oh where have you gone to, and why did you
> leave us?*
> *Your heart must be stone, to betray and bereave
> us.*
> *Faithless and faceless, all promises broken,*
> *Your name is a curse which will no more be
> spoken.'*

I called to the maid but she seemed not to hear me.
I swore faith eternal, and meant her no treachery.
Her own love was lost, she was fair beyond measure;
I wanted no more than to love and to keep her.

The wall might be high but not too high to
climb it;
By the grace of a tree I had soon o'erleaped it
And stood among tangles of brambles that tore me
And cried out again, but no voice came to answer.
No poppies lived in this garden, no roses,
No birds could feed of the thorns that possessed it.
Here was no maiden, but true desolation.
I sang with the voice of her own love returning:

> *'Oh where have you gone to, could you wait no
> longer?*

> *I had duties elsewhere, and no one vow is*
>   *stronger.*
> *I left you my name, now I cannot reclaim it.*
> *Thief of my honour, what's love when you shame*
>   *it?'*

Julianne wanted more, another stanza, surely there must be some resolution, some answer to such terrible questions; but he gave one last long resonant sobbing stroke to the strings, stilled them with the palm of his hand and bowed his head to the silence.

She looked at Elisande again, and again saw how her friend's eyes glittered, and wondered this time if it were anger or tears that made them so shine.

The low murmur of voices through the hall only emphasised the quiet. This time there was no applause, nor did Rudel seem to expect or want it. After a while he raised his head – and was that a glint of water on his cheeks also, above the dark of his beard? – and set his hands to the strings once more.

This time it was a ballad that he sang, an old tale of brothers who loved and fought till they had destroyed each other over a matter of honour. Briefly Julianne felt nothing but relief, that this would give Elisande time to collect herself. But there seemed to be a devil in the man's choices, or else there was a devil lurking in this cold fireplace; she saw d'Escrivey stiffen and pale till his eyes were no more than dark pits fixed on the jongleur. Behind him Marron too seemed discomfited, staring at his master and then turning away. The air in that black chimney felt suddenly unbreathable; Julianne wanted to jump up and leave, to sweep Elisande out with her and take them both away from these strong undercurrents that she couldn't understand.

There was no way to do it, though, they were trapped by their situation. Instead she tipped her empty goblet and tapped its base lightly on the table, to draw Marron's attention. He followed her thought quickly, and came bustling round to serve them all. That at least afforded some distraction; from the corner of her eye Julianne saw d'Escrivey take a slow, deep breath and shake his head slightly, as though denying some unspoken suggestion that he had made to himself.

That song ended with death and disgrace, a broken sword and a man condemned to nameless wandering. As its echoes died away in the great space above them Rudel passed immediately into an epic lay that seemed much more to the taste of his audience, that had them again singing with him in the chorus. D'Escrivey did not sing, but this time the relief was genuine; Julianne felt the tension ebb from him and so from her too, though Elisande was still looking tight and strained.

She'll answer my questions tonight, Julianne thought grimly. *Willing or otherwise, she will . . .*

And for a while, for a little while she did. After the jongleur had begged a second period of rest for his ragged voice; after Julianne had seized that chance to retire and been immediately and eagerly supported by Elisande; after d'Escrivey had sent the flagging Marron to bed also and himself lighted the girls back to their chamber; while they helped each other to undress, Julianne posed questions and Elisande answered them. For what little good that did either one of them.

'You know that man. Don't you?'

'Rudel? Yes.'

'And he knows you.'

'Yes.'

'How?'

'Oh, Julianne, everyone knows Rudel.'

'Sieur Anton doesn't.'

'No, perhaps not. Or not by that name, at least. But then, a man with Sieur Anton's history . . .'

'What history is that?'

'Don't you know about him either? You told me your father had made you learn all the families in the Kingdom . . .'

'I thought he had. I know who the Earl d'Escrivey is, but I know nothing about Sieur Anton. What is there to know?'

'It would be better if you learned that from him.'

'Perhaps; but as he has not told me . . .?'

'Perhaps because you have not asked. Ask him how he came to join the Order. You are such friends, I'm sure he'll tell you. It is his shame, but not his secret.'

Were they friends? Not as Elisande meant to imply, at least. Julianne liked him, he interested her – and she him, she was sure, in much the same way. But she was also sure that Elisande was trying to force a quarrel, to save herself any further questions.

'Well, perhaps I will, then. How do you know Rudel?'

'I've known him for years. All my life,' with a savage edge to it. 'He has not always been a jongleur.'

'What else, then?'

'What would you like him to be?'

'Someone who answers questions straight, for a start. That song he sang, "La Chanson de Cireille" he called it . . .'

'What of it?'

'If it hadn't been for you, I would have thought it just a melancholy *pastorela*. A strange one, and unfinished, but no more than that. But it made you angry, and it made you cry. Why?'

'If it hadn't been for me,' she echoed harshly, 'he would not have sung it. I didn't want to hear it, which is why he did sing it. Which made me angry. The song makes me sad, which is why I cried; which was why I didn't want to hear it.'

'What does the song mean?'

'It means that people go away. When they shouldn't.'

'Elisande, who *is* he?'

'He is called Rudel, seemingly, for the moment. He has had other names. He is a wanderer who denies his home. He has been a soldier, a farmer, a magician, a merchant, a messenger. Other things. Now he is a jongleur, and he's very good at that too.'

And who are you? was the next question Julianne wanted to ask, but that she'd tried before, with Elisande in a more peaceable mood, and had received no answer that satisfied. Tonight she was sure it would be waste of breath.

So, 'What is it that lies between you two?'

'A lifetime,' she said, on a sigh. 'And a death,' bitter again. 'One that can't be forgiven. He should not have done what he did tonight, it was a coward's act.' She flung herself down on her bed and went on hastily, 'Julianne, no more questions now. Let me sleep . . .'

Julianne asked no more questions; but she didn't sleep, and neither she thought did Elisande. She lay listening to the other girl's fretful silence and felt herself trapped within it, lost in a maze of mystery where every answer only baffled more. For once in her life she wished, she really wished she could have slept this one night alone.

They crouched in shadows at the foot of a greater shadow, and this was what they had come for, if they had not come purely to kill. Jemel could reach out and touch the upthrust of rock, could feel it gritty and cool and almost damp against his fingers' ends although the dew would not come till the dawn, hours away yet; he could tilt back his head and gape at half the sky, and see how the other half was occluded by the massive scarp with its massive castle atop. The castle itself he could not see from here. He and the others had watched all day from close cover, and he knew how it was set back on the height, above a steep talus of faced stone.

Jazra stood suddenly at his side, stretched up, set his hands to the rock and began to climb, swiftly and easily. After a count of five his feet were higher than Jemel's head, though Jemel had stood up also. Further along others were also testing themselves against the rock, shadows moving on black shadow.

'How far are you going?' he called up in a whisper.

A soft laugh from above, and his friend jumped down again beside him.

'We can climb this,' he said. 'Even with no moon and no stars, we could climb this; and we will have both.'

'With weapons,' a voice asked behind them, 'and in silence?'

They turned quickly, to find Hasan with them.

'Yes, and yes,' Jazra said.

'Good. But put a stone on your tongue, each of you, when the time comes. If any man should fall, he must not cry out.'

They nodded. He had said as much already. A stone in the mouth was better than a gag.

'The rock we can climb,' Jemel said slowly, 'there are many holds for hands and feet. The talus will be harder.'

'When we come to the talus,' Hasan said, 'we will have help. They will be ready for us. Not tonight, and not tomorrow night, but they will be ready when we come.' His eyes moved, up and up, towards the invisible castle. 'If we take it,' he murmured, 'we can keep it, and their grip on our land will be the weaker. But more than that, they do not know the value of what they hold here. The castle is strong, but that is the least of it. If we take the Roq, we take the Tower also; and then, if it is needed, the Ghost Walker comes to our people again.'

'Would you carry that?' Jemel asked, on a breath.

'If it is needed,' Hasan said again.

Not by you, he wanted to say, *you of all men need nothing more than what you are.* But Hasan had turned and gone, was making his way along the rock and talking to others of their party, men of other tribes. Jemel wanted to follow at his heels like a dog, only that his pride would not allow it.

Neither was it needful after the first moment, the first pang of loss. Jazra's hand touched his, and spoke in silence: fingers against the beat of blood in his wrist, and then knuckles touched to knuckles. *Whom I love, him do I fight for.*

Jemel turned his own hand and made answer, knuckles to knuckles and fingers to wrist: *whom I fight for, him do I love.*

9

Brothers in Arms

Fra' Piet thought Marron had faked his swoon on the road and his sick giddiness after, purely to escape the penance laid on him: for the sake of mutton broth, a night in the infirmary and another day's rest after.

Not that he said so, exactly. All he said was, 'I had not thought you so weak, Fra' Marron, nor so foolish,' but he made it very clear what he meant. Aldo particularly seized on what had not quite been said and said it himself, loud enough for Marron to overhear: 'A brother who is afraid of discipline,' he said, 'will be afraid in battle also. He can't be trusted. Like a brother who seeks his own pleasure, rather than sharing the duties of his troop . . .'

It wasn't true, none of it was true, but it was telling. Marron had to clench his jaws, not to shout or plead or scream his innocence; he had to hide fists in sleeves and hunch his shoulders tight inside his loose habit, to stop himself flinging punches. That would see him in the cells for sure. *Cool enough down there,* he could hear Fra' Piet's cracked voice now, *it'll do you good, little brother. And the time to consider your sins, your many sins, that will be good for you also; and the flogging that will follow, oh my brother, that will be best of all* . . .

Injuring a brother, weakening the arm of the Church Militant was almost the gravest offence a brother could commit; the penalties were correspondingly severe. Marron remembered asking about that once, when they were being catechised at the abbey to test their knowledge of the Rule: did it not weaken the Order more, he'd asked, to inflict a penance so harsh that there would be two brothers in the infirmary, where there had been one? Father Prior had smiled and shaken his head, and said that such a brother unchastised would weaken the Order every day, simply by living within it. He must make his peace with his superiors and with his brethren, he must repent before the altar of the God; and that repentance must be marked out on his flesh, in stripes.

So no, no punches. Marron filed obediently with his troop from prayers in hall to the refectory, enduring in dutiful humility all the way; once there he bit hard into his breakfast bread, tearing it between hand and teeth as he couched his wounded arm in his lap and feeling glad as he never used to be, as he seemed always to be glad now for the rule of silence while they ate. At least he was spared taunts at the table.

Despite his wolverine technique, ripping and gulping, Marron was none the less slow to finish; he was still chewing when a single chime from the bar that hung on high table had them all scrambling to their feet for grace. He stilled his jaws desperately, breathed through his nose and prayed for a chance to empty his mouth unnoticed as they cleared the tables after.

The God was not listening to him, that morning as so many others recently; or else the God really did find it an offence to see a man swallow after grace had been said. He could feel Fra' Piet's eyes on him, though he dared not glance up at the table's end to be sure. The half-chewed lump of bread was heavy on his tongue, too big to swallow whole; he worked it cautiously between his teeth, wished he could draw his hood up just for a moment, looked desperately for some other way to hide his face and saw none.

'Brother Marron.' That was Fra' Piet's voice, a summons he couldn't ignore. He turned compliantly towards his confessor, sensing doom – and as he walked past the line of his brothers, it seemed that the God was listening after all. Aldo's elbow jabbed at him maliciously, catching his wounded arm; Marron doubled up around the stabbing pain of it, but still had wit enough to turn his grunt of shock into a coughing fit. He coughed into his hand, spitting out the bread. Squeezed it between his fingers and straightened, letting his long sleeve fall down to hide it; lifted his innocent face to meet Fra' Piet's glare, and said, 'Yes, brother?'

'Your manners at table are unfitting to a brother. Mend them.'

'Yes, brother.'

'Meanwhile, your folly of yesterday has left you once more unable to share the work of your troop. Go, and find some service you are fit for.'

'Yes, brother.'

*

Sent away, dismissed from his brothers – and dismissed by his brothers also, by Aldo's sneer and several shrugging shoulders – Marron knew only one place else to look for some service he could offer, one-handed and inept.

Forbidden hunting they might be, but some of the knights had brought their dogs with them regardless. There was a kennel in the small court between the knights' and squires' quarters; this wasn't the first time that Marron had paused briefly to bid them good morning. This time, though, the first long brindled nose that snuffed at his hand had its reward, if a sodden mass of bread were a prize worth having. It seemed that it was, the way it was accepted with a gulp and a nudge and an insistent whimper for more.

Marron grinned, fondled silky ears, spread his fingers in apology and hurried away.

Up the steps and along the passage, a polite scratch at a closed door that for once brought no response. He scratched again, then opened the door and peered inside.

The room was empty; Sieur Anton was gone, and so were his sword and his armour. Briefly Marron felt bereft, unwanted here also. But he had perhaps not been expected here, and Sieur Anton was not a patient man, to wait on the chance of his coming. Marron went inside anyway, hoping to find some task he could do unasked to justify himself against Fra' Piet's later questions, how he had spent his day.

The rugs on the floor were dusty, but carrying them out into the air and beating them clean was no work for one hand. Casting about for something, anything else light but useful, Marron saw a small book lying on the window-shelf. He'd seen it before, packed at the bottom of the chest; now a touch of curiosity made him reach for it. He'd seen books, some here and many, dozens and dozens in the abbey's library at home, but never one in private hands before.

The cover was plain stiffened leather; when he opened the volume at random and spelled out the rubric at the head of the page, he realised that it was a missal. He was reading one of the prayers from the midday service.

The book was finely made, good paper well sewn into its binding, but the writing was strangely clumsy: the letters ill-formed and unadorned, the rubrics done simply in red ink with no gilding, some lines not of the straightest even to Marron's unaccustomed eye.

It puzzled him that Sieur Anton of all men should choose to keep – to treasure, indeed, because he kept so few things, each of them must be a treasure – something so poorly crafted; but as he went to close it the pages fell down before the cover, and he saw that there was an inscription on the fly-leaf.

He lifted the cover back again to see, and read it out slowly:

> *This book of true wisdom is a gift of love*
> *to Anton d'Escrivey on his birthday*
> *made by me Charol d'Escrivey*
> *by the God's grace brother to Anton*

Marron took a little longer to understand, even then; but that dedication was written in the same crabbed hand as the text on all the pages of the book. Sieur Anton's brother hadn't only given the volume, he had made it first: penned the words and sewn the pages too, cut and shaped the leather for the binding, done it all.

Marron knew his letters, but he knew too how much pain he had in writing them out, how he would sweat to produce four lines not half so well inscribed as these. The thought of copying out a whole book, so many pages so tightly crammed with words, made his fingers ache in sympathy while his mind gaped in awe. Monks did such work, they gave their lives to it by the orders of their superiors and in honour of the God; but there must have been months of labour even in so simple a volume, and for a nobleman's child to do it for love alone . . .

And this was, must have been the brother whom Sieur Anton had killed, or said he'd killed. The brother for whom the sword Dard had been made, which Sieur Anton said was Marron's now . . .

Oh, it was too much, too bewildering. Marron let the book fall shut, and then heard footsteps and voices in the passage beyond the open door; and took a hasty pace backwards and knew even as he did so that it was too short and too late because for sure that would be Sieur Anton coming now to catch him prying here, that was the way his life worked these cruel days, and he had not a word to say in defence or denial . . .

He was wrong, though. Not Sieur Anton but two of his confrères; and Marron wasn't trying to overhear but he couldn't help listening when he caught the knight's name mentioned, when he heard, 'D'Escrivey's left his door ajar. Not like him. Is he in?'

'Not he,' the other replied on an unkind laugh. 'He'll be

off playing knight-and-squire with that pretty young brother he's taken— Oh. No . . .'

They stood for a moment, two knights in white gazing in, while Marron stared mutely back at them. Then they walked on, and he heard them convulse with laughter; and felt his face flush furiously, while his hands clenched at his sides and he wanted to snatch up dead Charol's sword and go after, challenge them both, call them liars, call them to account . . .

And of course he did nothing so stupid, so fatal. He only stood and sweated, stood and hated until the trembling passion passed, until he was sure the passage was safe, was empty. Then he glanced around the chamber to check that he'd moved nothing that he'd not replaced, he'd left no sign of his presence; then he slipped out and closed the door firmly behind him; then he hurried away.

His mind surging with anger and confusion, he could focus only on the one thing, the need to justify his day. *Find some service you are fit for*, Fra' Piet had said; *afraid of discipline*, Aldo had said, meaning that he had dissembled yesterday to escape his penance. All he could think of was to go back to the stables, to beg Magister Raul for some work a one-handed brother could do, to show his confessor and his former friend and all his troop that it was not so.

At least he might win himself a smile there, if Mustar were in sight. With Aldo so poisonous against him suddenly – and he still didn't understand quite how that had happened, he could name it jealousy but it made no sense to him – and Aldo and Fra' Piet between them poisoning the troop, with Sieur Anton heedless or forgetful of him this morning, he felt the want of a smile.

He'd have run in search of that smile – or else to seem more eager, more obedient, heedless himself of dispensations – only that jolting hurt his arm as much as using it. Everything hurt his arm, today. He carried it as best he could, cradling his left elbow in his good right hand; but he still winced on every flight of steps up or down. Maybe the stables were not such a good idea after all. There was no virtue in begging for work he was clearly unable to do.

But he could think of nowhere else to go, and the anticipation of that smile drew him down through the castle to the brightness of the stable-yard; where he found neither Magister Raul's scowl nor Mustar's sun-dazzling smile but the jongleur Rudel's clever hands making a dazzle of their own from hard light and harder steel, as he stood bare-headed on the cobbles and juggled three blades that flashed cold fire as they turned and twisted in the glare.

He had perhaps only been practising or only passing time, but like any master of his particular trade he knew himself observed. He didn't glance round to acknowledge Marron, but he did straighten his back a little and set his feet more firmly, and he did nip a fourth knife from his belt and send that spinning into the shimmering cascade above his head. His hands seemed hardly to move at all, there was no need; the knives fell handle-down into his palm and leaped high again apparently of their own will.

Marron watched, fascinated and forgetful. After a minute Rudel tossed yet one more knife into the dance of light and steel, but that was one too many for his skill. His hands were suddenly snatching, his feet had to move to follow the dance, and soon two blades clashed in mid-air and fell out of the pattern, skittering away across the cobbles. One slid almost to Marron's feet.

Rudel laughed shortly, caught the other three and held them, then bent to retrieve the one in easy reach. Now at last he looked round, nodded to Marron and said, 'Toss that back, would you, brother?'

Marron stooped and stretched without thought. The sudden movement tugged at his injured arm, making him gasp aloud; he heard, 'No, wait, are you hurt?' but still fumbled to pick up the knife before he straightened.

'Only a little, sir,' he said, not truthfully; his arm ached with a cruel passion. Rudel was right there, taking the knife from him, gazing at him, frowning.

'You're the lad from yesterday, with the dung-cart.'

'Yes, sir.'

'I'm sorry, I should have looked first. A brother with leisure to stand and watch my juggling? I should have *thought* . . . How are you feeling?'

'Quite well, thank you, sir.'

'Hmm. Then I should hate to see you quite ill. You look – no, not so much drawn, perhaps, as ill-drawn. Apprentice work, and the colours poorly mixed. The arm's bad too, hnh?'

'Only sore, sir.'

'Sore enough that you have to hold it on, though. Let me have your girdle, and just slip that habit off for a moment.'

'Sir?'

'Do it, lad, don't argue. Here, I'll help, it's awkward one-handed . . . What's your name?'

'Marron.'

'Good. You were playing servant to the ladies in the hall last night, too, weren't you? When I would have said you should be sleeping? I remember, you were the only brother there . . .'

'Yes, sir. I, uh, I serve Sieur Anton, as he doesn't have a squire, and the ladies were his guests, so . . .'

'So he routed you out of bed in the infirmary to pour wine for them? Yes, that bears the true stamp of d'Escrivey . . . Now. If I knot the girdle round your wrist here, see, tight enough to grip but loose enough for you to slip off with your other hand; then I make a loop of the rest and that goes around your neck, so; that'll hold your arm so you don't have to. Comfortable?'

'Er, yes . . .'

'Good. Now, the habit goes back on over – no, you stand still, I'll do this – and your bad arm's underneath, so you can't use it even if you want to. What were you supposed to be doing this day?'

'I – I'm not sure, sir . . .' *Find some service you are fit for*, but the sling only emphasised what had been clear before, that there was none.

'Will you be my guide, then, Marron? This fortress tangles my mind. And I'm told there's a village down below, but I saw no sign of it from the road . . .?'

'Yes, sir, there's a village. You have to go round the hill to the south, but the track's easy to find.'

'Good. You can show me that, then, too. But the secrets of the castle first, I think. It'll give you something to do, at least. I know idleness does not sit well with the Order.'

'No, sir.'

As he spoke, the jongleur had been crouching over a bright-dyed leather scrip at his feet, stowing his knives within it. Now he stood up, lifting the scrip by its long strap; before he could slip that over his shoulder, Marron had reached out and twitched it from his fingers.

'Eh?'

'You are a guest of the Ransomers, sir, no less than the ladies. I'll be pleased to serve you,' *to serve you too, why not? I serve so many masters now,* 'but you must at least let me carry your satchel.'

'Well, then. Thank you, Fra' Marron, I will. Though most of your Order, I think, would call me and my kind something less welcome than your ladies. You are showing yourself to be somewhat of an unusual brother.'

Marron said nothing; Rudel laughed softly, sympathetically, turning his words from a gibe to a simple truth observed.

'That hits home, eh? Well, never mind. There are always some who find it no natural life for them. You must custom yourself to it; custom can be learned. We'll talk of that. But now, will you show me all the dark corners of this citadel? Old places I love, and some parts of this place I think are very old.'

'Yes, sir. But I'm new-come myself, I don't know them all . . .'

'Then what you don't know we'll discover together. Lead me, Fra' Marron. Lead me blindly when you must, I'll follow regardless . . .'

It seemed more to Marron as though Rudel led and he followed, though that leading was done mostly by questions, *what's down here, where does this go?* and, *how do we get up there?*

Nor were those all the questions that Rudel asked. His curiosity ran broader and deeper far than Marron's knowledge: how many brothers were stationed here and how many knights, how many of those made the permanent garrison and how many could expect to be sent elsewhere and how soon, how safe were the lands to the north where no roads ran and for how far did the Order patrol them?

Marron could give him no answers, and the questioning itself made him uncomfortable. He wanted to ask one thing in return, why the jongleur was so interested; but Rudel was a guest and he was only a guide, it was not his place to meet question with question.

'You must ask the masters, sir,' was all he said, all that he felt able to say. He wondered if perhaps in duty he should report to one of the masters himself, that so many questions were being asked. He was known to none of them, though, bar Magister Raul, and that man he thought would not listen. Neither would Fra' Piet, he was sure. Sieur Anton might – but still, it was only curiosity after all, perhaps all visitors to the Roq asked such questions . . .

He felt little easier when Rudel shifted his interrogation onto more personal ground. Why had Marron chosen to come to the Sanctuary Land, and why had he sworn himself to the Order to do so, why not come simply as a yeoman settler and be welcomed? Marron stammered over his father's name, and then could add little more to it; all the old certainties seemed to have abandoned him, so that he no longer knew why he was here or why in this habit.

The harder Rudel pressed, the fewer answers Marron

had to offer. He floundered, gestured vainly with his one hand, cast about for some distraction – they were in the kitchens by this time, and if the great kettles of onions and carrots weren't enough to catch the jongleur's eye there were always the massive bread-ovens, surely they were worth a word or two? – and saw a miracle instead, or he thought so.

He saw the lady Julianne's companion, Elisande. Running an errand for her lady, perhaps, or else dismissed from duty; whatever the cause she was here, lifting her veil heedlessly aside to munch on an apple. He saw her lick juices from the skin, and his own mouth watered; then she turned her head, and her eyes met his.

He bowed, partly good manners and partly to hide his smile of relief. When he straightened, though, he saw how Elisande was staring, no, *glaring* at his companion; and when he glanced to his side he saw how Rudel was meeting that with a cold gaze of his own. Marron understood this not at all. Perhaps she hadn't enjoyed the man's playing last night, but even so . . .

'Er, sir, my lady . . .' He didn't know the order of precedence here, who he should properly introduce to whom, whether a lady's companion outranked a jongleur twice her age.

'It's all right, Marron,' Rudel said quietly. 'Elisande and I are old friends.'

They didn't look to be friends. Even through the veil he could see how Elisande's face twisted at the word. She tossed the fabric aside and took another defiant, crunching bite of her apple; and then, chewing and speaking together in a way that shocked Marron because it would have shocked his aunt and earned him a cuff from his uncle – and the tone of voice another, if ever he could have managed such a mix of vitriol and contempt – she said, 'Indeed. He makes songs about the dead. It's a talent that touches us both.'

'I'm pleased that something touches you, my lady,' Rudel said, quiet yet, though Marron had sensed his sudden stiffening. 'Though I might wish that it had been your father's rod when you were younger.'

Elisande's veil was still disarranged, enough to show Marron one high cheekbone. Quite white that had gone, at Rudel's first sentence; the second made it red, a fierce flush that mirrored the glowing embers a brother was raking out of the bread-oven at her back. Marron watched him, not to watch her; never had he seen the task done so slowly, or so silently.

'You have no right,' she hissed, 'no right to *say* that! You, of all men . . .'

'Perhaps not,' though there was no hint of apology in his voice. 'But I think we ought not to debate what is right or proper or properly owing between us, you and I. It is too late for that.'

'Long ago, it was much too late,' she concurred bitterly. Then, startlingly, 'Forgive me, Marron. I should not have confronted you with this.'

Before he could stammer a denial, she had turned away, sweeping past the raking brother in a way that had him staring after her, making public all the curiosity he'd been trying so hard to hide. Nor was he the only one to stare; Elisande was out of sight and gone before Rudel stirred or spoke again.

When he did, it was to pose yet another question, one that had no bearing on what had just passed.

'Where does this lead?' he asked, and was already moving towards the doorway behind the ovens before Marron could collect his scattered wits and hurry after him.

'Er, only to the penitents' cells, sir, I don't think you ought . . .'

Too slow: Rudel had already set his feet on the stairs, and was heading down into the dark. Marron took a breath and followed.

They were not halfway down, though, before a rising sound met them, a low groan that swelled suddenly into a shriek. Marron froze, his scalp prickling coldly; after a moment he heard Rudel's voice just a few steps below him, low and tight.

'No, you're right, Brother Marron. We ought not. Up, I think, back up to the light.'

And once there, once far enough from the stair's doorway that the native noises of the kitchens quelled any other noise that might still be winding its way up from below, Rudel didn't pause; he strode on, leading his hesitant guide with just a glance around and, 'Now the village, if you would, Marron.'

'Sir, it's simple, turn to your left at the foot of the hill where the track runs, you don't need—'

'Even so. If you would?'

'Yes, sir.'

Of course he would, with so plain an order; and glad to have it, glad to get out of the castle for an hour or two. Never had the walls seemed so high, the stones so heavy nor the ways so dark. He thought the echo of a scream – not to be heard now, no, but only in their heads – drove them both, brother and jongleur.

Rudel was grim-faced and silent all the long and winding walk down, far from last night's minstrelsy or the curious companion of an hour before. Where the road forked, though, he paused, set his back to the sky-thrusting promontory that overshadowed them and shook his head once, hard. Then he turned his face upward, breathed slowly in and out, and said, 'Look, there's a hawk. Do you see?'

Marron squinted into the pale sky. 'Where, sir?'

'There.' A hand lifted to point. 'Come, your eyes are younger than mine . . .'

It took Marron a moment longer to find the dot that hung high in the air above them. Rudel's finger followed it as it wheeled on the wind, marking a slow trail that left no trace behind it, that the finest hunter couldn't follow; then the jongleur laughed abruptly, let his arm fall onto Marron's shoulder and pushed him gently on along the track.

It seemed to Marron as though, in stepping from the rock of the great scarp to the dust of the track, his companion had stepped out of one mood and into another. Or else the hawk's freedom had freed his soul, perhaps. Rudel pointed out and named other birds flitting about the low dry scrub, and imitated their songs in soft whistles; he spotted bright-coloured butterflies on the thorn-bushes, and signs of a snake's passage across the path.

Marron's mind found its own freedom, its own content: slipping back past time and travel, years back to long walks with his uncle in a more gentle country, the smells of rich earth after rain and the sounds of a meadow in sunlight, the quiet comfort of an adult voice endlessly patient with a boy's eager questions.

But his uncle had been ever a plain man, not seeing what the boy saw, having the knowledge but feeling none of the enchantment. Marron shook his memories away after a short time, rejecting their easy shelter for what was stronger and more vivid, the present smells of heat and dust and the immediate wisdom of a man who could find life, it seemed, beneath the harshest rock.

They turned one stone beside the track and found a scorpion, dark and smooth and glistening as the mud on a tidal bank, tiny and deadly, Rudel said, a creature with its own eternal enchantment in its coiled, poised tail.

Marron thought of rocks and things buried beneath rocks, small things, deadly things; to the scorpion its sheltering stone must have seemed a fortress. Sheltered beneath the fortress that overhung them still, somewhere within that rock was a man who had screamed this morning all unheard by any help, and how small and helpless must he be feeling, and how deadly his host?

But there again Marron's mind chose not to dwell, sliding swiftly on. Small things, deadly things under a weight of rock: the coolth of deep shadow made him shudder, the sun unseen was a candle waiting to be lit, and there burning in his memory was enchantment true, such a small flame and so fatal . . .

'Sir . . .?'

Rudel settled the rock carefully back in its former place, not to disturb its lethal tenant, straightened and said,

'Marron, would it be against your Rule if you just called me by my name?'

It was becoming a familiar experience, to be tossed suddenly and unexpectedly into confusion. This time, at least the question had given him a handhold, something to hang on to; he treated it literally, though he wasn't at all sure that it had been meant that way.

Like all his brothers – almost all – he knew the Rule by heart, from beginning to end. To learn it was the first task of every novice, and flagging memories were revived by its being read through once a week in the refectory. From beginning to end, though, was exactly and only how he knew it. He couldn't fillet a neat bone of instruction on demand. There was a great deal, he knew, about respect and obedience, the giving of honour where it was due; but as to the addressing of an older man not of the Order, not of the nobility, not of any rank that either Marron or the Rule could recognise . . .

'I don't know, sir,' he said, nothing more than that.

'You don't *know*? I thought you all knew every word of it . . .?'

'Yes, sir. I'll say it,' boldly, 'and then you tell me. "Listen, my son, to the precepts of your Master, and incline the ear of your heart unto them. Freely accept and faithfully fulfil the advice of a loving father, so that you may, by the labour of obedience, return to Him, Whom you abandoned through the sloth of disobedience. To you, therefore, whoever you are, my words are directed, who, renouncing your own will, take up the strong and excellent arms of obedience to fight for the true King, our Lord—"'

'Enough, enough!' Rudel was laughing, even as he

clamped a big hand across Marron's mouth to stem the spew of words. 'I understand you, lad. And yes, I have heard the Rule before, in all its piety and coarseness; and no, I do not wish to hear it all again. So let us assume, shall we, that it does not forbid your calling me Rudel, and progress from there?'

'Sir—'

'You're thinking that it would be safer to assume the opposite, that the Rule forbids most things and hence quite likely this too? Of course you are, I read boys' minds. Not girls',' and it was as though for a moment a cloud had kissed the sun, casting his face into shadow so that the lines and the pits of it showed only that bleak anger Elisande had woken in him. 'But, let me see, in that briefest of introductions you were enjoined two or three times towards obedience, were you not? And there is more, much more later. So how if I *order* you to assume, to believe, to be utterly certain that the Rule not only allows but requires you to follow my wishes in this? How then?'

'Sir, guests are sacred to us; but—'

'Good. You will call me Rudel, then, or I will send you to your confessor in search of a thrashing.' Even a jovial reference to Fra' Piet, made in ignorance, could still cause Marron to flinch; but if Rudel marked it, he didn't comment. 'Now, you had a question for me?'

'I did?'

'I believe so. We were looking at the scorpion . . .'

'Oh. Yes. Uh,' which had nearly come out as a 'sir', only changed hurriedly to a grunt as his muddled mind clamped hard down on the habits of his mouth, 'have you ever seen magic made?'

'Seen it? Marron, lad, I'm a jongleur. You have heard me singing for my supper, but I do have other skills to trade. I *make* magic. Watch . . .'

He stooped, to pick up three pebbles from the track. All three were smooth and rounded, much of a size, the size of chicken's eggs. He held them up, two in one hand and one in the other, letting his sleeves fall back to show his corded arms bare; then he tossed them into the air and began to juggle.

This was skill, to be sure, but not magic. Marron had seen so much and more at every fair he'd been to as a child. He'd seen men juggle flaming torches, four or five at once. He'd seen Rudel do more this morning, keeping four and almost five knives dancing in the air with never a nick to a finger. He bit back his frustration, though, and watched; and somehow didn't see when the pebbles changed, when they became not pebbles but eggs indeed, gleaming green-white ducks' eggs, twice as big. Neither did he see how Rudel cracked and split them, so that they opened in mid-air before his eyes with a trill of birdsong and a shower of sparkling silver dust like the soft scales from a butterfly's wing; and briefly he saw bright birds and butterflies rising from the broken shells, before they fell into Rudel's gentle hands and were only gaudy scarves of sheer silk that draped across his stilling fingers.

Rudel laughed, and looped the scarves around Marron's neck; their touch was soft as a child's fingers against his skin, a startling change from the rough wool of his habit, and it was a long moment before he moved to pull them off. Silks and colours were certainly very much against the Rule, that he had no doubts about.

He held them out mutely, stiffly awkward; but Rudel only laughed and said, 'Put them in the satchel, then, if you don't find them easy wearing.'

Marron did that, and then, stubbornly, 'I didn't mean tricks, or fairground skills. I meant real magic, true wonders . . .'

'Marron, lad,' and Rudel was solemn again, at least on the surface, though his eyes still glinted with laughter, 'I have lived all my life in this land where your God walked once, and not Him alone. I have lived a year in Ascariel. How could I not have seen wonders? I have seen the djinn in their strength, and other creatures too. Creatures less neutral, more cruelly disposed towards men.'

Had seen them, and it seemed wanted not to talk of them; at any rate he started walking again, briskly along the track. Marron followed quietly, until Rudel glanced back and asked, 'So what is it that you have seen?'

Marron wasn't sure that he should say. It might be a secret of the Order, what he had been shown in that damp cold chamber beneath the castle; so he said nothing until Rudel put his question another way.

'Did they show you the King's Eye, lad? Yes, of course they did, they greet you all with that, don't they? Well, don't let it hang in your own eye. That's what they want, they only do it to frighten you. Frighten and inspire, I suppose, but frighten mainly.'

Frighten him was mainly what the sight had done, to be sure. Frighten and inspire, yes; but awe and terror were so closely matched and so easily confused, and right now everything that the Order touched seemed to make him shudder, like a cold hand laid on him in the heat.

A deep breath that was almost a gasp at his own temerity and then, inevitably, 'Have you, have you *seen* it, sir?'

'I thought you meant to call me by my name.'

'I'm sorry, sir. Ru, Rudel, I mean. But,' all in a rush now, a frantic burst of honesty, 'I don't think I can and I'm really not sure that I should, and I *am* sure that Fra' Piet would say that I shouldn't, he'll make me pay a penance for it if I tell him that I have and I'd have to do that, I'd have to confess, it'd lie on my conscience else and fester there . . .'

'Gods, what do they *do* to you boys? No, don't answer that. I know what they do, I've seen it. All right, call me what you will. I'd ask you who you think I am, to be deserving of so much respect from a young devout like you, except that I know the answer to that one too. Just a shabby conjuror, a singer of songs and a teller of foolish tales; but a guest none the less, and so honoured. Isn't that right? You'd honour a barefoot beggar and never realise how much honour that does you, though your superiors know it too well. It's this urge to confess that worries me more. Can't you remember what it felt like, *not* to tell your secrets? When you were a child, Marron? I'll wager that nothing festered then.'

Yes, he could remember; but all those memories were painful to him now, because all those secrets had been shared with Aldo. Determinedly, Marron came back to what might or might not be a secret but was apparently shared with the jongleur. 'Have you seen the King's Eye? Sir?'

'Not as you've seen it, I fancy. How is it for you, shadows and glory buried away in some dark and hidden chamber?

Well, let me tell you, lad, it shines as brightly in full sun, in all the noise and sweat and fear of a war . . .'

For a moment Marron thought that was all he'd be granted, a glimpse of another man's secret too soon snatched away. But Rudel sighed, shook his head vainly against the persistence of memory or perhaps against the stupidity of man, and said, 'I was down in Less Arvon. Twenty years ago, this was, when all the songs I knew and all the skills I had were violent. I had taken service with the duke; the Little Duke he is called, you'll have heard stories about him. Well, some of those stories, I was there.

'It was a quarrelsome time; the Sharai infested the hills to the east of his country, and there was brutality and treaty-breaking on both sides. Caravans raided, castles taken and retaken. Prisoners slain, of course, that was the governance and practice of the war.

'The duke led an army himself, in the end, when it seemed that he might lose his borders. He drove the Sharai back, but of course he pursued them too far, he was always a hot-head. And of course the bulk of the men were left behind, foot soldiers can't keep up with cavalry in a hard chase; and privately I've always believed that some of his own family drew rein deliberately, to let us ride off into trouble. There was always a faction held that the dukedom would be better in younger and less impulsive hands.

'At any rate, there were fewer than two hundred of us with him when we finally got it through his skull that we rode alone. We were a long way into debatable lands, frankly lost, and surrounded by enemies; we couldn't see where the Sharai were regrouping, but of course they would be. That's how they fight, strike and retreat and strike again.

Remember that. And they're devils on horseback, those fine-boned little things they ride, faster than you can dream and they turn like dancers. Remember that, too.

'One thing we knew for sure, we couldn't go back as we had come. We sent outriders that way, to see if the army was following; the Sharai returned them to us, strapped into their saddles and missing a few pieces. Tongues and eyes and such. Not dead, though. We had to do them that kindness.

'To be true, I thought we were all of us dead men. White bones walking. Especially when the arrows started coming, out of dead land; we couldn't see the archers. We lost men and horses both; I think we'd have broken if we'd known which way to run.

'But we had a troop of brothers among our number, they'd been first in the field as always; and their elder, their confessor took a twisted candle and set it on a rock, and lit it. He mumbled some nonsense over it, I was close enough to hear and it was no language that I knew, I thought it some death-rite of the Order to take our souls to glory. Only then he held his hands in the flame, and it burned him not at all; and the light of it outshone the sun, filling the hollow where we were grouped and turning the trees to gold.

'Even the duke was amazed. I was nearest, and first to find my tongue; I asked the brother what this was. "You stand in the King's Eye, my son," he said, "and he will see us safe."

'And so it proved. No more arrows came, and that was blessing enough; but then he set that candle on his saddle-bow and led us back along the valley, and all the land glittered and shone and was empty. We had to walk, the horses were half-crazed and would not be ridden; but we met no Sharai and none of our army either, in a march of hours. The candle burned out at last, though one doubled taper should never have lasted so long; and then the brother cupped the last of its flame within his hands, and it burned there as brightly as ever it had and the light flowed out between his fingers.

'Where he led us, where we walked was familiar, and yet not so. Though the hills seemed the same, it had been autumn but the air was hot and crisp, stinging in our throats; and the earth and the rocks too were warm, and their touch tingled on our skin. Where we forded rivers, the water steamed and we could not drink it; it ran slowly, and glittered strangely. There were no birds, no insects.

'At last we came out onto the plain, and that too seemed empty of life until suddenly the brother flung his hands up, crying certain words I do not remember. The gold was gone in a moment and it was twilight, there were shadows and movement all around us and that was the bulk of our men, making what camp and what order they could without their officers.'

As he told his tale, Rudel's voice had deepened and changed its rhythm, the jongleur's art taking charge of his words to make a small performance of them, to play upon his hearer; that too had Marron shivering.

But it was a performance on the move, on the march; Rudel hadn't stopped walking. Neither had the sun, if that had legs to walk with. Higher than the castle now it stood, its light flowing down over them like the heat, like water, and shadows were fractional. It could lack only a few minutes of noon. Which thought, which memory made Marron glance aside, suddenly conscious of just where they were along the track; and yes, there it was still, the little altar that Mustar had erected. Only one of those blue stones on its slab now, he noticed, vaguely puzzled: who would take a stone, two stones, and leave the altar standing? Thrushes, perhaps, to break open a snail's shell. If there were thrushes in the Sanctuary Land, if there were snails . . .

He could ask Rudel, of course, that man seemed to know everything about the world of life they walked through; but it was only a brief curiosity, and he had something of more moment, much more moment to override it.

He would need to pray, and wasn't sure that Rudel would pray with him. Wasn't sure if he should ask, even. *Your God*, Rudel had said, and that was blasphemy, and he'd been so casual about it. Hadn't even noticed what he'd said, perhaps . . .

Marron had said his prayers with only one man head to head, only with Sieur Anton. That was a special experience every time and he didn't want it tainted, overlaid by memories of another man's voice and his own doubts about that man's faith.

Neither, of course, could he walk aside to pray alone; but there was a third way. If they hurried. The village was not far ahead now, no distance at all to quick feet and determination; and there was a temple there, listen, soon its thin bell would be calling its people in. Never mind the unfamiliar rite and the press of strangers' bodies, better to hide his questions in a crush. Better far to stand or kneel or prostrate himself in a place where he understood nothing, where he felt a stranger himself.

So *hurry, hurry* went his feet, and Rudel kept pace with him as the deep tones of Frater Susurrus impelled them both, it seemed, tumbling down from the high castle and pushing at their backs while the temple's bell pulled them forward.

And so they came to the village and through the village as the bells hushed, to the village square before the temple; and there they found confusion instead of order, high-pitched voices raised against the proper silence, fear where there should have been peace.

They found the people of the village, the old men and the children all in a pack, not filing into the temple to pray but babbling and staring. They found the priest in his beard stood before the open temple door with one arm out-thrust to bar it and the other lifted high as he called down the God's anger, it seemed, on the little group that stood huddled before him, a man and a woman with a baby in her arms.

Worse – worst, almost, of all the things that Marron could imagine to make this scene worse – they found his own troop of brothers gathered together in the square, all on foot around a single fretful horse, murmuring between themselves as Fra' Piet paced towards the temple steps, his hand already on the haft of his axe.

Marron hesitated, wanting to run to his brothers to ask what this was about but shy of their contempt or rejection, knowing how poisoned they were against him.

There was no matching hesitation in Rudel. The jongleur cursed under his breath and hurried forward, close to running before he reached Fra' Piet. The confessor had his hood up, so Marron couldn't see if he spared Rudel so much as a glance; but the two men reached the steps side by side, and matched their paces as they climbed.

Marron followed uncertainly, with many sidelong glances of his own. His brothers were mainly watching the priest and Fra' Piet, those who weren't cautiously watching the horse as it shied and sidled in their midst. Only Aldo was watching him.

He stopped before he'd set foot on the lowest of the broad flat steps; up there was no place for him. He could hear well enough from down below, he could learn the cause of all this.

'What is the matter here?'

That was Fra' Piet, naturally. Rudel seemed content now to stand back a little, perhaps merely to witness.

There was spittle on the priest's beard; more flew from his white-flecked lips as he said, 'Holy brother, most welcome come! See these dogs now, they are not of the faith, see . . .'

And he wrenched at the man's rough robe, where already it was torn open at the neck; and true, there around the man's throat was a leather thong with a blue bead threaded onto it, which was the sign of a heretic Catari anywhere throughout the Sanctuary Land. The Sharai scorned those beads, Marron had heard, the Sharai said that they knew each other and they knew their god as their god knew them, they needed no other sign between them; but all the tamed and conquered peoples wore them. By their new masters' edict, as much as their own will: it was useful to tell heretic from believer at a glance.

As now. The man couldn't deny it, and Fra' Piet's axe had already left his belt when Rudel's hand clamped suddenly around its haft, just a finger's-breadth below the confessor's grip.

The axe stilled, as did the two men and everyone who watched them. It was a stillness born of terrible tension; Marron thought the axe might snap, he thought unseen muscles heaved and strained and matched each other strength for strength, he thought something had to break and neither man would.

Neither did, but no more did the axe. Fra' Piet chose another path, too proud to wrestle for his weapon under the eyes of his men.

'You imperil your soul,' he said.

'Not I. There is a law, the King's law, that says such as these are as free as any in the Kingdom, if they pay their taxes and do no harm.'

'There is a law,' Fra' Piet rasped, 'the Church's law, that says such as these may enter no church, no temple, no chapel nor any place dedicated to the God, on pain of the Order's justice.'

That was true too, or so Marron had heard it; neither did Rudel dispute it.

'And is this the Order's justice,' he demanded, 'an axe on the temple steps and no one to speak for them, no one even to *name* them before they die? The husband, the wife and the baby too?'

'The penalty is death,' Fra' Piet said, 'for such as they. They would have polluted the God's temple with their presence.'

'It usually is death,' Rudel agreed, and how was it that

his voice sounded so measured and at the same time so sardonic, so condemning? 'For such as they. Whatever the offence. But their death is not yours to deliver, Brother Confessor. Your masters must have a word in this. The priest too, and the village headman. Who are these people, and why did they seek to go in to prayers to a god they do not follow?'

Fra' Piet hissed – *Be careful*, Marron thought urgently, *or he'll charge you too, jongleur, before the masters* – but said only, 'Spies. They are spies who seek to hide among the faithful.'

'The baby too? More likely they were afraid, under the shadow of your castle, and therefore sought to hide. Where is the headman?'

The headman was perhaps one of the dozen men who pushed past Marron then and hurried up the steps, all of them talking at once: to the priest, to Rudel, to Fra' Piet and to each other. In the babble Marron could hear nothing but the baby's wailing, which chimed cruelly with another baby's crying in his head, and the dreadful sound of that baby's silence after.

The debate on the temple steps came to a resolution, of a sort. The man was bound to a pillar and the woman also, though her hands were left free to hold her baby. They would all three be taken up to the Roq after worship, to face the preceptor's judgement.

The villagers filed into the temple; the troop followed at Fra' Piet's word; Rudel beckoned to Marron and they too went inside to kneel at the back, almost in the doorway, all the space there was.

Fra' Piet led the prayers himself, to spare his doubts about the native rite; let the villagers doubt and misunderstand, murmur and fall silent in the face of unfamiliar responses here in their own temple, so long as his troop was kept pure.

Marron, who could school his mind to the words and his mind's eye to the God – most of the time – when he prayed with Sieur Anton, could do nothing like it when Fra' Piet said the prayers. For all the confessor's own devotion, he had no gift to share it. His voice and manner made this a duty only, to spend the middle hour of a hot day kneeling among hot bodies and chanting words by rote.

Marron's arm ached, his eyes shifted, his thoughts barely registered when his mouth was speaking and when it was not. All his attention was out through the door at his back and focused on the world there, the three lives forfeit to his earthly masters. He had no doubt of their deaths; he had seen Fra' Piet's fierce righteousness work its madness on the whole troop, and he was sure the confessor's cold condemnation would do the same in the preceptor's court. Even the babe would die, for its parents' stupidity. And Marron had seen, heard, felt, made one baby die for Fra' Piet, and he couldn't bear another. He owed the world restitution, his own death or another's life to quiet that constant silence in his head; and no matter what the God might make of such a bad bargain, every choice that came his way was soured now, he had little left to lose that he could care for . . .

It still took him a long time to find the nerve, to make the first small movement: still on his knees but shuffling backwards, reaching blindly for the light. Only Rudel's head moved to track him; no one else could see except Fra' Piet, if he could peer over all those massed bodies and make out one that shifted against the sun's glare beating at the open door.

Marron met Rudel's questioning gaze with what he hoped was a telling look, a face that could carry several messages at once: *I have to do this*, and, *don't make a sound*, and, *thank you, I really enjoyed your company today*. He wouldn't, he thought, be having any more of it. No solace now, no hope of anything but loss ahead, and he'd lost so much already. Brave this might be, stupid it surely was.

Still, once moving, he wasn't going to stop. On his knees but stretching up, he saw Fra' Piet prostrate himself before the crude stone block that made the altar.

Now . . .

Quiet as he could, swift as he could manage, Marron stood and turned and stepped outside. From sticky shade to the dry burning glare of the sun; from company to solitude; from obedience to rebellion he went in a single pace, and never felt its moment.

Feeling nothing but urgency, Marron hurried along the temple wall to where the two prisoners stood bound to wooden pillars that supported the overhanging roof. The baby was asleep now, in the woman's arms; that was some relief, at least. Dark eyes watched him questioningly, and he pressed a finger to his lips, *be as silent as the babe, for your own lives' sakes . . .*

He fumbled inside Rudel's satchel, where it still hung on his shoulder; his fingers found the keen edge of a knife, gripped the handle and drew it out.

He saw the man's eyes widen, wondering, but he went to the woman first. Cut the thong that bound her throat to the pillar, stooped to free her waist and ankles. Quickly from her to the man and cut again, at throat and wrists and ankles; and then with a gesture led them down the steps to where Fra' Piet's horse was hobbled in the square.

Two strokes of the knife cut the hobble away; he straightened, gripped the bridle against the horse's prancing and beckoned the freed prisoners forward.

Can you ride? Oh, tell me you can ride . . . He had no language to ask them, but no need. The man swung himself up easily into the saddle and the woman followed, awkward only because of the baby. A touch of the man's hand on an arching neck, a murmur close to a flicking ear, and the horse quieted. For a moment the riders gazed down impassively, then the man reached to brush back Marron's hood, to see more clearly. His eyes narrowed and he nodded, *I have your face now, brother*; the woman smiled thinly as a twitch of the reins turned the horse's head away. Neither seemed much awed now by how near to death they'd stood, though they'd been craven before the priest.

Marron watched them leave, glad to see the horse walked till they were out of sight and out of hearing, not to make a noise that might be heard within the temple.

With them free and gone, though, the enormity of what he'd done descended on him in a rush. His hand was trembling as he stowed the knife carefully with its brothers in the scrip, as he slipped that from his shoulder and set it aside. There were other things than knives inside that scrip; a purse, for one. Forsworn already, outcast by his own choice, he could take it and run, abandon his habit before it was stripped from him and save himself the pains that must come soon; but no. He'd be a traitor to his oaths, his Order and his God, but he would not be a coward.

So he stood and waited there in the square, in the sun, until the soft sound of the responses ceased to murmur through the temple's open door. He stood and faced that dark square until he saw a figure move there, saw Fra' Piet emerge, stiffen, turn his head in search; saw his confessor all but run down the steps towards him, and moved not a muscle.

Met Fra' Piet's cold stare with his own, and answered his questions.

'Where are they?'

'Fled.'

'On my horse?'

'Yes.'

'How?'

'I freed them.' *For a baby's sake, that you had me kill,* but he wouldn't say that. Not here, not to him. To the preceptor, perhaps, or to anyone who might choose to ask why.

Fra' Piet hissed air between his teeth and asked one more question, while his hand reached down to the axe in his girdle.

'Is there another mount anywhere in this village?'

Marron blinked, and answered honestly. 'Only a camel, that I have seen; and that is old, and blind.'

The axe came free of the girdle then, and swung. The last Marron noticed was that the head of it lay tight against Fra' Piet's wrist.

PART TWO

The Road to Ruin

10

In the Dark

Dark: cold and dark.

Hunger, cold and dark.

Fear and hunger, cold and dark.

Pain also, he was hurting and frightened and hungry and cold; but all of those could slip away and be lost or forgotten as he lost or forgot himself, as his body came and faded, as his life did, jags and snatches. The dark was ever present, never lost. Even when they brought the light to see him by – twice they'd brought it now, brought it and taken it away and each time left a token to remind him, *here it was and now it's gone again* – even then the dark remained, lurking in all the corners, pressing in scornfully against that little light and rushing back like water at its tail.

Like us, he'd thought, *like us all, that little light: holding the Sanctuary Land but barely, sure of the God's purpose, sure of our doom or we should be, so little a light and the dark all around us, so strong and so constant, pushing, pushing . . .*

That had been a rare, a rational thought. Mostly he considered the dark, no more than that.

Memories came to him unsought, unwanted, unwelcomed. He found them like seeds in the darkness whether his eyes were open or closed, and they grew and burned and consumed themselves like blooms of fire, making his eyes sting, open or closed.

Nothing of his childhood, nothing of who he had been though he might have welcomed that as a field to walk in, smells and textures and voices that loved him, anywhere other than here.

All he remembered was moments, flashes, each of them limned in that absent light:

—the axe, Fra' Piet's axe and how he held it, a moment of stilled time: hand gripping just below the head so it was the haft, only the haft that cracked on Marron's skull, and was that cruelty or kindness?

—Aldo's face, so close: like waking up, that was, like waking up used to be when they could share a bed, when they used to share everything or tried to. But his face so close and so sad, this was not how it used to be; and his mouth saying something that his eyes were not, 'No, brother, he's stupid still,' while his eyes said, *oh my brother, where have we come to, you and I?*

—the face of Master Infirmarer and no charity in it today, only harsh assessment: fingers waking fire in his skull and in his arm, and voices that swirled and met like waters in a stream, now running fast, now spreading wide and slow. '. . . No, not well, but well enough. He'll do for you . . . How comes this to be opened again? I sewed it yesterday, and see, my stitches have been cut . . .'

'Likely he opened it himself,' Fra' Piet's voice booming and whispering, 'to escape work another day. No, leave it, Magister, I pray you. He is none of ours now, or will not be tomorrow. Let him bleed tonight, as a reminder.'

'He will bleed enough, though not I think tomorrow. A man must walk to judgement. Bind it up, brother, I will not sew again. Some we lose, and this one is small loss. One night in my cots here, I think, Fra' Piet, though he deserves it not; one night a penitent, as the rule is; he'll be hungry when he makes that walk . . .'

—not the walk they spoke of, but a walk he remembered, a stumbling rather, hard hands to drag him and steps going down: lamplight swinging, a corridor, a cell with an open door and a body, his body on its knees now and shivering already in a loose white tunic and where had his habit gone, had someone taken it and must he do penance for the loss?

—no face but a body, another body in white and not his because it was moving and he was not. There was light in the corridor, they had brought light and would not let him see; but he smelled dung and familiarity and heard a voice, a whisper, 'Here is bread, eat it slowly, slowly.' A hand guided his to find it, where he could not see despite the light. 'Here is water, drink it slowly. And here,' the hand pressed something into his, hard and round and cool it was, 'here is for tonight. Show it when they come, it will keep you safe . . .'

—no face but a body, and this one white and still and still not his. The lamp burned behind the visitor's shoulder and shadow cloaked all but the robe, but the robe and the voice were Sieur Anton's and he said, 'Stupid, stupid! Even I cannot help you this time, Marron. You have been condemned. The judgement is that you must be flayed tomorrow before the Order, and then cast out naked into the world.'

That judgement is right, his voice said, *I cannot dispute it*; but as his robe swirled to fill the cell and block all light from what his hands did, a weight dropped silently into Marron's lap. *For tomorrow*, the silence said, *if you should choose it. If you cannot bear what must come else . . .*

As Sieur Anton stalked away, a last fall of light from the warder's lamp showed a soft blue gleam in Marron's palm, where he still held what Mustar had left with him.

Time was a creeping thing, with little to mark it. There had twice been light, brought and taken; three times now there had been sounds. Twice Frater Susurrus had called to him, midday and sunset he thought those must have been; once he had heard a screaming that echoed down the passage and drove the chill deeper into his bones. That too had brought its memory, he and Rudel on the steps above, driven back by another man's agony.

Slowly, time had taken the numbness and confusion from him. He knew now who and where he was; he was Marron, Fra' Marron for one more night and no more than that, by Sieur Anton's word. He knelt in the dark in a penitent's cell, and felt not at all penitent: only hurt and afraid, cold and hungry and very much alone. Sometimes he felt saved, that also, he felt justified: a life for a life, he had repaid the debt and the voice of a wailing babe was stilled now within him. But that inner peace was fragile, too easily swamped or broken, he dared not touch it often for fear of losing it altogether.

He nibbled at bread and sipped water that he should not have, that Mustar had slipped to him; he stood to use the bucket and staggered, hastily knelt again and used it kneeling; and betweentimes he played with the two tokens he had been so carefully, secretly gifted, and understood only one of them.

Sieur Anton's gift was a blade, and the second such the knight had given him. Not a sword this time; a misericorde, a knife slender and short as a girl's finger but wide enough, long enough to serve. If the fear grew through the hours of the night, if the memory of a man's flesh ripped from his living bones proved too terrible, if he could not face those leather straps with their iron barbs or the shame that came after, if anything but death came after – well, he had a way to escape them. That was kindness, he supposed. Of a sort.

Mustar's gift was a bafflement. He knew what else it was, he'd seen it, it was heresy: a blue bead worn at a man's throat, a blue stone laid on a makeshift altar, the sign of their false god. Too large, too heavy for a bead, this was a stone like those he had seen Mustar set out in a pattern of three. *For tonight*, Mustar had whispered. He didn't know what that meant.

He rolled the stone between his palms, frowning. Mustar was a boy and a believer, still practising his religion despite the dangers; but would even he believe that a little stone might turn a man from one god to another? *For tonight*, he'd said. *Show it when they come*, he'd said. When who came? *It will keep you safe*, he'd said, but safe from what? Not from the Order, that was sure. If they found it on him, if he showed it when they came for him, he'd face worse than a flaying. He'd face the questioners first, it would be his screams that filled the ears of the penitents and their warders tomorrow. Mustar must know that. He'd taken a terrible risk himself, to bring it here . . .

For tonight. Show it when they come, it will keep you safe.

A blue stone, three blue stones and a blue bead . . . Marron thought again about the boy kneeling at his little altar, laying out his stones and saying his prayers. What did a slave boy pray for, a captive taken from his people?

And then yesterday, with Rudel, he had seen the altar still standing but only one stone left. A bird, he'd thought; but stones this big, this heavy were too much for any thrush. A crow might take one, he supposed, but a man could do it easier. Or a boy. Any man who followed the God would have scattered all the stones, destroyed the altar . . .

A man with a blue bead, come from somewhere, for some reason. With a woman and a baby, true, but not like peasants. They'd ridden like masters. Like Sharai, perhaps . . .? *Spies*, Fra' Piet had said, and he might have been right.

For tonight. Show it when they come, it will keep you safe . . .

Three stones could be a message. *Three days*, they could say; that day, the next day, and this. A man, a spy could take one, and that could be a message too: *we are ready.* A boy could take one, *we too are ready. For tomorrow.* And today that same boy could have taken the last, *come tonight*; and that boy could give it to a friend as a token, a sign to keep him safe . . .

Darkness and cold, hunger and fear and pain could make a young man's mind act strangely, see truth in nonsense. Marron shook his head, and winced at the soreness in it; he laid the stone down and tried to think clearly, to see that he was being foolish. He was weaving fantasies, no more than that.

But there had been three stones, and then one; and now he had a stone, and these stones were rare and dangerous, how many could there be?

For tonight. Show it when they come, it will keep you safe . . .

Marron groaned, in a whisper. His arm was aching badly after so little exercise, rolling a stone in his palms; when he touched the bandage, he found it sticky. He must be bleeding once again. Well, that didn't matter. He'd bleed worse tomorrow. If he had a tomorrow, if he didn't use Sieur Anton's gift to escape it . . .

No. Not that. That was a knight's trick which would ill become a knave. Or a brother. It might suit Sieur Anton's sense of honour; for Marron it was not even a question.

Frater Susurrus beat out the hour again; that must be midnight. All his brothers bar the watch would be before the altar now; like those of a true penitent his own lips started moving, saying the office in an unvoiced whisper, though it meant nothing to him. Broken oaths and a love that failed, a faith that faded as the days turned rancid in the heat: the Order would flay him and reject him tomorrow, it had no claim any longer on his loyalty or his soul. But the words came regardless, and with the words came a picture in his mind, one man he knew who would not be praying with the brothers. And there was a count in his head, *three stones to one, and a bead at a man's throat, a stone here now for me and all the garrison praying*; and there was a tremor in him that was more than a starved lad's fancy, a vision of some evil worked against the castle now and he the only one to know or guess it, and was he to know or guess it and do nothing? How many lives this time, to set with those he'd taken against those he'd saved?

He was moving almost before he'd taken the decision to move. He stood, and the darkness seethed around him. He grabbed at nothing and scored his palm on rock, leaned against it until the weakness eased, though it did not pass. Then he scabbarded the little knife in the bandage on his arm, where it could be held and handy; he gripped the stone tightly in his other hand like a token, a talisman, *oh, keep me safe, then. If you can . . .*

And he stepped without permission from his cell into the passage, which perhaps no penitent had done before him.

To one side he saw light, dimmed by distance but bright enough to his starved eyes; that must be the chamber where the lamp burned in its niche in the wall, where the warders stood on guard. Or knelt in prayer, he hoped, he prayed . . .

He turned the other way, not hopeful, walking slowly with his fingers trailing the wall. Closed doors meant empty cells; and then at the end of the passage one door both closed and bolted. For the questioners' guest, he supposed. No possible exit this way, though in honesty he hadn't expected to find one, he'd only hoped.

So he tracked back towards the light, ghosting past all the open doors, knowing that even in the dark he'd shine in his white to any penitents' eyes that were looking. Luck: some slept and the rest prayed, and none glanced up to see him.

He came to the chamber at the end, and was lucky again. Two warders there as before, but knowing themselves redundant – what man of the Order, however strayed, would challenge the authority that had sent him penitent here? – they prayed as properly as their wakeful charges, side by side and hooded, on their knees and turned towards the light.

Marron watched them from the passage, waited breathlessly until the rite had them bowing heads to ground and chanting softly; then he slid one cautious foot out into the chamber, and then the other.

His bare toes made no sound on the rock of the floor, his shift didn't rustle, not even the stench of his fear betrayed him. He reached the stairway, and took a moment to bow himself towards the light in gratitude before he slid on upwards, still placing each foot with care and doubly so after the staircase turned and he was blind again.

Into the kitchen, and suddenly warm; he paused for a moment by the bread-ovens, just to feel the waft of hot air on long-chilled skin.

Out past the latrines, and this way led to the great hall

and his gathered brethren but he turned the other, not so very stupid; what, should he burst in and cry danger to them all, with no more proof than a blue stone in his hand, betraying Mustar and himself?

No, he ran out into the open, where the breeze felt as warm as the air by the ovens, and up steps onto the high wall that circled the castle. By the God's grace the moon was high, giving him light to see by. Light to be seen by, also; but he knew where the guards were stationed, he should be safe enough here and he needed to be sure.

Movement caught his eye, where no one should be moving. He stilled, crouched, stared without breathing and saw white figures in the moonlight, others, darker, swarming over the wall.

That was his proof, his confirmation. He turned to go back down – and there was a man in front of him, dark-robed and deadly, a knife glinting light along its edges.

Marron gasped, flung his hand up desperately, and the man held his stroke.

'Show me,' he hissed.

Marron held his hand out flat, and the man took the stone from his palm. Looked at it, nodded, sheathed his knife.

'Come . . .'

The man half-turned, and that half-turn was enough. Marron slid the misericorde from his bandage and thrust blindly, felt a moment's grating resistance and thrust harder; there was a rush of warm wetness, the man made a quiet choking noise and slumped heavily, dragging the slippery knife from Marron's grasp as he fell.

*

No more caution now; Marron sprinted down the steps and through the castle, his arms flying as wildly as his feet, shoving at the walls to push him on faster.

At last the court, the final climb, the corridor he sought; he all but fell against Sieur Anton's door, shoved it open and stumbled inside.

'Marron! What in the world . . .?'

Sieur Anton was in his nightgown, had been on his knees; now he was on his feet, stepping forward and then checking suddenly, standing very still.

'Marron, what have you done?'

Marron had blood on his hands, he saw, as they twitched in his sight, beckoning like frantic claws. Blood on the once-white shift, too; the fabric was heavy with it, clinging. He hadn't known a man would pay such a gift of blood to his killer. Or he'd forgotten, rather: in the village they had bathed in blood, but he'd been hot mad then. Now he was cold, chilled, desperate as he gathered his shift and wiped his hands like a madman.

Sieur Anton, he realised, thought he'd used that little knife – as he had – but didn't know on whom. Didn't know, and doubted. He'd seen the warders, after all, who were placed to watch the penitents in their cells . . .

'Sharai,' Marron gasped. 'There are Sharai, climbing the north wall. I, I killed one . . .'

The knight needed no more than that. He seized his sword, drew breath for a bellow – and then held it, shook his head. 'All at prayer, yes? They'll not hear us from here. Marron, can you run to the hall?'

Marron shook his head. 'Not me, sieur.'

'Not . . .?' A momentary frown, which cleared quickly.

'Oh. In the circumstances, no, not you. But I must go to the wall and hold them, if I can . . .'

'Me too, sieur.' Bold as he'd ever been, Marron ducked across the room and snatched up the sword Dard from where it lay in its white sheath on the chest. 'You gave this to me, sieur, it is mine to use.'

'Surely, take the sword – but if ever you practised obedience, do it now. Run to the bell, wake the castle. If two can hold the wall, perhaps one alone can do it also – but neither can do so for long . . .'

Marron wasn't sure that he did still practise obedience, in anything or to anybody. This time tomorrow he would be dead to the Order, so why not this time tonight? He'd likely be dead for real in an hour's time, so why not in five minutes' time instead, and fighting with the knight?

But he didn't truly believe in death, or not his own; and he did still believe in duty, and in hope. Sounding the bell, rousing the castle was sensible. Nor was there anyone to do it bar himself.

Side by side, the two ran together. They met no one, saw no shadow shift; when Sieur Anton's hand moved in a chopping, urgent motion, *you go that way now*, Marron had no choice but to leave him and run on alone.

He'd never visited what they all called Frater Susurrus' Cell, but he knew where to find it: up and up, as high up as he could go, to the highest point in the Roq and in any of the country round about. At the top of the tallest tower there was a bell-shaped chamber of stone with windows cut wide and high at every quarter, open to each and any of the winds; and the shape bespoke the purpose, for there hung the bell that spoke the hours and called the Ransomers to prayer.

Oddly, there was no watch kept from that chamber, or none official. *Brother Whisperer keeps his own eyes open*, they said; but if that were true he must be blind or mute at night, for he was speaking no warning now. Marron leaped up the last of the stairs and plunged across the flat roof, tumbled into the bell-chamber and came up short against the awesome presence of the bell.

In the moonlight he saw it more as shadow than substance, but it was shadow with a voice, shadow that chose silence just for now; and even that silence pulsed at a level way below hearing, as the night breeze stroked the great bronze flange of the bell and so light a touch still drew a humming from it.

It hung from a frame wrought of timber and steel and stone, and high as that frame was – perhaps three times Marron's height – the bell's rim was still only knee-high above the floor. He couldn't imagine the weight of it.

Neither could he see how it was sounded. The bells he knew, from chapel or temple or abbey, all hung high in a tower and were rung by pulling on a rope; no rope could topple this massive thing, to make an invisible tongue cry against it. He reversed Dard in his hands, still sheathed, and struck at the great bell's flank with its pommel.

The bell sang, but softly: Brother Whisperer indeed, a throbbing chord that made his bones shake because he stood so close, made the stone floor tremble beneath his bare feet but would never reach down to where the Order prayed in the great hall so far below.

Still he hammered at it, twice and three times, desperately, uselessly, or so he thought; but there was suddenly another noise in the stillness of the chamber, a scuffling sound and then a figure moving against the moonlight, a small man in the robe of a brother stumbling out of the bell's shadow to confront him.

'Who strikes, who strikes my brother? It is not the hour . . .' His voice was loud, flat and slurred; his eyes were wide, his hands hard and calloused as they pawed and thrust at Marron, pushing him away.

'Brother, make it sound, there are Sharai below . . .'

'Who? Who strikes? It is my duty, mine, and this is not the hour . . .'

'Don't you hear me? There are Sharai on the walls!' But no, the man did not hear him, he only slobbered and shoved. Deaf, Marron realised, stone deaf and perhaps half-mad also after years of tending the bell too closely.

Marron backed off until he stood outside the chamber, on the tower's roof with his face full in the moonlight; he gripped the man's shoulder in his one free hand, his bad hand, and mouthed the words carefully. 'Sharai! Sound the bell, wake the castle!'

Still no reaction, and Marron was half-crazed himself now, frustrated and enraged by this stupid twist of fortune. He pushed the man back into the chamber, though it hurt his arm to do it; then he slipped Dard free of its sheath and held its blade to the man's throat, screaming, 'Sound it! Sound the bell!'

Whether he understood at last, or whether he was only trying to call help to himself in the face of a lunatic penitent with a sword in his hand and blood on his robe,

Marron never knew; but the man stooped, and straightened after with a rope in his grip. He hauled on that frantically, let the rope slide away between his hands and hauled again, and Frater Susurrus cried out full-voiced beside them.

No wonder the man was deaf. Marron gasped and staggered out into the night, pursued by the bell's roar. It made the air shiver, again and again; he thought his ears must be bleeding as his arm was, as he stumbled blindly down the tower's stairs and the terrible weight of sound shoved at his back and flowed around him in the darkness like falling earth or water. It could pick him up, he thought, and carry him down, roll him over and over and crush him utterly if once he lost his feet on these narrow steps . . .

Safely distant when he reached the tower's base, for a moment he felt stupidly safe.

Then he heard the mutter and rush to his left, brothers hurrying – all in order, though, in their well-drilled troops – running from the hall in response to the bell's alarum; to his right he heard faintly the clash and grate of steel on edged steel.

'Swords, swords! Sharai!' he cried to his left, to where the masters came pushing through the throng. 'Sharai on the north wall! Fetch swords!'

And stayed not to see that he was understood, but turned to his right and ran with his own sword light in his hand, shimmering like cold flame under the moon; ran to the foot of the stair that led up to where he had killed his first Sharai.

That man's body or another's lay sprawled across the

steps now. Above, atop the wall, he saw Sieur Anton like an angel of war, robed in gleaming white and shifting, dancing, all grace and strength as his sword leaped and spun, as he fought for his life and the castle's safety.

All along the wall, dark figures moved and massed. Only space up there for one at a time to cross swords with the knight, but others were descending, swarming down the same ropes they must have used to scale the height of the wall. The ropes that Mustar and the other boys must have let down for them – but no time to think of that now. Marron saw half a dozen dark-robed men drop down into the court, with others right behind them; and he left them all for his brothers, ran up the steps to fight beside Sieur Anton.

11

The Living Bleed

Every night the bell woke her with its sonorous, jarring call, but it had done that once tonight already. She'd muttered a brief prayer and gone to sleep again. Not a dream, that had happened, she was certain.

But now here came the bell again, thudding into and through her body, startling her up from the bolster; and not the regular call to prayer, three slow strokes and silence before another three. This was rapid, almost racing, a juddering incoherent cry from a man in a panic, she thought. She'd never seen a brother in a panic, except perhaps that lad Marron trying to pour wine with Elisande flirting at him around her veil; certainly they didn't panic without reason. This must be an alarm, *wake! wake!*

That was reason enough to have her out of bed and running to the window, trying to see through the carved screens and seeing nothing. Working the latches with a grunt and swinging the panels back to lean out, and still she could see nothing. Ink-black, soot-black shadows and silver lights where the moon touched a glint from the stone of wall or ward, nothing more than that. No torch, no running man, no hint of catastrophe.

Elisande was beside her, hanging out so far Julianne snatched anxiously at her shoulder; the other girl only glanced at her glitter-eyed, twisted her head awry in a vain attempt to see round corners and said, 'What is it?'

'I don't know. The bell . . .' It still went on, making the air thrum, making her teeth ache, setting her every small hair arise.

'Yes, Julianne,' with a hint of humour yet in her oh-so-patient smile, 'but why?'

'I can't see . . .'

No more could Elisande; but, 'Listen,' she said.

She was right. Dominant though it was, the bell's voice was so bass that it didn't drown out other noises; straining, she could just make out faint sounds of battle, the clash of weapons and men's voices crying loud.

Elisande was gone from her side before she realised. Julianne spun round to see her fumbling in the shadows beside her bed, hauling something from the pack that held all she chose to travel with.

'What are you doing?'

'Well, I can't go out like this,' and her fingers twitched hurriedly at the ties of her nightgown, tangled the bows into knots and gave up; she grabbed at the fabric and yanked it over her head like a child, wriggled and tugged and tossed it aside.

'Out where?'

'To see what's happening, of course. Do you want to sit

and fold your hands and wait to be instructed? You're not married yet, Julianne.'

That told, that was the killer blow. Julianne turned towards her own bed, her own clothes; but Elisande was already dressed in the same peasant burnous she'd been wearing when they met, was jamming her feet into boots and obviously wanted to be gone. Every dress that Julianne had brought would be too slow in the donning for Elisande's impatience, and hopelessly awkward if they found trouble out there, if they had to run or hide . . .

'Have you got another one of those?'

'Of course,' with a full smile this time, showing white in the gloom.

Elisande helped her with her own bows, dropped the burnous over her head and belted it with a length of rope. The stuff felt coarse and scratchy against her skin, and riding boots felt ridiculous beneath, but the choice lay between those and slippers, nothing more suitable.

'One thing else,' Elisande said. 'Take a knife,' and she held one out on her palm, handle foremost.

Julianne grinned mirthlessly. 'Keep it,' she said, turning back to her trunks and boxes. 'I have my own,' in this at least her father's daughter and no man's quiet wife, *not yet* . . .

Jewel-handled knives she carried, costume pieces with blunted silver blades, pretty adornments for a pretty wife if young Baron Imber should think her pretty or care for her adornment. But those were not the extent of her armoury. When a girl, any girl ran wild in the streets of Marasson, she did well to carry a blade or two, to prick men into manners; when that girl was the daughter of the King's Shadow, she had need and duty to protect herself. Julianne had been grateful more than once for the feel of a good sharp knife in her hand, and the knowledge of how to use it.

She pulled two now from their travelling-case, and couldn't resist flicking them neatly hand to hand in a juggler's shuffle before she thrust them into the rope girdle. Elisande nodded approval, and stowed her own blades the same way.

The lamp outside the door had burned out; they held hands on the darkness of the stair, and still for a while longer as they slipped through the castle, towards the sounds of fighting. Ghost-footed, the two girls made no more noise than the breeze, or so Julianne imagined. She couldn't hear their steps, and if not she, then who? Amid the row, the cries and clatter of the fighting up ahead?

Nor would they be spotted soon, she thought, if they were careful. These dun-coloured robes they wore, light enough to blend with parched earth and dust in the daytime, were dark and dull enough not to shine at night. Even with the moonlight full on them, and both girls were being wary to avoid that . . .

So they came as spies to where the battle was, in a long outer ward below the north wall. Elisande taught Julianne in dumb-show how to turn her knife in her hand so that the blade lay inward, against the soft flesh of her forearm and within the loose sleeve of the burnous, where it could be hidden but ready, ready but hidden, gleaming in no stray beam of light. Then they scuttled and crouched,

crouched and scuttled until they found a place to settle, against the buttress of a tower wall from where they could see easily but not easily be seen: deep shadow would guard them better than their knives might.

At first, crouching and scuttling, all that Julianne saw was a mêlée, a swirling chaos of dark robes, bright blades, pale faces and others not so pale. This close, the sounds were still no clearer: the great bell had stopped its booming at last, but the battle was all clash and grunt, gasp and hack and scream.

Once in the shelter of the buttress, though, where she could squat and be still in the squeeze between cool stone and warm Elisande, she pulled her long hair down like a veil of shadow across her face and gazed out through the tresses. Now she could see more clearly: she could distinguish the brothers in their shapeless habits from the men they fought, who wore a different style of robe and used curved scimitars, whose jaws were often dark with beards, whose heads were always covered. *Sharai*, she thought. Dozens of them, but no more than dozens; doomed, she thought they were. They must be, surely. A raiding-party, and what could be the point? There were hundreds of brothers in the castle, and a hundred knights also. She could see knights in the throng, standing out in their white dress and also in their swordsmanship, their strength and skill: meeting the Sharai on equal terms or better, it seemed to her, where the brothers only blocked and thrust in simple, well-drilled movements. Blocked and thrust and fell, that too, injured or dying or dead. Individually, Brother Ransomer against Sharai, this would have been a slaughter, she thought, and herself and Elisande only the least part of the prize; but fear ebbed quickly, as she saw no real danger. Even without the knights, sheer weight of numbers must have won this battle for the brothers.

Discipline was asserting itself after the shock of the sudden attack, she thought; or else she was beginning to understand what she watched, to see order where all had seemed random before. She saw how senior brothers, troop-leaders marshalled their forces around them, and how the knights did the same, urging men forward or calling them back, taking control. The Sharai had their own discipline also, but they were falling back, although there was nowhere they could run to. *Disciplined to die*, she thought, and hoped they thought the fighting had been worth it.

Elisande nudged her with an elbow, pointed with her chin. Up, up on the wall above the ward: Julianne raised her eyes, saw black and white in motion against the stars. A man in a white gown, nightgown, another knight he must be, fighting at the head of the steps there almost alone; only a boy at his side and a step or two below him in a stained white shift, his squire surely, and the two of them facing off half a dozen or more. The narrow measure of the wall made that almost a single combat, though, or two single combats side by side when a Sharai leaped from wall to steps to take on the boy.

Julianne wondered why the nudge from Elisande, why the gesture, unless it was simply to call her attention to some pretty swordplay; the boy and his master both were elegance itself against the more brutal hack and thrust in the ward below. Though they had space enough, and there was none down here . . .

No. Slowly, watching, Julianne recognised knight and squire. They were known, they were friends, or nearly so: that was Sieur Anton d'Escrivey, and the boy was Marron. Marron in white because he was under sentence, a penitent in the cells or meant to be, or did the Order free all its defaulters at the call to arms? Perhaps they did, though no one else was fighting in a like loose shift. Neither in a night-gown, as d'Escrivey was . . .

Nor was anyone else, knight or brother, climbing the steps to help them. Julianne had been observing with her father's eye, analytical, judgemental, as he would expect of her; suddenly she was herself again, watching people she knew and worried for.

She looked around, and there was the preceptor himself, standing aloof from the fray; if she asked, surely he would send men up to help? If the Sharai held the wall, they did after all hold a way of escape or reinforcement, and would remain a threat until they were driven from it . . .

She nudged Elisande in her turn, to say a silent, *come with me, we can help them*; but if the message was under-stood, it was wilfully misinterpreted. Elisande nodded, rose from where she squatted on her heels, and moved fast in completely the wrong direction. *Towards* the steps . . .

'Come back! Where are you—?'

Only a whisper, too soft and too late: Elisande didn't check her cautious but urgent progress across the ward, huddling low even as she leaped over bodies and skirted pools of blood, until she had found a new shelter in the shadows below the wall, in the crook where the steps climbed to the walkway.

Invisible she might be – only a pale blur of face against

black stone, and that only when she moved – but she was vulnerable too, she must be. Julianne could see the ropes hanging down from the battlements, where the Sharai must have descended the wall: how if more came down, only a few paces from where Elisande was lurking? Or how if those in the ward rallied and fought their way back, to climb up and make their escape . . .?

Julianne was on her feet by now, and following. Two were twice as easy to spot, of course; but it might be a master or a sharp-eyed brother who spotted them first, and brought men to their relief. If not, two could fight twice as effectively also. *And die with twice the loss*, but that was a thought for later.

Trying to look in three directions at once – forward to Elisande, left to where the fighting was, right to where the preceptor watched, though he was not watching her – Julianne forgot to look down. Her feet could never have picked their own way through such a carnage; she stumbled over a body's outflung arm, slid when her other foot came down in something greasy and fell with a squawk onto hands and knees. Looked round to see if she'd been heard, decided she'd been lucky – or its opposite, perhaps – and looked ahead to see more clearly what path she should follow to get to Elisande.

And saw Elisande fully, saw her step from shadow into moonlight, saw her arm stretch back and then hurl itself skyward; even saw – or so she thought – the flicker of a rising star that was Elisande's dagger spinning, streaking up from ward to wall.

Julianne stared upward, her eyes dragged behind its flight. A man, Sharai, stood against the stars with his sword-arm raised, frozen as it seemed, not slashing down as it was surely meant to. D'Escrivey it was who moved, whose own sword cut the night; the tip of it cut a throat neatly, the man toppled and fell.

Only for a moment, Julianne's gaze followed that fall, anxious for Elisande beneath it. Then a savage scream wrenched at her, jerked her attention up once more. Not the falling man who had screamed, he only thudded mutely to ground. She saw another Sharai – young by his cracked voice, though his face was just a beardless smudge in moonlight – crouched on the wall and staring down, then twisting to stare at d'Escrivey. And standing, trying to push through his companions towards the knight; and being blocked, hauled back, thrust to where someone was pulling up one of those dangling ropes.

Enough of watching. Julianne scrambled to her feet and hurried over to the wall's base, to find Elisande on her knees beside the body of a Sharai. The one she'd felled, she and d'Escrivey between them: she was pulling her knife from his side, and there were unexpected tears on her face.

'Elisande . . .?'

The dash of a rough sleeve across her eyes, no more than a shake of her head and a scowl for her friend, and a few hard words squeezed out from a full throat. 'No. Leave me. I have to give him grace . . .'

She reached to lay a hand on the dead man's brow, heedless of the blood that had spattered it; she began to murmur, to chant in a soft sobbing voice and a language Julianne didn't know. Elisande seemed not to know it well, either, or not to have used it for a long time. It was more than distress made her tongue pause and stumble and repeat. Her eyes were closed and her body rocked slightly to and fro, and that seemed to be ritual too, enough perhaps to carry her through where her memory failed her.

Julianne backed away, as she'd been asked to. She looked up, and saw that positions on the wall had been reversed; one Sharai was fighting to hold d'Escrivey back, to give his companions time to flee the trap the castle had become. One brave Sharai: he fought well, but she could see he was outmatched, and he'd have no chance to get away himself. At least one rope must be hanging outside the wall now; she watched men scramble through an embrasure and disappear.

D'Escrivey parried, feinted, thrust casually and his opponent fell. The knight stepped across him with Marron still at his back, still watchful. Together they walked to the embrasure, where d'Escrivey lifted his sword as though to cut the rope that Julianne couldn't see, that must be there; but he paused, and held his stroke. Murmured something to his squire and turned, looking down into the ward as he strode towards the stair. Julianne pressed herself back into the shadow of the wall; there could be no danger now, the last of the raiders were penned into a distant corner and she didn't want to be spotted and treated like an errant child, conducted back to her chamber under an unnecessary guard. Neither did she want Elisande interrupted in her quiet chanting. Whatever that rite meant, it meant something important to her friend.

When knight and squire both were away and out of sight — heading for the infirmary, she hoped, if those dark stains on Marron's shift were what she thought — she hurried over to the steps and up onto the wall, trying to look purposeful and entitled. Trying to look like herself, of course, nothing more. She most certainly was entitled, she was a guest here and no prisoner; and as to a purpose, she genuinely did have that. She still didn't understand this raid, so few men against a citadel so strong; and she hated ignorance with a passion, especially when it was her own. Her father had instilled that in her early: *always seek to understand, little one, always ask the question. Of yourself, of the world, of a stranger. And remember, the question is always, 'Why?'*

So she went high to see far, although heights frightened her; and when she saw the plains move and spark, she did understand.

All around the great promontory, the upthrusting base of rock where the Roq sat like a guardian bird – *great bird, black and red, ill-omened bird,* she thought – all around it seethed a shadow specked with light, a mass of men with flambeaux. Mounted men, she thought: too far below to see by the moon and those distant lights, far too far to hear sounds of hooves, but something in the way the shadow shifted said that there were horses under the men who held the brands.

There would need to be. What was she looking at, three hundred men, perhaps? A hundred lights at least, and far from all held flambeaux. There could be many times the number if they circled the scarp, if that was a besieging ring. They couldn't have brought up such an army on foot, not so secretly: however fast they'd marched, whispers of their coming would have run ahead.

Gripping tightly, staring down despite her terror at the

drop, she made slow sense of what she saw, as with the battle, finding shape and pattern and meaning in what at first seemed chaotic. Although those faint specks of light moved this way and that, although the river of shadow that bore the light bulged and broke and rippled at its edges, still like any river it had its flow; and that was north, away. This was an army in retreat that she was watching. Not in defeat, not in any hurry, but on the march.

There would be no siege, then. They'd meant to take the Roq with a sneak attack, so much was clear. A small party must have made the climb up the north face of the hill and then the talus and the outer wall, hoping to fight their way through to the gate and let the main force in. At midnight, while the brothers were at prayer and the watch perhaps less watchful . . .

With the failure, the army was retreating. Good general-ship, not to risk further loss on hope or improvisation: Julianne's father would approve, undoubtedly. So did she. Plan and strike, hold if you win and withdraw if not, to make another plan. Looking somewhere else she hoped, she fervently hoped. If the Sharai had taken Roq de Rançon, they no less than the Ransomers could have held it indefi-nitely; and that would have been the northern border broken, the shield-arm of Outremer. All of Tallis open to raiding or worse, Elessi as good as cut off . . . It could have meant the slow death of the Kingdom itself, or possibly not so slow. The Roq was the key, or so she thought it that night, and if such a key should turn . . .

Though she'd never so much as travelled let alone lived anywhere within the Sanctuary Land, still she was her father's daughter, she had his restless love. Tonight she had visions, a Sharai horde sweeping down all the length of the country, through Tallis and Less Arvon and hidden Surayon till it came to the gates of Ascariel itself, by which time there would be no man left to defend them. All terror and grief her vision was, all blood and fury: and all for such a small thing, a mark on a map, one castle lost from a land of a hundred, a thousand castles.

Only that the Roq was no ordinary castle, which must be why the Sharai were so keen to take it, sending so many men so far for a single fling of the dice; which was certainly why the King had given it to the Ransomers to defend. The best troops and the most of them, almost the only troops in Outremer who had no other role than to watch and guard and be ready to fight.

Watch and guard, fight and pray, she shouldn't forget the praying. Their enemy the Sharai general had not forgotten the praying. It took a cold mind, a cunning mind to come to people at prayer, she thought, with a sword in your hand. Cold and cunning the Sharai were, though, or were said to be: people with hidden hands. Desert people, those were the attributes they had to set against their hot and open country.

Patient people, also. She stood and watched them ride away, shadow and light and silence, and knew they would come again. And again and again, until her vision was a true seeing and Outremer was overrun. Even her father didn't believe they could be held back forever.

Despite the height she wanted to stand and watch for an hour, two hours, however long it took until they were quite gone, their little glimmer quite lost against the dawn. But men would be coming soon, she knew: brothers to clear the bodies from the wall, perhaps masters to see what she was seeing, an enemy departed. She still wanted to avoid that encounter, cold words and a silent escort to her room. Besides, Elisande was in the ward below and shouldn't be left alone too long, she thought, had perhaps been left too long already.

One last look and she turned to go; and as she picked her way across the fallen on the wall, one slumped figure reared up suddenly in front of her. His teeth gleamed behind his beard, his blade glittered in his hand, his eyes were white and shining; his pain was written on his body but his purpose too, that he meant to pave his way to paradise with one more infidel life.

She felt the haft of a knife cool against her hand, and didn't know what to do with it. All her training failed her, in one fatal moment. She stood utterly still before him, almost lifted her chin to make his stroke the easier, to say a swifter farewell to her father's plans and her own weary fears; saw the sword's fall almost as relief, a liberty unlooked-for.

And was hurled back by a blast of air made solid, an impossible fist of wind. Fell into an embrasure with a longer fall only a hand's breadth behind her, gasped and grabbed at the merlon to deny it – and no, she did not after all want to die yet, it seemed, or not by falling – and hung there gasping, staring.

Staring at a whirling rod of light and darkness, a spinning black rope that drank moonlight and sparkled gold, that stood not on the wall but a little aslant in the air between her and the Sharai.

She knew of course what it was, and was still startled

beyond measure at its appearing, too bewildered to be grateful yet.

So too did the Sharai know what it was. He let go his sword, which dropped with a dull clatter that was still resoundingly loud amid their silence: she wasn't breathing, neither she thought was he, and if the djinn breathed she had never been told so.

The Sharai dropped to his knees, which forced more than a breath, a grunt of anguish from him; Julianne thought, *that's enough, leave him, he won't harm me now.* And heard herself gasp again at the implications of that thought, the certainty this time that the djinni was watching over, protecting her. Even from her own foolishness.

The djinni – *Shaban Ra'isse Khaldor*, it had named itself, she remembered – either couldn't hear her unspoken thought, or else chose to ignore it. It moved slowly, drifting, she might almost have said, except that it moved against the wind and with definite purpose; towards the Sharai it went, cruelly unhurried, and his eyes bulged with terror. He flung his arms up – *don't*, she thought uselessly, *don't touch it*, remembering the boy who had done that, who had lost his arm in its spinning coils – and he opened his mouth to plead or scream or maybe just to make a sound against this silent doom, and never had the chance to do any.

The djinni touched him, only a little, only the tail of its twisting body touched his chest. So little but enough, more than enough. She heard a tearing, wrenching, snapping sound, and briefly saw the gleam of bone and then a rush of what was dark and wet. The man leaped, no, was snatched high into the air, simply by the force of what had touched him; for a moment he seemed to hang there spread-eagled, crucified in air.

Then he fell, struck a merlon and fell again. Would be rolling, had she cared to look, down the steep talus below the wall; and then no doubt falling once more, a longer fall all the way to the plain. No matter, he was dead before the falling started. No doubt of that, there had been a scooped-out hollow where his heart and lungs should have been working behind their cage of bone, where instead the ribs had been splayed like open fingers, empty hands.

Steady. It's waiting to hear you scream, she thought, *so do not.*

It was waiting for something, certainly, or else it had simply chosen to spend some few minutes of its eternal time standing or floating in the air there, slightly asquint to the world unless it was the world, as she felt, that stood slightly asquint to it. Waiting, she thought, more likely. Waiting for her. Not to scream, not now, the moment had passed. To speak, then. To speak to it. *What do you want of me?* perhaps, or any other question forced by the moment, a scream in little, a cry without thought. *Never ask a djinni a question*, she remembered. Advice taken too late to heart, but she wouldn't repeat the folly, if folly it had been.

Neither would she kneel, nor curtsey, nor bow. Not if it had tricked her before, as Elisande claimed. Guile was an invaluable tool, but it earned no respect.

So she stood erect and faced it; and she said, 'I am grateful, djinni: though,' just to make the point clear, 'I did not ask for aid.'

It laughed, that same cold silvery sound with nothing human in it. 'Neither do I claim a debt for it. Lady.'

'I must suppose, then,' treading oh so carefully through the tricks and traps of language, 'that your concern for me springs from some concern of the djinn, that is not clear to me.'

'Indeed you must. And it must remain unclear to you, daughter of the Shadow. Only this, I charge you: go where you are sent, and marry where you must.'

'You said that to me before. I do not forget. But,' daughter of the Shadow indeed, with all that that implied as evident as she could make it in her stature and in her voice, she said, 'it is my father's will that I obey in this.' *Not yours, spirit,* boldly written in her thoughts and she hoped on her face also.

'For the present, perhaps. I will say it to you a third time, Julianne de Rance, and also a fourth. Be ready. And remember, you stand already in my debt.'

Not for tonight, it had said that; neither for its last appearance on the plain, before her galloping horse. Only for the first time, for those careless questions of hers and its unresponsive answers. She was not sure she was prepared to acknowledge a debt for so little given or taken, such a small exchange; she was certainly prepared to say so, here and now, only that it gave her no chance to do so. Sparks of gold flew from its rope of a body, faster and further, till she flinched back for fear of being burned; it spun itself into a cord, a twine, a thread of black, and then it was nothing at all.

Nothing except a whisper, at least, a voice in darkness, thin as the wind: 'Tell Lisan there is one below she should also say the *khalat* for. The carrion-eaters will have his body and not leave a bone to be prayed over. His name was Kamaal ib' Shofar.'

'Do you know *everything?*' she demanded furiously — and choked, too late, and bit her tongue in penance. And waited for the djinni's laugh, its answer *yes* or *no*, its casual assumption of another debt; and heard only the wind and distant voices calling on the walls, softer voices closer, mingling with grunts and groaning, the occasional sharp cry as brothers carried their wounded to the infirmary.

What did they do with wounded Sharai? she wondered; and thought probably that there would be none, that a knife's silent work would relieve that problem wherever it occurred.

Thoughts of the Sharai fallen reminded her of Elisande, down there among those labouring brothers. Alone and grieving over the body of an enemy, chanting what the Order would surely call heresy, and within their own walls too . . .

She went down the steps far more quickly than she had come up them; and found Elisande not chanting now but still kneeling beside the body, too weary or too distressed to move. And she so active usually, so determined to see things done . . .

'Elisande?'

This time at least she wasn't sent away; the smaller girl lifted her head to look at her and even so much was an effort, her nod was exhaustion.

'I have, I have a message for you,' which she didn't dare not to deliver.

'How?'

'From the djinni,' and never mind how, she didn't want to say. 'It called you Lisan again, and said, it said there is another you should say the, the *khalat* for, is that right? A man who fell from the wall, whose body will be lost, it said. It said his name, but I can't remember now . . .'

'It doesn't matter,' Elisande murmured. 'They are all lost, here. They will get none of the rites that their deaths deserve. I will say *khalat* for them all. This one was special,' *this one I killed myself,* she was saying, 'but so were they all.'

'They were brave,' Julianne said hesitantly, 'but they would still have killed us, probably, if they had won the gate and let their army in . . .'

'Was that it? I wondered. And perhaps you're right, perhaps they would. There might have been a very great slaughter. Their codes forbid it, and so does their religion, but there have been so many killings now, on every side . . . These people were my *friends*, Julianne. I was their guest, they fed and sheltered me for a year, they visited me at my home . . .'

Where is your home? she wanted to ask, it seemed the obvious question; but what was more obvious yet, Elisande did not want to be questioned. Not now, not with tears running down her cheeks. Vulnerable she might be, feeling too much to keep her guard; but she was Julianne's friend also. So no, no prying questions yet. Besides, Julianne thought she might already have some answers and she didn't want to hear them just now, certainly didn't want them overheard.

'Not these men, surely?' she asked instead, innocently, stupidly.

'Their cousins, then. Men and women both, they gave me greater freedom than they give their own. And there are men here from so many tribes,' she said, her mind sliding off suddenly, sliding back to the blood and bodies that she knelt among. 'Beni Rus I have seen, Kauram and Ashti and the Ib' Dharan. This one is Saren, by his dress. These men should not be fighting together, it's so strange . . .'

'Come back to the chamber, Elisande. Come now, before there's trouble. You can say your prayer there, can't you? Where we're private?'

'Oh, yes,' she said. 'I don't *need* their blood on my hands . . .'

But still she made no effort to wipe it off; and Julianne had to help her to her feet, and support her across the blood-washed stones of the court until inevitably a brother did see them, and join them, and escort them firmly back to their quarters in the guests' tower.

Jazra was dead, and the tribes were in retreat. The night and Jemel's heart had turned to bitter shame, and he hated Hasan more than he hated even the infidels in their high castle, more than he hated any man save one.

Jazra was dead, a blood-brother lost in blood, and all their oaths were broken. They had sworn their lives and bodies to each other, in public by the fire and in private again and again, in their single shared blanket and their bodies' heat against the desert chill; but the fight, the night had made a treacher of him. Of them both, because Jazra had gone ahead where he should have waited, Jazra had fought and fallen because he was alone. A knife had come from below, and the man in white had swung his sword, and so Jazra fell. Because he was alone where he should not have been, where there should have been another blade to guard him.

This blade, his blade, sworn to that. It had been Hasan, Hasan himself who had held Jemel back from just revenge; and all oaths were broken, and if Hasan had ridden with the Saren tonight Hasan would have died for that, this blade would have found out his heart.

But Hasan was away, ahead, leading this withdrawal; and that too was shame, and he should die for it. And would not, because the old men – *old women* – of every tribe and every fire stood with him in this, said yes. *We came, we failed*, they said, *we pull back. At least for tonight. We will take fresh counsel in the morning.*

And so they rode away and left their dead like a badge of their shame, for the infidels to display or disgrace as they chose; and still each tribe's oaths were holding – for this night, at least – and he couldn't believe that it was happening this way. His body twitched and sweated as though he had fever, coldly, as he would sweat cold he thought every night now, without Jazra.

There had been such pride, such hope when they rode out, those weeks ago. The Sharai united, again and at last: all tribes together for this first great strike against the greatest of the infidels' castles. That would fall, they swore, and they would hold it; but one try, an hour's unlucky fighting and all oaths were forgotten, it seemed, as dead as his own.

Hasan had ordered torches lit as soon as the climbing party was seen to have breasted the walls, to show that the Sharai did not skulk in victory or defeat, he'd said. To draw the guards' eyes outward from the walls was the general belief, not to let them see the blades at their backs. But that was before, that was when the strike was certain and defeat was a word for the infidels to learn at the scimitar's point or else perhaps in the collar of a slave, those few who were let live. So great a castle, there were bound to be some who hid or were just overlooked until the blood-debt was well paid. *There's a time*, the old ones said, *when everyone wearies of killing. No matter the offence, to us or to our holy places; comes a time when there has just been blood enough.*

He didn't believe it, himself. He couldn't imagine blood enough to pay this debt, though that man in white and every infidel in the land were wrung dry of it and Hasan too, and all the tribes of all the men who stood by Hasan this calamitous night.

Jazra was dead, and he wanted to kill and kill until these watery lands were as dead as the high desert wastes; and then at the end, when he was the last man moving under the sun – *like the Ghost Walker*, he thought, and shivered, and spat superstitiously into the dust, giving water to the land to buy its favour, not to meet the Ghost Walker this night – he wanted to kill himself and be dead also, to seek Jazra in whatever paradise there might be.

12

The Lights of Judgement

On his knees again, hungry and confused and afraid again: Marron remembered that it had not always been like this, his life, there was a time when he had been comfortable and content, warm and fed and certain.

Only then had come his oaths, the fulfilment of a life-long promise, to follow his dead father to the God's war in the God's own land; and since then — *since Fra' Piet* his mind said as though one man, any man else could be to blame — nothing had gone easy or as it was meant to go. Blessed he'd felt once, but no longer.

Cold and afraid, hurt and hungry and very much in the dark, for all the sun that fell through high and narrow chapel windows to make a pool of light around him.

This time he was not alone, though, at least he had that to cling to. This was his judgement, he faced his accusers and each man's face was hard and set against him; but one man stood at his back, and gave his voice to Marron.

*

Last night, after the fighting was over, Sieur Anton had led Marron quickly, directly to his own chamber. 'Now, while my confrères are hot for a chase,' he'd said, 'before wiser heads preach caution and daylight and send them to their beds to wait for it. I don't want questions,' he'd said, 'or even questioning looks.'

'Sit on the bed,' he'd said once they were there; and himself had fetched water in a bowl, cloths and bandages from Marron knew not where.

'Sieur, should you not go to the infirmary? You're hurt . . .'

'And so are you; and no, neither one of us should go to the infirmary. I have everything we need. Show me your arm.'

Actually, Marron had not been hurt on the wall, bar a few nicks and bruises; fighting beside and behind Sieur Anton, he'd been largely protected by the knight's reach and skill. Only his arm had bled badly, and in the strange exultant giddiness afterwards he'd felt that to be normal, almost a part of him now, a sign he carried from the God or perhaps from Sieur Anton: a brand of ownership that he could mar but not mend.

Marred it was when Sieur Anton unwrapped it from its sticky bindings, a far cry from the clean cut it had been once, that should have healed quickly and left only a white seam for a scar. Now it was a fat and ragged mouth of red wet flesh, half-grown over before it was torn again and yet again, with a margin of pricked scabs where Master Infirmarer's stitches had sewn it closed and then been cut away to let it gape.

Sieur Anton had hissed softly as he wiped the blood away, had murmured, 'Best not have it stitched this time, lad, for fear the flesh should rot within and poison the whole arm. It'll not be pretty when it mends, mind, but keep it clean and mend it should.'

Strong fingers had held it firm against Marron's flinching as the wound was washed and dabbed with salve from a clay pot. *Horse-liniment?* he had wondered and not asked, biting back the giggle that the question carried with it. Then when the arm was bound again and the binding tied, Sieur Anton had stripped off his own blood-marked robe and it had been Marron's turn to wash and salve what cuts the knight had taken. No great hurt on him either, his own swordsmanship and Marron's blade at his shoulder had guarded him. One bandage on his upper arm and one around his ribs sufficed; then Sieur Anton had tossed furs onto the floor in a corner and told Marron to slip off his soaked shift, lie down and sleep.

'Sieur, I should go back to the cells . . .'

'Perhaps you should, but I forbid it. Come the morning, we will worry what you should or should not do. If you cannot obey your masters, try to obey me.'

So he had; and had slept, though he'd thought he would not. Come the morning, wrapped in a fur for decency, he had prayed once more at the knight's side and then served him breakfast in his chamber, fresh bread and milk fetched by another knight's squire. Marron had refused to eat himself, sick with nerves and giddy with memory and trying to make a point also, unless he was only giving a gloss of virtue to the sour-stomached truth. 'No, sieur, I am meant to be fasting. I can fast,' if he couldn't keep any other one of his vows, it seemed.

Sieur Anton had left him after that, ordered him to finish the milk if he would not eat and then to lie quietly on the bed for an hour. Marron had dozed despite the pain in his arm and his restless mind; then the knight had returned, had him dress again in the stained and filthy shift, and had brought him here. And now he knelt in the knights' chapel before the preceptor himself and half a dozen masters, the consistory court that would pass judgement on him.

Sieur Anton had told him little, only that scouts had ridden out at dawn to see if the Sharai had truly withdrawn or if they meant to attack again. And that Marron's trial was not postponed, that Fra' Piet had been required to stay within the castle to testify against him.

That testimony, Marron thought, had been damning. In truth, he had no defence. He had broken the Rule, acting in gross disobedience to save the life of a man who very likely was the spy Fra' Piet had named him, the woman and baby only a disguise.

But Sieur Anton stood behind him, and spoke for him: said, 'Masters, there is no dispute of this. Fra' Marron has been foolish, wilful and disobedient since he came to this place, and his acts of yesterday imperilled the castle and every man in it. Every man, and every woman who guests here,' which was twice damning.

'But Fra' Marron's acts of last night saved the castle, its garrison and its guests. That too cannot be disputed. The Sharai prisoners would not have told of the impending attack, even under question; they guard their tongues fanatically. If Fra' Marron had not understood what signs he had seen that day, if he had not broken his oaths again to leave his cell and give warning, if he had not alerted us all with his ringing of the bell, that raiding party would have won through to the gate and the Sharai would have ridden in among us.'

Marron shook his head slightly; that wasn't quite right. There was no proof after all that the prisoner had been Sharai, or a spy; it was only his own mazed mind seeing patterns where perhaps none lay to be seen. The man might have been quite innocent, a wanderer trying to keep faith with his god and protect his family both at once in difficult lands, difficult times. And it was Sieur Anton who had sent Marron to the bell – and the deaf brother there who had sounded it, but that was a quibble – and Sieur Anton who had delayed the raiders on the wall until more help had come.

But it was Sieur Anton too who had whispered one brief command to Marron before they came into the chapel here, 'You say nothing, boy. On your obedience, on your soul, keep silence!' He knelt with head bowed, held his tongue and hoped that twitch of honesty hadn't betrayed him. He was sworn to tell truth to these men, if they called on him to answer . . .

'Masters,' Sieur Anton went on, 'I know Fra' Marron cannot stay within your Order. He has broken your Rule too often, and too grievously. He cannot keep his oaths, it seems, and he will never make a Ransomer. But I plead with you, on my knees,' and the proud knight did indeed kneel beside Marron, 'be generous. He is a young man, a foolish boy; but he is a brave boy also, he proved that fighting at my side on the wall. And he is an avowed enemy of your enemies, although he lacks the discipline to remain as one of your brotherhood. Cast him out from among you, but do it gently. Do not punish him, more than the shame of expulsion is a punishment; respect his courage for his father's sake, whom Marron has tried and failed to emulate. His failure is not his fault. You ask much of your brothers; no man should be blamed for being too weak to meet your standards. Cast him out, but give him to me, whole and unharmed. I am in need of a squire; Marron needs a discipline less harsh than yours. I can teach him that much. Let me have him, and he may yet serve the God and the King in these dangerous times. I beg you, do not make a waste of his life, more than he has wasted it already.'

Sieur Anton fell silent then, rising to his feet; Marron risked a glance up, to see the preceptor glance to one side and then the other, gathering the masters with his eyes.

'Thank you, Sieur Anton. We will withdraw,' he said, 'to discuss this. Remain here, each of you.'

That meant Marron, and Sieur Anton, and Fra' Piet; and that last meant that Marron had to stay as he was, penitent and silent, not a word of gratitude or question. He glanced across to where Fra' Piet stood, quite still except for his thumb which stroked the keen edge of his axe, thrumming across it again and again, like a man giving rhythm to his prayers. To see even so much, Marron had had to turn his head a touch, enough to bring a warning finger on his shoulder from the knight who stood behind him; and Sieur Anton was right, he had no discipline, no strength to deny even the least whisper of temptation . . .

The chapel floor was cold and hard, his stomach churned and all his bones were aching. He wanted to raise his eyes to see the colours of light and paint around the chapel, and could not; he wanted to lean back against Sieur Anton's legs, and of course could not.

He was trembling before the masters filed back in, and only hoped that Fra' Piet could not see it, that Sieur Anton would not think it fear. They arrayed themselves before him, and the preceptor said, 'Fra' Marron.'

He jerked, as though a whip had licked his back. He had been whipped as a child, as a youth; this lash of voice, he thought, was worse.

'Your faults are many, your offence is grave. If you had done what you did and had not been of the Order, you would have died for it ere now. As a brother, you are sanctified to the God and we may not kill His servants; as a brother, you have betrayed the God and we owe you no duty except your life, if you were strong enough to keep it. His vengeance also He delegates to us, and neither He nor we are easy with a treacher.

'But as Sieur Anton d'Escrivey has said, you served Him well last night, though it cost another act of disobedience to do so. Because of that – because this reminds us that there can be virtue outside our discipline, for which humility we thank you – we are minded to accede to Sieur Anton's request. You must leave the Order, that sentence cannot be remitted nor should it be, you have no place with us; but you need not leave the castle, if you are able to stay and serve Sieur Anton with a better will than you have shown in serving us.'

Was that a question, was he meant to speak? Marron opened his mouth, ready to say *yes, your grace* and whatever more might be required of him; and was forestalled, Fra'

Piet's cracked voice insistent, incredulous, crushing his first faint breath of hope.

'Your grace, masters, he must pay his penance. The Order, all the brothers must see him pay . . .'

'You want to see him flayed, Fra' Piet?' That was Sieur Anton again, with a cold, condemning smile in his voice. 'Then say so, don't blame it on your brethren. And yes, flay him by all means. Strip the flesh from his back, leave him useless to me or any man else. Why not? Let's sacrifice a skilled young fighter to your offended pride, that would surely please the God unendingly.'

'He is only one man,' chill matched with chill, only that Fra' Piet was not smiling, probably could not remember how. 'The God calls us all to sacrifice. The penance must be paid, or all discipline will be lost. His troop saw what he did, so every troop will know by now. If there is no punishment, how can we look for obedience the next time a heedless, arrogant fool thinks he knows better than his confessor?'

'Marron is only one man, true; and yes, you can make an example of him if you will, to frighten others into a thoughtless obedience. But let word of that go back to where he came from, *he saved the castle and they flogged him half to death*, send his bones back maybe because of course you do not kill but sometimes brothers die regardless, and see how many more recruits that wins you. Do you know how desperate our case is, how few of us there are to guard this land? We have enemies on every border, and heretics within; we can ill afford to lose even one man, and if that loss means that we lose a dozen others, then it's a bargain that may cost us dear next year, or the year after. We fight for the God, we fight the Sharai; we should not fight each other.'

'Enough!' The preceptor, not shouting but making the chapel echo. 'You both forget your places. Fra' Marron is not the only one here who owes a duty of obedience; nor it seems is he the only one who forgets that, or finds it inconvenient. Sieur Anton, your rank does not set you aloof from punishment; neither does yours, Fra' Piet.'

The knight at Marron's side bowed low; on the other side and farther off, Fra' Piet dropped to his knees. Marron couldn't see, but he heard the sullen sound of it, and knew.

'Nor is this court entirely foolish, Sieur Anton, to be moved to mercy by the sight of a warrior unwashed; you could I think have brought the boy before us in a clean shift. It might have seemed to you more appropriate, given where we stand. However, I was saying, we are minded to an unaccustomed leniency in this matter. Other voices than yours, Fra' Piet, have called for punishment, for the due measure of the Rule's prescription to assuage the wrath of the God; but it seems to me presumptuous to assert the God's anger, where the consequences have been so beneficial. I have opened the King's Eye to see, and the army sent against us now stands some miles to the north and east. Magister Ricard has ridden out in force to harry it further, and I have hopes he may scatter it completely; he rides in secrecy, in the Eye, and will come upon them unannounced. However that may fall out, it is all but certain that this castle is in no danger now. None can say that would have been the case, had Fra' Marron prayed with his brethren last midnight and not been watchful in a penitent's cell.

'This, then, is my judgement: that having failed in your service to the Order but yet served the God well, Fra' Marron, you shall lose that title and the habit that signifies it; you shall lose the brotherhood of the Society of Ransom and be cast out from our number in the sight of all, never to be accepted again. But our gates shall not be closed against you, for so long as you serve the Knight Ransomer Sieur Anton d'Escrivey who has spoken for you. Are you content?'

'Your grace, I am content.' Easy to say, hard to find a voice to say it with, relief was choking him; but he did manage a whisper, enough.

'Very well, then. It shall be done this evening, after prayers. Meantime, you will return to the penitents' cells to wait and pray this last day in our company.'

'Your grace, is that necessary?'

'Oh, yes. Very necessary, Sieur Anton. One final day of our discipline, I think, before he must submit himself to yours. He is ours yet, until we relinquish him; and as Fra' Piet says, that must be done in the sight of all.'

Back in the dark, the cold, the hunger. This time, though, he had a bubble of warmth in his chest, the promise of hope realised. That was enough.

He also had a clean shift, tossed to him with mute disdain by one of the warders. It was a single length of worn white stuff, so thin it was near-transparent in places. The head went through a tear at the midpoint, and a length of coarse white cord tied around the waist held front and back together. Or was meant to. Marron had used hand and teeth to knot the cord into a double loop, a sling for his aching injured arm.

Probably that was disobedience, he thought, not to use the cord as girdle, as it was meant to be used; but he didn't care. He had only a few hours of hungry patient waiting now, shivering with chill and anticipation. And no, he was not going to pray as the preceptor had told him to. He had spent a long lifetime, it seemed to him, on his knees and only a moment last night on his feet, Dard in hand, his skin wet with blood and sweat and fear like a live thing in his gut, the battle like a storm all around him, making the very air shriek; and he knew which had thrilled him, which his heart had leaped to like a creature come home. Not like the slaughter in the village, when he had been mad, made mad: last night had been trained muscles and a sharp mind balanced behind a sharp eye, fear but not terror, thrill but not frenzy.

Last night had been what he wanted, what he'd thought he could find in his father's legacy, in his father's life. What he thought now he would find at Sieur Anton's heel, like a good dog rewarded: the chance to fight for the God he might still, might yet believe in, without the poison of dead babies and friends turned unkind, confessors too ready to kill.

So he'd whispered the due prayers at noon, and had allowed himself a smile in the dark at the thought of Sieur Anton doing the same, equally alone in his room. He thought the God would not begrudge the smile.

And he had not prayed since, neither dwelt on what was to come at evening prayers. That was hours away yet, and would last only minutes; after that a new life under a new master, a new chance, bitterness set aside . . .

*

Trouble came back to Marron with the soft glow of lamp-light and the soft sounds of feet approaching slowly, the daily delivery of bread and water, the emptying of buckets. Late today, he thought, but no wonder in that, given what had happened overnight.

The brother with the light and basket passed him by. No wonder in that either: he was disgraced, under doom of exile from the Order. Fasting was the least penance he could expect.

The brother came a second time with water, and again there was none for him. A third time the brother passed, and came not into Marron's cell even to empty his bucket; this time Marron was startled to recognise him as one of the warders from yesterday. Doing his own penance, apparently, for having been so slack last night, not seeing a penitent slip from his cell . . .

That made Marron smile again, briefly, when he was again left in darkness. But the smile was lost too soon, as he remembered that it was usually one of the Sharai boys who did this duty. Mustar had done it yesterday. A blue stone, *this will keep you safe* . . .

There had been nothing to keep Mustar safe. They had betrayed the castle, Mustar and others, he had seen them on the walls.

What had happened to them, to him? Marron didn't know, no one had said. Nothing good, though, surely. They might have died with the warriors, on the walls or in the court below; they might have snatched swords from the fallen and fought, and died with honour. Or they might be here, he thought, not penitents but prisoners awaiting the Order's harsh justice . . .

He had to know. Nothing he could do if he found them – in a cell with the door bolted, perhaps, they wouldn't be trusted as the brothers were – but he couldn't simply kneel here in patience waiting and not know. Mustar who had tried to save him might be just the other side of the rock wall there. Mustar who had saved him, who had stupidly saved the castle with a blue stone for warning to a friend . . .

Marron stood up slowly, groping for balance against the dizziness of hunger and darkness. He shuffled forward, feeling with his one arm for the doorway while the shift swung light and loose against his skin. Found it, and peered cautiously out. These warders might be more watchful, having seen their brother doing penance for his carelessness. It might be an order, even, *trust no more*.

But there was only the light at the end of the passage, a dim glow in the chamber beyond and no figure outlined against it. He took a slow, wary breath and slipped out, turned his back to the light and felt his way along to the next cell. The door stood closed but not bolted, as before, he found that with his fingers; this time he opened it and the cell felt empty, smelled empty too. No sounds of breathing, no response when he hissed a greeting.

Out again, and on; the next was empty too, and the next after that. No point now in going further, he thought; but he went further regardless, only because it felt good to be moving, to be one last time defiant. All the way to the end of the passage he went; and here once more he did finally find a door that was bolted against him.

And drew another cautious breath, took a grip on the bolt and moved it slowly. It ran back easily, with never a squeal of metal on metal; neither did the hinges make a sound as he eased the door open.

What he hadn't expected, at this darkest end of a dark passage where he couldn't see his fingers' tips an inch in front of his eyes, he hadn't expected light. There hadn't been a glimmer or a hint of it squinting through cracks in the planking or slipping between door and jamb.

It was the curtain which prevented that, the heavy, dusty black curtain that he sidled straight into because he couldn't see it, black against black in this dead darkness. But it billowed just a little when his shoulder caught it, as he stilled; and in its movement he could see it after all, or the edges of it as they spilled light.

He stood and breathed nervously in that narrow space between door and curtain, bewildered now. Only one solid, rock-sure thought in his head, and that was, *don't let the warders see, if either of them should look*. He pulled the door to at his back before gripping the felted curtain and twitching it aside, chancing a glance around it.

A cell, a larger cell: but more than that. Here was where the questioners did their work; their implements hung on the walls, their machines of wood and steel sat below.

No boys, but here was the man whose scream had met them on the stair, Marron and Rudel, whose screams he had heard again yesterday. Surely it must be him, that bruise-blackened and filthy figure which lay sprawled near-naked on a rank pallet in the corner, his back to Marron, his face turned to the wall. The man who had come, been brought here in a barrel, they said, though Marron had not seen it.

Neither had he seen instruments of torture before, but

nor they nor the man could hold his eyes quite yet. Not in this light, not when the light was there to stare at, to spark wonder and terror in his fuddled mind like sparks from a dull flint.

He'd thought that he knew magic, that magic was the King's Eye, lines of hot gold which branded pictures deep inside his skull. That must be holy magic, he thought now, sanctioned by the God like the preceptor's light at midnight; and this must be its opposite, devil's magic, witchlight. If this man came from Surayon as the rumour was, and Surayon was anathema, then nothing good could it breed. Which meant that the soft warm glow pulsing gently from a globe the size of a big man's fist must be something cursed, malevolent; and he should be afraid to stand in its creamy light, he should dread to look upon it for fear of the taint entering his own soul and damning him forever . . .

But it hung in the air without strings or wires and burned nothing at all if it burned at all; and it didn't seem to him to burn, it only shone, light without fire. How could he help but stare?

Or move? Before he knew it he had come all the way through the curtain and was standing heedlessly in the cell, directly under that ball of light with his head tipped back as if he were checking for those absent strings or wires; and he must have stirred the air or made some soft barefoot sound to declare himself, because the man on the pallet grunted and turned his head, and then cried out with the pain of that small movement.

The light died. Marron sighed softly, then whispered, 'I'm sorry. Do not fear me.'

'No? Why should I not?' The voice was a broken reed, as cracked and hoarse as Fra' Piet's, only that it kept yet some echo of humour in it; and despite the words the light came back, a little: a faint and pearly ball now, motionless and further off, where it would show Marron's face more clearly. 'Even boys can be fearful, and I am a fearful man.'

A man willing to play, it seemed, at least with words. Marron thought him not at all afraid, once recovered from that first moment of discovery, a stranger standing in his cell, in his surely forbidden light.

The light showed both their faces, and they both gazed in silence for a while, assessing, guessing. Marron saw an old man gaunt and strained, unshaven and little fed; what the man saw, he didn't say.

What he did say, he whispered through swollen, broken lips; he said, 'Well. You're not the boy, you're not any of the boys whom they allow to wash and water me, sometimes. You're certainly not the boy who slipped me an *ayar*-stone yesterday. But you don't choose to dress like a brother either,' with even a hint of mockery, he could manage so much, to say that he knew Marron was not dressed this way from choice. 'Perhaps you're right, perhaps I shouldn't fear you. I'll try not. At any rate, you don't look like a boy who'll run to tell your masters of my wicked light. Or am I wrong? Should I burn you where you stand? Who *are* you, boy?'

And the light flared fiercely, too bright to look upon; Marron twisted away and saw hard shadows shift across the floor, as if the light had followed his movement. He was the one who was afraid, as he was meant to be.

He straightened, turned back to face the man and said, 'My name is Marron. I am, I *am* a brother here,' though for only a few hours longer, 'and I do not believe your light can harm me,' or surely the man would never have come to this, starved and tortured in a hidden cell, surely he would not have let it happen?

The man laughed wheezingly, and the light faded to a comfortable glow once more. 'No? Well, perhaps you're right again, Fra' Marron. Perhaps it is only a toy, though it could damn me; but likely I'm damned already.'

As Marron was likely damned also, if anyone should hear of this. Sieur Anton he thought would be no more forgiving than the preceptor, if he heard that his squire blinked at devilry.

But blink he did, deliberately stepping forward under the globe of light. Mustar had given this man a stone also, an *ayar*-stone, that must be what he meant; it had to be significant. *My friend's friend*, he thought, trying to understand it.

He knelt beside the filthy pallet, and said, 'Sir, can I help you? In any way?'

The man's mouth twisted, something like a smile it made. 'You're a strange brother, Fra' Marron, and not only in your dress. If you're not a trick of those questioners of yours, more subtle than their usual. You could pass me a drink of water.'

'Sir?'

'Over there.' A nod towards a flask and a goblet, little more than an arm's reach away; the man lifted an arm to show how it was shackled to the wall, a clinking chain which made that reach impossible. 'This is as subtle as they can manage ordinarily, to leave it just a finger's length beyond me.'

The wit was as dry as the mouth must be; talking clearly pained him, but he talked none the less. In these past days the man must have screamed a lot, but talked hardly or not at all. Marron poured water into the goblet and held it out – then looked again at the state of the man's hands and held it to his lips instead, tilted a little, watched how eagerly, how greedily the throat gulped the water down. He refilled the goblet and helped the man to drink it, then used the hem of his shift to wipe up what had been spilt on chin and bare chest.

Dabbing gingerly with the damp cloth at stains of blood and sweat on the man's face, he said, 'What's your name, sir?'

'Ah. No. No questions, Fra' Marron. You might yet be a trick.' The voice was stronger now, but no less caustic.

'No, sir. I am, I am under a doom, to be expelled from the Order.'

'Indeed? Even so. No questions, please. You can call me Jonson. You're not supposed to be in here, I take it?'

'No, sir. I was looking for someone else . . .' And hadn't found him, or any of them; and was trying not to worry about that, not to see Mustar and the other boys dead in a pit. Perhaps they'd climbed down the ropes and fled to freedom . . .

Perhaps not. It was as much to distract his mind as to allay the man Jonson's suspicions, certainly not at all from curiosity or any genuine wish to know, that Marron asked, 'Sir, your hands – what happened to your hands?'

Jonson lifted them, gazed at them more dispassionately than Marron could, seeming to consider exactly how twisted they were, how bent the fingers. 'Clever men, Fra'

Marron, they have made for themselves clever machines. But they are still stupid about people, they still believe pain can overmaster anyone, if there is enough of it for long enough. They are wrong, I have told them that; but they will not believe me, you see.'

Marron did see, and had no trouble believing. Men like Fra' Piet, the questioners must be. They would be confident; *just a little more, another day and he will break, he must.* Especially with a prisoner, a victim like Jonson, a man not ashamed to scream. Screaming was weakness and weakness meant victory, tomorrow if not today. It was cruel ignorance, but constant failure, constant deaths still would not show them so.

'What can I do, sir?'

'Go away. If they find you here, they'll have another to try their machines on. You taint your soul by speaking to me. Infection spreads, and must be cauterised.'

It was true. A Surayon witch might corrupt the holiest brother, with honeyed words and secret spells; heresy at the heart could destroy the Ransomers and all Outremer from within, the worm in the apple, poisonous and deadly. Cast out or not, if they thought him tainted they would never let him go. He might have escaped a flaying in the hall above only to encounter what was worse and far worse down here in the cold, where all that was warm was the betraying witchlight . . .

'May I give you one more drink before I leave you?' He wanted to do more, but there was no way.

'No – but leave the flask within my reach. That will explain the missing water. With luck they'll blame it on their own carelessness.'

And would never stop to think that he couldn't have poured from a flask nor gripped a goblet, however close they left it? Well, perhaps. *People believe what's easiest*, his uncle used to say. After midday service sometimes, as they went back to food and the fields; Marron's aunt would shush him then, and glance round anxiously for priests or listening neighbours.

Marron set the flask where he'd been told to, rose to his feet and made his way to the curtained door. He wanted to leave good wishes, but that was stupid, pointless. This man was going to die – soon, and in terrible pain – and they both knew it. The best he could manage was a warning, 'Sir, that light you make,' *that magic you make, in defiance of the God and the law*, 'you should take more care . . .'

'I do, ordinarily. You surprised me; you work that door very quietly, Fra' Marron. The questioners are not so careful. Even though that curtain muffles sound. That's what it's for, to keep me from disturbing your prayerful duties.'

If so, it didn't work too well, Marron thought, remembering the cries in the stairwell. But then, without it, perhaps those cries would have scoured the kitchens also, and soured the soup . . .

He bade the man Jonson a respectful farewell – he might be Surayonnaise and heretic, he was certainly a witch, but he was still a man; he hid a great courage behind his craven screaming, and that spoke to Marron far more forcefully than even his long-trained soul could recoil from – and backed out of the cell as cautiously as he had entered, through the curtain first and then through the door, letting no fall of light betray him. Neither any sound:

he took slow pains with the bolt, to be sure it whispered into its bracket. All but blind then, he counted off the empty cells till he came to his own, confirmed it by the smell from his bucket, and knelt quietly in his place as though he had never strayed a little inch from his due obedience that day.

His mind strayed, further than his body had; his mind was up in the castle and down on the plain, seeking Mustar. And further, far further, looking for hidden Surayon: looking to see if anyone there wept and wailed for an absent man, a wonder-worker lost to cold Ransomers, unransomable to them or anyone.

And found nothing, of course, except his own doubts and dreads; and so settled back into chill and hunger once more, into the sharp aching of his never-mending arm, into unhappy anticipation of what was to come.

Brothers came to fetch him out, before the great bell sounded for evening service. Not to take him to the hall, not yet: only to an antechamber where they stood silent guard over him, making no comment even about his sling and his flapping shift, until the call to prayer pushed them all to their knees, sound made solid.

The brothers recited the prayers in a soft chant. Marron joined them in a whisper, not to add to his known faults, but it was all rote. Today he could feel only bitterness towards the God and all men who worshipped Him, who tortured and killed and called it worship.

When they were done they waited, once more in silence. At last the high doors to the hall swung open, the preceptor, masters and knights filed out; Magister Rolf and Magister Sewart, the two Masters Confessors stepped aside from the procession and stood in the doorway to the antechamber, not deigning even to glance at Marron.

Then it was time to stand, to follow them back into the great hall; to walk all the length of the aisle between the gathered brothers, to feel their hidden eyes on him, to stand and then kneel before the steps to the altar with his head uncovered, a public sign of his disgrace.

The masters between them declared his faults, gross disobedience that amounted to treachery against the Order and the God; then his mitigation, that his later understanding had perhaps saved the castle, and that he had fought well and bravely on the wall. Justice condemned him, justice reprieved him; he was to be stripped and cast out from the Order, to make what way he could in the world unblessed by brotherhood.

The two brothers who stood watch behind him ripped the shift from his body, tearing it in two between them; they took the girdle also, that had made his sling. Naked, cradling his bad arm, he made that long walk again the other way, head as high and feet as steady as he could manage.

And so out of the hall and all the way through the castle, and no sign of Sieur Anton to succour him; only the harsh silence of the brothers at his back, and the sidelong glances of the brothers who stood watch on the walls.

In the wide yard before the stables was a vast pile of wood, with small kegs beside. He didn't understand that, but his curiosity was almost dead within him, drowned by dread. Sieur Anton had changed his mind or the court had changed his sentence: he was not to serve as squire after all, only to be thrust out alone, afraid, anathema . . .

The guards at the gate opened it, still with no word spoken. He walked through, heard it slammed behind him; and lifted his eyes to face this new world, wondering who he was now, where he could go, what he might do to survive in this unkind land.

And saw the knight some few paces off, standing waiting for him.

Sieur Anton had brought clothes out with him, tunic and breeches and soft boots, begged or bought from another knight's squire.

'Sieur, thank you . . .'

'Don't,' the knight said. 'Not yet. I lied to the court, Marron; you will find my discipline at least as stern as theirs, and no easier. If you can't practise obedience to me, I will have no use for you; and I won't keep you simply for your own sake.'

'I can obey you, sieur,' simply, honestly, from the heart, 'and I will.'

'We'll see. Here.' Soft bread and an apple pressed into his hands, the good and the bad, and if this was Sieur Anton's discipline Marron wanted more of it, a lifetime's more. 'Eat, and listen. You are my squire, given and sworn; you can sleep with the other squires and the servants, or you can sleep in my room as you have before. Either way will cause you trouble, because of whom you serve. That choice I leave to you.'

'Sieur, if I sleep with you—'

'In my room, Marron.'

'Yes, sieur — may I pray with you also, at the hours?'

'I would insist on it. Is that your choice, then?'

'Please, sieur.'

'Good. You will suffer for it, I warn you now; but that cannot be avoided.'

Neither apparently was it going to be explained, but Marron wasn't worried. He thought squires and servants could teach him nothing now about suffering; he thought life itself had little more to show him.

'One last thing. There is to be a ceremony of sacrament in the stable yard, after the brothers have taken their supper. That will not be easy for you either, but regard it as the first test of your service: you must be there.'

'Sieur, where you go . . .'

'Hmm. Within limits, I trust. I shall be there, but we cannot stand together. Stay it out, Marron, that is all. It is needful. Now eat. I am not accustomed to repeating myself.'

Nor was he likely accustomed to having his servants speak to him with their mouths full, which was why Marron had been standing with his hands held rigidly at his sides. Only his nose was twitching with an ill discipline, alert as always to any scent of food after a fast, while his mouth ran wet and his words slurred.

'Yes, sieur. No, sieur . . .' *Whatever you like, sieur*, so long as Marron could tear and chew and swallow, bite and savour as though the wolf in his stomach were arbiter over his head also, and ruled his manners.

He heard the knight laughing, and didn't mind that now. Neither was he anxious about what might come this evening, despite Sieur Anton's warnings. He was brother no more; the Order had no direct authority over him now, only through the authority it had over his master – what authority Sieur Anton had elected to give it – and it was always careful in its dealings with the knights. What harm could be done him, if he stood through another rite? A ceremony of sacrament: that might mean anything. His own profession had been a sacrament; so was confession, and a man's last prayer before a priest, and any number of little rituals between. It was kind of Sieur Anton to be concerned, but not necessary . . .

So he thought, young and hungry as he was, young and forgetful. Until he stood in the yard among the other squires – who were already nudging and whispering, giving him dishonest words of welcome then crushing back to make an uncomfortable space for him to stand in – while Sieur Anton was drawn up among the knights, each of them shining in their white in the torchlight. One man in every ten held a torch, masters and knights and brothers drawn up in their ranks; so many shadows flickered and danced across his eyes it was hard to see anything clearly, but still Marron could see more than he liked or wanted.

The Order stood in its order around that mound of wood, the squires and other servants squeezed in where they could; the preceptor stepped forward from the line of masters and raised his hand for silence. Every eye was on him, and not Marron alone was holding his breath to hear.

'The night gone,' the preceptor said, his voice harsh and carrying, 'treachery near handed this fortress to the enemy.

Only the God's grace protected us.' *And me*, Marron thought rebelliously, but did not breathe. 'Those who betrayed us were our own vassals, kept by our kindness, their lives within our gift. Which lives are now forfeit by our law, and may the God have mercy upon them, for we shall not.'

That was all. The preceptor gestured and stepped back; a brother with an axe took his place in the light, breaking open the kegs that stood arrayed. He set the axe aside and lifted each keg one by one, pouring viscous oil over the heap of wood and tossing the empty kegs onto the pile.

It was the preceptor himself who took a torch and hurled it, setting the oiled wood ablaze.

Two burly brothers came out of the stables, through the only clear path in that crowded yard, dragging a small figure in white between them. One of the Sharai lads, Marron saw, his hands bound behind him.

'No . . .'

It came out as little more than a groan, inaudible in the sudden murmur of many voices. Marron drew breath to cry aloud, to push forward and shriek against this savagery; and was suddenly seized from behind, lost his breath in a startled gasp and twisted round to see Rudel standing there.

'Don't be a fool,' the jongleur hissed in his ear. 'You can't stop this. Watch, and remember . . .'

Marron fought the man's grip for a moment, uselessly, and then subsided. Rudel was right, he would only make more trouble for himself and perhaps for Sieur Anton too, and to no effect. Nothing he could do to stop the Sharai boy being picked up and swung between the two brothers, too numbed it seemed even to struggle; nothing to prevent his being thrown through the air and into the roaring flames.

Marron sobbed, but that too was lost, this time in the howling as the boy writhed and burned. The brothers went back to the stables, came out with another boy.

Mustar was the fourth. Marron's eyes were not too dazzled by tears and firelight, his mind not too dazed to know his friend. Again he tried to twist free, and again Rudel held him still; and all he could do then was stiffen and stare, bear witness and swear a silent revenge.

At least Mustar struggled and cursed, before he was fed to the fire. Then he screamed, agony and despair, and that long dying cry seared itself into Marron's skull. *Remember*, Rudel had said, needlessly; this could never be forgotten, nor forgiven.

There were perhaps a dozen boys brought out from the stables, a dozen survivors of the night, though Marron had stopped counting before the boys stopped dying. Some might have been quite innocent; there had been fewer surely on the wall with ropes.

When the last of them was still, when only the flames were moving, the Ransomers were dismissed, by the preceptor's word. They filed back through the narrow way into the castle; Marron barely noticed that the jostling throng around him had dispersed also, until Rudel shook him gently back into himself.

'Remember that, lad, but don't dwell on it. This is a cruel country.' *These things happen*, he was saying, as though they must, as though they always would. He sounded like Sieur Anton. Perhaps all men sounded that way after some years in this cursed-cruel country; perhaps he would himself. 'Now, will you speak with me? Privately?'

Secretly, he meant; they were private already. Marron thought that he didn't want to hear any more secrets, he held too many as it was. He wanted to be new, reborn, he wanted to start again, Sieur Anton's squire and nothing more. 'Sir, I ought to . . .' What ought he to do? He didn't know. Seek out the knight, he supposed, or else run to his quarters and find work there, sweep or tidy, polish Josette and see if Dard's edge were true yet after last night's exercise . . .

But there was no strength in his legs to carry him, no strength in his will to defy Rudel. It was so much easier simply to stand here where the heat of the fire tightened the skin on his brow, where the smell of charred meat was all that was left him of Mustar, one last reminder like a whisper from his spirit, *this they did to me . . .*

Standing meant listening: the jongleur assumed a consent he had not given. But listening was easy too, words were fugitive, he wouldn't have to remember them . . .

'Marron, you have been in the penitents' cells, yes? Today and yesterday?'

'Yes.' Answering questions wasn't hard, he could do that and still think of Mustar, still watch for faces in the flames. All magic was light, it seemed, so all light should be magic. There should be signs, he wanted signs to show one young soul gone to paradise, if the Sharai knew the way to any such . . .

'You remember when we went down the steps that day and turned back, when we heard a man screaming?'

And went out and down the hill instead, and saw the missing stones and the bead at the man's throat, and so from there to here, and so Mustar burned. 'Yes.'

'Do you know, did you learn where they are keeping that man? While you were down there?'

Broken hands and blood, all his bones showing, they have been kind to him. 'Yes.'

'Tell me where. Tell me all you can: where they hold him, how they treat him, how often he is—'

Seen? Visited? Treated? Marron could tell him a lot, perhaps, more than the man expected; but, 'Tell me why,' he said instead.

'Because I want to help him, get him out.' A great confession but no great surprise, not now.

'That's heresy.'

'Treason, I think; but yes, it's a capital offence,' and they were talking about it in the light of an execution-pyre, and each turned his head towards the flames, as if to feel again the heat against the eye, the almost-pain of it this far away. 'For both of us if you help me, if we are taken. Will you?'

The screaming of him, and the hands; Marron's thoughts were blurred, it was hard to remember that there was a difference, Jonson in the cell and Mustar in the fire. Both had screamed, both had had hands. The rope that bound Mustar's had burned through more quickly than his flesh; Marron had seen him stretch his arms out in the flames, and his hands were burning claws clutching at the light, and always would be.

Marron meant to say yes already, he thought he must; simply listening made him guilty, so why not? So much for being newborn or innocent, starting afresh; Sieur Anton would condemn him before the court himself, if ever he found out. Secrets and lies already, oaths as good as broken – *I can obey you, sieur, and I will,* but not in this – and him not two hours old yet in his new service . . .

First, though, 'Tell me why,' he demanded again. 'Why risk so much, what is that man' – Jonson, but that surely was not his name, and Marron should have had no chance to hear it in any case – 'what is he to you?'

Rudel smiled, spread his hands. 'I am from Surayon,' he said, 'and so is he.'

13

Where She is Sent

The girls had seen the light and heard the screams, but they'd known what was coming long since, after a day's hard labour among the wounded.

Blaise had brought their breakfast that morning, and seasoned it with news of armed parties riding out to scour the country. He'd been grim and bitter, his mouth twisting on the words, a fighting man forbidden to fight last night and unable even to ride this morning, held back by duty. Julianne had felt accused and hadn't resented it, unfair though it was; she knew that sense of being wasted, of being seen as useless. Too well she knew it already, and would she thought learn many finer nuances in her life to come.

Not today, though. She'd been determined on that. As soon as they'd eaten, she and Elisande had made their way to the infirmary dressed in her plainest gowns, those she could most easily sacrifice. Master Infirmarer had been in no position to turn the girls away; he had too many injured

men on his hands. There were always more men wounded
in a night battle, a wicked disproportion; more yet could be
expected, brought back from Master Ricard's expedition;
and the Order's strictures allowed that caring for the sick
and injured was fit work for women, acceptable even to a
Ransomer in time of need. The girls were guests, to be
sure, and should not work – but they were needed. Two
competent pairs of hands down below freed two men to
stand guard above, lest the Sharai come again.

So yes, Julianne and Elisande had been permitted to
help, if not made exactly welcome. The worst of the
wounded had been given what crude treatment was possible last night, in a hurry and by lamplight; lesser injuries
had received a quick binding and short shrift else. Now by
day was the time for care and skill and patient examination,
and while Master Infirmarer and his brethren occupied
themselves so, Julianne and Elisande could go from cot to
cot with water for wounded men to drink and more to
ease the unwrapping of last night's bandages, to wash away
the caked blood beneath. No one had cared or even noticed
when they pushed their awkward veils aside, except for
those few who had refused their aid altogether, who had
turned their stiff heads on stiff necks and refused even to
look upon them, far less suffer themselves to be touched by
female hands.

As the hours had passed, Elisande particularly had not
been content simply to ferry water and prepare the injured
brothers for other men's ministrations. She had doctored
minor wounds herself, applying salves and bandages, teaching Julianne to do the same. To her obvious frustration,
she'd been forbidden to assist in the surgery, which took

place in an inner room that was all lamplight and shadows, knives and hot irons and screaming. Elisande had tried to bully and then squirm her way in, calling that she had some knowledge of such treatments that might benefit them all, surgeons and patients alike; but that door was closed firmly against her.

When the noon bell sounded even work in the infirmary had slowed and the less grievously injured had knelt beside their cots, to whisper prayers in echo of the master's lead. Elisande had gestured with her head then, Julianne had nodded; the two of them had slipped outside and just walked for a while in the still shadowed air of the courts before going back to their chamber to shed their filthy clothes, wash the blood and stink from their skins and offer their exhaustion some rest.

Elisande had slept for an hour, Julianne not at all, only lying staring at the patterns of shadow on the ceiling, seeing pictures of the night gone by and the morning that had followed: battle and death, an army defiant or else simply philosophical in defeat, a hundred separate hurts in the men she had helped and no joy even for the healthy. She had not thought it would be like that.

There had been no survivors among the invading Sharai, not one. She had asked, once, only to be certain: were wounded prisoners taken elsewhere, some more secure place of treatment? The man she'd asked had laughed at her, and she'd read the truth in his laughter, in what he would not say. There were no prisoners, wounded or otherwise. A knife to the throat, perhaps, as she'd speculated on the wall, or a club to the skull to save blunting good steel: war without quarter. They called themselves the

Ransomers, but it was the land they came to ransom, with their lives if necessary; they offered no ransom to the Sharai.

When Elisande woke, they'd dressed and eaten quickly and then gone back to the infirmary, taking a brief detour on the way just to look into the north ward, just to satisfy a curiosity barely spoken between them. All the bodies were gone, and brothers were swabbing blood from the flag-stones; an hour's sunlight to dry them and there would be no trace remaining of all last night's death and terror. Elisande had murmured something under her breath, a last benediction for the Sharai fallen who would have no other rites said over them, and then both girls had turned and gone on their way.

The wounded had overflowed the infirmary, filling two dormitories besides. The girls fetched food and water to them, changed dressings, spent a good deal of time only sit-ting by one cot or another, speaking to the men who lay there or simply listening while they rambled and drifted in and out of consciousness. More than once Julianne found herself holding a young man's hand, playing sister or mother as best she could as his injuries overcame him, as he slipped slowly into death. She'd have washed and prepared their bodies also, she had no fear of the dead; but that she was not allowed to do. The brothers had their own rituals, it seemed, which were private and not for female under-standing.

Julianne also had her own private needs. Eventually she'd slipped away alone, and good fortune or some higher power had brought her shortly to the door of a small chapel. Like the great hall, this too had a gallery; she'd climbed the steps and knelt in the shadows above, not meaning to pray, only to be quiet for a while.

But her eyes had been distracted by unexpected colour and gleam. Lamps and candles had burned in the chapel below, showing how the walls were painted; everywhere she'd looked she'd seen images of the saints and their deaths, images too of the God's victory here and throughout the Sanctuary Land. The glory of Ascariel glimmered gold behind the altar, and the vessels that stood there were certainly silver where they were not gold.

Looking and looking, she'd seen at last that she was not after all alone; a man had been kneeling close beside a pillar, as far within its shadow as he could come. She'd been doubly glad then that she'd come up into the gallery.

She'd not been able to see him at all clearly; but even so there'd been something about him, his bare head and the way he held himself, his dark clothes that were none the less not the habit of a brother. She'd been fairly certain she could put a name to him.

Then another had come into the chapel. Again bareheaded, this time in a habit but again not a brother; him she'd been certain of.

He'd knelt beside the other man and touched his wrist, bringing a gasp, a jerk of the head, almost a shrinking away.

'Do you know me, child?'

'Yes, Magister Fulke.' Only a whisper, but Julianne had heard it perfectly; there could be no secrets spoken before the God.

'Good. But you need not call me so; that title is reserved for the Order.'

'Please? If I may . . .?'

'Well, but you must answer me a question, then. Why did you forsake us? Brother?'

'I did not, Magister. I was, I was cast out . . .'

'No, tell me true. Why did you forsake us?'

Blaise had begun to weep, then. Marshal Fulke had waited, patient as the God Himself; it was Julianne who'd moved, to rise and slip away. There could be no secrets spoken before the God, but this history was not meant for her to hear, and she would not spy.

She'd slipped soft-footed down the stairs, and gone back to her work among the wounded. It was only later that it occurred to her to wonder quite why Marshal Fulke had so deliberately sought out her sergeant, what he might have offered the man in exchange for his story, or what further service he might demand.

Inevitably, spending so much time among the injured, both girls had heard all the news of the day: how, following the scouts, a small army – half the garrison – had ridden out to surprise the enemy; how it had been the captured stable-lads who had let down ropes from the wall to give the raiders entry; how the surviving boys had been put to cruel question since.

How they had spoken of a new leader among the Sharai, a man who sought to unite all the tribes against Outremer. Hasan, they said was his name.

How they were condemned, out of their own mouths convicted; how they were all to be put to death that night, as justice and the law demanded.

*

About Marron no brother spoke at all, nor would speak when they asked; except the one who cleared his throat and spat wetly onto the flags of the floor, rasped, 'Treacher,' and turned his head the other way. Marron was a worry, but not a great one. They'd seen him last night, free and fighting and then walking from the ward with d'Escrivey, very much like a squire at his master's side. That surely meant that he'd been reprieved, that he would be forgiven his act of rebellion in the village that even the strictures of the Rule hadn't stopped the brothers gossiping about; the girls had had the story from Blaise, who'd had it from a dozen different men in a dozen forms but little different one from another.

Julianne had been sure, at least, that Marron was reprieved. Or at least had tried to seem so, to herself as to her friend. Elisande had grunted, 'So where is he, then? I want to look at his arm,' and had asked again, and had again got no answer.

At close of day, in that little time of shadows after the sun had sunk below the castle wall but not yet to the horizons of the guards above, Elisande had taken Julianne by the elbow and tugged her discreetly out of the infirmary.

'What is it?'

'Before they start that bell ringing, and no one listens to us. Come on. Put your veil straight, and look demure . . .'

Through the castle to the kitchens; and from there down a narrow turning stair into darkness, into the hard bowels of the rock, one hand feeling for Elisande and the other for the wall when she could see neither, only a hand's span from her nose . . . Julianne had known what this place was, no need to ask. And before they reached bottom she'd known why Elisande had brought her here, and why she'd brought also a scrip filled with linen and ointments.

They'd come from darkness into light: a small chamber, an oil-lamp, two brothers on guard by another doorway. Not armed except with staves, but alert; and very surprised to see two women on the stair and firm of purpose.

'We have come to tend to Fra' Marron,' Elisande had said, brandishing her scrip. 'We understand he was hurt in the fighting last night; his arm will need dressing, at least . . .'

All so convincing, so likely, so legitimate; and all so wasted, because both guards had shaken their heads together, and one had said, 'He is not here.' Short of snatching up the lamp and pushing their way past to check every cell in that dark passage behind the men, there had been little the girls could do but nod and climb the stairs again. Elisande had tried a little more, one more time with the single simple question, 'Can you tell me where he is?' and had received no more satisfaction than at any time this day. The man had shaken his head again, just as the great bell had thrummed its first calling strokes through the stone above their heads; he'd shaken it once more, emphatically, touched a finger to his lips and turned towards his brother. The two of them had knelt, casting their hoods over their heads but facing each other so that, almost knocking heads as they bowed, they'd entirely blocked the way through to the passage they guarded. No chance to slip by them; Elisande's eyes had spoken her frustration. Even so she'd lingered a little, squinting in what light there was, peering down the passage as though she thought she could see through dark and rock and all to find whom she sought there.

As they returned to their chamber Julianne had spoken her conviction again, that the boy was well or well enough. 'Not in the infirmary and not in the cells, that brother wouldn't have lied to us, he wouldn't demean himself so. Marron's not badly hurt, then, and he's not badly in trouble . . .'

And others were, which was why Marron was a worry but not a great one. Others were death-doomed, irretrievable: their names not known and their faces hardly glimpsed and not remembered – only stable-boys, after all, and she'd seen so many through the years; why should she have made an effort with these lads, how could she have known? – but their trial a great weight on her regardless, and on Elisande also, a crushing weight they'd carried all the day and could not put down now.

And so the day and the evening that had followed. Blaise had brought their evening meal himself – no spare hands to serve them, he'd said, that jongleur Rudel scrounging a meal with Blaise's men, and he'd never known such a thing happen in the Order, that guests should go unattended – and had delivered a fierce scolding for seasoning, once he'd learned why their gowns were smeared with dust and wetter, deeper stains.

Elisande had borne it snarling, Julianne with an unnatural patience – at least so Elisande had said afterwards, when they were alone, that her patience was unnatural; she'd managed a half-smile and a nod, 'Yes, it was taught me,' – and at last he'd gone. To be with his men, he'd said, and left unspoken the reason why. Young men, some of them: were they fretful, cold with the thought of the thing to come, Julianne had wondered, as she was herself but would not say so, or not at least to him? Or did they want to watch? Young men could be fierce; and they were Elessan, all of them. A hard people, hard to themselves and harder still to others. The Sharai were their enemy and the God's also, branded so bone-deep, soul-deep. There would be little mercy in their hearts in the face of Sharai treachery.

Blaise might even want to watch himself, she'd thought. Having missed the opportunity to fight. That tirade he'd unleashed on Elisande and herself had sounded more resentful than anything else. He was a warrior trained and ready, there'd been a battle, he'd had no part to play in it; and what had been his own clear charge he'd clearly failed at, to keep Julianne safe and safely distant from the fighting. Blood-letting cooled a fevered body; for a fevered spirit, someone else's blood might be enough.

So they'd known it was coming, that glow of light reflected from the walls, fierce red on dull; and foolishly, stupidly, she'd thought she could simply turn her back to the screened windows and wait, see nothing and pretend that nothing was all she knew.

She hadn't thought about the screaming. Certainly she hadn't expected the cruelty of how it was made, a chain of single links: how one boy had died before the next was burned, and each one's screaming was the story of a life from bright sudden consciousness to exhausted end, and each brief silence after was the loss of life.

Some man must have made that decision, one at a time: the preceptor himself, most likely. For the cold satisfaction of his men, or else for the added suffering of the boys who must wait; or else for both. She'd tried to think of it as an affirmation, each boy declaring his death to the sky or to his god and not one being lost in another's agony; she'd tried and failed, it had been too much to ask of her. She'd only suffered, sobbed with each separate scream and each sudden silence, and her only victory had been that she had not screamed herself. Unless that had been her father's victory, and not hers at all . . .

At last, at long last there had been no more screaming, and the stretching silence had been washed over by a hissing whisper. When she'd wiped her wet face and sore eyes – on her veil, of course, and what else was it for, of what use was it if not for that? – and looked around, she'd seen Elisande standing silhouetted against the dim red shadows at the window.

Saying that prayer again, she'd guessed, the *khalat*, speaking the boys' souls to whatever paradise awaited them, if any. If there were any world beyond this, somewhere less savage, if that was not just a lie fed to the ignorant and unlucky to keep them subservient to their masters' unkind law. She doubted it herself; but in the end she'd done what little she could, she'd walked across to stand beside her friend and offer her own unspeaking respect to the ritual, in the hope that it might mean something at least to Elisande, though it came too late to help herself and was far too small, far too late to help the dead.

Standing so, with folded hands and not a movement in

her except her gulping throat and gasping breath, determinedly not closing her eyes to the fading light of the fire outside, she thought at first that it was only her blurred sight that made the light dance in the pattern of the screens across the window.

Then that it was a sudden flare from one of the lamps, shifting all the shadows to flickering confusion.

Then that it was an insect's wings battering the air too fast to see, and the body of it invisible in the intricacies of dark and light that pierced and shaped the screen.

She thought so, or hoped so in defiance of what she thought, what she expected from the first quick hint of strange, the catch of nothing at her eye. It was only when blur and dance and flicker stretched to a shimmering worm a finger's length and longer, a finger's width and narrowing like a taper, like an over-fine image of a finger; only when she saw how it drew spangles of light together to weave itself a body; only then did Julianne take breath and clamp her throat hard around a thin steel wire of a voice that she barely recognised as her own. 'Djinni Khaldor. This is – an unexpected visitation,' she said, though she wasn't even sure that it was true. After the tensions and terrors of last night and the long weariness that had been today, after the monstrousness of the fire that guttered still in a courtyard too close, out of sight but not out of hearing, she felt too exhausted to be surprised by anything.

True for Elisande it was, though, so much at least. That girl gasped and jerked her head around, needed a moment of blinking to find the hover-and-spin aglitter, the thread of distortion of light and air that was the djinni this night; and then needed a moment more to stiffen herself to the task before she stepped deliberately between it and Julianne.

'Had I been expected,' the djinni said, and its voice was as large and as quiet as before, seemingly quite unaffected by the form it chose to take, 'you would have waited in vain.'

'And to our loss, I am sure,' Elisande said, though she sounded as though she meant that not one jot. *Careful,* Julianne thought, Julianne's fingers said against her friend's wrist, just the lightest touch for such a solemn message, *don't let your anger confuse your words. You know these creatures, how subtle they are,* and Julianne was still a nervous pupil, clumsy and uncertain. Even so there was something she must say, something she had to learn, though she wouldn't batter at the djinni with questions as her soul was crying to.

'Not so, but there would have been no purpose to my coming. You would have known already what I sought.'

'Even so. People like to be asked, sometimes,' and now suddenly Elisande had the voice exactly, as she had used it before: respectful but not subservient, determined to speak and treat as an equal without harbouring any delusions that equal she was. 'Neither could we have gifted you that thing you seek, had you not come here to collect it . . .'

'It lies not in your gift, Lisan of the Dead Waters; neither is it a thing to be collected, except that there is a debt.'

That meant it spoke to Julianne – impossible to tell with no face turning between them, no clues of body for even her high-trained eyes to read, and oh, how she resented its immunity – and it wished some service from her. Again, neither aspect of that was a surprise.

The only possible surprise lay in the answer that she gave; and again, perhaps, the only one surprised was Elisande.

'A debt unacknowledged,' Julianne said slowly, 'is no debt at all.'

Now it was the turn of Elisande's fingers to speak to Julianne's, *careful, careful! You don't know these creatures, how powerful they are*, even as the djinni replied.

'That is true. Similarly, though, a debt acquired in ignorance is still a debt. It may be forgiven, but not ignored. And those who choose to trespass into a society they do not understand should not seek to deny the consequences of their choice.'

Julianne nodded, bowed almost, the point confessed; then she turned her face deliberately towards the dying light beyond the windows and said, 'I was wondering just now whether the Sharai were right in their beliefs, in the god they worship and their prospects of paradise hereafter. It occurs to me that though nothing mortal-bound can know, the djinn might have that knowledge.'

'Daughter of the Shadow, the djinn are mortal also. Of a kind. Time will not touch us, but still we can be slain. And no, we do not know the gods, neither the truths behind their promises. All faith is hope, no more; I can offer you nothing else.'

Not true, it had offered her kindness, and she valued that. Now there was a debt she did acknowledge; this must be what she had wanted, she thought, to have her own reason for saying yes. Why she should have wanted to, except for some curious sense of honour that the djinni itself seemed to recognise and respond to, she couldn't say.

At any rate, she felt relief far more than anxiety as she said, 'Tell me what you want, spirit, and I will do it if I can.'

Elisande choked, span round, laid the palm of her hand across Julianne's mouth too late. '*No!* Djinni, she did not mean – Julianne, you *can't* . . .'

Julianne reached up, took her friend's hand in both of hers and held it calmly, almost patted it. 'Yes,' she affirmed. 'I did mean it, and I will do it. A blind promise, I know, to a creature of guile and subtlety; none the less, I make it willingly. There is a debt.' *Now.*

'Go where you are sent, Julianne de Rance, and marry where you must.'

That at least, at last was unexpected. She bit down hard on any question, steadied her mind and said, 'Well, I will; but—'

'I have not yet said where I will send you.' It waited then, for a long, slow beat that echoed unbearably in Julianne's mind; and it was laughing as it went on, 'Go to the Sharai, daughter of the Shadow.'

More than unexpected, this was startling. Questions teemed on her tongue, and were swallowed with difficulty. There had to be a way to ask without asking; she was too muddled to find it, but Elisande not, it seemed. Elisande said, 'That was the duty you laid on me, at our last meeting.'

'It was.'

'There must be a reason,' enunciated oh so carefully, not to have it sound as if she were asking, 'why the djinn would see Julianne and me both among the Sharai.'

'There are many reasons, Lisan, and two that I will tell you. Human children take the care of their friends upon themselves; if I send Julianne into lands and among a people that she does not know, it seems to me likely that you will travel with her. She calls me subtle; I do not know if this be subtlety, but you have not gone alone.'

'I do not wish to go to the Sharai.'

'No, but I wish it, and others will be glad if you do. You can tell the imams at Rhabat that the *khalat* was properly said for the dead in their time of dying.'

'It was said. That is enough.'

'For their god, perhaps, if god there be. For the comfort of their families and the satisfaction of their priests, not so. It should be known. Also, Julianne will find her father there.'

Her *father*? Elisande's nails dug deep into her wrist; she gasped, wrenched her hand free and said, 'I did, I did not know my father was there.'

'He is, and he will be; and he will be in great danger. You can save him, though it might be better if you did not.'

'Djinni . . .' This was too much for her; what it said made too much sense and no sense, it left her reeling. 'I wish that you would tell me, straightly, what it is that you would have me do.'

'I have told you that, three times now. Once more I will say it, but not here.'

'At least tell me how to find them, then, where my road should take me . . .' That was a plea, desperate as it began, almost shouted; but she let it die, thinking that a demand for information was a question in all but name, and the djinni might treat it so, might assume another debt as fair exchange.

All it said, though, was, 'Lisan can tell you that. She

can show you, she is your road if she will be so. For now, fare well.'

This time no thunderclap, no sparks; it dwindled only as it had grown, to a petty agitation of air and light, to an absence. She wondered briefly what a djinni's body was, how it was made or how many ways it could make itself, what more it could be. Only briefly, though.

My father . . .

She turned to Elisande and said, 'Will you come?'

'I do not want to.'

'You said that.'

'I am not free, Julianne . . .'

'No more am I,' she said. Duties weighed her down, promises conflicted; she had sworn obedience to her father, but for her father's sake she would break that oath, and any. 'I am going. Alone, if I must.'

'You cannot. You said yourself, you do not know the road; nor do you know the customs of the people, nor how to travel in the desert. You would die, long before you saw Rhabat.'

'Even so. If my father is in peril . . .'

'We are all in peril.' Elisande's fists were clenched, and her face also; Julianne could not read her thoughts. But, 'Well,' she said at last, 'I must betray someone, it seems. Many people, perhaps, and disaster may come of it. But I cannot let you go alone. Besides, I might be less welcome here once you were gone. Doubly so, once for my own sake and once because of you. I do not want to find myself in one of those cells they are so fond of. So yes, if you must go, I will show you the way of it.'

Julianne kissed her then, once for love and twice more

formally, on each cheek, another promise sealed and this one not to break.

How they should leave — how to escape might be a better way of putting it — was another question, and she was out of the practice of asking questions tonight. Morning would be soon enough. Then she would have other questions too, she would try once again to learn just why Elisande had come here, and why she was so reluctant to move on. Two questions with one answer, most likely, a purpose not achieved; but what that purpose was, Julianne determined that she would learn. Tomorrow.

For now, she took herself to bed. Elisande aped her, undressing silently, putting out the lamps, lying down in the dark; but Julianne lay a long time with her eyes wide open, staring at things she could not see, the vaulted ceiling not truly one of them; and she didn't ask but she suspected that Elisande aped her in that also.

Both girls slept through the bell next morning, slept through the hour of service and could have slept later still. Julianne could have spent half the day in bed. Her conscience touched her with a sharp question, though — was she resting, or hiding? — and the answer had her up in short order.

She nudged Elisande out of bed also, sweetly smiling to rub the salt of her virtue in deeper; but they were both soon glad that she had. Julianne fetched in the cooling ewer of water that waited on the landing, left by a brother before the bell; they washed and dressed, and almost immediately heard footsteps on the stairs outside, a cough, a finger scratching at the curtain.

'Come.'

Blaise it was who came, which Julianne knew already; his tread was unmistakable, heavy-booted against the soft shuffle of the brothers' sandals. This was the second morning running he'd come with a tray in his hands, bearing their breakfast; the second morning she'd seen him blushing, fighting to keep his eyes unfocused as if he trespassed somewhere sanctified, entering his lady's chamber before ever she'd deigned to leave it. *And he nearly did catch us in our beds,* she thought, *and what would he have done then, if I'd called him in? Died of shame, most like . . .*

'Blaise, good morning. Are you our servant once again?'

'My lady, I took this from the brother who was bringing it. I have a message for you. His grace the preceptor would welcome a visit from you this morning, if you are at leisure.'

'As he knows perfectly well how much I am at leisure, I take it that's a summons. Can you tell me why?'

'No, my lady,' he said stolidly, meaning, she thought, that he knew perfectly well and would not tell. Because he'd been ordered not to, or because it was not his place to do so; either one would fit.

'Did he mean immediately?' she asked, with a hint of the plaintive in her throat and her eyes on the breakfast-tray. She *was* hungry, after a weary day and a wakeful night. Diplomacy said to hurry, but . . .

'Immediately you have breakfasted, I think, my lady.'

Of course, the preceptor was a diplomat too. She nodded, placated.

'Did he mean me as well?' Elisande asked.

'I could not say, my lady. He asked me to bring the message to the lady Julianne.'

Which clearly meant *no* in Blaise's mind, but Julianne had a mind of her own, and was determined to assert it.

'Of course, you as well. You are my companion, my chaperone,' with a wicked smile, *perhaps I need the protection of a chaperone, perhaps no girl is safe with His Grace the Preceptor* . . .

Elisande grinned back over her shoulder, as she took the tray from Blaise.

He waited outside the chamber while they ate; neither girl hurried. The bread was good and the honey sweet, the sheep's milk rich and nutty and the preceptor a busy man; he would neither waste half an hour of his time nor begrudge it to his guests.

When they were ready, Blaise led them to a part of the castle they had not visited before, unless Elisande's private wanderings had brought her here. It was all new to Julianne.

Another ward, another tower: but here the stone flags were covered with rushes, to mute the sound of Blaise's boots. A brother on watch opened the door to the preceptor's private apartments and bowed them in, unless he was averting his eyes from even veiled women; it was subtly done if so, and Julianne couldn't tell.

The room they came into was a fine, a classic example of what her father called costly austerity when he was feeling generous, religious hypocrisy when he was not. The furnishings were simple, but of that simplicity that cost dear: the chests and chairs were unadorned but of high quality, made from woods brought from the homelands, hundreds of miles at great expense. The rugs on the floor were plain, colours of earth and straw, colours of humility; they were knotted silk of a style that Julianne had seen rarely, traded from Sharai who had journeyed in the uttermost east. The walls had been washed a soft white and carried no decoration save a pair of woven hangings – Ascariel, they depicted, the golden city in light and darkness, and even in darkness it lit up the night – and the looped sign of the God, not jewelled or chased as she had seen done in Marasson, but beaten with great craft from a weight of solid gold.

The room was empty. The brother at the door bade them wait, and refresh themselves if they would; goblets of glass and silver stood on a chest, with a flask beside. Elisande sniffed it, and her eyebrows rose.

'*Jereth,*' she murmured. 'The Sharai make it, from herbs and berries. It's . . . uncommon, in Outremer.'

In Marasson, also. Julianne had tasted it once, as a small child, just a sip from her father's glass. She remembered the flavour still.

Elisande lifted the flask and poured, two small measures; then she looked to Blaise, and her eyebrows asked the question.

'Thank you, no, my lady. I was not invited.'

He stepped outside, and the brother closed the door.

Julianne took the goblet Elisande passed to her, bent over it, inhaled – and was briefly young again, excited by everything, thrilled to be taking treasure from her father's hand. She tossed her veil aside and sipped, and the taste was exact, a moment of sour herbs that twisted the mouth before sweet fruit soothed it. *Like medicine,* she'd said the first time, and her father had laughed at her; but she thought the same now. There was bitterness there, not quite disguised, and the memory of that lingered longer than the dulcet. As though the asperity were the purpose of it, and the sweetness only there as an allay. And yet the balance of the two was unimpeachable, a touch more of either would have done it irreparable harm. It was a drink for adults, she decided, with a sigh inside; and yes, it made her feel a child again.

'This is – exceptional,' she said.

'I am glad.' It was the preceptor's voice, soft, mellifluent and at her back, where she had thought there was only wall behind her.

She turned more sharply than she would have wished, and saw how one of the hangings still billowed, where he had come through a hidden door. A doorway, at least: not a door, she would surely have heard the hinges. His sandals, on these rugs – that she could forgive herself for, if he'd been trying to walk silently. Which she was sure of. This man she thought did nothing without thought, without deliberate intent.

He stood before her now, only a long arm's reach away and he had long arms; and a mild gaze, a benevolent smile, silver hair and a bald crown, the God's own tonsure given to a faithful servant. He was the image of a peaceable religious, and she believed that image not at all. And rightly. *This is the man who ordered all those boys burned alive.* And stayed perhaps to see it done, or sat in here and listened to their screaming . . . Or maybe he'd been reading or praying or sleeping, maybe he'd heard not a single cry of it, maybe he'd put it completely out of his mind. It made not the slightest difference.

She reached to draw her veil over her face again, but the preceptor forestalled her. 'Please, not while we're private. Primitive customs are for primitive people. We have offered you poor entertainment these last days, I fear,' he went on, 'and it's too late now to improve our reputation in your eyes; but a gesture, at least, a touch of how we'd sooner treat our guests . . .'

'You have lost no reputation with me, your grace,' she said.

'Meaning that we had none to lose?' His smile, his voice, all his manner said that he was teasing; but oh, he was sharp, he struck uncomfortably close. 'Come, sit down; you worked yourselves to exhaustion yesterday on our behalf, at least you must rest today.'

His gesture as well as his words included Elisande; she said, 'May I not pour you some *jereth*, your grace?'

'We call it monks'-wine here, child,' and the reproach was so gilded even Julianne was hardly aware of it, 'I suppose because it is not – quite – forbidden by the Rule. But no, I thank you, I do not take it myself. Please, sit.'

She did, they both did, close together on a settle. *Like children*, she thought again, with a twinge of irritation, *come to be disposed of by their father.*

Because that was what was happening here, she realised suddenly, even before the preceptor said it directly. He was making dispositions. It was implicit, twice implicit in what he'd said already. She really should wake up or he'd have her dancing to his delight, only that his voice lulled her so . . .

'There is no way,' he said, 'properly to thank you both for your labours yesterday, so I am cast already as an ungrateful host; and I regret, I deeply regret that I must add to my failures in that regard. But your father sent you to us, Lady Julianne, for your protection, to ensure your safety; and the attack on this castle two nights since has thrown that safety into severe question.' He didn't say, he didn't need to say that it was her own actions that night that drew her into real danger; again, that was implicit. 'I have been considering the situation since, and I am afraid that I have no choice in this. The Sharai may return in greater strength, to invest us or assault again; for your welfare, I must send you forth. I will detail a party to accompany you. The road is not perilous, but neither is it invulnerable, and your own men are no longer enough. There are traders here too, bound for Elessi; you can all travel together. The greater numbers, the greater safety.'

Julianne nodded slowly. 'How soon, your grace?'

'As soon as may be. Tomorrow, if you can be ready.'

'Your grace, I can be ready today, if you wish it.' *I'm ready now, I'd ride out as I am and never look back, never see or wish to see your pleasant face again except in nightmare . . .*

'All the better. Shall we say after the noon heat, then? If that will give you time enough to prepare? You could be some miles on your way before nightfall, and perhaps a day earlier in Elessi.'

'Of course. I am sorry if we have caused you worry; your hospitality has been generosity itself.'

'Not at all. Hospitality is the heart of the Rule; in serving you, we have served the God, which is all our purpose.'

And did you serve the God last night, with your fire? She'd have preferred an easy answer to that question, something she could live with, a sigh and a sad shrug, a simple 'no';

unfortunately, even without asking, she knew that he would say yes, and mean it.

The preceptor gave orders at the door: knights and troops to be detailed, the traders alerted. Then he returned to his guests, and they sat and drank and talked of other things. Her life in Marasson, a little of Elessi, though each time he turned the conversation that way she turned it back. When she arrived there would be soon enough to learn its ways. If ever she did arrive there . . .

He asked no questions of Elisande, which was some small relief. Julianne still had her own questions, but this was no place for her to ask and he no man to hear.

When their goblets were empty he offered to refill them, and she declined: pure politeness on each side, they both knew the interview was over.

She stood, so did he, so did Elisande. They made their formal farewells, he promised to see them on their way himself, she thanked him graciously for the courtesy; she adjusted her veil and turned towards the door, which was opened before she reached it, the brother there bowing deeply or else avoiding the poison of her gaze, as before. She swept past, Elisande at her back.

Blaise brought them back to their chamber, a watchful escort who made them both mute. As soon as they were alone, though, Elisande said, 'Well. That makes it easier, I suppose.'

Indeed, easier for their escape, to fulfil her promise to the djinni and embark on some blind adventure; but it would be no easier for Elisande to leave this place. The frustration and distress of that was laid clear and heavy in her voice, denying each one of her words.

14

The Corruption in the Blood

All night Marron had been trying to sleep with a deadly secret, to pray with a heresy in his head.

I am from Surayon.

From Surayon and free, still free because Marron had not denounced him, and would not.

I am from Surayon, and so is he; and the bare announcement was so shocking, Marron hadn't even recoiled. Hadn't even stared, had only stood numbly while the words settled in his head. Even Jonson had not admitted so much; he'd had a little more care for his much-abused body, and a little less trust in a chance-met boy. Not so Rudel, who had betrayed them both, himself and Jonson, given them over into Marron's hands; and Marron's hands were not strong enough to hold them, and so all three would suffer, he was sure.

He had tried to sleep, and could not; had tried to pray, and could not. Then he had tried to hide it all from Sieur

Anton, though very much doubting his ability to do that also.

'Marron, don't mumble the prayers in future, they're not a lesson for impatient boys to babble through.'

'No, sieur.'

'You were restless all night, too. What kept you from sleeping?'

'Nothing, sieur, I don't know . . .'

The knight had sighed. 'Marron, didn't I tell you not to lie to me? Show me your arm.'

Well, there had been some truth in that at least, though his silence was a lie. The arm had been painful all night, if not as painful as his conscience. As he'd gazed at it this morning, as Sieur Anton had pushed back the sleeve to expose it, they'd both seen how it was swollen on either side of the stained bandage, how the tight skin shone; how beneath the skin darkly vivid and telltale streaks ran out to reach almost to his elbow, almost to his wrist. When he'd tried, he couldn't bend his fingers.

Sieur Anton's breath had hissed softly. 'That's not good.'

'No, sieur.' It had been frightening, truly.

'It needs care, but not from me. I won't even unwrap it. Take it to Master Infirmarer, Marron, for his opinion. Right now, I think.'

'Oh, please, sieur, no!' Being frightened had not seemed so bad, in comparison. 'There are, there are so many others hurt, worse than I am . . .'

'Perhaps; but even so, someone with more skill than I should look at this. It's been denied the chance to heal too often, and some poison has got into it. Why do you not want to go to the infirmary?'

'Sieur, Master Infirmarer might not want to treat me. I am not a brother now.' He had been cast out, in utter humiliation; he couldn't have borne that rejection again, so soon.

'He will treat my squire. I am sworn to the Ransomers still, if you are not. And they are sworn to serve all those who fight for the God, whether they are of the Order or not.' And then, against Marron's stubborn silence, 'Would you rather lose the arm? That may happen yet, if we leave this.'

'Sieur, will you, will you come with me?'

The knight, his master had laughed shortly. 'No, I will not. You are not a child, Marron. I will order you to go, though, if that makes it easier for you. Remember, you have promised me your obedience.'

'Yes, sieur.'

Another laugh, more kindly in the face of his misery; and, 'We can wash and dress first, though. And eat, I would not send you fasting to such a trial. Can you fetch a tray without spilling it, or shall I send another lad?'

'I can fetch it, sieur.'

And had done, had fetched it and carried it away again, had done all for his master that a squire should though it had cost agonies of pain, agonies of anxiety; and now at last, too soon was making slow steps towards the infirmary, cursing his arm and all its long history of mistreatment, cursing himself and everyone except Sieur Anton who'd caused the wound to start with.

Nearly there despite his dawdling, he turned a corner and found Rudel sitting in an embrasure with a small reed pipe in his mouth, moving his fingers over the holes but not blowing, making no sound at all.

'Marron, good morning.' The greeting was cheerful enough, though the eyes were watchful.

No more so than Marron's. *I am from Surayon*, he'd said, and little more.

'I have to go to the infirmary. Sir.' Still no easy *Rudel*. He never would have found that truly easy, with a man twice his age and many times his experience of the world; he might no longer be a brother here, but the lord God help him, he wanted some distance today.

'Yes, I thought you might,' a casual smile hinting that there was no mystery at all in this meeting, only a little thought, a little care and a willingness to wait. Also no pretence that this was not deliberate. 'How is the arm?'

'Not good, sir.' Sieur Anton's words, because he could think of none of his own.

'No? Show me.'

Well, that was better than showing Master Infirmarer. Marron eased back his sleeve, displayed his arm with its distorted, miscoloured flesh.

No hiss of breath this time, and no anxiety on Rudel's face as there had been on Sieur Anton's: only a thoughtful interest, a slow consideration, and then a finger lifted to touch gently, first here and then there.

'Does this hurt? And this? How if I press, is that worse . . .?'

Marron bore it with nods and grunts for answer, trying not to flinch even when that careful finger sent a surge of pain all through his arm and on through every bone of him, making him dizzy and shaky on his feet.

'Steady, lad.' Rudel's strong hand gripped his shoulder, held him still until his head cleared. Then the jongleur's head lowered to the bandage, and Marron heard him sniff deeply, once and then again.

'Sir?'

'You've a malaise in there, lad, it's been too long left unhealing. And Master Infirmarer will do little enough for it; he can't stop the sickness, only wait till it's stenching bad and then cut it off. At the elbow maybe, at the shoulder more like, if he waits.'

Marron didn't question Rudel's judgement. Blindly believing, his first impulse was to ask again for company. 'Sir, would you come and talk to him? He won't listen to me, but . . .'

'No more to me, lad. I'm a jongleur, remember, and he's a proud man. What do I know of men's bodies, or the poisons that corrupt them? What could I possibly know, that he does not? But in any case, there's no need. That's what Master Infirmarer would do for you, he'd leave you with a paddle or a stump. I can do better. Come with me.'

He walked off along the passage, away from the infirmary; Marron hesitated only a moment before following, though he breathed doubt as much as hope. What indeed could a jongleur know, that the Master Infirmarer of the Society of Ransom did not?

I am from Surayon. There was only that, the ultimate declaration of sorcery, heresy and treason. It wasn't much, to build a hope upon.

But no, in honesty, that wasn't all. There was the man himself, and the confidence of him: last night the confidence to trust, this morning it seemed the confidence to heal. To diagnose, and then to heal – and Marron hadn't doubted the diagnosis, so why doubt him now?

Because he's a jongleur, because he's from Surayon, because he's the Order's enemy and my master's enemy and must be mine also . . .

But still Marron followed him to a small windowless chamber that stood dark and empty, a storeroom lacking stores. Rudel pushed the door to behind them; it grated along the floor and its hinges squeaked, and when it was closed there was no light at all.

'Now,' his voice said in the shadows, 'we need at least a glow to work by. Don't be scared, boy. You asked me once if I'd seen magic, do you remember? The true answer to that is, never in the dark . . .'

A soft-shining ball of light floated between them, above their heads. Marron glanced at it briefly, then gazed levelly at Rudel.

'Well,' the jongleur said, 'I see that you're not scared. Of course, you've seen the King's Eye, haven't you? No reason why you should be, then; but I've known men twice your age who pissed themselves when I conjured a little light, and then refused to admit it after. Refused to admit either part of it, the light or the piss . . .'

He'd seen more than the King's Eye, though that was enough and more, far more than this. He'd seen the preceptor call forth the sign of the God in flowing blue light every night before service, and set torches aflame with it after. And, more nearly, 'Sir, I have seen this before.'

'What?' Rudel was very still suddenly, and his little light burned brighter, burned hard into Marron's eyes.

'This light, sir. I have seen another man do this,' and was

not apologising for it, standing squarely to the truth and glad for the chance of it, for the change.

'When have you— Wait.' Rudel reached for his shoulder – *wrong shoulder*, but Marron wasn't going to say so, certainly wasn't going to show how much that fierce grip hurt him, even so high on his bad arm – and said, demanded, 'You saw him, didn't you? You saw Redmond!'

'I don't know, sir,' more truth, 'but I saw the man in the cells. He wouldn't tell me his true name.'

'And no more should I have done. Forget it, if you can,' though he must have known that Marron could not. Any name would have been hard to lose; that one, not possible. 'Only tell me how it happened, that you saw him. You must have caught him unawares, surely, if he made a light like this. He wouldn't have known to trust you . . .'

There were other questions there, how Rudel knew to trust Marron, and whether he was right; but all Marron said was, 'Yes, sir,' and then briefly the story of his last afternoon.

'So. Two from Surayon, and you have met them both now. And betrayed neither. That's your life forfeit, Marron, if not your soul.'

'My soul too, sir,' he said, stubbornly insistent. All his life he had known this, that the God condemned black heresy and all who harboured it. The death that came first, in the fire or otherwise, the justice of the Church was only a forerunner.

'I don't think so, lad. Truly, I don't. But never mind now, eh? You've given us your silence; I don't ask for your faith too. Let's see what I can do for you instead, shall we? Give me your hand.'

The hurting one, he meant, the one that already looked swollen and discoloured as the arm above it was, worse than an hour ago. Marron held it out, though even so much movement was painful and only the pain said that it was still something of his, so stiff and awkward it felt, like a length of wood clumsily grafted onto living flesh. Rudel took the weight of it in one hand while his other unpicked the knot of the bandage and peeled that away, pulling sharply when it stuck to itself and to the open wound beneath. Marron let out a hissing whistle, the best he could manage for a scream; the jongleur apologised distractedly.

The arm looked very bad. Even the muted light of Rudel's magic couldn't hide the streaking in the flesh, even the pain that blurred Marron's eyes and made his head swim couldn't stop him seeing creamy yellow pus in the gaping wound. No balm, no horse-liniment would cure this now. Hot knives, he thought, were all his future held; and would Sieur Anton keep a one-armed squire?

Rudel's thumb stroked down all the length of his forearm, and left a numbing coolness where it touched. Again, the other hand, the other side; Marron sighed softly, as the pain receded.

Again, this time with all the fingers spread, spanning the open mouth of the wound. Rudel said, 'My friend in the cell below could do this better.'

Not with those hands, Marron thought, remembering. And opened his mouth to say so, and gasped instead; not with pain this time, nor the fear of it, but only with surprise as a warmth flowed from Rudel's fingers, flooding through his arm like water, soothing, cleansing.

He closed his eyes against the prick of tears, and turned

his head aside. And condemned himself for cowardice, turned back, looked down deliberately to see how those damning streaks receded as he watched, how the skin of his arm paled from purple-red to pink.

'Sir, what are you—' No, that was foolish, he knew what; but, 'How are you doing this?'

'We have a certain skill, with living flesh,' Rudel said. 'I cannot knit the wound together, time must do that, and your own strength of body; but I can drive the poison out, and subdue the pain of it for a while.'

'Is it magic?'

'I suppose it is. Or knowledge, rather; but that's what magic is. An understanding of what lies under the surface of the world. I can see more clearly, or deeper than you do; my eyes are not defeated by the surface of a thing, when I choose to see beneath it. And what I can see, I can work upon.'

All this time his hands were working, touching, stroking; more than Marron's arm was tingling now with the warmth that ran from the jongleur's fingers. All his body pulsed with it.

'There. That's as much as I can manage,' and indeed Rudel was sweating, seeming to shiver as he released Marron's arm, as he stepped back and pushed his big hands through his damp hair.

'Sir, thank you . . .' Marron's turn now to touch that arm, in wonder at the lack of pain. The wound was there still, like a dark hole ripped unkindly and gaping red at the edges; but the sickly glint of pus had dried to a colourless crust, and the streaks that had warned of evil working within had reduced to a little redness, a little local swelling.

'Others could have done more. If you're careful, though, it should heal now. Come, let's put that bandage back. Fresh air would be better, but we don't want your master asking questions.'

'No, sir,' fervently. 'Please, what am I to tell Sieur Anton? He told me to see the Master Infirmarer . . .'

'Lie to him, Marron. I'm sorry, but you must.'

Marron nodded unhappily. It was a small deception next to the great secret that Rudel had burdened him with, but still it hung upon him, souring the wonder.

Sensing that, perhaps, Rudel said, 'Marron, let me tell you something about Surayon.'

'Sir, I don't want to—'

'If you are to help me – no, that's too fast, I won't assume it, but if I am to ask for your help, you have to know a little, at least. A little of the truth. There have been a great many lies told about us. Lies that justify what has been done to my friend below, and worse things done to others.' Rudel settled himself on the floor, and gestured to Marron to do the same. He sank down cautiously against the opposite wall, cradling his arm against a pain that didn't come.

'When Outremer was won,' Rudel began slowly, 'when the Ekhed were overrun in the south and the Sharai driven back into the desert, it was the King's voice – the Duc de Charelles he was then, before he took the Kingship – it was his voice that divided up the land. His voice against the Church, largely. He had led the army, all the separate armies; he was overlord, he had kept the commanders focused on the great goal, Ascariel. Without him they would have broken apart long before, warred between themselves, seized what land they could and likely lost it all within a year or two as the Sharai tribes picked them off, one by one. A rotten fruit will fall to ruin. But de Charelles held them all together, with the great aid of his friend, the Duc d'Albéry.

'Then he seized Ascariel, and the Church Fathers claimed it for their own as soon as the news reached them. If they had been given the Holy City, they would have taken all Outremer.'

'Would that have been so bad, sir?' It seemed to Marron that the Church Fathers had hegemony over the home-lands, in despite of kings and courts. Pomp belonged to the princes, power to the priests. That was the way of things; even his uncle's lord, the Baron Thivers, deferred to the presbytery whenever his tenants looked to him for judge-ment. No one protested overmuch, beyond a little ritual grumbling when a decision went against them. It worked, he thought; why worry?

'Imagine your preceptor and his like, ruling the Sanctuary Land as they rule this Order. It would have been catastrophe.'

Marron thought about it briefly – and nodded. He'd seen little of Outremer yet, but he had seen Fra' Piet lead his troop against a heretic village, and he had seen the pre-ceptor's justice just last night. This was not, after all, the homelands. He knew that many, perhaps most of the people in this country did not hold to the true faith, as the Order defined it; but the very ground here was still holy to them, as it was to the Church. They still insisted on their right to worship their gods in their way. How long would the preceptor have tolerated that? There had been massacres enough in the early years, before and after the fall of Ascariel; under the rule of the Order, which at this distance was the rule of the Church, there would be massacres still, and many of them. Barren villages, razed temples, deserted towns . . .

'De Charelles had been fighting the bishops all through the campaign, as much as he'd been fighting the Ekhed or the Sharai. There were plenty riding in his train, and they wanted to burn every unbeliever that they passed. He kept them in check until Ascariel, but even so much wasn't easy. Afterwards would have been impossible, if they had been ceded the authority they sought.

'Technically, though, they weren't there as emissaries of the Church Fathers, only as vassals of their temporal lords; so de Charelles summoned a conclave and divided up the territory, without inviting any of the bishops in. By the time the Fathers heard about it, they were far too late to react. The thing was done: de Charelles was King by acclamation, the states of Outremer were established and they none of them belonged to the Church.'

Tallis and Elessi, the northernmost states, the head of the hammer – and Roq de Rançon on the northernmost border between the two: the pivot, the stronghold, the nail that gripped the head.

Below Tallis, Less Arvon; below that Ascariel the state, with Ascariel the city at its heart. Rudel was right, who held Ascariel held Outremer, their hand it was that gripped the hammer. The King's hand it was, and always had been.

Between those two, though, between Less Arvon and Ascariel lay a range of mountains, thrusting like an elbow towards the coast; and in those mountains lay hidden Surayon, the Folded Land, which must have been all but hidden even before it was Folded: buried in its valleys, a tiny state so unlike its sisters, so weak, a runt, a gesture . . .

'He had to placate the Fathers somehow, or they'd have been fomenting rebellion among the faithful just when he needed to look to his borders. He was King; he gave the dukedom of Ascariel to his son Raime, which was almost as good as giving it to the Church. A pious man, even then he listened to his priests more than to his father. Since then, with the King in seclusion – well. There are few Catari remaining in Ascariel, despite all the amnesties, and every temple follows your order of service. Other, older traditions have been denounced, and none would dare revive them.

'The King knew, I think, that this would happen; and he knew that there'd be trouble with Less Arvon. The Duke of Arvon was a fiery man then, and his son the Little Duke is worse. They give no credence to the Church, and little respect to Ascariel. That's why the King created Surayon, and gave the principality to the Duc d'Albéry: to act as a buffer between them, a cool head and a cool voice. Rank without strength, a man both sides could listen to without distrust.

'The Duc d'Albéry had been first squire, then friend, then counsellor to the Duc de Charelles. But de Charelles became the King and went immediately into his seclusion, without warning or explanation; d'Albéry became Princip of Surayon, which brings its own seclusion. Time passes, and men change.

'The Princip was always a curious man. More probing than prayerful, he has been called. Not good at taking things on faith, and always interested in what was new, always asking why. Which might be another reason the

King gave him Surayon, to make an uncomfortable neighbour both north and south. Arvonians are great traditionalists, as the Ascari are religious; perhaps the King thought d'Albéry could be both a peacemaker between them and a thorn in their sides. It makes little sense to my eyes, but the King's mind is a mystery, and not only to me.

'The Princip might have been a bishop himself, if he hadn't been born to land and high position; he had the inclination as a child, he spent some years of his youth in a monastery. He might have been a Church Father himself by now, if it hadn't been for that questioning mind.

'It was that brought him to Outremer, I'm sure, more than loyalty to his friend or service to his God. Especially not service to the God. He made a good soldier, but he hated the war with a passion; he pushed for the amnesty at Conclave, and was first and most thorough in its implementation.

'So Surayon became a haven for displaced Catari, a place of refuge. First state to trade with the Sharai, too. And the Princip talked to all these people: believer, unbeliever or heretic, there were no questions asked at the borders but plenty in the palace. He brought in scholars and friends from the homelands to talk to them also. When the Fathers protested, flirting with heresy they called it, he brought in bishops and priests too – but they were mostly friends of his before they were ordained or acquired rank, and his habits of question are infectious. They were none of them blindly obedient to the commands of the Fathers, nor to the teachings of the Church.

'That was a long generation since. We are anathema to the Church now, and to our neighbours, north and south;

but the Princip protects us, and we go on learning. We *are* heretics, Marron, by your Order's definition: you must understand that. We don't worship your God in your way. Neither any god of the Catari: we are heretics also to the devouts of the Sharai, of the Ekhed, of them all. But the Sharai treat us more kindly than our own people do. We share knowledge, we share trust, we share our children even; and so we can do such as you have seen this morning, some of us. Some can do a great deal more. It's not evil, it's only understanding; and that's Surayon, that's what we are. We will not shy from any question, so long as it leads us towards truth.'

This was the man, Marron struggled to remind himself, who only ten minutes since was urging or ordering Marron to lie for his own protection. Truth must be a flexible concept, in Surayon as elsewhere.

But he thought Rudel was mostly speaking true here. What he'd said was not so different from what the priests said about Surayon, only that they thundered it as blasphemy. The bones at least were the same, though the living spirit they described could not have been more opposite.

And it didn't matter, anyway. True or false, neither image was real, not to Marron, not there in a room at the Roq that day. What was real was his arm, rotten with corruption an hour since, halfway to healthy now; what was real was the man Redmond who called himself Jonson, who lay in blood and filth with broken hands in the cells below; what was real was the ashes of a great fire, the burned bones of children.

Rudel was quiet now, seemingly waiting for him to speak. Marron hesitated, opened his mouth and found his lips unaccountably dry, had to pause to lick them before he tried again.

'You said,' he began, knowing that he damned himself with every word he said and meant to say, 'last night you said that you wanted to rescue your friend.'

'Yes.'

'How can I help?'

It wasn't difficult to collect black habits for disguise. Marron had been ready with excuses, with lies hot on his tongue, but there was no need; the vestry was so busy no one had time to ask questions. Men from several troops were all drawing fresh clothes at once; Marron simply picked three habits from a pile and walked out with them. Rudel lingered, talking to one of the brothers briefly before he followed, back to that convenient storeroom.

With habits thrown on over their other clothes and a spare thrust under Marron's girdle, giving him a shape he'd never owned, with hoods drawn up to hide their faces they walked through the castle, through the courts, through the kitchens quite unstayed.

There was still no guard at the head of the narrow stair, no interest from the brothers at work by the ovens. Marron held his breath a little as they slipped into the shadows of the stairwell, but this time no screams rose up to meet them. Fingers brushed the curve of rock on either side, soft boots made little noise on cautious feet beneath their habits; none the less Marron found himself longing for sandals. Treachers, he thought, should tread more softly than they knew.

At the last turning before the chamber below, just where

a little fugitive lamplight made a visible shadow of Rudel, he stopped. One hand retreated inside the habit, slipping free of the sleeve altogether; Marron guessed it must be fumbling for something Rudel carried inside his everyday clothes.

After a minute, the empty sleeve filled and the hand reappeared. It held something clenched within the fingers now; something that began to glow, to pulse with light as Marron watched, to beat clear and blue with the steady rhythm of what might be Rudel's heartbeat, was far too slow and steady to be his own.

Rudel opened his hand, and it was a blue stone that lay there on his palm, an *ayar*-stone Marron thought, though he had to squint to see. Whether Rudel invested it with that light, or whether he used his skills simply to draw out the stone's own subtleties, Marron couldn't tell. A stone that shone, that was all he knew, something obviously far greater than a sign of faith.

A stone that fell, as Rudel tossed it; but it almost flew, it fell more slowly than it ought, as though the air were honey-thick around it. Struck a step and bounced, higher than a stone should; and the stone sang as it struck, unless it was the stone of the step that was singing.

It rose and fell, struck and bounced and sang again, a different note this time, high and bright and resonating sweetly with the first as it lingered. Marron felt a thrill in his bones at that music, he felt almost transparent in the pulsing light; it was an effort to remember that there were guards below if none above, that they must be alerted, wondering, suspicious. That this sudden, unexpected touch of wonder had made a nonsense of the creeping so quietly down this far . . .

He reached to touch Rudel's sleeve, an unspoken question. The older man raised an arm in response, *wait, and trust*; then, as the glowing stone vanished around the curve of the stair, leaving only its singing light behind as a guide, that same arm gestured slowly, *forward now*.

Marron followed Rudel, his nervousness overridden by the summoning music. Down the last steep steps and into the chamber below, and yes, there were the guards: two brothers standing rapt, entranced, their eyes wide and unblinking, gazing at the stone as it hung impossibly in the air, as the light of it flared and faded and flared again, as the music throbbed and echoed in that small space.

It wasn't only shock or wonder that held them so still. Their faces were quite vacant; it was as though their spirits had been snatched from them, leaving only coarse and empty flesh to occupy their habits as they stood. They seemed to notice nothing when Rudel walked casually between them, into the passage beyond. Marron stared at the stone, as they were staring; and he too felt the call of it, felt his own will drawn forth, draining his muscles and his mind till he was lost almost in the beat and rhythm of the light, of the song . . .

'Marron!' A hand gripped his neck, and shook him gently. He startled, shuddering; turned his head to find Rudel. There was a smile on the man's face but tension beneath, some urgency in his voice as he whispered, 'Come, I need you to show me where my friend lies. Close your eyes, if the *ayar* is too strong for you . . .'

'Yes, sir,' uncertainly. He could close his eyes, but what about his ears? The music called to him, as keenly as the light. He pulled his hood lower over his face for what small protection that could offer and took a step, two difficult steps towards the passage.

And checked, turned, went back; fighting against the summons of the stone, he walked tight-legged and determined to where the oil-lamp burned unregarded in its niche, its gentle yellow light quite lost in the fierce glare of blue.

Marron picked it up, gazing in at its pale flame, using that as a shield against the pervasive, seductive pulse in the room around him.

'Good lad,' Rudel called, his voice soft, barely audible above the high wordless chant of the *ayar*-stone's song. Marron didn't know why he was bothering to be quiet still; he thought thunderclaps and lightning would not call those men back from wherever their lost souls wandered. 'You're not as mazed as you seem, are you?'

Yes, I am, he thought, all but stumbling over the hem of his habit as he tried to walk with his eyes still fixed in the lamp's flame. The stone's song rang in his skull, a chord constantly changing as if it sought, as if it reached to find and draw him back into its spell again. He struggled to focus his swimming mind as his eyes were focused, feeling his way, glad when Rudel's big hand closed on his sleeve and tugged him into the shadows of the passage.

The light and music followed them, but less overpoweringly now; after a dozen paces he risked lifting his eyes from the lamp and saw Rudel laughing at him. There was a kindness in the laughter, though, and something close to admiration in the nod that followed.

'Well done. And I'm sorry, I'd forgotten that you would be as vulnerable as they. It takes a strong mind to fight off the lure of an *ayar*-stone awoken.'

'What of the penitents?' Marron asked in a whisper, his anxious eyes darting to the doors of the cells.

'There are none. They were all released yesterday: a special dispensation, by order of the preceptor. They were lucky; his need for men overruled the need for discipline.'

It was true, the cells were empty. Or their doors were closed, at least; he didn't open any, to check inside.

Only at the end of the passage was the one door still bolted, speaking of its prisoner within. Marron reached for the bolt with his free hand, forgetful for a moment, remembering his injury only when Rudel forestalled him with a touch.

'I told you to be careful with that arm.'

'It doesn't hurt, sir.' *Not any more.*

'Even so, you should rest it. And keep it hidden for a few days, if you can. Don't let your master see how much improved it is. Now, the stone will hold those men till I release them and they'll remember nothing, they'll only be surprised how quickly the morning has passed them by; but someone else may come, so fast as we can, lad, though I fear that'll not be fast . . .'

Rudel worked the bolt as he spoke, easing it back from its bracket. He pulled the door open and grunted in surprise, facing a black blankness.

'What . . .?'

'It's just a curtain, sir.'

'Oh.' Rudel pushed through, with Marron following. The cell was in darkness, no witchlight from the prisoner today; Marron raised the lamp high, and the flickering glow showed them all the walls of the cell, lined with the instruments of question.

Again, Rudel grunted. 'Where—?'

'Over there, sir.' Just a pile of rags, it was hard to see that there was a man among them. Rudel muttered something under his breath, which might have been a curse or a spell; when he touched the lamp it flared far brighter, an unnatural white light driving sharp-edged shadows around the cell.

Then the big man moved, crossing the cell in quick strides to fall on his knees beside the stirring prisoner.

'Redmond.' No hiding the name now, no point to it; Marron was as committed, as guilty as he. 'Redmond, how bad—?'

The man on the mattress pushed himself up slowly onto one elbow, with a clink of chain. The rags fell away, answer enough; Marron heard Rudel's breath hiss from his mouth, matching the prisoner's own harsh, effortful breathing.

'You, is it? And my little friend.' His voice was weaker than yesterday, even; Marron put the lamp down, making shadows dance, and poured water into the goblet that had been set again just out of reach.

Rudel took the goblet, and held it for the man to drink; shaking, Redmond spilt as much as he swallowed. Then, 'This is foolish, Rudel,' he said.

'No. This is necessary. What, should I leave you to the tender brethren's care? Should I stroll contentedly about my business overhead, and give never a thought to all your pains? Or to your future?'

'I have no future. Which being true, the more reason why you should not risk yourself. Nor strangers, who don't know what they chance,' with a glance across at Marron.

'He knows enough. Enough to choose. Young men were

always idiots. Remember? But you have as much future as any of us, Redmond.'

'Or as little,' dryly snorted.

'That, too. If we're not here, though, they can do us little harm.'

'And how will you remove us, shall we just walk out through the gate?'

'Better than that, we can ride. You and I, in brothers' garb. A party leaves this afternoon for Elessi. A mixed party, knights and brothers and private men-at-arms, to guard a pair of girls. The Shadow's daughter, and her companion. Had you heard?'

'I heard she was on her way. Not here.'

'Well, here she is; and sent away now, since the Sharai raided two nights since.'

'Did they?' That struck home, it seemed, far sharper than the other news. 'Hasan?'

'It's said so, yes.'

'Well. He failed, I presume.'

'This time. Thanks to Marron.'

'Indeed?' Another glance, and this time the hint of a smile to follow, in so far as his twisted mouth could manage that. 'But this is politics, and young Marron is impatient. I am sorry, Rudel, you were explaining your plan, I think?'

'That's it. This party is put together hurriedly; the talk earlier was that it would leave tomorrow. Now it is today. There will be a deal of confusion; it will not be hard for you and I to hide ourselves among them. Then we ride out, we slip away at first camp, and no one here knows that you have gone; not till tomorrow at least, and I will leave something that should confound them for a day or two longer.'

'A simulacrum. Good. Rudel, that is an attractively simple plan.'

'But?'

'But I cannot walk.'

'Ah. Your feet, is it?'

'As my hands are. Neither can I ride.'

'Well. I can do something for those. For the moment . . .'

'Not for a day's ride, Rudel. Nor even half a day. Nor for the flight after that. I am dead, boy, I have accepted that and so should you. The best kindness you could do me now would be to help me cheat their questioners.'

'*No!* It is not, it cannot be that bleak . . .' Rudel thought scowlingly; Marron watched him, watched the prisoner, watched the door. And took a moment's pleasure, though only a moment's, to hear Rudel called 'boy'.

Then, 'We will still make the attempt,' Rudel declared. 'I can help you out of here, to a place of hiding. Then, this girl is Julianne de Rance, she must have baggage; she must have a baggage-wagon. So will the knights, those lordlings are fussy about their dress. Or there are traders travelling with the escort, wagons again. One way or another, we will find a way to move you. In a box, if need be.'

'You're a fool, Rudel. Better to leave me, I'm quite prepared to die.'

'I'm not prepared to let you.'

'Stupid. It will happen; it will be here if you leave me, it may yet be here if you try to take me. Then like as not it would be you too, and you must not risk yourself.'

'I'll be careful,' Rudel promised, laughing. Fluent liars they were, Marron thought, these men from Surayon.

'Sir,' he murmured, too soft for either man to hear. Tried again more loudly, more boldly. 'Sir . . .'

'Yes, Marron?'

'Someone will see us and ask questions, if we carry him through the kitchens.'

'We won't need to carry him. As with your arm, so with his feet; I can heal somewhat, and hide the pain awhile.'

'Yes, sir,' because he'd known that already, he only wanted to have the man about it.

'Ah. You think I should stop arguing with my stubborn friend here and do what good I can, is that right?'

Of course it was right, and of course he could not say so directly, except by a fierce flush. 'There is, there is danger, sir, as long as we are here. You said so . . .'

'The questioners came early today,' the man Redmond said from his pallet. 'That's why I'm so weak. I couldn't light a firefly just now, Marron. But they won't be back till tomorrow, and no one else visits me. They probably won't be back,' correcting himself swiftly. 'Even so, the boy's right. Set on, Rudel. Don't worry with the most of me, just work on my feet. The rest I can bear.'

For how long was a question Marron dared not ask aloud, and neither he thought did Rudel. The man looked in no condition to be stowed in a box or hidden on a baggage-wagon; but men could endure much, when death was the alternative. Even a man who screamed so much where it could do no harm to scream, might bear the same pain in silence where that might save his life.

Rudel pulled the rags away from Redmond's body. The ankles were shackled as well as the wrists, Marron saw. That would stop prisoners reaching for water with their feet, he supposed; then he saw the feet themselves, and thought the shackles quite unnecessary.

Cruel boots, that man must have been wearing. He wondered what even Rudel's magic could do, against crushed and twisted bones and mangled flesh. *Not much*, had to be the answer. It hadn't healed his own wound, after all, only sapped the poison. If there were poison in those feet, it was the least of all the harm done to them.

Even so, Rudel took them into his lap, held them in soothing, smoothing hands and began to croon under his breath. The fierce light dimmed, letting dull yellow lamp-light fill the cell again. All Rudel's focus, Marron realised, all his attention was on his work; there was nothing to spare now for better seeing, and no need to see more than he had already.

Marron let his eyes drift around the walls, trying at first to make out what each separate instrument was for and how it worked. Learning too much, understanding too well – *there, that wooden box with the wedges, that must be the boot that wrecked those feet. One at a time, too, that's worse. Take it apart, build it afresh around each foot in turn. Let the man see, show him how it works. Then adjust to fit. Adjust the foot, that is. With those wedges, driven home by hammering, look, there's the hammer . . .*

Enough of that, very quickly. He slipped over to the curtain and beyond it, to stand with the door half-shut and his head peering around, watching the passage.

Watching the end of the passage, if he was honest: where blue light still beat to the rhythm of Rudel's blood, from where music still sounded, thin at this distance but still distinct, still striking home. The stone at least was not weakened by Rudel's distraction. Perhaps its power was inherent, then, and not endowed . . .

How long he stood there, he had no idea. Time was impossible of judgement anyway, here where they were buried so far from sunlight; and he lost the touch of his own body, even, knowing nothing but the pulsing call, the song's high summons until there was again a hand on his shoulder, shaking him, jerking him back into himself.

'Marron,' Rudel said softly, 'I can use your help now.'

'I was,' *I was caught by the stone again, not so strong as you named me after all*, 'I was watching, in case anyone came . . .' He could lie too, why not?

'I know.' *I know what you were doing*, Rudel's smile said, *or what was being done to you.*

Marron went back into the cell at Rudel's heels to find Redmond sitting up on his mattress, gaunt and pale still but looking better by far than he had, when? When Marron left the cell: ten minutes ago, an hour ago, whenever.

'We need to make a simulacrum,' Rudel said, 'something to confuse whoever comes, so that for a day or two they think they still have Redmond in their chains. I can do this; but first I must open those shackles, without breaking them. I can do that too, but it will take time. What I want you to do, Marron, is collect whatever you can find in the cell here that could be man-shaped, or any part of a man. Metal or wood or rag, it doesn't matter; I can cloak the truth of it, but I need something to work on. Pretend you're making a poppet, for your sister to play with. It needn't look real, or anything close to real. Man-size, that's all that counts. You know how children pretend.'

'Er, yes, sir . . .'

He'd never had a sister, but Aldo did; they'd made toys for her, figures scratched together from twigs and straw that had delighted her past reason.

This was different, though, hugely so. He looked around, trying not to see purposes now but only shape; and still felt stupid, expected the men's laughter as he reached for giant tongs that were hanging on one wall.

A brazier stood below them. Heated, they could tear a man's flesh from his bones; Redmond might know that too well, by the fresh bubbled scars on his chest. But never mind knowing. They were an arm's length or longer, and jointed; they might make a pair of legs for a foolish figure.

There were wooden staves for arms, so much was easy, and a great iron ball so heavy he could barely lift it, that could be a head. A body to join them all together, that was not so simple; he gazed, thought, finally scooped up a double armful of the rags that made Redmond's bedding and his clothing both. He laid out the largest, heaped the rest atop it and sat down to knot them all together.

A glance across as he worked showed that neither man was watching. Rudel had wrapped both hands around one of the shackles that held Redmond's wrists; Marron thought he was staring at it, staring through his own fingers at the crude iron ring. Except that his eyes were closed, he could be seeing nothing. It was Redmond who was staring, at the top of his friend's head. Could these men see into each other's skulls, to read their thoughts?

Marron turned back to his own task, something he

could do and was determined to do well. *At least let them not laugh, not that . . .*

Knots and twists of rag: he bound the tongs to the loose body he'd tied together, and then each of the two staves that were to be its arms. The iron ball was harder, he couldn't see how to fix that to the rest so that even a child could pretend the figure was whole: *this poppet's been beheaded*, he thought, and swallowed a tight little giggle.

And shook the stupidity out of his head, and looked around again; and saw rope, a thin coil of it in one corner. Fetched that and set about weaving a simple net, looking up only when a metallic click snatched at his attention.

That shackle was open, he saw, though he couldn't see or guess how. Locked or riveted, either way it should have resisted the force of a man's hands, and Rudel hadn't even been trying to force it.

Magic, he thought, without even a shiver of wonder any more, and turned back to his weaving and knotting.

When he was done, he wrapped the net around the ball – *hair and a beard*, he thought, stupid again, close to giggling again – and tied all the ends to the rag body of his grotesque poppet. He couldn't play with it, he couldn't so much as make it sit up, the iron ball was far too heavy; but lying down as it was, it looked – well, actually it looked ridiculous and nothing remotely like a man, but he'd done what had been asked of him. That, at least . . .

There had been other sounds from the corner where the pallet lay, where the men were: clicks and rattles, murmuring voices. When he looked, he saw that Redmond was free at last of his chains. More, he was moving with Rudel's help, struggling slowly to his feet.

That should not be possible, even on this most impossible of days. The man's feet were still wrenched far from human shape; Marron ached in sympathy, just looking. He couldn't imagine the crippling agony of such ruin, far less the agony of standing on them.

But Redmond was standing, and showing no pain. He did lean on Rudel's arm, but Marron thought that was only for balance, for support against a dizzying weakness.

'Good,' Rudel said to him. 'How does it feel?'

'It doesn't feel at all,' said softly, said almost with a chuckle.

'Well, you'll suffer for that later; but it should see you out of here now, and on your own feet. Now, Marron. Good,' again, as his eyes ran over Marron's creation where it lay on the floor. 'That's perfect. Can you lift it over onto the mattress?'

'Yes, sir.' Or not lift, exactly, but lift and drag, slowly, with great care against the fragility of the knots. One stave-arm did slip free of its bindings; Marron flushed, muttered, gathered it up and forced it further into the mess of rags, tied it in more tightly.

'Marron, I said to rest that arm, remember?'

'Sir, you said to make a man-sized poppet for you.' *Remember?* – but he wasn't up to insolence of that degree. Not yet.

'All right. But be careful. If it bleeds again, it could poison again. Now come here and take my place, help to keep Redmond on his feet.'

*

Not a heavy task, that: the man was lighter than the poppet without its head or felt so, bird-hollow bones and no flesh.

'Your arm?' Redmond asked, and there was more strength in his voice than anywhere in his body, and his voice was thread-thin and empty.

'A wound, sir,' and Marron shook back his sleeve to show the bandage; he had seen so much of this man's pain, he owed that much at least. 'It won't heal . . .'

'It's not been given a chance to heal,' Rudel grunted from where he hunched across the figure on the mattress, looping shackles over staves and tongs as though they were wrists and ankles, as though the slack iron gripped tightly. 'Torn open, ripped open again and again, at least once deliberately, not to let it heal.'

'You, uh, he, uh, Rudel has made it better, though . . .'

'For the moment. Like Redmond, you will pay later; and both of you deserve it. How could you let this happen to you, old fool?'

'Some busy steward knew me. Can you credit it? Forty years on, I was playing trader with wagon and ribbons and no beard to my chin and still the idiot stands there stammering, "The Red Earl, Redmond of Corbonne, oh, sir, call out your guard . . ." What could I do?'

'You could have killed them all,' Rudel murmured, in a tone that denied his own words, *of course you couldn't*.

Marron believed both, that the old man was capable of it but never would. Marron, frankly, knew himself to be gaping. Redmond of Corbonne? The Red Earl, the hero of the great war declared heretic, renegade ten years later, one of the few Surayonnaise anathematised by name and known by name even back in the homelands – the Red Earl, this patchwork starveling creature?

Marron held a legend in his arms and did not, could not believe it.

Which Redmond knew, could clearly read on his face. The dull eyes glittered for a moment, as he whispered, 'Never mind, lad. All dreams die. Now watch, this might amuse you. Don't be scared . . .'

He nodded towards Rudel and the figure; Marron wrenched his head that way, though not his giddy thoughts, not yet. This was the Red Earl: a master, a monster in battle, who had ridden his horse knee-deep in blood through the streets of Ascariel, who had shielded the King himself from the spear of the High Imam on the steps of the great temple and then hewn the Imam's head from his shoulders; a great and heretical monster fit to frighten children with, who had been corrupted by his overlord in the Folded Land, who had with his own hands killed every last true priest trapped in that unhappy land when the evil Princip closed it off from the world by his wicked charms . . .

Scared? Why would he be scared, who had seen so much magic done today and other days? Marron frowned, and watched more closely what Rudel was doing.

Rudel was kneeling with the figure, that absurd poppet in his arms like an overgrown child or a sick companion. He had the great head of the thing cradled against his neck, somehow holding the weight of that iron ball between shoulder and chin; he was whispering to it, while his hands stroked all over, wooden arms and body of rags and the long metal legs of it.

As Marron watched, he spat onto the rough iron and rope of its head; and then he let it go, he pulled himself away and stood up.

The figure stayed sitting as he had left it, a mockery in chains. The head should have fallen then, the whole thing should have toppled over and torn itself apart, and did not. It sat like a man, leaning its weight on one arm; and when it did move it tried to stand, it tried to follow Rudel.

And was stopped by its shackles, which should have fallen from its limbs and did not, though they had no flesh to cleave to.

Marron gasped. Only Redmond's grip on his arm kept him from stepping back, only the Red Earl's whisper of a chuckle stopped him from pulling free and running. *See? I knew you'd be scared*, the chuckle said. Marron shuddered and stood firm.

'Well?' That was Rudel, and the question was aimed at him.

'Sir, you said, you said it was to fool whoever came. It does not,' his voice dried, so that he had to cough and lick his lips and try again, 'it does not look like the Earl Redmond to me . . .' Nor like any living thing, human or otherwise.

'No. Not yet, and not to you. Neither will it. But bring him close, Marron, help him over here.'

The last thing Marron wanted to do was to get any closer to that animated thing, where it was standing hunched over, at the limits of its chains and pulling. But Rudel's eyes were on him, and the echo of the Red Earl's chuckle was in his head yet; he forced his reluctant feet forward, while a cold rank sweat prickled all his skin.

Closer and closer, slower and slower but closer still, almost to touching distance; if it weren't for the shackles, the thing could reach and touch him. Not that, but Redmond did reach out and touch it, lightly on what should have been its elbow; then he drew his hand back, spat on his fingers and reached to touch again.

'Now,' Rudel said softly.

And now the thing changed, or seemed to. Marron could still see tongs and staves, but he could see also a shimmer around them, a glassy transparent flesh. The soft and greasy padding of its body acquired hard ridges of ribs and a glimmer of skin, though that was all seeming, it was rags yet. Rags and illusion. Even the head, that impossible weight balanced on what could not possibly hold it, even that cold iron had the image of a face across its net of rope, hints of hair and beard. And yes, that might be Redmond's face, if anyone's . . .

But it wasn't, not anyone's at all; this was a thin and useless magic, it couldn't fool a blind man in the dark. Marron opened his mouth to say so, if more politely, and was forestalled.

'You see what you expect to see, Marron lad,' Rudel told him. 'You made it, you know what it is. You see a hint of the charm, but only a hint because your mind knows what lies beneath. Everyone sees what they expect to see. The guards, the questioners expect to see Redmond, and they will. For a while, they will. Even when they apply their instruments, they'll see and hear what they expect, because nothing else is possible to them. They *know* they have him here, they know they burn and mutilate a man; and so they will.

'Now. Two brothers came down here; I don't believe anyone was watching, but still three should not walk out together. You go up first, Marron. Give me that spare habit, go back to the storeroom and leave yours there, and then be about your duties. And thank you.'

'Yes, sir. Er, what happens next?'

'For you? Nothing. You are your master's squire, nothing more than that. Say nothing, try to remember nothing. Pray for us, perhaps, if you do pray, if you must. Otherwise, I hope that the next you know is gossip in the servants' hall, when at last they notice that one or other of us is missing. There will be a deal of disruption in the castle after that, and I suppose they will think to track along the road to Elessi, but I don't believe they'll find us once we're gone.'

'Earl Redmond won't go far, sir, not on his feet . . .' Even with two days' grace, say. Mounted men would catch them in a spare hour, Marron thought.

'No; but if we can't run, we can hide. The men of Surayon are well-practised in evasion, Marron.' *We have hidden our whole country, remember?*

Really Marron didn't want to leave, he felt he was being cut out of the story half-told. Rudel was right, though; he shouldn't linger with the men like a conspirator. Let them go, let them get away, forget he was ever a part of their escape. Otherwise it might be himself taking a turn in this cell, facing the questioners, naked and afraid. He thought he would do more than scream; he thought he would betray them all, if any one of those instruments were used on him.

He kept his head low and held his breath as he sidled

through the kitchens, but no man showed any interest. As far as he could tell, he wasn't seen either going into the storeroom as a monk or coming out as a squire; and as a squire, again he attracted no notice at all until he reached Sieur Anton's chamber.

Where he was greeted with a bellow of righteous fury, 'Where in all the hells on this earth have you been, Marron?'

'Sieur, you sent me to the infirmary.' Quite true, he did.

'That was hours ago!'

'Yes, sieur. There are many men there, hurt worse than me . . .' Also true, and equally as deceptive; and then quickly, before the knight asked a question he couldn't misdirect, he said, 'Have you been looking for something, sir?'

The travelling-chest stood open and half-empty, with heaps of clothing scattered across the bed and the floor.

'Yes, I've been looking for you. Pack for me, Marron. For us both.'

'Sieur?'

'The lady Julianne rides to Elessi today—'

'Yes, sieur.'

'You knew?'

'Gossip, sieur. Among the squires.'

'I thought you'd been to the infirmary? Well, ne'er mind. Word moves faster than the wind, in this place. Did the gossip say who escorts her?'

'Her own men, sieur,' repeating Rudel's words while his mind raced, 'and a troop of brothers, and knights beside . . .?'

'Knights and their squires,' Sieur Anton said briskly. 'Pack; then run down to the stables. It will be a dreadful scrimmage, especially with the lack of stable-boys to help. Every knight's man will be out to see his master's needs are serviced, first and best. Be sure that you succeed. I shall want one of the destriers, Alembert I think, ready an hour after prayers; and you will need a mule. There will be a wagon for the chest. If you can't carry it alone – and don't, don't even try – ask another squire to help you. That's all.'

'Yes, sieur. Uh, should I pack the mail shirt, or—?'

'Don't be a fool, Marron. This isn't a jaunting-party. I shall wear the mail.'

15

A Snare in Shadow and Sun

Julianne had come one last time to the midday prayers, and had insisted that Elisande come too: 'We've got to look good. Virtuous young women, obedient to the God, the Church and our parents.' That had won her no more than a snort, but she'd gone on determinedly, 'We don't want to give them any reason to doubt us, anything that would make them watch more carefully than they will in any case.'

'They will in any case,' Elisande had iterated. 'No matter how pure and good we seem to be. They're delivering the young baron's wife, the countess-to-be; you'll have his men about you and all these sworn brothers, all of them with the scent of Sharai blood hot in their nostrils still; what else are they going to be but watchful? That's what they're *for*. Going to service today won't make them any less so.'

'Well, it might,' Julianne had said, knowing the weakness of her own arguments but convinced none the less that she was right, that any small allaying gesture would help. She still didn't see how they would ever slip away;

there she must rely on Elisande, who was smilingly relaxed about it, *not a worry, don't trouble yourself, they'll all be looking the wrong way as we pass. You wouldn't believe how many wrong ways there are, that a man could be looking . . .*

'Please, Elisande?' Julianne had said at last. 'Maybe it's unnecessary—'

'Absolutely it's unnecessary,' from her friend, which was when she knew that she had won.

'—But please? Because I ask it, if you can't see any better reason? Because I think I ought to go, and I don't want to go alone . . .?'

That was insistence, cloaked by diplomacy; and at that appeal, Elisande had finally subsided with a nod.

So they had come, and had found Blaise also in the gallery, already on his knees with his bare head bowed; he'd looked as though he had been there some time, as though he had come to pray privately before ever the bell had called the brothers and their visitors to worship.

Elisande had stretched out a hand to brush imaginary dust from his shoulders, *see how long this good man's been at his prayers?*

A nudge, a stern glare that had threatened to dissolve into a giggle; Julianne had grabbed her friend's shoulder, gripped it tightly, tried to pretend that she was simply pushing Elisande into her place. And had failed utterly, to judge by the sparkling grin she received in return; and had given up, and bitten down on the back of her own hand hard enough to leave white marks behind, until the resurgent giggles subsided. And then had wanted to take Elisande's hand, simply to do the same to her; but that deceiving girl had been already kneeling at the balustrade, as pious-seeming as Blaise himself, *this is what you wanted, isn't it?*, and there had been nothing Julianne could do but join her.

Afterwards, Blaise stood when they stood, and stepped aside to let them leave first. Seeing his cap gripped tightly in his hands, thinking how many of the brothers and knights below had knelt and prayed with their hoods thrown back, she wondered vaguely what had come of Master Fulke's great mission; she'd heard no more of it, since that first thundering sermon.

Well, thundering sermons had that effect more often than not, especially on young and bullish men. A surge in the soul, an answering cry, a fire that burned for a night – and then the cool bleak light of morning, the drudgeries of duty and the fire burned down to ash. Preaching rarely lasted. Even the famous sermons that had ultimately led to all of this, the great call to arms in the homelands a lifetime since, even those had been only the key that opened the gate to let the people loose. According to her father, at least. Too many younger sons landless, ambitious and bored, he'd said: they'd seized the priests' sermons for their own excuse, as a chance for rewards far greater than the God's content. Not fine words that had kept them marching and fighting through scorch and freeze, disaster, starvation and disease.

Hot enthusiasm had faded, perhaps, or else was being turned to cold and careful plans; or had been forgotten altogether, perhaps, with the Sharai raiding and the countryside to scour, herself to be escorted safely on. An order such as the Ransomers needed an enemy; perhaps that had been Fulke's true mission, to give them unity and purpose, and this sudden rising of the old enemy had driven out any need of a new. Surayon might be safe for another generation, if the Sharai came back . . .

'Not so long a rest as we had thought, sergeant,' she said. 'I trust your men are not too disappointed?' The castle likely offered little in the way of recreation, but more at least of comfort than the dusty road. If she knew soldiers, they'd have been glad of that.

'My men have not been resting, my lady,' he answered, with a touch almost of outrage in his voice, as though she had offered interference and insult both. 'I have had them drilling with the brothers, every day since we arrived.'

'Of course you have.' If he wanted an apology, he could look for it in her tone; she would not give him the words. But if she thought she knew soldiers, she should remember that they had sergeants too. In this case a sergeant who was blatantly disappointed, who would have liked to respond to Master Fulke's call and go riding against the heretics of the Folded Land; who would be doubly disappointed – if she knew sergeants, if she knew Blaise at all – that he'd had no chance either to fight against the Sharai. 'Well, at least they'll see Elessi sooner than we expected yesterday. We'll all be glad of that,' she said, sowing more seeds of deception.

'Yes, my lady. Shall I send someone to help you with your packing?'

'No need for that. Elisande and I have seen to it.' Blaise had been shocked from the first day, that she'd brought no female servants with her. There'd been women along the way, happy to do her laundry for the sake of a few small coins, but it had still offended his sense of what was right. He'd been constantly anxious, she thought, that she might ask some unsuitable service of his men. She'd almost yielded to the temptation a time or two, just for the pleasure of seeing his face. 'I'm sure the brothers will bring my chests down, when the wagon is ready for them.'

One of her chests was actually a little lighter than it should be. The gowns she and Elisande wore yesterday had been given to the village women to be washed, and were not yet returned. It was no great loss; they'd have been spotted still, most likely: it took the hand of a mistress launderer to wash blood from linen without leaving a stain. And she had gowns enough and to spare. Let the village girls have the good of them, if they could find an occasion to wear such things or a market to sell them in.

She and Elisande went back to the guest chamber one last time, where they found the usual light midday meal set out for them. After they'd eaten they rested, or Julianne did, or at least she lay down and pretended. Elisande stood at the window, stiff and silent; facing her failure, Julianne thought, still without knowing where the failure lay. For herself, she was preoccupied with what lay ahead. The desert, the Sharai, her father: all daunting, and such a veil of confusion obscuring the journey and the point of it. Her father in danger, and she could save him, the djinni had said – *though it might be better if you did not*, it had said that also – but that foretelling had been granted her only as an inducement, encouragement to go. It was not the purpose. *Marry where you must* – but it was the Baron Imber she must marry, and she would not find him among the Sharai.

She didn't understand, she could make no sense of it; but she would go, for her father's sake, as much to defy as to obey the djinni. If she, if they could slip away from their escort unnoticed, and evade the search that must follow. They'd stand a better chance on horseback, Merissa's speed would serve Julianne well; but she couldn't outpace even the heavy destriers of the knights if she were double-loaded, and they had no mount for Elisande. Besides, taking a horse from the lines would make the escape far more diffi-cult, well-nigh impossible. No, best to go afoot, cover what ground they could and then hide up, hide and hope. Elisande knew the hills and the ways of the hills, that was to their advantage. And it would be hard territory for trackers, worse with the dust in the wind. They had a chance, at least. Perhaps the djinni would watch over them, it was so keen to see them on their way . . .

So she lay, and pondered, and had little rest; then a brother came, hunched and puffing heavily from the stairs, to say that the wagon was ready for their baggage, and the litter was ready for themselves – *your gracious presences* he said, but *the baggage of your bodies* he meant or seemed to mean, from the way he kept his hood up and his face down, avoiding the corruption of any exchange of eyes – and the preceptor himself was there to bid them farewell, and would they please hurry?

Not that he said that last either, but it was very much implicit in his bowing and ushering motions.

On the landing outside another brother waited to help with the chests; again he hid his face, but he was a scrawny figure of a man, she thought he had been leaning against the wall for support the moment before she emerged. Well, let him struggle with the weight of her goods, it would be fit retribution for his prejudice . . .

Down the stair and across the court with Elisande, down the long narrow ramp to the stable-yard; and here indeed was the preceptor as promised, and the much-cursed palanquin with her faithful bearers standing by, and remembering the steep and terrifying drop to the plain she was glad to see them there.

'Your grace, this is kind of you, when you must have so much else on your mind.'

'Nothing supersedes the proper courtesies to guests, Lady Julianne. I would allow nothing to do so in any case, when they have been so thoughtful and generous as yourself.'

Proper courtesies indeed; all this was second nature to them both. As they exchanged good wishes with gently mannered tongues, her eyes above her veil were busy surveying all the activity in the cobbled yard: the traders who were taking advantage of the escort to accompany her to Elessi, as they thought; that escort itself, brothers and knights and their squires, their horses and their baggage-train. Chaos it could have been, in Marasson it would have been; here it was disciplined chaos at least, noisy but organised.

At last the formalities of her leave-taking were satisfied, on both sides. She curtseyed one final time to the preceptor, he bowed and handed her into the palanquin; Elisande followed with a minimal curtsey of her own, and pulled the curtain down at her back.

The noise flowed up around them, horses and men

passing, heading towards the gate; Julianne heard d'Escrivey suddenly bellow above the clamour, sounding at the very end of his patience.

'Marron! Where have you been skulking?'

'Sieur,' into that sudden silence that always falls around a furious man in public, 'a brother asked me to help carry the ladies' baggage . . .'

'Indeed? And did I not ask you, command you even, to give that arm *rest*? Are you stupid, as well as wilful . . .?'

Any further exchange was lost to her, in a sudden rattle of hooves. The boy Marron was never out of trouble, it seemed. Those brothers must have grabbed him as he passed; he was too young, too new to his role as squire to refuse politely, even despite his wounded arm. Well, he'd learn. Under d'Escrivey's scathing tongue, doubtless he'd learn quickly.

The litter jerked and lifted; Julianne settled back against the cushions, finding herself glad that those two were in the escort. The knight was a knowing charmer, the boy an innocent one; she enjoyed the company of both.

Then she remembered she'd have little enough time to enjoy that company, and might have sunk into anxiety again except that Elisande beside her picked up a flask, uncorked it, sloshed, sniffed and unexpectedly beamed.

'Surely not?'

'Yes, indeed. A parting gift, from the preceptor who will miss you so very much. But this really is kind of him.'

No, not that; merely practised. She'd have done as much herself. She was extremely glad, though, that he had done it.

'My lady,' Elisande at her most graciously subservient,

'may I pour you a morsel of monks'-wine, as we know it here?'

'Are there goblets?'

'There are. Two.'

'Then yes, thank you. And will you join me?'

'Lady, I will, by your esteemed favour.'

As the curtains masked the drop itself, the *jereth* helped to mask her fear of it; but only somewhat, and only from herself. The litter rocked and swayed, they struggled to keep their goblets level, not to spill the precious little that tipped and ran within the bowls; and as the curtains swung away sometimes from the litter's side to remind her of the fall, how far it was, how little held her back, so Elisande's laughter and the bittersweet taste on her lips and tongue were still not always enough, sometimes it all peeled back to leave her naked.

Before they'd reached bottom Elisande had an arm round her shoulders, tighter than friendship, and was saying, 'What is it, Julianne, why are you so afraid?'

'Afraid? I'm not afraid, don't be stupid, I don't know what you mean . . .'

'Of course not; but why?'

A sigh, and, 'Give me some more *jereth*, and I'll tell you.'

'Finish what you have first, your hand is shaking. I'll not have you spilling this, you don't appreciate how rare it is.'

Not so. She appreciated how rare it tasted, and more: the power of it to draw her mind down to this simple act of sip and swallow, how the flavour of it filled her and possessed her so that for long moments from the first sharp touch on the tongue to the slow fading sweetness in the throat there was nothing else, nothing that mattered, only this. Now there was rare indeed, anything that could make her forget herself, her father, this foul descent . . .

She swallowed obediently, and felt the hot gold-and-green of it all the way down to her stomach. Elisande allowed her a dribble more, which she only gazed into: blood-dark it was and flecked with darkness, the colours of the herbs long lost in the berries' juices.

Then, 'I fell from a roof, once,' she said shortly, to Elisande's expectant silence. 'High places, long drops – they've scared me ever since. Nothing feels solid, when you can see what lies beneath.'

After a moment, Elisande laughed. 'Don't go to the Sharai, Julianne. They won't welcome you, not if that's your idea of a story told.'

'I don't like to talk about it.' Nor to remember the falling in the dark, how she hadn't screamed even then, how she'd bitten her tongue so deep to stop it; how the stars had spun about her, each of them wanting to watch her down-coming.

And after, how she'd never climbed again: how she'd tunnelled rather, how she'd become a creature of streams and cellars, turning her back on the light and air of the high walls and the rooftops. That especially, she didn't like to talk or think about.

Elisande sighed. 'Well, come to the Sharai, then, Julianne. No towers, no roofs. No heights, except at Rhabat; and you must go there, but you needn't climb, except inside. Just don't look out of the windows. And if they can't teach you to be comfortable up high, perhaps they'll teach you how to be comfortable inside a tale, whether it's your own or someone else's. Then I'll ask you what you were doing on the roof, who you were with and who you were chasing, or who was chasing you.'

'I won't tell you. I'm sorry, but— Elisande, I've never even told my *father* . . .'

For a moment, the other girl's eyebrows said she was impressed, as she was supposed to be; then she lost it, her face stiffening suddenly. 'Julianne, I've never told my father anything important, not since I was a child. No one does, do they? No one should, at any rate. Fathers are for hiding things from. Friends are for sharing with, at least the stories after.'

Julianne shook her head; she'd never had that kind of friend. *Nor that kind of father*, she thought, surprising herself with just a hint of regret. Daughter of the King's Shadow was a role, a position for which her father had made the rules and she'd grown into them like a well-trained sapling, bending to order and yielding as much fruit as she could bear. She'd never thought of keeping secrets from her father, until she had to do it; ever since it had been a burden of guilt to her, a silent betrayal and an extra reason for obedience thereafter.

On level ground at last, where dusty track merged with dusty plain, Elisande recorked the flask of *jereth* just as they heard hooves, a single horse cantering up to the palanquin, slowing down.

'A secret,' Elisande said. 'Practise with your sergeant, pretend he's your father; he stands in his place, does he not?'

He had before, when they were on the road to the Roq; now she thought not. She thought that whoever commanded the contingent of Ransomers commanded the caravan, which meant he commanded her and Blaise also.

'My lady?'

'Yes, sergeant.'

'I have spoken with Master Sharrol. He believes we might make eight miles today, if we pushed on till dark; but there is a convenient village at six miles' distance, where you can be decently housed and the men may camp. There is water and perhaps a little forage for the cattle also. He believes we should stop when we arrive there, and I agree with him.'

'Master Sharrol commands, does he?'

'Yes, my lady,' with reproach in his voice, as though she should have known that. 'He is deputy weapons master to Master Ricard.'

Which meant a lot, clearly, to Blaise, and carried some little of the same weight with her. Everyone who knew the history of Outremer knew the name of Ricard; no guarantee that his deputy would be an equal man to him, but at least a likelihood that he would be of the same type. A certainty, surely, that he would be more than fit to see a caravan such as this safe to its destination. Alas . . .

'Very well. Thank you,' and she didn't even pretend to give her own consent to the arrangement. Let them think, oh, *please* let them think that she was content to have all ordered for her, no hint of rebellion, not a trace, not a question of it in their self-contented minds . . .

The dust rose and the sun sank, in the world outside their curtains; Julianne felt cocooned in swathing softness but no, not safe, not that. She was not. She had to break out of this and fly, like any imago: that was the opposite of safe.

'How will we ever—?'

'We will. Trust me. I have some craft in moving quietly, unseen.'

So in truth did she herself, though city streets and palaces were her habitat. Out here, she'd follow Elisande's lead. For that at least she could be grateful, that she didn't have to go alone . . .

Unexpectedly, the gentle swaying of the palanquin was stayed; after a moment, the bearers set it down. Elisande knelt forward and peered through the gauze, then shook her head.

'Wherever it is we're stopping for the night, this isn't it. Just a pass. But no one's moving . . .'

Julianne nudged her aside, to look herself. A wide pass or a narrow valley: hills rose on either side. The traders with their ox-wagons were all at the rear; as the dust-cloud cleared she saw Blaise's men on foot ahead of her, and beyond them a column of black and white on horseback, brothers and knights. There was confusion at the head of the column, but she couldn't see what had caused it. Not trouble, she thought, not an ambush. She couldn't imagine what else would halt them, though. Not the djinni again, surely; other traffic, perhaps, causing an obstruction if the road narrowed further?

Here was a rider, neither black nor white, headed back towards them: Blaise again, coming to report.

'My lady?' He sounded hoarse, more from excitement than dust, she thought.

'Yes, sergeant. Is there a problem?'

'A messenger, my lady. An Elessan, from the Baron Imber's party . . .'

Startlement robbed her of breath; she took a moment to steady herself, glad of Elisande's sudden grip on her arm, before she said, 'What party?' *What baron?* she wanted to ask also, but could not.

'They are only a few miles from here, my lady, on their way to fetch you. This man was riding ahead, to warn the castle of their coming; Master Sharrol is sending him back, to say that we are on the road already. We will meet them at the village where we intended to halt.'

That made sense; men on horseback might reach the Roq before nightfall, but this slow caravan could not. There was no point, in any case, in returning, except to greet her promised husband – *or his uncle*, it might very well be the other Baron Imber, insisting on all the proprieties – in more suitable surroundings than a military encampment . . .

It was only her father's rigorous training that allowed her even so much judgement. For the rest, her mind was a whirl of muddled emotion. In all her anxieties, all her darkest imaginings, she had never anticipated this. She'd not forgotten but had allowed herself to overlook the messages sent to Elessi by her father and the preceptor both. They might miscarry, they would surely be delayed; the count would be in no hurry to send for her, knowing her safe in Roq de Rançon . . .

But she'd been wrong, it seemed, three times over; or else she'd simply been hopeful, where no real hope existed. Deluding herself, pretending like a child that bad things, the worst thing simply would not happen . . .

Well, it had happened. One Baron Imber, or very likely the other, would be waiting for her an hour's travel down the road. Where did that leave their secret intentions, how could they possibly hope to slip away now?

'It changes nothing,' Elisande murmured, her words no more use than her hand that stroked Julianne's arm, trying to soothe away the tensions that made her tremble, trying and failing. 'There will be more men, that's all. Tripping over each other, challenging, arguing, jumping at shadows . . .'

Julianne nodded, grateful for her friend's effort, but she believed none of it. This was disaster, this was the end of her promise to the djinni. It meant her father's lethal danger, though she didn't know how; and it meant her own life taken from her, forced into a pattern of others' deciding. *Marry where you must*, she remembered bitterly, and could have laughed except that she felt so empty. Hollow, nothing left even to rattle and ring inside her, to make her body sound.

Well, let it be, then. Others had worse lives – *and shorter*, flames and cries in the night and both died slowly, slower still in her memory – and she was well trained for this, for her loss of joy. She didn't need even contentment; she could be ruthless with herself, as she must.

She stilled her trembling by a conscious effort of will; she sat cool and upright on her cushions, swaying only as the litter swayed as the bearers picked it up, as the column moved ahead.

'Julianne, are you— Are you thirsty?' Elisande asked after a while, meaning something else altogether. 'There is still some *jereth* left,' *and it's good for more than thirst,* her voice was saying.

'No, keep what remains. We'll keep it for my husband,' and here was a wonder, she could say even that without bitterness, without any feeling at all. 'It will make a fitting greeting, don't you think? A betrothal-cup, a drink of something rare,' *and if it's his uncle meets us we'll keep it yet, I think . . .*

'The Baron Imber,' Elisande said thoughtfully, 'is being given something more rare than *jereth*. I only hope he knows its true value.'

And she followed that with a kiss on the cheek, sudden and impulsive; Julianne smiled at her, said nothing and felt nothing, or persuaded herself so.

There was a lulling, a soothing in the motion of the litter; it took her back to the days of her smallness, when nurses were big and rocked her against their shoulders, or set her in a rocking cradle.

Her father was enormous then, those times he came to see her. He would swoop without warning, throw her in the air and make her squeal. He was enormous still, she thought; and still he threw her about with little warning beyond what she had known all her life, that this was what he did. This time, she thought, she would not squeal. Neither would she scream, nor sulk. She would run away, if she could; the djinni, she thought, was bigger even than her father, and so could throw her further.

If it were not frustrated, if the dead weight of the Baron Imber, either one, did not hold her heavy at his side . . .

*

Lulled, soothed, she could almost lose herself in dreaming despite the prick of such thoughts; time flowed by her and she was little aware of it, with Elisande silent at her side.

At last, though, the palanquin was set down again, and this time there were buildings all about them, simple huts of sun-baked mud. And here was Blaise again, dismounted now, saying, 'My lady, this is the best shelter we can find for you. There is a bed at least, and I have men drawing water.'

'Thank you, sergeant.' She stepped out, with Elisande at her back; looked around, saw groups of peasants standing, staring. Wondered which had been displaced to give her this roof for the night, and did not ask. Said only, 'Where is the baron's party?'

'Just ahead, to the east of the village. Master Sharrol has said that we will camp to the west. The baron will visit you, I am sure, when you have refreshed yourself.'

Yes. She was sure of that, too. And with men watching the road both east and west she thought they would be more than lucky, they must needs be blessed if they were to escape tonight.

'Will you bring up my luggage, please, sergeant? We should change our dress before the baron calls, I had sooner not meet him in my dust.'

'Of course, my lady. It may take a little time.'

She nodded. The more time the better; she was in no hurry to face this meeting, whichever Baron Imber it might be.

The hut was bare indeed, four rough walls of mud bricks and a roof of matting overlaid with mud, all of it cracked and gaping under the hard sun's weight; she really didn't trust that roof at all. Rain must fall sometime in this god-forsaken country, else why the dried-up river beds? When it did, she thought this hut and all this village would, must melt away in a run of filthy water.

It wouldn't be tonight, she was clear on that; but she could see skylight through the glimmering cracks, and she was not clear at all that the roof's own weight of dust and dryness might not drag it down atop her as she slept . . .

Only that she hoped not to be sleeping, of course, she hoped to be slipping secretly away from Blaise and the baron both. She gave her hopes no credence, no stamp of reality; no true vision, they were nothing to be clung to, only wisps and vapours in her mind's eye. But still, it was a simple choice. She could try escape, or she could lie here like a good girl and have the roof fall in on her, now and forever after . . .

There was one small window in the hut, set in the wall opposite the doorway, letting in light enough to lift the gloom of shadows if not her own gloom: light enough to show the simple bed, a straw pallet on a timber frame that was probably an expression of great wealth in such a place as this. Lacking anything else to look at, she looked out of the window and saw how the ground dropped away to another of those winding dust-trap gullies that would be a running river in its season, if that season ever came again. Beyond was a gentler slope flecked green and yellow, the villagers' starveling gardens.

Footsteps and a grunt at the doorway, which might or might not have been asking permission to enter: when she turned around they were coming in already, two men carrying her biggest chest. It had taken no time at all, she thought, regretfully. Then the men set their load down and straightened slowly, black habit and white tunic, and she recognised first one and then the other.

Not a man, the one in white, little more than a boy: 'Marron,' she said, 'should you not be serving your master?'

'He has ridden ahead with some of the other knights, my lady. He left me no orders . . .'

So the squire had made himself useful, helping the brother hump her chest along. Both parts of that were strange, she thought. Marron had helped with the loading also, back at the castle, and had been berated for it. And why was it a brother at the other end, when Blaise would presumably have given orders to his own men to see to her comfort?

She found an answer, part of an answer, simply by looking. The brother had his hood up and the rim of it hanging low across his face; but he forgot to keep his head down as he stretched and grunted, easing his back as though the weight of the chest had been too great for him comfortably to bear. Light fell in to deny the hood's shadows, she saw nose and mouth and an unlikely beard, the glitter of immodest eyes, and—

'You!' Elisande gasped beside her.

'I indeed,' he agreed, bowing to her; and then he turned and walked out of the hut, and only then did Julianne manage to see through the habit to the true man beneath. No brother he, that was Rudel the jongleur . . .

Elisande had been quicker, and as ever she was quicker also to confront. Julianne would have thought about it, wondered, sought the chance to ask a private question later; true to her father's teaching, *never act in haste, never show impatience or surprise.* Elisande lacked such a father, so much was clear: she was straight out after Rudel, through the doorway before his shadow had cleared it.

Julianne followed, to find the two of them still moving away from her. Rudel had remembered his guise and was walking like a brother, specifically like one of those brothers who would not look at women; he crabbed along the roadway, his head twisted awry and his shoulders turned to his small companion. Who stalked at his side like an angry bird, her hands matching her voice, gesture and tone both stabbing, accusing.

'. . . following me, is that it? Creeping at my tail, first in one shape, now another? This is *ridiculous!*'

'If it were true, it would be.' At least his voice wasn't cringing, as his body was. He sounded almost as angry as she did, though very much more under control. Julianne gazed about, as casual-seeming as she could, and saw no man close enough to overhear. Anyone might be lurking in this building or that, though, or following close behind. There was no swifter way to declare that you had something to hide, than by twisting to look over your shoulder; she wouldn't do that. Elisande might be careless enough to give herself away – herself and the jongleur: they both had their secrets, manifestly, and it seemed that each knew the other's – but Julianne at least would be more cautious.

'Oh, and is it not true?' Elisande hissed now, loud enough for half the village to hear if it were listening. 'I was there, and so were you; I am here, and behold . . .'

'You overvalue yourself,' Rudel replied: deliberately soft, Julianne thought, an obvious rebuke that could only make Elisande the angrier. 'I had a reason to go to the Roq, and

I have a reason to join this party, and you are neither of them.'

Elisande seethed, but at least she did it silently, giving Julianne her chance to catch up. She slipped her arm through her friend's, trying to disguise the sharp grip she took of the smaller girl's elbow, the little warning shake she gave it; then, loudly, she said, 'Brother, thank you for bringing my chest. Elisande, will you come and help me? We must find fit dress to greet the baron when he comes, and I fear the gowns will need a good beating before we can wear them, this road has been so dusty . . .'

That earned her such a glare, she had to swallow a bubble of laughter for diplomacy's sake. Rudel bowed to her, and moved away; and now she could look back, turning Elisande as she did so. She saw no danger, no eavesdropper: only Marron walking off in the distance with another brother, too far distant to have heard anything.

Elisande fell stiffly into step beside her, still twitching with fury. Julianne wanted to learn what it was that lay between those two, how they knew each other and what their secrets were; very badly she wanted it, but this was not the time to ask.

She steered her friend quietly back into the hut, and lifted the lid of the chest. Blinked a little to see how crushed her dresses were, she hadn't thought herself so bad a packer; but the road had been rough and no doubt the men had been careless, tossing and bumping the chest as they heaved it on and off the wagon. She sighed and stooped, lifted out the topmost robe and gave it a rough shake, said, 'You should wear this, the colour will suit you admirably . . .'

*

An hour later they had washed, more or less, in cool and cooling water; they had stood like peasants behind the hut, draping their chosen dresses across dry thorn-bushes and beating them with twigs till the swirling breeze carried no more dust away than it brought with it; they had come in coughing, gritty, laughing at their own foolishness, having to wash again.

Now they sat, washed and dressed and veiled with virtue, primly side by side on the bed, leaving the chest for their awaited visitor the baron; now they heard voices, footfalls, heavy men in heavy boots approaching, and for once Julianne couldn't tell at all what her friend was thinking but for herself she was thinking dread, cold and darkly private thoughts.

Shadow in the doorway, a tall man stooping low, calling before he entered: 'My lady Julianne?'

Both girls stood; she replied, 'Come in, sir. I am Julianne de Rance. This is my companion, the lady Elisande.'

Gracefully, he turned that stoop under the lintel into a low bow. 'Karel auf Karlheim, my lady, ladies both. Cousin to the baron-heir.'

Ah, was that how they managed it, then, how they drew the difference? The baron, and the baron-heir? That still was not to say which one led this reception-party, but all knowledge was useful. 'You are welcome, sir.' Which he was, she decided, as he straightened – cautiously, wary of the roof not a hand's-breadth above his head – and the light fell full on his face. A cheerful young man he seemed, which was one characteristic she had definitely not learned to expect of an Elessan. Neither in repute nor in her experience did they smile overmuch, but this Karel was grinning widely, relaxed and easy as he gazed about him.

At first his eyebrow spoke his thoughts, quirking humorously; then, 'My lady, there are some few of us come to make our bows to you, and Master Sharrol too; I think perhaps this is too small a court. Forgive the discourtesy, but if you would honour us by stepping outside . . .?'

'Too late.' A growling voice and another shadow made another man: one who stood a full hand shorter, who did not need to duck this doorway, though his shoulders were broad enough that almost he had to sidle through it.

The jaunty Karel lost his smile in a moment, or put it aside, rather; stiffened and set his face and voice to duty, named the newcomer to her like a sentry cut from stone: 'My lady, the Baron Imber von und zu Karlheim, brother-heir to the Count of Elessi.'

This much she knew, they had met before; though whatever else her father had made of her she had been a child still, and like a child what she had seen most of, what she best remembered was the scar like a livid red rope, like a living scarlet worm that hung on his cheek with its head buried behind his ear and its tail winding down into his beard. His head was shaved, and his eyes seemed too small in his face, too small for the mass of him generally.

Like Karel, he wore formal robes as if this were indeed a court; unlike Karel, his strong fingers plucked at them to lift the hems above the mud floor. That much she saw as she fell into a full and courtly curtsey, heedless of her own dress that had seemed apt before and did not now, seemed almost an insult to his sense of what was fit for this meeting.

Her heart sank with her, that it was this baron and not the other; she hoped she was schooled enough to hide her feelings as she rose again.

'My lord baron, you do us honour . . .'

'I do my duty,' he interrupted her, his voice as heavy and insistent as his body. He gazed scowlingly about him, and no, she could not ask him to sit on the chest as she had meant to; but she had no time to think of any other arrangement, because a third man appeared in the doorway and Karel named him too, almost a repetition and a great surprise.

'Lady Julianne, the Baron Imber von und zu Karlheim, son and heir to the Count of Elessi.'

What, *both* the barons? Automatically she hid her startlement beneath the practice of good manners, flowing down into another curtsey, perhaps a little deeper this time and held a little longer, as befitted a woman greeting her promised husband, a future subject greeting her future lord.

He was no more than a shadow to her yet, a name without a frame, a figure glimpsed half-hidden behind his uncle's bulk in that ill-built, ill-lit and increasingly cramped hut. As she rose, keeping her eyes submissively lowered against her rebellious curiosity, she let one brief prayer flicker across her mind, that he would be made more in his cousin's mould, less in his uncle's.

He spoke her name and more, he said, 'Lady Julianne, this is a kindness from the God, that we meet even an hour sooner than I had looked and hoped for.' His voice was neither the cousin's nor the uncle's, younger and huskier than the one, less abrasive than the other; she lifted her head and saw that his face also was entirely his own. He stood taller than his uncle, an inch or two shorter than his cousin. The last of the sunlight touched him where he stood in the doorway, making his blond hair shine, and his soft short beard. She knew his age, of course, from her father: he was twenty years old, a son come late to his parents after many daughters. His smile still held the shyness of a boy's.

For a moment they held each other's gaze. In all her wondering, her imagining of this encounter, she had never expected to feel a thrill course through her, a physical jolt that made her nearly cry aloud; but it was there and there it was, it happened, and she could have wept for the wonder of it. She could have knelt and gabbled her gratitude to the God and her father both for their mutual care of her, this gift quite unforeseen.

She gasped behind her veil, reached desperately for some politeness to return to him – and was granted no time to find it, because his uncle the elder Baron Imber shifted impatiently and rasped, 'This is ridiculous. Out, all, why do we exchange courtesies in a hovel? A sty?'

He chivvied them with great waving motions of his arms, as though they were a gaggle of geese or servants, and lost his own dignity in doing so. Elisande clutched suddenly at Julianne's arm, and her face and her fingers between them said, *this shouldn't be funny, I know what this means to you and I shouldn't even be close to laughing, but oh . . .*

Except that Elisande didn't know, she appeared not to have registered any least little part of the epiphany that had swept through Julianne like a summer fire on a mountain, unpredictable and deadly. It scorched her still, quiescent but hot yet; confusion clouded her, as ash might fill the sky from that burning mountain. And yes, it was ridiculous, as all this scene was ridiculous, and like her friend she should have been fighting laughter, and was not. All she fought was the desire, the need, the hunger to look at him again; she was dizzy with it, and she would not.

His uncle gave her the excuse she needed, a reason to resist the haunting question, *is he looking at me yet, looking again, is he strong like me, can I be stronger?* His uncle, she thought, had probably been in a temper all the long ride from Elessi, at having to collect what should have been delivered; certainly he was in a stiff fury now, and directing it at the man in a master's robe who stood outside.

Used as she was to the subtleties of Marasson, where even the slaves dealt in soft words and hidden meanings, this was fascinating; it held her eyes, her ears and almost her attention, almost drowned the intense and crucial murmur, *is he watching, what is he seeing, do I give myself away?*

She thought this might be a feature now, from here to the end of her days: an ever-seeking after his attention, never satisfied by constant awareness that she had it all already.

She thought she might not mind that, proved it so.

'. . . I'll send to my camp, and have the lady's tent erected there,' Baron Imber, the wrong Baron Imber was saying, not bothering even to lower his voice, while every muscle of his body shouted outrage. 'She will be mother to the heirs of Elessi, if the God grants her grace; how could you think to house her in a pit?'

'Better quarters in a village than a tent in the Order's camp,' Master Sharrol replied smoothly, with no hint of offence taken. 'My brothers have forgone the company of women, baron; some would feel themselves forsworn, to have one sleep among them.'

'But not if she sleeps in shit, to save their precious sensibilities? How if she came to harm in the night, how then, would they not be forsworn then also? What of your oaths to safeguard and protect?'

'The Order will be watching the village all night, baron.'

'You'll watch an empty village. I'll take the girl into my own custody, sir, where I can be sure of her.'

'No, my lord baron.'

That last came not from Master Sharrol, it came from Julianne: surprised her nearly with the speed and the force of it, never mind the impertinence. He spun around, glaring; she dragged in a hard breath and tried to palliate her refusal, too late. 'Forgive me, sir, but my father sent me into the care of the Ransomers, and their preceptor set me in Master Sharrol's shadow. It is still for him to make disposition of me, unless he choose to relinquish me formally tonight?'

She said it soft as soap, and still saw the barb sink home. Master Sharrol twitched, even, before he replied. 'The morning will be soon enough, I think. We have already made our dispositions, as you say. Believe me, baron, the lady Julianne will be quite adequately guarded, if not quite bedded down in the comforts to which she is accustomed.'

Julianne thanked him, rewarded him with a gentle laugh. 'I am a soldier's daughter, sir, though it is a long time since my father went to war with a sword in his hand.' It would not hurt, she thought, to remind them not only of her father's past, but his current position also. *Think on that, and quarrel no more*, she was saying, as she said, 'I find no hardship in sleeping more roughly than I am used to; I can enjoy it, with my friends around me. Certainly I anticipate no danger,' *except from him, that lingering tall boy I will not look at, I'll have him look at me and look and look* . . .

'You'll do as you're told, girl.'

'And as I have said, my lord baron, my father told me to put myself in the hands of the Society of Ransom. Where I lie still, until they give me up.'

'Yes, your father,' and here it was at her back, that young man's hoarseness that might sharpen or blur further, depending on mood and moment; and still she would not look, not yet, not quite, though she blessed him for the interruption. 'How did it come that your father left you to make your way alone to Roq de Rançon? We had heard him more careful than that.'

'The King summoned him, my lord baron,' *my* lord baron she wanted to say, and did not – quite – dare. Besides, the man should declare himself first, and with more than his bright eyes in a dim room. What colour were they? Green, she thought, but light played games in shadow, and her mind had been greatly shadowed when he came.

'Even so, a delay of a few days to see his daughter safe; the King would not have begrudged him, surely . . .?'

And now she did turn suddenly, to let him see that her laughter was teasing only, no malice in the world; and his eyes were green or grey, the sun was behind him and she couldn't be sure, but she said, 'I know nothing of the King's grudges, sir, but the King's summons I do know,' though in all honesty this was the first time she had seen it. She would not tell him that. 'When the world tears open, a fool would not speak to it of delay.'

'My lady?'

'I saw the wind rip the road apart,' and she would show Elisande how she could tell a story, when she chose to, 'and the sun's light burn in the gulf it made, as though all we see and touch were tissue laid over liquid gold. The horses were terrified,' and her bearers too, the only time those solid, laughing men had let her down; not set her down but dropped her, and cowered wailing in the dust, and she had been terrified herself also, though she would not say that either. 'There was no voice, but my father listened to it; and then he spoke to my sergeant,' quickly, roughly, making plans for her without wasting the time it would take to explain them to her. 'He calmed his mount,' with an old soldier's exemplary horsemanship that she could never match though he had taught her all her life to ride, 'and left his baggage with us, left us there; he rode into that flaming light, and it sealed itself behind him and was gone, with not a sign remaining,' except the chaos of their party that had taken an hour to recover.

'Say it plainly, girl,' from the other Baron Imber, the uncle of her man.

'My lord, that is as plain as I can make it. The King opened a strange path that day, and my father took it. I know no more than that.'

One thing else she did know, as the younger baron, her own Imber reached to touch her for the first time, laying his hand lightly on her shoulder like a token and a promise both: that it would be hard, much harder now to run away tonight, although she must.

16

Speaking True

The Order's discipline was its greatest strength, Marron had heard that and heard it. He had seen it for himself two nights since, when the Sharai attacked the castle: it was discipline in battle that had driven the invaders back, not his sounding the alarm. He could have called forth as many men and seen them slaughtered, if their obedience and training had been weaker or less ingrained.

But that selfsame discipline was a danger also, it made the Order dangerous to itself. That he saw tonight, when he saw how easy it was for two strangers to hide themselves among the brothers. Dress a man in a habit, and it was the habit that men saw. An unknown face meant only a man from another troop, it raised no questions where several troops travelled together; a man with his hood thrown over his face was a modest man or a man at prayer, to be made way for or stepped around. One brother might have ridden all day beside Rudel and never asked a question. In fact Rudel had moved around, a little time here and a little there, a lot on his own beside the wagons, giving no man the chance; but chances were that he could have sat in state on my lady's chest all the way and still no man would have challenged him.

And if one man, two men – two Surayonnaise, yet, one a prisoner fleeing and one whose face had been seen and seen around the castle in other dress than this – if two men in a small party could sit over a fire apart and never be approached, then so could two dozen, more. If Marron were Sharai, he'd have his women weave black cloth and sew habits by the hundred . . .

But Sharai he was not, nor brother now. Squire, yes, and already a traitor to his master as to his God, holding secrets that broke every oath he'd ever made; and he tried not to stare at Rudel's fire as he saw to Sieur Anton's horse and his meal and his errands, and he tried not even to remember what he knew, and he failed of course at every turn.

Failed also to feel guilty. Regretful he felt, and anxious, but guilty not. It was no just way to treat a man, what Redmond had been put to in that cell; whatever the laws said or the priests taught, the place had stunk of wrongness and this rescue was a virtue.

Marron was to have no further hand in it. 'Forget us now,' Rudel had told him, after Marron had freed Redmond from his cramping nest among the lady's gowns and helped him to the camp. That had been a nervous walk for both of them, but again no one had questioned it. A squire lending an arm to an ailing brother: not a common sight, perhaps, but nothing disturbing.

'Forget us now,' Rudel had said, striking sparks to light his solitary little fire. 'See to your master's needs, and your own. We'll be away once the camp is settled; nobody will see us leave or miss us once we're gone.'

'Which way will you go, sir?'

'Down that dry gully, I think, that runs by the village. I can mask men's eyes, so that they do not see us; but those banks run high, they'll give us extra cover. It's not your concern, though, lad. We're grateful for your help,' and a grunt of agreement from the exhausted, trembling Redmond, 'more than grateful, but your part is over now. Let us go, and see to your own content.'

Well, he would, or he would try to, but not he thought until this night was over. His duties were finished for the evening; Sieur Anton had eaten, had watched Marron eat, and had then walked over to the Elessans' camp.

'No,' he had said, 'you may not come with me. The young baron was a companion of my brother's for a time. I am – shall we say uncertain of my reception? I will not cower in the camp here, though, and avoid them. They will think what they will think, but I had rather let them see my face and think it. I doubt much will be said, if I am there and in my white. The elder baron may have a few rough words for me, but he is rough with everyone.'

'Sieur, I should—'

'You should *not*. Amuse yourself, Marron; play with the other boys if they will have you, but don't play at dice with the sergeant's men, or you'll lose every penny in your purse and your purse besides.'

'Sieur, I have none.'

'No? Oh – no, of course not. Here,' and a small leather pouch had flown into the air between them, giving him no choice but to snatch at it one-handed.

He didn't dare throw it back, but tried to give it. 'I wasn't begging, sieur . . .'

'I know. That's why you have it. Don't be difficult, Marron. It's a knight's duty to see to his squire's wants, and a boy in camp wants money. Gamble if you like that, but only with my confrères' lads, they won't strip you unless you're stupid; and visit the traders first, let them have the best of it. A sword you have, but you could use a good knife to match it. Don't wear Dard, by the way. No one will touch it here.'

And so he was gone. The purse-strings were knotted, but loosely; Marron picked them apart, worked the mouth wide and slipped a finger in. Eyes and finger both told him there was mixed silver and copper in there, thin coins with nipped and broken edges, fit wealth for a young squire's purse but not a knight's. Sieur Anton had been ready for this.

One camp they might call it, but in truth it was three. Outermost were the brothers' cooking-fires and their horse-lines, and the hard ground between where they would lie in their habits, in their troops, and sleep sword to hand till they must rise for prayer or guard or other duty in the night. Then came the knights with their tents and chests and servants – though Sieur Anton had no tent, only a blanket-roll and another for Marron to spread at his master's feet – and lastly, closest to the village, the traders had set their wagons in a circle and a bright fire to burn at the heart of it, invitation to all.

The dour brothers were poverty-sworn, the knights wealthy but well-equipped already; the villagers, the natives would have little to spare. But *the habit makes the man,* one of his uncle's sayings and too true he thought to be funny; the habit had near broken Marron in its efforts to make a brother of him. Any business was better than none, he supposed; and likely the traders lit their fire in any case, whatever company it brought them.

Fire, and food: he could smell what he hadn't smelled in weeks, hot meats roasting over an open flame. He'd eaten just, but Sieur Anton's notion of a necessary supper was little improvement on the Order's, only hard bread and harder cheese. Marron's nose would have drawn him closer even if he hadn't had money in his hand and his master's injunction at his back to push him on. There was a gap like a gateway left between two of the wagons; Marron walked through into the fire's welcome.

And was greeted by a gust of laughter that made him check, until he realised that it wasn't aimed at him. He wasn't the first to have been summoned by light and smells, far from it; there was a cluster of young men and boys dressed as he was and standing with their backs to him, all their attention focused on something he couldn't see. Squires from the knights' camp: some he knew by sight, a few by name, though none by any gesture of kindness. Sieur Anton's warning had proved true thus far, that the master he served might bring him enemies through no fault of his own, but would certainly bring him no friends.

He moved forward less eagerly, stretching to peer over the press of heads and shoulders. A sudden shrill screaming sound was followed by another ripple of laughter and movement, nudging elbows and a brief surge; he was still too far back to make out what so amused them. One of the taller lads glanced round at him, though; recognition fetched another laugh, a short bark with no hint of welcome in it. A hand gripped his tunic, rough enough to jerk his arm – aching once more after the weight of the lady's chest with Redmond in it – and hard enough to make him yelp.

Again the same laugh, and, 'Here, make room, boys. D'Escrivey's monkey has sniffed his brother out . . .'

Blushing, struggling, trying hopelessly to protect his arm in the jostle, Marron was pushed through the crowd; his eyes were smarting when they thrust him out into clear space again, which only made him blush the more. He cupped his elbow in his other hand, trying to look as though he only crossed his arms, and blinked rapidly to clear his gaze.

'Don't cry, little monkey,' a voice advised him, cruelly cheerful. 'See, your brother's here . . .'

What Marron saw was a boy his own size, his own age, one of those few he could put a name to. Lucan this was, squire to Sieur Merival, but far from the dignity of his service now; he was choked with laughter, painfully doubled over, and he seemed to have a small black cat on his leg.

No, not a cat. It turned its head; Marron saw a little wrinkled face, almost human and inconsolably sad. Its mouth opened and it screamed again, provoking a chorus of laughter and further advice. 'Greet your brother, Marron, he greets you. Has he been watching you with your master, pretty monkey?'

Marron was only confused by that last, until he saw how the animal's paws – like hands they were, tiny but fully formed, fingers not claws – were clenched in Lucan's breeches, how its hindquarters worked against the cloth. Then he understood. He had seen dogs act so in their excitement, until they were kicked away.

No one kicked this creature, but a man's hand reached over and plucked it up; a man's voice said, 'Enough. There's meat over yonder, if you lads are hungry and have a copper or two to pay for it . . .?'

If they were hungry? They were young, all, and had probably not fed so much better than Marron; their masters might be less abstemious than his, but were likely less generous also. At any rate, their sudden rush away said that they were hungry, and that they had coppers to pay. Marron was left alone this side of the fire, alone with the man and his creature.

The man was a trader, that much was clear: the rich fabrics of his clothing said so, as did their condition, faded and patched, stained and ingrained with the dust and the sweat of the road. His creature perched on his shoulder, chittering and playing with a leash that was knotted one end around its neck and the other around its owner's belt.

'No appetite, boy, or no coins?'

Marron lacked neither, only the others' urgency and any desire for their company. Besides, curiosity was burning a question in his throat. 'Sir, what – what *is* that?'

'Haven't you seen a monkey before?'

He had not. He had heard the word, as he had heard of gryphons and oliphants and harpies; he thought he had seen a picture in a bestiary at the abbey, but this looked nothing like that.

'Well,' the man said, 'now that howling pack has dispersed, perhaps he'll be a little calmer. Sit yourself here, and take him.'

Sitting was awkward, trying neither to jar his arm nor to make a show of it; the effort drew a grunt from him, though no more. The man placed the monkey in his lap, but it leaped instantly onto his shoulder. Warm fur he felt, then sharp little fingers gripping his ear; its face peered at him, liquid eyes and sorrow and so very like a brother, he thought, all in black and only its suffering face to show. He felt more twinship than kinship, far more than the brotherhood the boys had mocked him with, and he was very aware of the purse clutched still in his hand. If the man had suggested a price, he'd have given it all, right then.

If he'd given it all or any of it, he'd have had Sieur Anton to face later. 'I gave you money for a knife, boy, and you bought a *monkey* . . .?' It didn't bear thinking about, but he'd have done it anyway.

'His name is Caspius,' the man said, reading Marron's thoughts on his face, which couldn't have been difficult, 'and he is not for sale. Don't waste your breath in asking.'

'No, sir.'

'And mine is Almet; and yours is—?'

'Oh, Marron . . .' absently, as he offered the monkey a finger to clutch at like a baby, except that the skin on its palms was quite dry.

'Marron. And you serve a knight called d'Escrivey, did they say?'

They had said so, he remembered, though not straightly. *Where a trader gleans, there are no secrets worth the picking after.*

'Anton d'Escrivey, would that be?'

'Sieur Anton,' he replied sharply, instant defence of his master's honour; then, 'Yes, sir,' quietly, turning his eyes to the monkey again.

'Well, he was sure to surface, sooner or later. A man like that can't stay buried, he's too good to lose. Here, boy, that monk's taken a fancy to you; and you to him, I can see that. Keep a hold of this, would you?' He untied the monkey's leash from his belt and looped the end around Marron's wrist, his bad wrist, but did it so light-fingered that there was no pain, only a moment's surprise that the man had noticed and remembered and cared enough to be careful.

The trader Almet walked out of the circle of firelight, and was gone; the monkey Caspius screamed its anxiety at the dark, and tried to scamper after. Marron drew it back by the leash, as gently as he could manage, and soothed and stroked and tickled until the agitated little creature quieted, relaxed, at last curled itself contentedly cat-like in his lap, clutching at his hand with all four paws.

Marron's purse lay on the ground beside him. He didn't remember setting it down; he must have done that quite unthinkingly, playing with the monkey.

And Almet must have seen it. Indeed, Almet had probably seen through the leather and counted every coin in it. *If a trader refuses to sell to you, watch your purse.* One of his uncle's more sour sayings; Marron grinned at himself, at his own folly. Of course the monkey was for sale. This was part of the bargaining. Leave the boy alone, let him fall absolutely in love with the creature; he'll pay more, he'll pay anything . . .

Only he wouldn't, not now. The trader had misread him, for a wonder, had not known enough. In that first moment, yes; but the immediate bond had proved too fragile, it had been snapped by what came after. Caspius was only a monkey now, worth a smile and a stroke but no more. The surge of sympathy had been lost; Marron didn't wear the habit of a brother any longer and had no brothers among them, or none that loved him. He served another master now, and burned to learn his story.

When Almet came back, he brought a wooden platter piled high with steaming hacks of meat, and a bunch of grapes in his other hand.

'Would you rather feed yourself, lad, or the monk? I doubt you can do both one-handed.'

Indeed. Caspius was already capering from knee to shoulder, shrilling for food; Marron held the leash out mutely. Almet took it with no sign of disappointment or surprise, only a grin and, 'That hungry, huh?'

'Uh, no, sir.' *Yes, sir,* but he was having doubts suddenly, how far that purse would run. He must buy a knife, and a good one; best to curb his appetite, and be sure.

'Meaning yes, sir, but you want to save your coppers? Eat, boy, you did me a favour. Gossip carries value, more than a mouthful of meat is worth.'

More than a mouthful of meat was what Marron took, in the end; more than a handful, a bellyful. And then licked fat and juices from his fingers, wiped them on dusty grass and took Caspius back, and did feed him grapes till the little monkey fell asleep.

As though that were a sign, *time for business*, Almet said, 'That's not a thin purse, Marron, for a squire sent off to play. Your master cares more for you than for your clothes, seemingly?'

Marron blushed in the darkness, though he thought Almet was poorly placed to criticise anyone's dress. 'These clothes were begged for me, sir; I wore . . . another style, two days ago.'

Almet laughed. 'I guessed it, lad. I was joking. But for a boy taken up, as you must have been, who I'd guess had no coin of his own – and only two days ago, was it? Those others are quick, then, to make mock of you – I still say that's a kind purse to play with.'

Sieur Anton is generous, he wanted to say, *and those others are liars*; but this was swamp, all swamp about him, and he was uncertain of his path. So, 'There's no gold in it,' that was response enough.

'Even so. Come, Marron, what did he send you for? Not a monkey, so much is obvious; I really wouldn't sell you Caspius, if it meant the wrath of your master on your head. So what, then?'

'Sir,' with a sweet sigh of relief because he took no pleasure in these games, nor did he play them well, 'do you have knives?'

'Do I have knives? I'm bound for Elessi, and the boy asks if I have knives?'

'They might make all their own . . .'

'True, they might; but they do not. And just as well, for their own health and mine also. They have craft in Elessi, and no art. A good blade needs more than strength, it needs some beauty. Wait one short minute, Squire Marron, and

I'll show you such knives as will make your heart weep for
longing . . .'

And so he might have done, but that he knew already the
weight of Marron's purse. He fetched out no jewelled hafts,
and no chased steel; a rack of plain daggers and poniards he
brought, old and new and all of them well-made, sturdy in
the grip and needle-sharp.

Marron knew that, for he tried them all. Only one he
tried twice, though, only one he came back to for a second
look. That was the oldest in the rack, its ivory handle
cracked and streaked with use.

'A fine knife once, and a fine blade still,' Almet murmured, at his side. 'These others are its inferiors, only that
the grip is as you see it, past repair. I should replace it, but
a knife is a whole thing, and never so good patched. I
wouldn't have said this, lad, but stay with that one, if you
stay with me. There are other men here who would have
knives to show . . .'

'No. This is for me,' *if we can agree* he should have said,
his uncle would have, he did not. 'How much do you want
for it?'

'No more than you can afford, boy. I'll not rob you. I
can't sell it for the blade's worth, so throw that purse over
and let's see. It needs a good sword to match it, mind,' as he
tipped coins into his palm and fingered through them.

'I have a sword.'

'A good one?'

Two: one good enough, one startling. He could simply
have nodded the question away, but he thought he owed
the trader more; was sure of it when he saw what coins

Almet kept, and what he put back in the purse. Cracked handle or not, the knife was a bargain at that price.

'Sieur Anton gave it me, it was his brother's . . .'

Almet stiffened, his eyes widened for a moment; then, 'You should probably not boast of that, lad. Oh, I know, you did not mean to boast; but it were better not said at all, for your master's sake and your own.'

Marron looked down, petted the sleeping monkey in his lap, then lifted his head again with sudden determination. 'Sir? Can you tell me the truth, about Sieur Anton and his brother?'

'Marron, anyone who knows Outremer can tell you the story that Outremer knows. Whether it's the truth, that's for the God to judge. Do you truly not know the story?'

'I am new-come here, sir. I only know what my master has told me, and he tells it harshly against himself.'

'So does everyone. This is a harsh country.'

'Please, sir?'

'Well. You should know the facts, at least, and they are quickly told. They were close brothers, Anton and Charol, they loved each other better than many brothers do, when there's only one estate to share between them. But there came a day when both of them went missing; their father sent his men to search, and they found Charol's body, killed with a single stroke, and his sword gone. His brother, too. Duke Raime put word out to find Anton, to have him answer to this; but when he was discovered, he had already sworn himself to the Ransomers. He admitted his brother's death, but his life belonged to the Order and could not be forfeited. Rumour says that Charol caught Anton with a boy, and Anton killed him to keep that dishonour secret.

It's only rumour, but if ever he denied it, I've not heard. That'll be why your friends are so unfriendly; Sieur Anton's squire must be Sieur Anton's boy.'

And it seemed he left a question hanging, *tell me the truth of that?* Whatever Marron owed him, though, he owed him not so much. Not even a denial. Whatever passed between his master and himself was private to them, and not for roadside gossip.

So he said nothing, and at last Almet asked, 'Where is your master tonight, then? If I'd known I rode with Anton d'Escrivey, I'd have sought a glimpse of him before this.'

'He's gone to the Elessan camp,' Marron answered shortly.

'Has he, though? He's a bold man; he'll find few friends there, I fancy. Or anywhere, even so far from his home estate. The name d'Escrivey carries a heavy weight these days; his kind will forgive much, but not this. I'll be interested to see how well he bears it.'

'You will find, sir, that he bears it very well,' and Marron was spilling the shrieking monkey and up on his feet and the knife was there in his hand, his fingers clenched about that cracked haft almost hard enough to crack it further. The blade glittered in the light, but all the movement on it was the fire's dance.

'Ah. Your pardon, lad; you are sworn to him, of course. I spoke unthinkingly.'

'You spoke with your heart, I think, sir.'

'Aye, that I did – but don't make a quarrel of it, boy. I have asked pardon; and you're half my size,' and he stood himself to prove it, bending as he did to scoop the monkey up onto his shoulder, 'and hurt besides. I won't fight a one-handed child. Nor would your master want you to fight me.'

That was true enough. The noise across the fire was ebbing, people were turning to stare; Marron took a deep breath, turned the knife in his hand and thrust it into his belt.

'That's better. How bad is your arm? There are people here with some skill at mending wounds.'

'Thank you, sir, it has been treated already.' Treated and treated, and mistreated too; it was aching badly now.

'Fair enough. Don't go cold on me, lad, for a careless thought; I'm a careless man. I've seen most things, and most people in these lands. It's curiosity keeps me moving. I admit it, I'm curious to see your Sieur Anton; is that so bad?'

Marron hesitated, then shrugged awkwardly, one-shouldered. 'No. I suppose not.'

'Good. We recover some ground, at least. How were you hurt?'

Another hesitation, then the twitch of a smile, and, 'Sieur Anton cut me, at sword-practice.'

'Did he, though? I should have guessed it.'

'Sir?'

'You have all the signs, lad, of a boy cut by his master. Even to trying to hide the hurt of it. Now come, there's money yet in this purse of yours,' and he stooped again, retrieved it from where it lay forgotten on the thin grass, tossed it to Marron. 'Will you spend it with me? I have other goods that might interest a youngster.'

'No. Another night, perhaps,' but Marron was remembering that there was more than a trader's wagon to interest him just now. 'I think I'll walk for a while.'

'As you wish. Don't go seeking your master with the Elessans, though. Leave that meeting for cooler heads.'

The trader turned away, caressing his monkey as he went; Marron nodded a belated thanks for his wisdom, felt a moment's pang for the loss of the monkey – so easy a relationship, defined by grapes and affection; that sadness an illusion, only the natural falls of its face, no more – and looked for the nearest way out of the circle of wagons.

The knights' camp was deserted, save for a few servants gathered around the last of the cooking-fires. Sieur Anton would find most of his confrères also visiting the Elessans, Marron guessed, and doubtless glad of new faces, old friends to talk with. He paused briefly to check that no one had disturbed his master's things – and his own, his one thing, the sword Dard; his fingers touched its haft lightly, *I've a brother-blade for you now* – and again at the horse-lines, to be sure that their mounts were settled and content.

Glad to have no other duties there, he hurried on to where the brothers were camped, and saw before he came to it that Rudel's little fire had been scuffed out, and that the two men were gone.

That was good, that was truly all he needed; but in itself it was only information, not reassurance. And he knew which way they meant to go, and he had nothing else to occupy his mind. There was no reason why he shouldn't wander back towards the village, a young squire at a loose end with his master elsewhere and neither friends nor chores to claim his time . . .

He tried to walk slowly in the starlight, not to be obviously seeking. Back past the horses and the knights' comfortable camp, past the traders' circle and the laughter of young men at play; before he reached the village, he found the dry and sunken watercourse.

Stars were brighter or more fierce, here in the Sanctuary Land; they seemed bigger somehow, as the moon did also. Though it lay a tall man's height below where he stood, Marron could see clearly how the absent river's bed was crazed, silt baked hard under the sun and only softened by the overlay of a season's dust. The banks were steep, and tangled with thorn and scrub which cast their own confusing shadows down. A man would have to stand where he was, right on the edge, to see clearly if anyone moved along it.

Marron himself could see no movement, but the watercourse turned and twisted sharply, following the lie of the land. There was security in that, too; no one could watch more than a short stretch. Similarly, though, no one in the gully would see a watcher on the bank until they were close, too close, coming round a sudden corner to be caught . . .

Rudel might need him after all, he thought, to strike ahead and warn of trouble waiting. He stepped out faster, finding a track that ran straighter than the watercourse but touched its bank often enough that he shouldn't miss the two men. They ought not to be so far ahead; Redmond would be stiff and slow, still carrying the pains of the cell on broken feet, despite Rudel's healing magic. Marron's arm told him the truth of that.

He scanned the track as far as he could see, and made

out no figures on it; whenever he was close enough he peered down into the gully, forward and back, and saw no one.

He strained his ears as well as his eyes, as he came below the quiet of the village. The rowdiness of the traders' circle was behind him; was that the murmur of male voices ahead, or only the low whisper of a breeze in the bushes?

Voices, or the sound of a spring welling up in the watercourse, undefeated by the summer sun?

Voices it was, he was sure. He left the path to follow the bank and there they were, two black robes and two paler faces gazing up, gazing directly at him.

For a moment the picture of them seemed to smudge somewhere behind his eyes, a mist falling inside his head, a tingling touch that stilled him where he stood; then there was a sough of breath released and Rudel's voice rising to greet him, more exasperated than pleased despite his good intentions.

'Marron. What are you doing here?'

'Sir, I came to see you safe away. I thought there might be guards on the bank, up ahead . . .'

'If there are guards,' the soft voice came back to him, 'we can deal with them. We can walk straight past, and they'll never know that we were here. The trouble that we face now, there *is* someone ahead of us; but not guards and not on the bank, down here in the gully . . .'

'Who is it?' meaning really, *how can you tell?*

'That I can't say, I cannot read so much; but two, and not moving.'

'I could go and see, sir.'

'You could. I shouldn't let you, but – well, you do have

a knack for making yourself convenient, Marron. When you're not making a stupid nuisance of yourself. Can you act the innocent squire?'

'Yes, sir.' *Been doing that all day. And will do, all my service still to come . . .*

'Go, then. Quiet as you can, but don't creep. And don't peer, and don't come directly back . . .'

Marron strolled the bank like any boy excused to idleness, and it wasn't he who crouched and tried to hide in darkness. Scrub shadows fell confusingly across the river's bed, and it was hard to see without staring, but he spotted them at last, two thin figures hunched under a thorn-bush—

Or thought he did. He blinked and squinted sidelong, trying to be certain of them; and the longer he gazed the harder it was to see clearly, to find clothes or faces among those shifting, blurring shadows.

It was making him dizzy, so much wasted effort, as it seemed to him suddenly, trying to outstare a thorn. There was no one there, it was only a trick of the dark; and oh, he was giddy with it, he needed to sit down . . .

And did, and laid his head on his good arm where it folded itself across his knees, and when he closed his eyes the prickling in his skin died away and his mind steadied, a little. Though it was still hard to find any one thought that didn't slip and dissolve when he touched it except for that one strong, forceful shout of a thought, *nobody there, there wasn't anybody there, only the light and the shadows and the earth beneath . . .*

And so he sat, and didn't move again until some harsh

whisper cut through the web of bafflement that held him. The ground was suddenly solid again and his mind was clear and he had seen them, two of them, local lads by their dress, simple robes and lengths of dirty cloth wound around their heads . . .

He stood up, cautiously for his arm's sake and the more so for fear of that dizziness returning; and heard the low sounds of voices in the gully, tight with a barely leashed anger, and one of them was a full-grown man's for sure and he rather thought Rudel's.

So he went to see, moving slow and shy and wary. There were four people standing in the watercourse below him now, two in black robes and two in dusty dun. Rudel and Redmond, yes, and that pair of lads – except that no village lad would outface armed brothers as one of them was doing, standing hands on hips and glaring, hissing, spitting in a whisper.

No lad at all, indeed. That was the lady Elisande, under those coarse rags; and the other, when he rubbed his eyes and squinnied, the other was the lady Julianne, with her long hair coiled up and hidden beneath the turban that she wore.

'. . . Why should I tell you?'

'Not tell. Ask, I said.'

'Worse. You of all men, what right have you to order my comings and goings?'

'We will discuss my rights later,' Rudel said, and it was a wonder to Marron that he kept his voice so quiet, so much passion was in it. 'For now, we will *all* leave this place, and we will do so together.'

'Before we do,' Julianne said, cold and clear and with an

edge like a diamond, 'may I know who my companions are? Truly? You are something else than a jongleur, Rudel, and I think neither one of you is a Ransomer.'

'Later,' he said again, with a gesture of sheer impatience. That might not have been enough for Julianne, by the way she stiffened; but he turned away from her, glanced up and said, 'Marron, are you still fuddled?'

'No, sir,' though the truth was, *yes, sir, all this fuddles me.*

'Good. This is farewell, then; take our thanks, and go back to—'

Back to your camp, back to your master, back to your life, but none of that was said. Redmond tugged urgently at Rudel's sleeve, Rudel's head jerked around, Elisande gasped and twisted, all three of them reacting to something Marron could neither see nor hear; but whatever sense it was that warned them, this time it came too late.

'Who's that?' The voice beat at them from the dark, from the far side of the gully. 'You there, boy . . .'

Marron froze; his white tunic betrayed him and betrayed them all, making an easy target of him under these bright stars. Now he could see his challengers, three men emerging from the night in disguising black, brothers on patrol. They strode to the gully's rim, still fixed on him but no chance that they would not see the others down below.

Unless he ran, unless he drew them off . . .

He spun around and leaped away, winning a bellowing shout that was echoed on this side of the watercourse. Some man unseen among the huts of the village above him: twisting his head to look back as he ran, he cursed himself. If those three were to follow him, of course they must cross the gully; of course they would do it here where they were closest, before another of its sudden turns could force them further back. So there they were, stood right on the edge now and not staring after him but down into its shadows. At Rudel and Redmond and the ladies; and all Marron had done was bring more trouble to them.

He saw that, he saw another party of men come from the village, and then he felt his foot snagged by a thorn and he saw the world tumble.

Instinct thrust his hands out, both his hands, to catch his weight as he hit ground; a moment after the jar of contact, he felt the leaping pain released in his arm as that thrice-cursed wound split open yet again.

For the space of two breaths – one gasp, and one sob – he lay still; and through all the shouting and the throbbing and the blurring shock of his fall he heard one voice clear, Rudel's: 'Go on, go on! I can hold these, we can turn back but you go . . .!'

And then he was up again with a thrust and a stagger and a yelp of pain as he used, as he had to use that damned arm to get himself moving; and the three men on the gully's bank were not so much climbing or leaping down, more slipping and sliding and in their minds as much as their bodies so, he thought, seeing how their heads rolled and their limbs hung slackly. Dizzy and cut loose he thought they were, seeing nothing, caught in a brutal maze . . .

No time to wonder at it, though. Nor to worry about the others in the gully, whether that mazement would be enough to see them away and free or else back in camp but undetected, if that was what Rudel had meant. The patrol from the village was coming after him; they either hadn't noticed what was happening below them, or else they weren't concerned. They wore dark tunics, but not the brothers' black.

And Marron wore white and was easy, too easy to spot; and was slow, too slow after that fall, not destined to escape.

So he drew his knife and waved it high above his head, glanced back again and cried them on, 'This way! They went this way . . .' and plunged forward headlong, trying to seem hound and not hare.

There were lights beyond the village, tents and bright fires burning; more men, many more men gathering and gazing at the noise, starting to run. That must be the Elessans' camp. He picked a path between that and the gully, trying to come not too close to either.

It was a race, but not for him to win: only to see who caught him first, the men who followed or those who came down to intercept. A hand snatched at his shoulder, missed its grip and grabbed again, sending another jarring pain down his arm to wake his wound to fire; he gasped, stumbled, almost fell. Turned his eyes upward to the bearded face of the man who had run him down, who was barely breathing hard despite the chase, and panted, 'Sir, sir, they went that way,' gesturing onward with his knife.

'Who did? I saw no one. Who are you?'

'Marron, sir, squire to Sieur Anton d'Escrivey.' That checked the man's scowling disbelief, at least for a moment, though by the way his face changed it had not made him Marron's friend. Marron went on urgently, 'There were men here, Sharai perhaps, I do not know; they wore Catari dress. I came on them back there, below the village, and they drew knives on me. I think I wounded one, see . . .'

He showed the man his knife, with blood clearly on the blade; the man grunted, and peered ahead into the dark.

'How many?'

'Three that I saw, sir . . .'

Another grunt, and then a gesture that brought his own men closer. Those from the camp had reached them also, big men, all bearded, all suspicious.

'Catari, three, the boy says. Sneak assassins, Sharai, by the sound of them. One is bleeding, perhaps.'

Blood was dripping from Marron's fingers, but he kept that arm down at his side and hoped, prayed almost that no one would notice in the dark.

'Three Sharai? Why is the boy not dead?'

'They fled, sir. Not from me, I think,' in swift response to their scornful laughter, *three Sharai assassins to run from one bare-chinned boy? We think not* . . . 'Perhaps they heard you coming, sir?'

'Perhaps they did. Well, we will pursue; you will go to the camp,' and he was passed from that man's strong and painful grip to another's, 'with Barad to escort you, to have your own hurt dressed. There is blood on your sleeve.'

'Yes, sir,' and a cut in the fabric also, though he'd made that himself as he ran. Anyone looking closely would see that the cut did not match the wound, that the wound bled independently, that there was still a blood-soaked bandage between the two to prove it. That didn't really matter, as he'd made no claims about it – 'no, sir, I was hurt before, the Catari's knife didn't cut me' – but he hoped to keep anyone from seeing so much. Blood on his clothes and a fresh bandage, he hoped that would be enough even when the searchers returned with no Sharai.

They might of course return with the ladies, or with Rudel and Redmond, or with both; that was out of Marron's hands.

His escort was a tough Elessi of middle years keeping a watchful grip on his good arm, making little pretence of assistance. Lord, but they were a suspicious people . . .

In through the circle of watch-fires that contained the camp, to where the tents were ordered in neat lines: a suspicious and disciplined people. Marron sagged a little against his escort's hold, though not with any fixed purpose in mind. The man's hand tightened in response, still more guard than help.

Then, for the second time tonight, the same question flung at him from the dark, and with almost the same exasperated tone: 'Marron, what are you doing here?'

The voice this time was Sieur Anton's. So was the shadow, the walk, the body that stood before them: making no challenge, but obstructing the way so that Marron's escort had perforce to stand still, and Marron also. It was a precise gambit perfectly executed, and again was all Sieur Anton.

'You know this boy, sieur?'

'Indeed. He is mine own.'

'Your name, sieur?'

'Anton d'Escrivey, of the Knights Ransomers. What has happened, why is my squire bleeding?'

The man's fingers slipped from Marron's arm, his tongue stumbled and slipped on his words; he said, 'The boy surprised men in the village, sieur, Sieur Anton . . . He says he saw them off, we are searching now . . . By your leave, sieur . . .'

A bow and a sharp turn, and he was off without waiting for Sieur Anton's casual wave of dismissal. Marron thought he saw the man make a surreptitious sign as he all but ran away from them, the sign of the God but as the peasants, as the superstitious used it, a ward to fend off evil.

'You will become used to that,' Sieur Anton said, sounding a little weary, a little amused, nothing more. 'Now, Marron. Men?'

'Catari, sieur. Three of them, they might have been Sharai . . .'

'They might have been local here, and of the faith. People do live in this village, though they seem to have melted tonight.'

'Yes, sieur, but these carried knives drawn. Before they saw me, even . . .' He regretted the lie bitterly, but it must be complete, one story told to all and stood by regardless of who came to challenge it.

'Ah. Hence all the fuss, I take it,' because fuss there was and spreading through the camp now, single men and squads of men hurrying east and west. 'You there!'

'Sieur?' A young sergeant stiffened, almost saluted; it seemed that Sieur Anton had more reputations than one.

'Has anyone thought to check on the safety of the ladies?'

It was an order, politely disguised; this time the sergeant did salute. 'I will do so immediately, sieur.'

'Good. Take some men,' *just in case. This might be a feint to draw us out, to draw our eyes away . . .*

Marron flinched. Those men would find no Sharai, no threat – and no ladies either. They'd scour the village, rouse every camp, search the night by torchlight. Two girls afoot could neither flee nor hide from so many men.

Nor could Marron do anything more to aid them; they must face their own reckoning, as he must his.

The sergeant hurried off, leaving Sieur Anton frowning at his back. 'I ought to go myself,' he murmured. 'But the Elessans wouldn't welcome me, unless it came to a fight. And as usual, someone has to see to you, Marron. Are you always going to be this much trouble?'

'Sieur, I can see to myself . . .'

'I don't think so. Did they cut your arm, these men of yours?'

'No, sieur.' Here at least he couldn't lie, not even by misdirection.

'The old hurt once more, is it? Come with me, then. Even Elessans must travel with a surgeon, for all that they value their scars so much. He won't make it pretty, but I fear that arm never will be pretty now. We'll have it stitched again, at any rate, if it's clean enough within. I am tired of seeing blood on your sleeve.'

Stitched it was, after it had been bathed with something caustic, a liquid that burned on first touch and burned hotter as it bit deeper. The surgeon was a sour man who scorned Marron's first startled gasp and sneered at the trickling tears that came after; as he threaded his needle with coarse gut, he tossed over a pad of foul-smelling leather. 'Bite on that, puppy, if you can't hush your yelping. I've no patience with the weak.'

Sieur Anton took it from him, though, with a brief shake of the head. 'You don't need a gag, lad. Here, give me your hand – no, the other, fool. Hold onto mine, that's right, and squeeze when you must. As tight as you need to, you can't hurt me . . .'

By the time the stitching was done, Marron had his face buried in Sieur Anton's shoulder and his teeth clenched in the knight's clothing, a gag after all. He'd not made a sound, though, nor moved his wounded arm from the surgeon's table; he thought he deserved credit for that, till he opened his wet eyes and saw how the surgeon's free hand still clamped his wrist, Sieur Anton's his elbow. Marron hadn't felt their weight at all, for feeling the fine silver fire of the needle bite and flow around the duller burning of his weeping wound.

When it had been bandaged one more time, and this time strapped tightly to his chest at Sieur Anton's insistence so that he could neither move nor use it, the two of them headed back towards their own camp. Marron at least yearned for his blanket-roll and sleep without dreaming, a black hand to ease pain and anxiety both, some short relief from this long night's work.

'Can you walk, or must I carry you again?'

'Of course I can walk, sieur! Or you must leave me, if I can't . . .'

'Of course.'

And he could walk: though before long his incompetent feet were stumbling, misled by his deceived and stupid eyes, and it was or it seemed to be only Sieur Anton's hand laid on his neck that kept him upright. So light a touch and so much strength to be taken from it, there was magic in this, surely . . .?

Lights and men moved about them in the dark, voices

called, low and harsh and guttural. Three times they were challenged by patrols with weapons drawn; the third time was among the huts of the village, and the man who called them to a halt was that same young sergeant Sieur Anton had sent to check on the ladies' welfare.

'Oh – beg pardon, Sieur Anton, but . . .'

'Not at all, you do right; you should let no one walk these streets untested. I take it the ladies are safe and unharmed?'

'Sleeping soundly, sieur – at least, I hope so. One woke when I went in to check on them, and she's a tongue like a blistering hogweed.'

Sieur Anton laughed. 'May she be blessed with a complaisant husband, then. But do your work quietly, sergeant, to save yourself further abuse. The lady Julianne is no Elessan yet, and she may have more strictures saved up for you if you disturb her sleep again.'

'My men are sworn to silence, sieur,' and he himself was speaking in a mutter, standing close. Sieur Anton laughed again, but softly, before he steered Marron on with a touch more pressure from that hand at his nape.

Marron didn't at all understand the sergeant. How could he think the lady Julianne had sworn at him, when the lady Julianne – Marron knew – was not in that hut or anywhere near the village now?

Unless she and her companion had after all not fled. He didn't know where or why they wanted to go, but the danger of discovery might have driven them back. Though he thought he'd heard Rudel cry the opposite, that the ladies leave while he and Redmond stayed . . .

There still wasn't anything he could do, to learn the

truth or affect it. Neither did there seem a need, for tonight at least. His body only felt the heavier, with one anxiety lifted from him. He was half-asleep already when they came to their encampment, and Sieur Anton's hand was actively propelling him along.

Not for the first time, what was proper was quite reversed between them; squire stood idle, dazed by weariness, while his master unrolled his bedding for him and advised him at least to take his boots off before he went to sleep.

Marron only blinked.

'Oh, for mercy's sake . . . Sit down, then, boy. Easy now, don't jolt that arm . . .'

And the master pulled off the squire's boots, unbuckled his belt, set it aside and saw the lad rolled into his blanket and drifting into sleep, though he grumbled under his breath all the while.

That was the first thing Marron remembered in the morning, the low monotone that had seen him off to sleep: '. . . and how I am to haul my own boots off I am not entirely clear, this is what I keep a boy for, or I thought so. Marron, infant, how can you be so *young* . . .?'

The monotone, and then the kiss. That was the second thing Marron remembered, a touch of dry lips and the brush of stubble, second and last before the welcome topple into nothing.

He thought about that briefly, before the other events of the night came back to him. There was confusion then and fear for himself and others, too many possible consequences; he opened his eyes and sat up with a jerk, too fast, waking his throbbing, stinging arm to fierce life.

Sieur Anton's place was empty, his blanket thrown aside. Marron struggled to his feet and gazed about him, saw the camp a flurry of squires and servants packing up and thought he'd best do the same, though his mouth was dry and his stomach grumbled with hunger.

He was struggling to roll his master's blanket one-handed when he heard his name called. His master's voice: he looked up to see Sieur Anton striding urgently towards him, with a deep frown on his face.

'Marron, leave that. You are sent for. Come.'

'Sieur, where—?'

'The baron wishes to speak with you. Make haste.'

Sieur Anton had already turned away; Marron hurried to catch up to him. Had he thought his mouth dry before? Not so; now it was dust-dry, desert-dry, and all his fear was for himself.

For a minute, it seemed he was to be told no more. But Sieur Anton slowed his pace briefly, glanced down and said, 'The Elessans found no trace of your Catari, boy, either last night or this morning when they looked again. Nor could the dogs find any trail of blood beyond your own. The baron will question you; be sure you do not lie to him. He has a truth-speaker with him.'

His voice was cold, heavy with suspicion, striking a chill deep into Marron's bones. Worse almost than his news, and that was fearful enough.

It was a shorter walk than Marron expected or hoped for, not half so far as the Elessans' camp. At the near edge of the village, a group of men was standing; just as Marron spotted them, Sieur Anton paused.

'Here. Drink a mouthful of this.'

He held out a flask; Marron took it with gratitude, tipped it to his mouth and choked violently. Not water, some fiery spirit that coursed through him, burning.

'The lady Julianne and her companion have vanished,' Sieur Anton told him softly. 'You will be questioned vigorously. Be prepared; and, Marron, *tell the truth*!'

No more then: only a hand on his shoulder, driving him forward, that might look to others as though it were a guard against his fleeing, that in truth – he hoped – was meant to encourage, to reassure. He could find no other reassurance.

Certainly there was none in the men's faces that greeted him, nor in the one woman's. The half-dozen men, dressed in costly, sombre austerity, gazed at him as though he were a felon convicted already, brought for sentence. One stood slightly forward, shaven-headed, scarred and scowling, gripping his sword's hilt as though he would willingly carry out that sentence himself. Perhaps he would.

The woman stood to the side, with them but not of them, not allowed so much licence; and she was the surprise here, and the cause of Marron's most dread. She was robed as a Catari, bronze-skinned and black-haired as a Catari, but her face was unveiled; her face was terrible. He thought at first that she was diseased, a leper or worse. Coming closer, he saw that the stains disfiguring her cheeks and jaw were made of man, an intricate pattern of tattoo; and the mark on her brow, that was man's work also, the sign of the God set there with a hot iron, branded bone-deep. All her skin was puckered around it and her eyes were sunk beneath, glimmers of blue in pits of shadow.

Her face was terrible, but it was not her face that scared him so. It was her calling. He had heard tales of Catari truth-speakers. They had a magic, the stories said, to cry a lie whenever they heard one; and he could not, he dared not tell truth here.

'This is the boy?'

'Yes, my lord.' Sieur Anton nudged Marron down onto his knees, with a discreet hand under his arm to help against the jolt of it.

'Very well. You, boy, you will tell us exactly what you know of last night's events.'

'Yes, sir. Sieur. My lord.' Did he mean now, this moment? Apparently he did; no one else spoke or moved, at any rate, so Marron took a breath and began. He told his tale again, his spur-of-the-moment invention that seemed less and less plausible each time he repeated it, that had had men running and shouting in the darkness but was only a ghost in daylight. Wise like any grown boy in the ways of lying – lessons learned hard, under his uncle's rod – he added nothing and altered nothing, though he could surely have made a more convincing story of it if he'd been free to think again.

Unrevised, it was a tale soon told, and greeted in silence. By their faces, when he dared to look, not one of these men had believed a word of it. And rightly so – but no, he had to forget the truth and focus on the lie; if he didn't believe himself, how could he make anyone else believe him? He didn't so much as glance towards the truth-speaker, for fear of seeing his lie writ as large as her life upon that dreadful skin.

Kneeling, waiting for the next demand, he heard instead

a sharp hoarse scream come from the village, followed by a low eerie wail that sounded barely human, those few moments before it was cut off. Marron shuddered; no man else reacted, except for a hint of displeasure that twisted the baron's mouth, contempt for the weakness of the one who screamed.

'My nephew's bride,' the baron said at last, 'has run away in the night. Do you know aught of that?'

'Nothing, my lord.'

'Strange. You cry an invisible enemy, what time the girl disappears; you throw all into confusion, and you wish us to believe there was no collusion between you?'

'My lord, the lady Julianne was seen and spoken to by your own man, a half-hour after I was attacked . . .'

That dissembling protest won him a glare from the baron and a cuff from Sieur Anton behind him, hard enough to make his skull sing. Punishment or warning, *don't try this man too far.*

'That man had a conversation with moppets,' the baron growled, 'with rags and ropes, it seems. Are you some man's moppet also, boy? My woman here will try the truth of you. Imber, you stay. Your honour is entangled here, and it stains my soul to watch this.'

The tall young man behind him nodded a blond head slowly, though *mine also* was written on his face. Another at his side – taller yet, and darker – touched his arm, *I'll stay with you.*

Marron watched the elder baron leave with others in his train, the younger remain and his friend also, and cared nothing for any of that. All he cared for was the rustle of the woman's skirts beside him, drawing near; the touch of her hand on the nape of his neck, cold and hard her fingers and so unlike his master's last night. Chill doom, he thought they spelled. They would pick truth from the strings of his body as a jongleur picked a tune from the strings of his mandora, and there would be no more mercy in these young men when they heard it than there had been in their senior when he demanded it.

Moppets, he'd said. Moppets were children's toys, but they were also – *rags and ropes* – the tools that Rudel used to make his simulacra, poppets he'd called them, his devil-dolls that sat and moved and he said looked like the people they pretended to be. Perhaps they talked so too, or seemed to . . .

Marron was making more sense of this morning's news, slowly, slowly, and just when he didn't want to, when he needed to stay bewildered. Rudel and Redmond must have gone to the ladies' lodging and set their poppets there to fool the guard; which meant that yes, truly, the ladies were gone. And he could say all that, he could be forced to, betray himself and the ladies and the two men too and so die, uselessly, too late . . .

Cold and hard her fingers, cold and hard her grip; she laid her other hand atop his head, pressing down. His mind spun, as though he were dizzy-drunk and sick with it. He closed his eyes, but that was worse: colours he had no name for oozed and pulsed behind his eyes, spread and shrank and left lingering shadows in their wake.

Even so, it was an effort to force his eyes to open again, a greater effort to make them focus on a pebble on the ground before him, to see at least one thing clearly and cling to that.

It would have been a greater effort still, an impossible

effort to focus his mind also on her voice, on the questions she thrust at him in a limpid, liquid, lilting, lisping voice where even the words seemed to change shape inside his head. He heard them, yes, he knew they were there; but he could not listen to them, nor keep his thoughts even a beat ahead of his voice as it slurred in answer.

'Marron, do you hear?'

'Yes.'

'Do you lie, ever?'

'Yes.'

'Will you lie to me?'

'No.'

He heard himself and was conscious of what he'd said, but always that little too late. Whatever this was that she did to him, however it was done it bore out all the stories that he'd heard. She could ask him anything and he'd tell her true, he couldn't help himself.

'Did you see three men, strangers, outside the village last night?'

'Yes,' he said, he heard himself reply; and was briefly amazed until he caught his own thought a moment later, a picture-memory of three men indeed and all of them strange to him, not of his troop, the patrol of brothers sliding down into the gully.

'Were they Catari men?'

'I don't know.' Well, and that was true too, he hadn't been close enough. It was most unlikely, there were no Catari brethren: he could say that, he could assert it, he could swear it, even, but he couldn't know for certain about these. There should be no Surayonnaise either in the Order's robes, but two had stood in that same gully last night.

'What of the blood on your knife, did you cut your own arm to claim the blood Catari?'

'No.' No, he hadn't cut his arm, he hadn't needed to; only slid the blade up his sleeve and smeared it with what oozed freshly from his much-abused flesh. He'd been proud of that, pleased with himself even in the heart-pounding frenzy of the chase.

'Did the lady Julianne ask you to aid her escape?'

'No.' She'd said not a word to him.

'Did her companion do so?'

'No.' She neither, only worked her dirty little spell in his mind to muddle him as this woman was now, leading his thoughts in a slow dance, invading what should be private beyond any spying . . .

'Do you know where they are gone?'

'No.'

'Ask him if he truly fought last night, if he truly wounded any man.'

But that was not her subtle voice, invested with her magic. It was a man's, blunt and brutal; and like a great stone heaved into a still pool it shattered what spell the woman had woven, what bound Marron's tongue to her quest. She gasped, and he felt a tearing pain as she lifted her hands suddenly from his head and neck. He toppled sideways as if there were nothing now to hold him upright, hit the ground hard and lay there retching, curling up around his roiling stomach as his mind plunged sickeningly toward a spinning darkness.

Dimly, distantly he heard the man again, 'Ask him!'

'I cannot, now,' she said above him, and she too sounded sick and hurt, her voice no liquid binding now, only a stammering stranger. 'See him, he could not speak again. You have broken it.'

'Enough.' That was Sieur Anton, no question of it, one word was plenty; and these were Sieur Anton's hands on his shoulders, lifting him gently back onto his knees, holding him steady, drawing him back from that dreadful abyss. 'He has answered enough. He spoke the truth.'

'Perhaps. I would have liked more.' That was another, not the first man to speak. 'My lady Julianne is missing—'

'—And this boy knows nothing of it, he said as much. Or do you doubt your woman's talents?'

'No, only her wisdom in the questioning. But you are right, Sieur Anton; my disappointment makes me harsher than I like. Is the boy unwell?'

'I do not know. He is hurt and frightened, shocked . . .'

'He will recover.' That was the woman again. 'We are both hurt. None should speak, save I alone. He needs rest.'

'As ever; which, as ever, he may not have. Set your men to searching, my lord baron, call out your dogs to find your lady's trail; I will see to my squire.'

His arms shifted, ready to lift. Marron squirmed, wriggled, almost fought to push his master from him. 'No, sieur, let me be . . .'

Startled perhaps by this unexpected rebellion, Sieur Anton made no further move. Marron reached his one free hand blindly back towards the knight, gripped his sleeve and pulled himself cautiously, wobblingly to his feet. Swallowed against his rising bile, and squinted into the light until his eyes found the young Baron Imber.

'My lord,' he said falteringly, 'I am sorry, but I do not know where your lady is gone.'

'Easy, lad. I believe you, though my uncle may not.'

'Then let me help you search, let me show . . .'

'There is no need,' the baron said, with the hint of a smile in his voice; and Sieur Anton rising beside him said, 'No, Marron. A one-armed boy would be of little use, even on muleback, and you have nothing more to prove. Come, make your bow to the baron,' and his hand on Marron's neck did that for him, bending him low to his stomach's great danger, 'and let be. You would likely fall from your mule in any case, and lose yourself also. We will go back to the camp, and then to the Roq again; it is decided. This party goes no further, until the ladies are discovered.'

'Sieur . . .'

'*No*, Marron. Obedience, Marron. Yes? God's truth, I wonder how you have lived so long . . .'

The sickness passed, though not the dizzy memory of it; the walk back to camp helped, as did his fumbling efforts to pack his master's goods, though Sieur Anton did more to help than his rank properly required. They were ready to ride before the other knights; in the delay, Marron said, 'Sieur, someone should check that the ladies' baggage has been collected from the village.'

'No doubt someone has. It is hardly my responsibility, nor yours.'

'No, sieur, but everyone might think thus. Whose responsibility is it, with her ladyship's companion missing also?'

'I do not know. Do you want me to run and find out?'

'No, sieur. Let me go. One look is all it needs, and the walk would help my head. I feel better, walking . . .'

'Oh, go, then. But don't linger, I won't wait. You could find yourself with a longer walk than you fancy.'

'No, sieur,' pretending that meant, *no, I won't linger*, when they both knew that in truth it meant, *no, sieur, you wouldn't leave me to walk.*

He didn't hurry, neither his legs nor his belly would allow it; and so much was true, that walking was better than being still.

The traders' circle was broken, the oxen harnessed and the wagons drawn up in line. The village beyond was empty, as it had been almost since their arrival. Of the faith the people might be; trusting they were not.

Then he came around a corner to find the headman's hut, where the ladies should have slept the night. He was genuinely looking to see if their baggage had been forgotten, in case Redmond had sought to hide once more within that awkward chest; he thought he might perhaps find Rudel here.

Instead, he found the young sergeant who had reported speaking with the lady Julianne last night.

He found the man naked and spread-eagled, crucified across the doorway to the hut: his arms high and his legs wide, wrists and ankles nailed to the wooden frame. He was gagged with a belt, perhaps his own; Marron remembered that wailing cry so quickly silenced.

Marron took the baggage on faith, along with Redmond's absence and Rudel's. He wanted only to turn and walk away, but the man's eyes held him, wide and white and agonised.

His body was all blood; it ran down his arms and down

his chest and legs, it pooled around his feet, too much to soak the dust and disappear.

I spoke to her, his eyes said, *I did . . .*

Marron nodded.

The man's ankles had been shattered by the dull metal spikes driven through them – iron tent-pegs, Marron thought, perhaps – so that he sagged against those that pinned his wrists and screamed behind his gag, screamed all but silently; and arched upward to put his weight on broken feet and screamed again, sagged again until he could neither bear the pain of that nor breathe, and so he arched again.

Help me, his eyes demanded, *this is too much, too cruel . . .*

Marron's hand moved to his belt, where his knife lay couched. His fingers gripped the hilt; the man's eyes focused on them, with unbearable intensity.

Slowly, slowly Marron uncurled his fingers, moved his hand away and shook his head. He couldn't speak, he couldn't possibly explain; but he had to be so careful. He'd been incredibly lucky this morning – and *yes, incredibly lucky*, he didn't believe in so much luck and he wished he could see into that woman's mind, because he thought the truth-speaker had deliberately helped him lie – but he daren't risk any more questions, not so much as a single further doubt. He'd have been seen for sure, coming into the deserted village alone. Let the Elessans only return to find a body with a knife-wound to the heart where they had left a man alive to suffer for his fault, and Redmond's life and Rudel's were forfeit again, as was Marron's own.

So he turned and walked away, trading one stranger's life for three he valued more, if little more.

17

Where She Must

There were lessons in humiliation, lessons and lessons; Julianne thought she might never now be free of learning this.

The night had been all breathless adventure at first, deliberately so: wings over time to make a child of her once more, those days and nights she'd slipped off with unsuitable friends to scout the rooftops of Marasson, later the cellars and sewers. So long as she focused on that and played the irresponsible girl again, she could do this and enjoy it, almost. So long as she kept a fierce grip on herself, her trembling fingers, her torn and treacherous mind . . .

Taking almost nothing with them — the flask of *jereth* and a blanket each, knives and food and water, silver and gold and little else; Elisande told her that all her clothes would be useless, so why carry the weight? They could go dirty till they found something clean — they had dressed to confuse, to look like boys from any distance, and slipped out of the hut by the window at the back. There was no guard at their door, Julianne had insisted on that. With friends to the east and friends to the west, she'd said, with men watching to the north and the south and the village deserted, she needed no further protection; she would not be treated like a prisoner, she'd said, to be guarded night and day. Besides, she was entitled to some privacy, she'd said, rustling her skirts in a way intended – and successfully so – to make her auditors blush.

So, no man at the door. But there would be men none the less in the streets, or rather the single street and the few alleys that made this hamlet; they were likely compromising their agreement by watching the door from a distance, men at every corner.

Out of the window they'd gone, then, she and Elisande; a quick scramble over the sill and a drop to ground and then a low-bending shuffle, almost a crawl sometimes as they'd used their hands to find their way through stones and scrub till they came to the dry river bed.

More scrub and thorns on the steep bank down; Elisande had tried to run through them, slipped and fell and rolled to the bottom with a muted squawk. Julianne, ever practical, had sat down and slid like a child, lying flat to let the bushes pass above her and laughing breathlessly, silently in the moon-made shadows.

Laughter that had died quickly, with a touch and a motion of Elisande's hand, a whisper no louder than a breeze: 'There are men in the gully. Be still.'

Still she'd been, a moment of chill terror before she'd remembered who and what she was: no child but daughter of the King's Shadow, and what was there, who was there here that she should fear? To be discovered and detained would be a concern certainly, an inconvenience, a problem; with her father's life at risk – *if* she could trust the djinni, and she must – it was a problem she would strive to avoid. But not from fear, no . . .

She'd turned her face to Elisande, shaped words on a gentle breath of air. 'I don't hear them.'

Elisande had shaken her head, *neither do I*, or else, *that doesn't matter*, perhaps both. 'Two,' she'd murmured. 'They were coming; now they've stopped.'

'Guards?' Julianne had asked, pointlessly: how could Elisande know, and what else could the men be?

But she'd asked anyway, and, 'No. Not guards. I don't know, they mask themselves . . . Hush, here comes another, on the bank . . .'

Her tugging hand had drawn Julianne down, deep into the shadows beneath the scrub; and so Marron had found them and then seemed to lose them again, but the men had come along the gully regardless and Elisande had gasped softly, and then risen up to meet them.

And one had been Rudel and the other was apparently called Redmond, a name that resonated through this land's history but must, surely must be coincidence because he'd been old and weak and shuffling, no kind of legend.

Hard words there'd been, between her friend and the jongleur – though that style was no more the truth than the brother's robes he wore that night; she'd challenged him on that, and not been satisfied – and then there'd been the guards finding them and falling slackly unconscious before they could do more than cry an alarm; and that had been

Rudel's work somehow and he'd done his own shouting then, to set them running as Marron had run already.

Even then, she hadn't wanted to flee. But there'd been more than her pride at stake suddenly, more even than her pride and her father's life. Whoever Rudel and Redmond really were, they'd brought another element to the night's adventure, a sense of greater danger which Elisande at least had recognised. Whoever Elisande really was, to know them well enough to curse them as she had . . .

So when Elisande's hand had snagged hers and tugged, she'd run with her friend along the gully. At least the blanket-roll roped to her back had been light and the peasant's robe easy to run in, though they'd kicked up choking clouds of dust and her boots had kept catching in cracks in the mud below the dust, so that she'd stumbled often and nearly fallen more than once.

For a while they'd run with the sounds of pursuit in their ears, though not pursuit of them. The twists and turns of the absent river's bed had led them away from that, away from the village and the Elessans' camp both; only once had Elisande pulled her urgently to a halt and then whispered a warning, guards ahead on the gully's bank. For a minute they'd stood still, silent except for her own panting breath and her friend's, irritatingly easier to her ears; then Elisande had gestured her on again at a slow walk. She could see the men who watched, standing shadowed against the stars; somehow, despite the bright sky, the men had not seen them.

Once past, they'd jogged on again until she'd simply had to rest, jerking at Elisande's arm to tell her so; she hadn't had the breath to say it. Her friend had nodded, gestured her to sit and crouched beside her, patient for a little while. Then she'd murmured, 'We should get out of this gully anyway, it's leading us off our path. We need to head more northerly.'

They'd clambered up the bank and found themselves in a wide bare valley, high dry hills all around them. Elisande had picked the direction, north and east, and set the pace, a slow walk at first that Julianne could match with comfort.

They'd found the road again, and crossed it: 'I wish this were the other side of the gully,' Elisande had murmured. 'This is how they'll come, looking for us. But we had to come back to it; north and around, it's further but that's the only safe way from here. I'd never get you through the mountains, not on foot and in high summer.'

There was an unspoken implication there, that alone she might have taken the mountain route and survived it. Julianne had been resentful, briefly – *sorry to hold you back, Elisande* – before she'd remembered that she owed the other girl a greater debt than this. If a little condescension was all the levy that her friend demanded, then she was getting guide and companion at a cheap cost indeed.

Besides, Elisande was probably right on both counts. She was hardy and experienced, very likely she could cross a mountain range afoot; Julianne was certain that she herself could not. She'd been having trouble enough in all honesty simply keeping up on the flat, now that the sight of the road had spurred Elisande to set a faster pace, a rapid walk that broke almost into a jog wherever the ground sloped even marginally downhill.

It was the sky, she'd thought, that wore her down. More than the thought of what she left, all she was running away from – a reluctant promise and a dreaded life, all thrown into question and confusion by her first meeting with that man, young man, tall man, heart-stealing thief of a man from whom she was also running away, though it rived her to do it – or the anticipation of what she ran towards, a mystery that might prove a monstrous betrayal if the djinni were false: more than all of that, it had been the sheer weight of sky that had dragged at her muscles and starved her of breath. So broad, so cold a canopy, the stars like chill candles and mind-sickeningly far away; her head had been bowed, she'd only watched her feet but still she'd felt it, still she'd hauled the great compass of it with every weary, aching step she took.

The hills had been no help. Black shadows or grey-glittering slopes of rock, either way they'd held themselves apart, they'd left it all to her. Elisande, too. She was wise, she was skilful, she had the knack to walk beneath the sky and not be touched by it; she was mean, she was selfish, she'd chosen to let her friend, her poor suffering bewildered friend drag all this weight alone . . .

Well, no further. She was going to sit, she had sat; the sky could drape itself about her like a robe, like a tent fallen in on itself, it could do as it willed but she would carry it no further, nor follow clever, cruel Elisande . . .

'Julianne— Oh, I'm so sorry. You're exhausted, I should have seen it sooner. You're right, we must rest. Not here, though. We must find some kind of shelter; if they search this way, we'll need a place to lie unseen. See that next hill, can you make it just to there? The night lies about distance, it's not as far as it looks. And you've done really well, it'll be dawn in a couple of hours and we've gone all night, that's excellent. Far better than I expected. So come on now, on your feet and just this last little stretch, we'll play beetles and find some rock to hide behind, some shadow to lie-up in. Here, take a sip of this first, it's the *jereth*. That'll put some fire in your blood. Water when we get there, yes? You'll never have tasted better, but you have to earn it first . . .'

And she had earned it, with the sharp sweet flavours of *jereth* in her mouth to speak to her of the world as it was, no weary fantasies to mock her now. She'd known herself to be only a tired girl trying to lose herself in a harsh and mocking world, seeking to hide from the one man who had ever drawn her, whose voice and face sucked at her like a lodestone; and the sky was the sky and the night the night, convenient darkness that would prove too short, and nothing more than that.

And no, that hill had not been closer than it seemed, it had been further away, it was Elisande who lied; and every step had been an effort even with her friend's strong arm to lean on, and when at last they'd reached it and found the broken well and the path up and the little cave where the path ended, she'd felt no curiosity, none of Elisande's piqued interest, only relief that it was there and it was empty and she could lie down now, which she had done and had then done nothing more.

She woke reluctantly and late, to the feather-touch of sun on her face and the far weightier touch of memory on her mind, its physical proof on her body. She lay still because every muscle felt stiff and sore and cruelly overused; she didn't open her eyes because even her eyelids were too much for her this morning, if morning it still was.

Sun about her, stone beneath her, a hard bed but it would do; there were noises also, distantly the knocking of rock on rock, but that could wait.

She let her thoughts run back, to see again everything that she'd done yesterday, everything that had happened to her and around her. Leaving the castle and meeting the Barons Imber, elder and younger both; leaving the village and meeting Rudel and Redmond in the gully, in disguise; leaving them – and leaving Imber, but she wasn't, she *wasn't* going to dwell on that, on him, on his face and manners and charm and the touch of him in her head and heart where she'd thought no man would ever touch her – and making that long trek through the night with Elisande, which had brought her here . . .

And where was here, exactly? Her eyes opened without permission, without any intent on her part; she saw a blaze of light and turned her head away, grunting at the effort of even so little movement, the stab of pain in her neck.

She saw light and shadow, no more than that; blinked, squinted against the dazzle and saw rock walls, a shelf of rock, a few small things on the floor and no more than that.

Sitting up took an age, against the aching stiffness in her body. She thought she could feel every bone in her spine creaking in protest. She tossed aside the second blanket that covered her, which Elisande must have laid there when she rose, and then looked around again. A small cave, with only one thing more to be seen in it, the sign of the God

Divided hewn into the wall. She tried to see that as an omen, but couldn't make it work. Wasn't she turning, running away from all that that implied?

No Elisande. That sound of stacking rocks some way away, below, assumed a new importance. So did standing up.

Had it ever been so hard? Well, yes. Once, twice, often. After she fell, that long slow silence down and down: after that, stirring a muscle, setting a foot outside her bed had been a dreadful thing, impossible. The sense of panic, the incoherent rush of terror – like a rush of air, and the gilded ceiling of her room darkening, spinning, rising up to greet her – had taken weeks to pass. Or not to pass, to be taken and closed away, locked in ever smaller, further places in her mind till it was lost, not forgotten but hidden even from herself.

And there had been other times, of course, times when she was ill or hurt or sore from a tumble off a horse, more sore than this; of *course* she'd felt worse than this, her legs had been more rebellious against her will and balance harder to find. And she was not a child any more, nor was she an invalid, and she still had her pride, she refused to let Elisande see her so weak. Nothing but a night's march, after all, and there would be men hunting for them ahorseback, this was no time to play the girl . . .

So she stood up. And cracked her head against the roof of the cave, and swore; and rubbed angrily at the sore spot on her skull, and made it hurt the worse. And saw the length of cloth that had made last night's turban lying on the floor beside her blankets, and stooped to pick it up and wrap it round her head again, and was still wrapping and tucking as she walked almost doubled over out of the cave's mouth—

And reeled, straightened with a gasp that was nearly, nearly a scream, and staggered back against the face of the cliff, her hands grasping at stone behind her as her head spun and she screwed her eyes tight shut against the sun and the wide view of hills and the long, long drop that she'd come so close to stepping over.

She hadn't seen it last night, what with the dark and her numbing exhaustion and Elisande on that side of her, holding her arm tight and talking, talking. She'd known that they climbed, of course, but she hadn't realised just how high nor how steep the path had been, how there'd been nothing on the other side of Elisande.

Steady now, steady . . .

She stood braced against the cliff, feeling for the solidity of rock, trying to borrow a little. She felt the breeze move against her face, she listened to the clunk of stones below her; and at last, oh so slowly, she forced her eyes to open.

Looked only at her feet, where they stood firmly on hard dusty rock. There, that was good. Took a step sideways, with her hands still clinging and her back dragging along the rock. Better. Excellent, indeed. One step, and now another. And a third; and so on down the track, step by cautious step, she could have counted them all the way, she took such care about them.

At last the track turned, away from the wall of cliff on her left. For a moment she hesitated, reluctant to lose that hold she had: with her world so shrunken – cliff-face and path, her feet on the path and her eyes on her feet and nowhere else – it was a wrench to step away, to break out from what was so very secure. Besides, stepping away meant stepping into space, she knew that, it meant falling and falling . . .

But the path stepped away, and the path was not falling; *trust to the path*, some little whisper of sense in her head suggested. So she did. And no, did not fall, because there was no drop now, only good dry dusty ground on either side of the path; this was the valley floor, and she stood and walked upon it.

And lifted her head with a gasp, with a sigh; and saw Elisande now, and saw what she was doing to make those noises, *knock knock* of stone on stone.

Remembered now, a picture plucked from last night's maze: a heap of stones not worked but gathered, and the path that ran from it lying silver in starlight, clear to be seen though nothing used it now, Elisande had said, stooping to brush with her fingers' tips at sand and dust. *This was a well*, she'd said, *and those who used it must have lived above, come, let's find what home they've left us* . . .

It looked more like a well now, or a little more: a dark narrow slit of a hole in the earth, with the stones set to make an awkward, jagged wall around it. Elisande's face shone with sweat beneath her turban as she laboured full in the sun's eye, lifting another stone and dropping it where it might almost fit, grinding it against its neighbours until it almost did.

'I'm no builder,' she panted, straightening as she saw Julianne, 'but this should hold a while. It'll serve to mark it out, at least; and make some windbreak, to hold the dust at bay.'

'Do we need water?' Julianne asked, meaning, *do we need to spend our time and effort repairing wells when we're running, when we're hunted, when we have to be moving on?*

'Sharai manners,' Elisande said, replying to what she had meant and not said. 'Desert habits: you never break a well, nor leave one broken. Learn that, Julianne, it's important.'

'More important than being caught and taken back? If they saw no water here, pursuers might give up for their horses' sake.'

'Yes, more important,' Elisande said flatly. 'Water is life in the desert, life for all. You'll be grateful to your enemy and your family's enemies, every time you drink untainted water. That's how it has to be.'

'This is not desert, and the Sharai are a long way from here.'

'Even so.'

'Well. Is there water, have you tried it?'

For answer, Elisande picked up a pebble and tossed it into the dark. A second later, a soft splash came back to them. The two friends gazed at each other, in contradiction but no hostility; then Julianne sighed, and sat down, and said, 'Where will we find them, then, how far must we go?'

'Look.' Elisande crouched at her side, swept the ground smooth with the flat of her hand and then drew quickly, one-fingered in the dust. 'Here is Tallis, here is Elessi; these are the hills that border both, where we are now. East and south are the mountains, like a spine that divides Outremer from the desert and the Sharai. I don't think we could reach them, whichever route we chose. I can look like a Catari but you cannot, not with that hair and that skin of yours; and all those petty barons are so jealous of their land, they'll stop and question any stranger. Even if we did reach the mountains, I don't believe that I could take you through them. It's harder land than this, no wells and steeper climbs; the passes are higher than these hills.' *Further to fall*, she was saying, and Julianne heard her.

'So we go north and east, we go around the mountains and come down to the desert. It'll take us weeks longer on foot, though we might find horses somewhere. That road is the Kingdom's border for a while, before it turns south towards Elessi. Out here they pay no taxes and offer no allegiance, though they don't make war either, they don't invite the attention of the Order. They're wild folk, nomads mostly, but they breed horses, they don't ask questions and they do like gold. We might even strike lucky. That raiding party that attacked the Roq – no, it was more than that, it was an army – but we might run into them and find ourselves an escort all the way. We can't go into the desert alone in any case, we'll need a guide . . .'

Was it lucky, to meet a Sharai war-party? Perhaps it was, now that her world had turned around, now that she was a reluctant fugitive in a land and a life that bewildered her. Imber was a golden vision trapped behind her eyes, as bright and hot as the sun; he must be held there, hidden and wrapped in a grief she had to keep private even from her friend.

Questions, though, she could surely ask questions; and now was the time to look for answers from Elisande.

'Rudel and that other man, Redmond,' she said slowly. 'Who are they? Truly?'

'You know who Redmond is,' Elisande replied, smiling slightly. 'He is two men, and you know about both. He is the prisoner from Surayon, who was being tortured in the cells at the Roq; and he is Redmond of Corbonne, who was known as the Red Earl.'

Julianne nodded, as though there were nothing momentous in any of this. 'And Rudel?'

'Rudel is also from Surayon.'

'And not a jongleur?'

'Not only a jongleur, though perhaps he should have been. He has some skill in that direction.'

'And you?'

'Oh, I too am also from Surayon. But you know that, don't you? You must have worked that out . . .?'

'Yes, of course. I just wanted to hear you say it. I'm tired of secrets, Elisande.' *Tell me your true heart's wishes, and I won't tell you mine. If you're lucky . . .*

'I know. I'm sorry. But I gave you hints enough, I thought. I couldn't actually say it in the castle. Words are birds, they fly upward and around and you never can tell quite where they'll settle . . .'

'Did some jongleur teach you that?'

'Rudel did.' Said flatly, as though she resented the reminder or the fact itself, that something of his had become something of hers.

'Who is Rudel?'

'A man who thinks he has some authority over me.'

'And does he?'

'No.'

If the next question was obvious – *so who are you, Elisande?* – Julianne thought the answer was also; she thought she'd be told, *I'm a girl over whom Rudel has no authority.* Instead she said, 'What will they do now, Rudel and Redmond? When we were discovered he said they'd turn back; but they wouldn't find it so easy to pass unnoticed a second time, not with all the guards alert and so much fuss . . .'

'I don't know what they'll do,' Elisande said, losing the stubborn cast of her face all in a moment, looking fretful and concerned and suddenly very young. 'There is a thing we can do, a talent we have to confuse men's minds so that they don't see what is in front of them, I suppose you'd call it magic. Not everything they teach about us Surayonnaise is false . . .'

Julianne saw another anxiety spring to life in her friend, and put an arm around her shoulder. 'Not everyone in Outremer thinks that all magic is demons' work, Elisande. And I grew up in Marasson,' *I have seen things done greater and worse.* 'Is that what you did to Marron, when he came along the bank?'

'Yes. I didn't know who he was at first, and then I wasn't sure if he was safe to see us. That boy confuses me, I don't understand his loyalties. Rudel did the same to the Ransomers, only harder, he's stronger than I am and the need was great. And I again, later and lighter, to the men who watched the gully. But everything has its limits; we can only touch a few at a time, three or four at most, and it's a struggle if their minds are focused. Rudel might, he *might* have been able to maze the guards and lead Redmond away again, but I'm not sure. I think perhaps they'd just sit quiet and wait for another chance. But that's in his hands now, there's nothing we can do. We have to look after ourselves,

Julianne, and make our way to the Sharai. That's all. Remember the djinni . . .'

'I haven't forgotten the djinni. Nor what it said. Must we move on today?'

She'd tried to keep her voice even, *just another question, no more*, but by the look that Elisande gave her — part sympathy and part frustration — she hadn't succeeded. Probably it had sounded like a plea, perhaps a child's whine.

'Better not, I think. We won't have left much of a trail on this ground, but even so they may ride out this way. We'd best hide up for the day, and move at night. That cave's as good as anywhere. You can't see it from down here, only the path, and we can brush that out at least a little.'

Perhaps you shouldn't have built the well up, so that it stands out so clearly man-made; but Elisande had not said what she might have said, *you're too exhausted to go on, one night's march has worn you out, you have to rest today*, so all Julianne said was, 'Whose cave was this, do you think? That's the God's sign they've cut into the rock up there . . .'

'Oh, some hermit, some mad monk. The land was full of them, after the King's armies claimed Outremer for their God. Every desolate hill had its religious. The local people brought them food and begged a prayer of them in return, though like as not they only got a curse. But the wild tribes raided here, sometimes the Sharai. The hermits were all killed, or driven off. With luck, your baron will find so many caves he won't search out ours, or else we'll be long gone before he does . . .'

Oh, her baron, searching for her: what must he think, that she had fled from him? Julianne gazed bleakly westward and pushed herself to her feet, aching more in heart than body though her body ached cruelly.

'Let's go up, then, they will have been early on the road.'

Elisande produced bread and oranges from her pack, and they sat in the light of the cave-mouth to eat, far enough back that Julianne could see the view but not the drop and didn't need to look at all, her hands so busy with tearing, peeling, segmenting.

'We've food for one more day, if we're sparing with it,' Elisande said. 'After that we must hunt, track down some people to beg from, or else go hungry,' but she said it cheerfully enough. Julianne understood that going hungry was not a serious option; her friend was confident of her hunting ability, even with nothing more than a knife, or else she was sure of finding company in these drab and empty-seeming hills. Or else both, very likely both. She might have been walking for weeks or months already when Julianne met her, living off the land or its people; admittedly Less Arvon and most of Tallis were fatter lands than these, but they were probably less charitable also. There'd been feeling in her voice, when she spoke of the petty barons' jealousies . . .

'Why did you come to Roq de Rançon?' Julianne asked her. 'It wasn't to rescue Redmond, he followed us.'

'No, Redmond was – a coincidence, an inconvenience. Like that damned djinni. I don't *want* to go to the Sharai!' suddenly, vehemently. 'Not now. Neither do you, do you? Of course you don't, except for your father. And the djinni could save him, if he needs saving; it could pick him up and bring him here in an eye-blink. But it wouldn't do that, of course, oh no. The djinn don't interfere with humankind, they're far too grand. Except when it pleases them, apparently, they just spin up out of the dust and send us off with no warning, and without even telling us *why* . . .'

'Elisande.'

'Yes?'

'Why did you come to the Roq?'

'I came to collect something, if I could. If I could get at it. Something we need to have safe in Surayon, if only to stop the fanatics, the Ransomers, men like Marshal Fulke from putting their hands upon it. Or that Baron Imber – not yours, the older one. Those men could destroy us; they have the means in their hands, if they only knew it. I wanted to pick it up and walk off with it, and leave them still not knowing; but I hadn't managed to get to it, and then they brought Redmond in and I *know* him, he's my friend, he was kind to me when I was a child, when kindness was what I needed more than anything. So I was – distracted; that's why I didn't want to leave, I couldn't bear to leave him. And I hate not knowing what's happened to him now, whether he got away or not . . .'

'What about Rudel?'

'Rudel can look after himself.'

'I mean, why did Rudel come to the castle?'

'Oh, the same as me, largely; he didn't trust me to take care of this thing we wanted, so he came for it himself. But actually it would be safer with me, that's why I came. It was stupid of him to follow me. Stupid, and typical . . .'

'What is it, then? This thing?'

'Just something they shouldn't have, that we could make good use of.'

'A weapon?'

'Of a sort.'

'Elisande, enough of secrets!'

'No. Not yet. Not till we're a lot further away from the castle.'

'Why, don't you trust me?'

'Of course I trust you. I have already, with my life; I'm Surayonnaise, remember? A Surayonnaise witch, they would burn me if they knew. But this is more important, and you're part of their world; if you dropped a hint to your Baron Imber . . .'

'Elisande, I'm running away from my Baron Imber. Remember?'

'Even so. This is not safe knowledge for you to have; not yet, and maybe not later. We failed, Rudel and I; that thing is still there, and fatal to us. It may still be there in a month, in a season, in a year. Where will you be then? Perhaps in Elessi, back with your baron, if your father sends you there. Enough of secrets, you said; I won't give you this one, then, that you might have to keep from lord and husband and friends and all.'

'You've given me enough of those already,' Julianne said, but grumpily, giving in.

'Then rest, under the weight of them. Seriously,' in response to a darting glance, 'you should rest. We must walk the night away.'

'What will you do?' Julianne asked, knowing only that *rest* was the one certainty, the one word she could be sure not to hear in response.

'Scout an hour, maybe two. There must be a village somewhere; those old mad hermits were not that mad, to live where no one would ever bring them bread or questions.'

'Elisande, if they see you—'

'If they see me, I am a goat-boy strayed from my goats, and much in need of a whipping. But in this heat? They will be resting. Like you. I will be a shadow among their sheep-folds. Just to see what kind of people they are, which god they follow. Whether there are horses we can buy or steal. Or camels, we will need camels later, though horses would be better on this ground. Sleep, Julianne. Dream easy, and don't worry about me. If we're lucky, I'll bring a rabbit back.'

Well, she wouldn't worry, then. Why should she, anyway? Elisande was in her element out here. Skin like bark – smooth bark, smooth and soft and oiled – and sapwood muscles beneath, she could walk all night and carry her friend too, rebuild a well and scout and hunt under the sun's hammer while that same friend and all the world else was dozing . . .

Well. Every jewel has its setting. Julianne was competent too, in her own place, and sometimes as quietly assertive. She would not resent Elisande's competence here; indeed, she would doze, as she'd been told to. And wake stiffer than before, no doubt, gall to that resentment that she did of course not feel.

She crept into the cave's shadows, where the rock below her was cool though the still air was warm. Too warm for a blanket now; she lay atop both, for some padding against the rock. And closed her eyes, stretched herself into some semblance of a sleeping figure – *like a tomb*, she thought, *here lies Julianne, lost and alone where even the djinn could not find her* – and her mind spun her back to Marasson, to cool statues under high domes, and she lost the thread of even such foolish thoughts, and did sleep.

And woke to find that the sun had moved on so that its light slid across the cave-mouth without striking even a little way inside. She sat up in the dimness, remembered not to stand; thought about crawling to the mouth to see if there were any sign of Elisande's returning, remembered the long fall that waited for her out there and decided against.

No hope of sleeping more: her rested, restless body told her that. She wondered how the hermit had passed his time here; in prayer, presumably. That was not an option for her. She reached a hand out and traced his God-sign with a finger, running it along the loops, round and around again. Dust powdered down, and little flakes of rock; a sudden gleam of gold leaped out.

No, not gold. Golden light, looking bright only against the shadow of the wall; pale it was by the sun's measure, but rich none the less. The colour of gold dissolved in milk, she thought. And warm, warm against her finger's tip . . .

Puzzled, she bent close to look, while her finger went on working. Dust and splinters fell away, the line of light stretched and ran; it flowed like milk, all through the crude-carved channel of the sign. And met itself and flowed on, round and around again as her finger had gone before it, though she'd snatched that back now. Warm enough before, too hot to touch the light looked suddenly. It was burning, almost too bright to look on; she squinnied her eyes, trying to see rock behind the light, and failing.

'Oh, the God's grief,' she murmured huskily, wishing that Elisande was back. 'What have I done . . .?'

No answer from the wall, only that pulsing, flaring light running and running in its stony path; nor from any god either. This she had to deal with herself.

All right. There was a hermit – *a presumed hermit, but let's presume the hermit, please . . .?* – who must have had some power, some magic, a contact with his God. This was what he did when he wasn't praying, he cut his God's sign into the rock and made it shine, an affirmation of his faith. And the power was not his but the God's, it survived him and lay latent in the rock, in the sign, until some other finger, her stupid ignorant finger was enough to wake it . . .

Yes. That made sense, if anything could be called sense in that fierce light, those pulsing shadows.

Of its own accord – no will, no choice of hers, surely – her hand rose again towards the light and the heat of it. Call it power, call it magic, call it living prayer: whatever it was, it had a wicked allure. She wanted to touch it now, in its glory, even at the cost of scorched fingers. Call it a girl's curiosity, call it her father's training, she needed to know how such a thing felt against her skin. Whether it really would burn her, or if the God had a care for even his most doubting subjects . . .

She touched: and no, even the flowing star of light – like a comet dragging its tail, she thought, and the light fading where it had burned and gone but never fading to darkness before here it came again – even that did not burn her. Her fingers tingled as it passed; she tried to cup it in her palm but it flowed on unregarding, seeming to pass through the flesh and bone of her.

Only a tingle and that pleasant warmth, she could get no touch of it else. Neither any touch of rock. Her fingers pressed further, deeper and a long way deeper than the sign had been chiselled; she could see rock still above her hand – though it was getting harder to see that, harder to see anything beyond the glow that spilt out of the blazing sign, poured out around her breaching hand – but she couldn't find it with her stretching fingers.

This was absurd, she must be dreaming; and yet she was not, she knew that with uttermost certainty. She pushed her hand slowly into the liquid light, without causing the least eddy in its run. The tingling feeling moved up to her elbow as gold washed over it, she lost sight of her hand altogether, and still her fingers clutched at nothing—

—until something clutched at them.

Julianne screamed.

Not a hand that held hers, nothing so human: more like a rope it felt, a hot rope. Or a snake, or a tendril of some grasping plant. Something flexible, that wrapped itself tightly around her hand and wrist. Her fingers clenched instinctively but couldn't grip it, couldn't get a purchase; they just seemed to sink into the thing as if it weren't there at all. When she tried to tug free, though, it clung like riverweed.

Sobbing for breath, sobbing for sheer terror, Julianne set her teeth and pulled. Slowly and steadily she drew her arm back from wherever it had gone, back through the glow and into the cave again.

Something else came with it.

She'd known it was coming, she'd been able to feel the weight of it, the resistance all the way. It was at least passive resistance, though, dead weight. Like pulling a pig of iron, she thought, rather than a living pig; at least it didn't pull back. Whatever it was, she'd rather this than the reverse, that it draw her through light and absent rock into its impossible place . . .

At first she saw it as a darkness, a shadow in the gold and a shadow on her skin, nothing more than that. Then, as her arm came free of the light's tingling touch, she saw it indeed as a rope, or a tendril, or a snake.

Just its tip was coiled around her hand and forearm, its thicker length went stretching back into the glare and back further, where she could not see; she only knew that there was more, much more of it than had hold of her.

She grabbed at it with her free hand, trying to peel it from her arm, but again her fingers found nothing solid to cling to. It was like clutching at smoke. Smoke that held its shape, but writhed and roiled within that intangible skin: beneath her panic Julianne's mind found a memory, another creature that fashioned itself with that same violence, by forces that she could not comprehend.

The djinni . . .

But no. Surely this was not the djinni, not any djinni: that creature's touch was lethal. She remembered the boy on the road, the man on the castle wall, both of them with their bodies ripped open to the bone. All she felt was pressure on her arm. Though she had heard that the djinn could shape themselves from anything, so why not from harmless smoke . . . ?

No. Still, not a djinni. She was sure. Something of the same world, though, something of spirit: and malignant with it, malevolent, she was sure of that also. It lay hot against and around her flesh, but her soul was chilled by its touch.

She scrambled awkwardly to her feet, gut-cramping fear keeping her crouched low below the roof as she backed slowly towards the cave-mouth. Her mouth was stone-dry, even breathing hurt; she couldn't have screamed again if screaming were guaranteed to bring rescue.

Every step she took away from the flaring wall, she had to drag against the weight of the thing that had roped itself to her arm. Its dark smoky shadow surged and seethed through the golden light, the gateway; and then suddenly it was a rope no more, its weight was gone from her, it was a great swirling mass that flowed and folded itself into a solid form at the back of the cave.

Julianne gasped; released, her stinging arm fell dead at her side. She clutched at it, drew it up and cradled it against her breast for a moment, then turned and plunged out into the sunlight.

Heedless of the fall so close at her side, conscious only of a far greater terror at her back, she leaped recklessly down the path, barely catching her weight on one foot before the other was stretching ahead. Stones skittered over the edge and her thoughts also teetered on an edge, on the very edge of a long, long fall; flight had released the pent-up panic in her bones, so that it was hard to think at all, hard to do anything that was not pure animal . . .

But animal she was not. She was daughter of the King's Shadow, and trained to do more, to do better than run. That training was a net which contained her even through that jarring, desperate descent, a net she could cling to, so that at the foot of the cliff she could halt, and did. She could straighten herself, and did; could even turn, to see what it was that she fled from.

And did.

And saw it coming after her, smoke no more; now it was something black and chitinous, a beetle perhaps though a beetle of grotesque size, balanced on too many sharp fast legs and with great claws extended, mouth-parts moving behind them as though it chewed already on her flesh. And it had an idol's head above the insect mouth, red burning eyes and horns rising high: half-beetle and half-devil then, and either half inimical and deadly.

What did she have, to meet such a monster?

Knives. Two knives, and her arms and knives together too short by a distance to reach past those grasping, tearing claws . . .

Julianne turned to run again, all training useless to her; but had gone no more than half a dozen stumbling paces before she was aware suddenly of a figure rising from the shadow of a rock ahead. She drew a sobbing breath to scream her friend's name, to tell her to run also, to run the other way, knives and courage were useless here; but staggered to a halt again, seeing that this was not Elisande who stood before her.

It was a man, a young man in Sharai robes of midnight-blue, and he had a bow in his hands and an arrow nocked already to the string.

He snapped something, a word she didn't know, but his gesture was unmistakable: a jerk of his head, to the side and down.

Julianne dived to the ground behind another rock, poor protection if the creature came after her, but she had no greater hope: neither knives nor speed would save her now, only the young man and his arrows offered any chance.

And the first of the young man's arrows had flown already as she dived, and his hands were busy with a second, notch and draw, aim and fire and pull another from the rope that made the belt of his ragged robe. He had a blade hung there also, a long curved scimitar, but he like she must know that if this devil-beetle came to sword's reach, the fight was over.

She followed the flight of the second arrow, saw it strike the creature's gleaming black armoured body and glance off, fall away. She could see no sign of the first, and presumed that the same had happened. Well, that was likely it, then. *The eyes, aim for the eyes*, but she thought he was already; and if he could shoot no straighter than this – and he had time for only one more arrow to prove it, or the thing would be on them – then she might as well decide to die now, and choose a god to pray to . . .

Briefly, she tried to be that cynical, that calm in the face of catastrophe. Her body betrayed her, though, shuddering with dread; and if her mind was praying it was only to the Sharai and not his god or any, *oh please, one more arrow, make it tell this time* . . .

He seemed to be praying too, holding that arrow in his hand and moving his lips above it while the creature scuttered ever closer. At last, though, he fitted it to his string and seemed not to aim at all, only to draw and release in a moment. Perhaps he had no hope and the arrow was only a gesture, as the prayer had been; or perhaps the thing loomed so large before him that he thought he could not miss.

And perhaps he was right, because he did not miss; neither did this arrow skitter off that unnatural chitin. It flew straight and true, and struck the creature not in either eye but between the two, below the bony black horns.

Julianne thought she saw sparks fly as it struck, sparks of gold.

The creature had no human mouth to bellow; but its jaws worked, and a shrill screeing sound hurt Julianne's ears. She clamped her hands over them, which helped not at all; then she saw the young man drop his bow, draw his scimitar and run forward. She opened her mouth to shout, *no, don't be a fool, stand back and use more arrows . . .*

But he'd never hear, above that scratching scream; and likely he wouldn't understand her anyway. So many tutors she'd had as a child, why had none of them ever taught her Catari?

Briefly, she thought she should draw her knives and go after him. But her short blades could add nothing to his sword, if that were not enough; and even it might not be needed. The creature was swaying, toppling already, its dreadful shriek fading to a moan; that single blessed arrow could be enough on its own account. For certainty's sake or for the pleasure of the kill, no more than that, the Sharai skipped lightly over a drooping claw and thrust his blade in through one of the creature's wide red eyes, thrust deep into its terrible skull. Julianne stood and watched as the fire died in that eye and the other, as the spindly legs collapsed, as the rounded body slumped and rolled. For a moment the head sprawled in the dust, those dead eyes seemed to stare directly at her in accusation, *you brought me through, to this*; then the gloss on the body clouded, what had seemed so strong and real turned back to smoke and held its shape only weakly. What little breeze there was stirred and broke it; the thing drifted like dust and was gone.

The young Sharai grunted, looked at his blade and seemed to find no blood, no mark, no sign at all. Even so he wiped it, he all but scrubbed it on his robe before he sheathed it, before he stooped to reclaim his more potent arrow from where it had fallen to the ground when the creature faded.

Slowly, on legs that she was determined not to allow to tremble, Julianne walked forward to join him. He glanced at her and she saw that he was younger even than she'd thought, younger perhaps than her own Imber, little more than a boy. He smiled effortfully, more shaken than he wanted to admit or her to know; murmured something soft and sibilant, gazed almost blankly at the rocky ground where his fallen enemy was not—

—and then turned abruptly back to her, his eyes widening. He said something more, sharp and demanding.

She shrugged, tried a difficult smile of her own and said, 'I'm sorry, I don't understand you.'

His hand touched the hilt of his sword, and she wondered if it would be her more earthly blood that next tainted his blade.

He held his hand, though; instead he scowled, seemed to fumble for words, at last said, 'You are not Catari. Not a boy.'

'No.' No, and no again. 'My name is Julianne. And thank you, you saved my life . . .'

He shrugged, and turned his face aside. 'Cover your head. Woman.'

Her head was covered already, by the turban that had

helped to deceive him, hiding her long and lustrous hair. She knew what he meant, though, and quickly unwound one end of it to wrap around as a makeshift veil. *There, is that better?* she wanted to say, sardonically, *does that distress you less?*

Instead, 'Forgive me,' she murmured placatingly. 'I am new to your land, and your customs.'

'You dress as a boy.'

'I know. It was . . . necessary. But,' with a sudden, unexpected shudder to say that she too was more shaken than she wanted to know or admit, not at all her father's daughter but only a girl too recently terrified out of her wits, 'what *was* that thing?'

''Ifrit,' he said shortly.

'Ifrit. Of course. Spirit like the djinn, but never neutral as the djinn were meant to be, always cruel, savage, terrible . . .

'It, it came out of the rock . . .' She wasn't going to say that she'd pulled it through, that it was her own curiosity that had so nearly brought disaster to them both.

He grunted and cast his eyes up the path towards the cave, as though he meant to climb it.

This time, Julianne did speak against his intent. 'No,' she said firmly. 'There is no room up there to use your bow,' *your magic arrow,* 'and besides, there are no more.' It had needed her arm, she thought, to make the breach, the gateway through that spinning light. Nor did she want the Sharai to see the light, the sign of an alien god alive and blazing. This was difficult enough already; stupid with aftershock – or so she told herself – she couldn't think how to talk to him, whether to hold him here or hope to see him go . . .

*

Blessedly, she didn't need to. There was a sudden scurry of footsteps behind them – deliberately loud, she thought, that girl could be as silent as a soaring hawk when she chose to – and the Sharai twisted round, his sword grating free of its scabbard in the same movement.

Julianne was slower, dangerously slow; Elisande could have died spitted before she'd even seen the stroke.

But Elisande was faster, in mind and body both. Her face was discreetly veiled already, as Julianne's was, with the tail of her turban; and she was standing quite still, quite unthreatening and more than a long sword's reach away.

Not a word to Julianne; she spoke to the Sharai, and in his own language.

He answered her, she spoke again, and suddenly there was a formality even in the way that he stood, almost a deference in the way that he listened.

No more that Julianne could do; she backed away until her legs came up against a rock, and then she sat on it. Her knees were trembling; aftershock for sure, she could think of nothing but the creature, the 'ifrit, how dark and terrible it had been. How close to death she'd come. She closed her eyes; that helped not at all, so she opened them again and watched the sere pale blue of the sky, wondering how long it would be before rain came to this forsaken country.

'Julianne?'

'Yes, Elisande?'

Rapidly, not to let him follow: 'His name is Jemel. He was with the war-party that attacked the Roq, but he left them in anger, he would not so much as keep the horse that he was riding. He had a friend, a lover I think, who died on the wall; it may have been my knife that killed him. I have not told him that. He has agreed to guide us through the desert to Rhabat; my grandfather's name is worth that much, at least. How did the 'ifrit come?'

Julianne blinked: so much information so quickly, and the question hard at its back. She recognised the technique, was not – quite – caught by it, but would not equivocate anyway.

'The God's sign, on the wall in the cave. I touched it, and it glowed with light: light that I could push my hand into. The 'ifrit caught hold of me, and came through when I tried to pull free . . .'

'Ah. Well, he wants to go up. We must, I think; but we follow him, do you understand? We stand in his shadow now.'

Yes, Julianne understood; that, and the chagrin in Elisande's voice. Her grandfather's name was not all-commanding, then.

She might have asked what that name was, but did not. She followed Elisande, who followed Jemel; and when they came to the cave there was no light running in the God's sign, no smoky shadows in the dimness, only rock and dust and their blankets and small goods strewn about.

Elisande reached to touch the gouged rock where the sign was, but held her hand a fraction short, before Julianne could call out to warn her.

'How could it . . .?'

Julianne had no answer to offer her; nor did she seem to expect one. There was another brief, incomprehensible conversation between her and the Sharai, which Elisande translated. Jemel had agreed that they would not move on till nightfall; there might be other Sharai about, from other tribes than his. It would be better, safer, not to be seen by such. He would keep watch at the cave-mouth, and Elisande with him.

Julianne withdrew. Let them talk, let Elisande sate her curiosity, brandish her grandfather's name, come as close as she might or as close as she dared to that fierce, dangerous young man. Julianne would take the blankets and make a nest for herself in the cool at the back of the cave, as far as she could get from them and from the rough-hewn sign that drew her eyes, drew them and drew them until she screwed them tightly shut and turned her head away.

'Julianne?'
    'Unh?'
    '*Julianne . . .*'
    'Yes, what is it?'
    'Riders.'

She hadn't meant to move. She hadn't moved for a while, not for a long time, and would have been just as glad never to have moved again. Now suddenly every muscle in her itched and twitched, she wanted to be up and running; already she was at the cave-mouth, crouched behind her friend.

'Who are they?' Elessans, brothers? Sharai, or some people other?

'I can't see, there's too much dust. But they're coming up the valley from the south.'

Which meant that she didn't need to see, any more than Julianne. *From the south* meant *from the road*, meant men sent to chase them down and bring them back. Too late to do anything except sit exceedingly still and pray to pass unnoticed, in dun and dirty robes among these dun and dirty rocks.

And so she did, so did they all until,

'Dogs!'

'What?' Julianne's head jerked and her eyes stared, despite all resolutions.

'They've got dogs with them. See?'

Julianne lifted her hand to shade her dazzled eyes. She saw first the dust-cloud down on the valley floor, and never mind how high, how very high she sat, she had neither time nor temper to mind it now. Men and horses, yes, shadows in the dust; and little shadows to the fore making their own little trail of dust, and yes again, those were dogs.

'Sekari hounds,' Elisande said, better used to the light and the habits of the country. 'The Catari princes breed them, for hunting ground game . . .'

'I have seen Sekari.' Tall lean dogs they were, with sharp noses and fine, beautiful silky coats of sand and white. All the fashion they'd been for a while among the Marasson nobility; her father had refused to let her have one as a pet. *They are hunting animals, not lap-dogs*, he'd said, and fetched her home a puppy suitable for a girl, a little wriggling, licking thing that had sat on her knee and slept on her pillow, claimed her love and never quite made up for her disappointment.

'If I'd known they had dogs with them . . .'

'You could have done nothing about it. I do not think you can confound the noses of a pack of dogs.'

But she, oh, there was something she could do. She stood up, despite Elisande's hissed warning; she walked, no, she stormed down the narrow path with no thought at all for her weariness or for the long drop that had once so sucked at her mind and courage.

She stood beside the well, and waited. After a minute Elisande joined her, laden with their blanket-rolls and waterskins; Julianne spared her only the one brief glance. Jemel must be lurking still in the cave, and so farewell to their guide. She turned her gaze back to the building dust.

The dogs came first, baying their success, sniffing and circling restlessly around the girls, pressing close against them; Elisande stroked curious noses and tugged gently at long ears, made little fussing noises while Julianne stood stiff and unresponsive as rock, still waiting.

Then came the horses, with the men that rode them; one led the others by several lengths. That man reined in, jumped down and left his mount to his companions' care, striding forward through the scattering dogs. A shrill whistle called them away, but Julianne would not move her eyes to watch them.

The man – tall and young, lithe and strong – wore a scarf of silk wrapped around his nose and mouth, against the cloying dust. Julianne was vaguely conscious of the irony as she met him bare-faced, her turban torn away and left on the path not to give him any impression of disguise; she could find no pleasure in it.

He stood before her, and seemed to hesitate a moment before he unwound the scarf that veiled him. Blond hair and soft blond beard, hair and beard and skin all overlaid with grey now, with that creeping, insidious dust; when he spoke there was dust in his voice also, that coughing would not clear.

'My lady, I am glad to have found you . . .'

'Do you hunt me with dogs, my lord baron?' she cut him off, at last allowing her outrage its escape. 'With *dogs?*'

And she lifted a hand and slapped him, hard and fast and furious, raising her own little cloud of dust that might have had her laughing another day, in another mood.

'Am I a hare or a deer,' she went on against his startled silence, against the rising murmur of his companions, 'or a runaway slave, to be hounded down this way? Am I an animal?'

'You are a runaway girl,' Imber said quietly, 'in rebellion against a lawful contract and your father's will. If you were an Elessan yet, and in Elessi, you could be whipped for this. If my uncle were here and saw you strike me, you would be whipped regardless.'

'I think not.'

'You don't know my uncle,' and there was a touch of a smile to his face and voice both, before he stilled it. 'He may yet demand it, when he hears; but I can protect you from that, at least. If you ride back with me now.'

'What if I refuse? Will you set your dogs on me again?'

Remarkably, he blushed; and ran a hand through his matted hair where dust and sweat together had made a glue, and said, 'Julianne, I am sorry about the dogs; but they were the swiftest way to find you before my uncle could. I had meant them as a gift, to make you happy . . .'

There was something in him then that touched her, a yearning regret that laid wreck to her anger despite herself. Bereft, she said nothing, only gazed at him: at the marks her fingers had made on his cheek and at the lustrous eyes above that were green or grey or somehow both at once, fringed with lashes of gold . . .

'My lady,' he said, formal again but still quiet, still private, 'is a marriage to me so terrible, that you must flee me after an hour's meeting? After you have come so far in obedience to your father?'

Yes, she thought, it must seem like that to him, that it was himself who had driven her away. What could she say to deny it? Nothing; and so she said nothing at all, only gazed in her sorrow at his own until he bowed and turned away, calling rapid orders to his men. He did not look at her again except the once, when he handed her his own scarf to veil her face, and his eyes were all grey now and turbulent with an understanding that was oh, so cruelly mistaken . . .

They shared a horse for the ride back, she and Elisande, while the man whose horse it was clung to another's stirrup and jogged beside. And sweated and gasped, and cursed with what little breath he had to spare, Julianne thought, cursed fey and fanciful girls in general and herself in particular; and those would be Elessan manners, she fancied, more common than his master's.

Though if not from the nephew, he might have learned them from the uncle; she was not looking forward to facing the elder Baron Imber. Being required to run away, being seen as an impetuous child who could not tolerate her father's plans for her, that had been sufficient humiliation, she'd thought. To be hunted down with dogs was worse, far worse; riding back with Imber's men packed close about her, their eyes scornful above their ill-concealing scarves, worse yet. The way everyone stood and stared as they came to camp, their very silence a contemptuous jeer, that was intolerable; and yet she tolerated it with her head high and her hands not even clenching on the horse's reins, not to startle the animal.

The uncle, though – she thought the uncle might be very bad indeed.

There was little left of the camp now, barely enough to merit the name. All the tents had been struck, bar one: that the tallest and the longest where the barons both had toasted her last night, together with a company from all parties, Elisande and Elessans, Knights Ransomers and Master Sharrol.

Men-at-arms were gathered in groups as before, but now their mess-fires were cold and their packs stowed in piles; their curiosity had turned sour, their nudges were sly and this time she was glad not to overhear what they muttered to each other as she passed. It must be as bad for Imber, too. If a girl would sooner flee than marry, what did that say about the man?

Squires came running to the horses' heads, gawping at her in her peasant's dress. Imber swung out of his saddle and came back to her, helping her down and then taking her arm to conduct her into the tent, a sop to her pride that only fanned the fires of her humiliation. Her jaw clenched behind the veil, as she walked stiffly at his side.

The canvas doors were tied back, to let some little air inside: not enough, she thought, walking into a stifling, stagnant wall of heat. It had been the same last night, an hour of desperate discomfort and not only because of the elder Baron Imber grunting and scowling, the impossibility of saying anything that mattered to the younger.

She thought this tent might be marked in her memory forever, as a place of distress of body, mind and spirit all at once. The elder baron was not there now, but that brought only momentary relief; he would surely come. And when he did, oh, when he did . . .

The tent was quite empty, even the long trestle table and the benches packed away, where the men would have eaten last night after she and Elisande had withdrawn. Women ate separately, it seemed, in Elessi. Only the frame and its cover were left standing: to give the nobles of the party some privacy, she thought, more than shelter from the sun. No one in their right minds would choose to sit in this suffocating air when a breeze was blowing outside, though it bore all the dusts of the desert.

Imber sent a boy running for a chair; she sat, and gladly. The same boy fetched fruit and juice; she was grateful, as much for something to do as for the refreshment. She peeled and segmented, ate and drank discreetly behind her veil while Imber politely turned his head away. And the silence was desperate between them, and both of them were only waiting; they had nothing to say to each other that they could say.

At last, too soon, there was a thunder of hooves and a cloud of dust and the storm broke all about them.

Imber's uncle came striding into the tent with a riding-whip in his hand, and the dark look of a man who meant to use it. Elisande's hands tightened on Julianne's shoulders, from where she stood behind the chair; actually — after one brief, shaming moment of quailing inside, of wanting to beg and plead, *don't beat me, don't hurt me* – Julianne thought her friend stood in greater danger than she did herself. Even the Baron Imber von und zu Karlheim, brother-heir to the Count of Elessi, would not whip the daughter of the King's Shadow. Certainly not before she was wed to his nephew, when she was only promised. A promise could be revoked by an angry father, and other trouble could follow. But *if you cannot whip the lady, whip the maid*; Elisande had no father to protect her, or none that she would lay claim to. Julianne was ready to beg, to plead if she must, though she thought it might do little good.

No need, though: Imber was ahead of her.

Ahead of his uncle's explosive temper, indeed; before the older man could do more than snort at the muggy heat and cast his riding-cloak aside, he said, 'Uncle, thank the God; they are both safe, and back with us.'

'Safe, is it? I would not say they were safe . . .'

'No, but I would.'

'Oh, and would you? Making fools of us, leaving moppets in their beds that cost me the life of a good man . . .'

Moppets? Julianne glanced up and back at Elisande, saw her shrug, then saw her startle behind the veil – she at least seemed to understand, though Julianne knew they had left nothing in their beds that might have looked like sleeping girls, they hadn't thought to do so.

Imber stepped forward, between Julianne and his glowering uncle; said, 'I know you are angry, but this is not a time to be thinking about punishment. It was a girl's foolishness, no more, she won't try to run again . . .'

'She will not,' the other rasped. 'I'll be sure of that. Girl's folly, was it? Well, you'll make a woman of her, then, see if that engenders any sense in the creature. We ride for the Roq immediately, and you'll marry her tonight.'

'But my father . . .'

Her own thought, or at least the one that had risen furthest from the jumbling chaos of all her thoughts; but not her voice, she hadn't recovered breath enough to say it.

It was Imber, either playing shield for her still or else voicing his own genuine concern, she wasn't sure; and it didn't matter, because she was grateful to him either way, and his protest was hopeless either way.

'Oh, you can have another ceremony at the palace later, with all the pomp and nonsense my brother wants. But she'll be married before the God this night, and we'll see if she's still so flighty when she belongs to you.'

'My lord baron—'

'Not I, apparently; but he will be your lord, girl, and you'll go on with him as you ought, or bear the pains of it.'

'My lord,' she tried again, 'I think my own father might have cause for complaint, if I am wed in privity and haste to the damage of my reputation, and he not there to see it done . . .'

'Girl, you have done your own reputation more damage than even a wedding may quickly undo.' That was surely true; she blushed at her ineptness, to have gifted him so easy a score. 'As to your father, he sent you to us to be wed; when and how we choose to do it is our own affair. He made his choice, not to accompany you.'

'The King summoned him, sir.'

The choleric baron only shrugged sourly. 'We all hold

our lands and honours in gift of the King, girl. If your father chooses to dance attendance upon him, that is his concern and none of ours.'

That was so inaccurate and so unfair, she actually found herself gaping. Before she could respond, though, she felt Elisande's fingers dig deep in warning, heard her murmur, 'Julianne, go where you are sent, and marry where you must.'

Too loud a murmur; the baron said, 'So. Listen to your attendant, girl. She may yet save both of you a whipping.'

What more he might have said, and whether young Imber would have argued further in her defence or her father's, she was not to learn; they were interrupted by the sound of riders, then by another man's shadow in the doorway.

Imber's cousin Karel: he nodded to the elder baron and the younger, and bowed courteously to her.

'My lady, I am delighted to see you restored to us. We have been anxious for your welfare.' Was he being sarcastic? She wasn't sure; his voice was graciousness itself, and the smile that backed it seemed honest. She decided to treat him in like manner.

'My lord, I am sorry to have been the cause of so much trouble.' Neither he nor the elder baron had seen fit to ask why she had fled; they must be as certain as her own Imber, that it was only to escape marriage to him. Well, let them think so. *Go where you are sent, and marry where you must*: it had seemed so simple an instruction once, but its force had changed a second time. The djinni's warning would still send her to the Sharai, if she and Elisande could contrive it; but if she must marry Imber first, then so be it. Perhaps their guard would slacken, once the thing was done.

If she could only bring herself to leave her Imber, once the thing was done. It had been hard enough the first time; she doubted her own resolution. Perhaps he would treat her badly, so that she could remember the dogs, her outrage at being hunted, that would help . . .

'Enough of this. Karel, we ride immediately, back to the castle, before sundown. Alert the men.'

Her own men brought up her palanquin to the tent's door. She was glad of that, not to have to face any more staring except for Blaise's, and he was more puzzled than vindictive. He told her that the other camp was broken already, that knights and brothers and traders all – the traders in complaint, he said; vociferous complaint, she understood – had headed back to the Roq, only he and his men remaining. Then he fought a silent war with young Imber, to hand her into the litter; remarkably, he won it, and in the brief time that he was close to her he murmured, 'My lady, are you quite well?'

'Quite, thank you.'

'I mean, well content, I mean . . . I could send a man, have him look for your father . . .'

'Blaise, thank you, but there's no need.' *What, can one man find him and fetch him before tonight, before I'm wed, before I'm a baroness?* 'I am content enough,' she said; and there was a massive lie in that, because on her conscience she should be far from here and travelling blindly, going where she was sent. And another because the man she was to marry was being so stiff with her, was so visibly hurt, and her heart ached for his. And yet, and yet: if she must marry – and even the djinni had said that she must, had ordered her to do so – then this would be the man, the boy she chose. This was not how she would choose to marry him, neither the place nor the style nor the time; but still some part of her, some small and foolish voice was murmuring contentment to her bones.

There was something between Blaise and her bearers as they set out, some conspiracy of concern. The bearers were wide-eyed, twitching and miserable; the sergeant rode close beside the litter, as though to guard against some risk that all the Elessan soldiery could not prevent.

The road took them back through the village, back past the hut they'd not slept in – *moppets? Elisande had understood that and she must remember to ask, but not now* – and suddenly Blaise was sidling his horse closer still, leaning it almost against the palanquin, and she could see nothing past him until the horse reared suddenly, screaming, startling him and her and startling the bearers too, stilling them for a moment in their nervous trot.

Now she could see the hut itself through the panel of gauze, her window onto a harsher world; and she could see something nailed across the doorway. Briefly she thought it was a man-sized moppet, until it moved and she saw that it was a man.

The litter skittered beneath her as the bearers shied like the horse, away from that dark figure whose mouth could make no noise around its gag, whose eyes glittered like a bird's eyes, unreadable, accusing.

Julianne couldn't swallow a sudden gasp, couldn't hide its cause; Elisande peered past her, frankly curious.

'What is it, what's—? Oh. I see. Are you all right?'

Now she had to swallow, and do it a couple of times before she could manage a reply. 'Yes. Yes, I am. Why would they, what had he . . .?' Something that concerned the two girls, obviously; no accident, that he should be stretched out to die across their doorway.

'"The life of a good man", the baron said . . . It must have been him found the simulacra in our beds.'

'What simulacra? The baron spoke of moppets, but we left nothing . . .'

'I think Rudel and Redmond took shelter there, when the cry went up. And they knew us gone, they could be sure someone would look to see if we were safe. There is a way we know to make a poppet that will stand and move and perhaps speak a little. That can muddle a man's mind.'

'Is Surayon magic all about lies and deceit?' she asked, sharp with the vision of what that poppet's work had done.

'Not all. And it was not the magic that crucified the man. That was your husband's work,' sharp in her turn, in defence of her people.

'Not him,' *please, not him.* 'His uncle.'

'Little difference. The Ransomers torture my friend, the Elessans execute their own. Is it any wonder that we draw a veil between our land and theirs? Or that we lie, yes, and deceive, and hide, and kill in secret if we must, to keep ourselves protected and apart?'

'No, Elisande,' only weary now, all passion fled and only wishing herself back in Marasson: not for the first time, and she was certain it would not be the last. 'No wonder at all. Will you lie to me, too, when I am an Elessan?'

'Oh, I expect so,' but her hands said not, drawing her friend close and holding her so as the litter swayed beneath them; they said she was lying already, which was the best comfort of that bad and bewildering day.

She dozed then, and woke still in Elisande's arms, her body stiff and sore again when she sat up, or tried to. Oddly, her feet were higher than her head; she fell back, and the other girl caught her.

'Where are we?'

'Going up. Don't look,' and Elisande's hands prevented her, holding her tightly.

'To the castle?'

'Yes.'

Of course, to the castle. Where else? Her mind felt numb, stupid with more than sleep, with the loss of hope and an unexpected shadow growing. There was only one other question she could think to ask, and the answer was just as obvious.

'The djinni didn't come, then?'

'No, sweetheart, the djinni didn't come. Did you think it would?'

'Not really. It might have, though . . .'

'I told you, the djinn don't interfere. They're not concerned with the ways of men.'

'But it has interfered, it saved my life. Twice, I think. And it told us to go to the Sharai, both of us, that's interference too. And we can't, we're prevented; and you said I owed it a debt, it would make me obey, and I *can't* . . .'

'I know. I don't understand it either. But it said you must marry, and the baron says so too; perhaps this is what it wants first. I don't know . . .'

*

And so on, talking in circles while the litter was carried ever higher; then the light was taken from them as they passed through the castle gate, through the passage and the tunnel beyond. They came back to late sun in the stable-yard, and were set down. Neither of them made any move, they only sat and listened to hurried voices beyond the curtains.

Eventually a hand reached to draw the curtain back, a hand with a black sleeve, a brother; she looked past him to see the preceptor himself gazing at her with some compassion, though little good that would do her.

'My lady. This is . . . unexpected.'

'I know. Forgive me . . .'

'Child, you are as welcome as you were before. But Baron Imber has spoken to me, and there are matters we must discuss. Will you come to my rooms?'

'Your grace, again, forgive me. I am tired,' exhausted, rather, and fretful as the child he named her. 'May we not speak here?' There was little enough to say, after all; she had no choices left.

'Very well. Will you alight?'

She did so, glad of the silent brother's arm to help her out, and then of Elisande's slipping around her waist to keep her from falling.

'The baron has – ah, asked,' *demanded* he meant, she understood him very well, 'that you should be married to his nephew here, tonight. I am not enamoured of this haste; nor, I am convinced, would your father be. I understand that the circumstances are unusual, and I am prepared to allow it. Lacking your father's consent, though, I have insisted that I must be given yours. I would not see anyone forced into an unwilling marriage within my walls. So how say you, my lady? Shall I refuse the baron?'

Here was a chance from nowhere, a choice unlooked-for; but oh, she was so tired, and she couldn't bear to face the baron's anger a second time. 'No,' she said, despite Elisande's sudden tug, *say yes, say yes . . .* 'My father sent me to be married; I think you can take that for his consent. It was my own foolishness that caused the baron's anger, and this haste. I will not resist him further.'

'Very well, child. If that is your true desire.'

'Thank you, it is. Your grace?'

'Yes?'

'Will you conduct the ceremony yourself? Please? My father would appreciate that, I think . . .'

He smiled, with more warmth than she had expected. 'You flatter me, my lady. Perhaps I flatter myself, but I hope you may be right. I have known your father for many years now, and I admire both him and his daughter. None but I shall marry you, be assured of that, if you must be married here.'

'I think I must, your grace. Again, I thank you.'

'No need. Come, let me take you to your room; you need rest. And food, I think. I can see half through you, and that is more than weariness . . .'

Her room for now, perhaps: for this brief time, and no longer. But she was glad to see it, gladder still to lie on the bed and shut her eyes, see nothing at all.

'Julianne, wait.' Elisande touched her lightly on the shoulder, plucking at the coarse and dirty robe she wore. 'Take this off.'

'I don't care about their blankets,' she muttered, throwing an arm across her closed eyes to shut out the light, the world the better.

Elisande laughed above her. 'No more do I, but I care about you. Take this off and turn over, you'll rest the easier. I promise.'

She grumbled, but she hadn't the will to resist; she was stripped quickly and firmly, then rolled onto her stomach.

'Now just relax.' Cool fingers touched her head, on either side. Julianne remembered Marron in a daze, guards slumping unconscious into the gully; she jerked away, though it cost her a stab of pain in her neck.

'Is this more of your magic? I don't want it . . .'

'No, love, it is not. And don't say that so loudly, not here. Not anywhere, this side of the desert. Just lie still, and let me ease you.'

She was rearranged, her head pillowed on her folded arms; then those fingers wove through her hair and worked her scalp lightly, soothingly. Moved down to massage her neck and then her shoulders, kneading, digging deeper with a wiry strength. She yelped; Elisande chuckled.

'It won't hurt for long. Don't fuss, trust me.'

She muttered ungratefully, biting down on another yelp as Elisande's fingers seemed to sink right into her body, plucking on fibres stretched tight beyond bearing. Gradually, though, she could feel her muscles relaxing, unwinding almost under that hard pressure; her mind also started to drift, tension falling away, anxieties lifting. Her thoughts lost their focus, only following the smooth, slow rhythms of Elisande's hands, gentler now, moving lightly down her back. She felt warm, comfortable, easy; weariness flowed through her body in waves, in irresistible pulses, there was nothing she could do but ride them, down and out and away . . .

When she woke, the room was darker. A blanket covered her; she lifted her head to see Elisande moving around, lighting lamps.

'The preceptor has sent food,' her friend said, smiling down at her.

'How long have I been asleep?'

'Not long, but long enough. Come, sit up and eat; we've time for that, but not for idleness.'

Elisande glided across the floor towards her, making a deliberate show of it; Julianne said snappishly, 'Why are you wearing my best dress?'

'I'm not, I'm wearing your second-best dress. You don't want me looking shabby at your wedding, do you? I chose that one for you,' setting a tray down with a grin, and nodding towards the big chest in the corner. 'Though I had to give it an almighty shaking, and I still haven't got all the creases out. I think I can guess how Redmond left the castle, and how he came back again, if they have come back.'

Creased or not, the gown draped across the lid of the chest was one of Julianne's favourites, though Elisande couldn't have known that and it was something more than clever of her to have guessed. The gown was quite simply cut, not at all appropriate for high courtly occasions but absolutely right for a quiet marriage in a Ransomer castle, where luxury and immodesty both would have been out of place. Its deep-sea shades would bring out the green that she loved in Imber's eyes, suppress the grey and give a golden sheen to his hair; and had Elisande thought of that also, how much did that girl see?

Like the preceptor, she saw the emptiness in Julianne's belly, that much was certain; and the tray was heaped high with temptation. Cold meats and candied fruits, pickles and preserves, fresh fruit and fresh white bread . . .

'Have you—?'

'Yes, I have. That's all yours. So eat it.'

So she did; and when she and the tray were finished, the latter as empty as she felt full, they shared the last of the flask of *jereth* between them in a private toast, only their eyes bespeaking what they drank to.

Then Elisande played servant girl, helping Julianne into the gown and dressing her hair, persuading her into a little discreet jewellery and finally arranging her veil so that it conformed to custom, she said, but hid nothing of her friend's great beauty.

There was no glass in the room – nor probably in the castle – so that Julianne couldn't check the honesty of her words; all she could do was blush and threaten Elisande with a hairbrush, and tell her not to be so ridiculous.

'What's ridiculous? You might as well deny that you have two legs, Julianne, or an impossible father, or a loving heart.'

'My father's not impossible.'

Elisande only looked at her, with just the slightest quirk of her eyebrow.

Julianne had to swallow a giggle. 'Well, anyway. You're as pretty as I am.'

Elisande seemed to consider that for a moment, before allowing thoughtfully, 'I make a very pretty boy.'

That cracked clean through all Julianne's reserve. Her laughter choked her; Elisande had to pound her back before she could catch her breath, and then put her disarranged veil in order again, all the time scolding like an old and privileged nanny, which only threatened to dissolve her once more.

'Stop it,' she pleaded, wiping at wet eyes with her fingers because Elisande wouldn't let her use the veil. 'Enough. What time is it?'

'Time you were a-marrying that boy.' Elisande took her hands and drew her gently to her feet, linked arms with her and stepped towards the curtained doorway. 'He's quite pretty too, mind,' she added judiciously. 'Though you should take a razor to him. I don't like beards much in any case, and as for that fluff of his . . .'

'Elisande, *stop* it . . .!'

The timing had seemed casual, and was exact. As they left the chamber the great bell above them struck the first of its calling-strokes, to summon the brothers to sunset prayer. They walked slowly – 'Let everyone else hurry,' Elisande murmured, 'this is your day and your hour, they'll wait for you' – down the stairs and across the ward beyond, seeing black-clad figures scurry ahead of them.

And so into the shadows of the castle proper as the bell boomed again, and as its echoes died away there was only the scurry of sandals to be heard in the passage, and that fading also.

They came to the great door of the great hall just as

Brother Whisperer sounded its last single stroke; but this time that door was not closed against them, nor did they turn aside towards the stair up to the guests' gallery.

Elisande's hand squeezed her arm, just once, for courage; Julianne stepped forward, and the two girls walked into the main body of the hall.

Flambeaux burned in sconces on every pillar, to light their path. Brothers knelt in dark ranks on either side, rank after rank; beyond the black were two of white, the knights of the Order in their places.

Lifting her head, Julianne saw all the masters arrayed in line before the altar. In the centre of that line stood the preceptor; below him, on the lowest of the steps, two other men were waiting, watching her.

Karel, there to support his cousin, and of course that cousin himself: Imber, dressed in the best that he had brought, not wedding finery but soft green velvet that would enhance both his eyes and her gown. She thought she could see his eyes even at this distance, shining with hurt and with hope.

Told herself not to be foolish, this was no jongleur's romance; it was real life, rich with promises to be broken and dreams left brutally unfulfilled.

None the less she walked forward with an extra impetus, certainty added to pride, to claim this much at least of what was hers, at least for this little moment.

They stood side by side on that bottom step, just a pace apart. On the other side, Elisande's hand was lightly linked with hers.

The preceptor lifted his arms and she heard a soft shuffling sound at her back, as all the knights and brothers rose to their feet. A movement snagged at the corner of her eye; stealing a quick glance, she saw people standing all along the walls also. Squires in white, servants in whatever were their finest dresses, traders in many-coloured clothes. She wondered vaguely if Marron were among the squires, if d'Escrivey had joined his confrères for once or if he kept a solitary vigil above, if indeed he'd come at all.

Less vaguely, she wondered if Rudel were here, and if so in what guise, as bright jongleur or hidden brother?

There must have been a signal given, by the preceptor or another master, but she didn't see it. All together, though, the Ransomers began to sing, and her bones thrilled to the sound of their massed voices.

It was the regular evening service, begun with a common prayer to the God; only that in honour to her or to the occasion, it was to be sung rather than spoken. Deep bass and rising tenor, the voices cut to the heart of her, and her hand tightened on Elisande's. Involuntarily her eyes moved the other way, to find Imber where he stood that short step away, his body in light and shadow. And caught him glancing at her: their gazes locked, and now her stomach too was churning, although she could not read his thoughts.

After the prayer, the responses: a single voice calling high and tuneful, a thundering reply. Tears pricked behind her eyes; she had to blink hard, and when her sight cleared she had lost Imber, he had turned his face forward and a guttering shadow hid even his profile from her.

So she too looked to the front, and then she understood the soft gasps she could hear from the sides of the hall. The sign of the God hung massively above the altar, and a cool blue liquid light was flowing through the endless double loop.

'Beloved brethren, we all of us serve the God: those who bear arms in His service and those who may not, those who guard the Sanctuary Land and those who work or dwell or travel within it. Just as precious, to Him and to us, are the women: for without them, He would have no servants and we no children. It is always a blessing to see a marriage performed, doubly so when it is a wedding of two high houses, whose sons will be the leaders of men in their generation. I feel thrice blessed this night, that I may act in such a rite . . .'

The preceptor's voice was as mellow and musical as the singing; but where that had beaten brazenly in her blood, this lulled and gentled Julianne. She was happy to let the voice simply pour over her like warm honey, she felt no need to listen.

Her eyes were drawn back inexorably to the God's sign, to the light that flared there. *Like the light in the cave,* but this a light divided: two lights that chased and never met each other even where the two loops joined, two lights of different shades of blue that pulsed to different rhythms.

The preceptor's hands beckoned; she and Imber took one pace forward together, climbed another step. Elisande remained below, with Karel. Julianne missed the comfort of her friend's touch; she folded her hands demurely below her ribs, and lifted her head to watch those lights again.

It seemed to her that they ran more slowly now, but pulsed the brighter. She could feel her own pulse under her fingers; one of those lights was beating in time with her body, she could see the match and sense it also.

The other, it seemed to her, was beating a little faster. She glanced sidelong at Imber and locked her hands together, to be sure that neither one would reach out to take his wrist, to test him.

'The God blesses all his children, but some He looks upon with especial favour. This His son Imber, heir to the County of Elessi; this His daughter Julianne, earthly daughter to the one known as the King's Shadow . . .'

Was she earthly? She didn't feel so, she felt luminous and unconfined. She felt she was that light, dancing in the God's grace; her eyes she thought must have turned to blazing blue, fiery pulsing blue, as Imber's also, surely.

'Take hands, children.'

She heard that but she didn't move, couldn't move, seemed not to have command of her body, so rapt she was, so caught by the spinning lights. Imber it was who reached across the gulf between them, who bridged it with his arm, whose slim hand claimed one of hers; his fingers lay lightly in her palm, forcing nothing, making no claim of strength. Her skin tingled at his touch; she thought of the cave again, and dared not grip tighter for fear of what lay deep in her, in him.

Now the lights ran together, still two but joined, two comets on the same fixed path. She felt his pulse and saw it, both at once; willed her own heart to beat more quickly to match his, and saw and felt it happen.

*

'Step up, and give me your hands.'

She did not want to do that, she wanted to still time and hold this moment forever, not to risk the loss of what was wonderful to her. Again it had to be Imber who moved first, who drew her up after him and gave her hand with his. She sighed softly as the preceptor broke the link between them, his soft skin against her fingers where she wanted only Imber's.

Above and behind him, the two lights stilled: one in each loop of the God's sign, both close to where the two loops joined. Beating, pulsing together, waiting.

'These rings I give you, as eternal witness that you are pledged, each to each and unto death. Wear them in faith, and trust in the God whose sign they make together, two become one.'

A cool band of gold, slipped onto the smallest finger of her right hand; another onto Imber's left. The preceptor lifted both their hands high, then touched them together so that gold met gold.

The two lights blazed and melted, each into the other; and then there was only one that flowed and burned too bright to look upon, before it faded like a flower dead too soon. She felt its going like a silence falling, and was bereft.

'Kiss her, child.'

And he did; his dry lips brushed hers, and she saw no lights now except his eyes, and they were grey and doubtful.

Never mind the singing, never mind the lights nor what went on beneath them; this was still a normal evening service, there would and must be a sermon. After one more exultant prayer, she heard shuffling, rustling sounds behind her, and knew the congregation to be kneeling. Imber's hand reclaimed hers. She walked slowly backward in pace with him, back and down with Elisande's touch unexpectedly on her spine to guide her; at the foot of the steps they too knelt, and she tried one more sideways glance. Nothing, only his profile again, again in shadow. If he sensed her eyes on him, he didn't respond.

Marshal Fulke gave the sermon, another clarion call to arms, against the evils of Surayon. Julianne wondered how Elisande must feel, hearing herself and all her people condemned as heretics and witches. She schooled her face to stillness, and listened with only half an ear. She had other things on her mind this night: questions and anxieties that racked her, hopes and fears for herself and others and one great burning desire – entirely for herself, this, to quiet the trembling that ran bone-deep within her; except that it wasn't, it couldn't be, it had to be shared or it was nothing at all – that only served to confuse her further.

After the service, after the last great stone-shaking cry had dwindled to a single sobbing note, losing itself in its own faint echo and finally engulfed by silence, the masters came down the steps in two files to pass between Imber and Karel, or else between her and Elisande. One or two, she noticed, drew up the skirts of their robes not to touch – not to be defiled by? – the gowns of either girl.

Only the preceptor remained above. Behind her she heard the congregation shuffling out, but she stayed as she was, on her knees and held by the hand. Because Imber did, because she didn't know what else to do.

It was Karel and Elisande who moved first, of the four of them: friends who stood and reached down, offered hands and help in rising.

With that assistance, she managed to stand up and not let go of Imber, nor look directly at him. His turn, if he would; she would not.

The preceptor came down the steps, his arms spread in pleasure.

'Excellently done, Imber, you will take a treasure home to Elessi. And you, my daughter: you have joined a famous name to a famous house. Only the best will come of this, the God will bless you both. Now come, Julianne,' and he took her hands, both of them, denied her any touch or sight of Imber as he turned her gently, deftly away, 'let your lord away to feast with his men; no doubt they will want to pledge your name and his. I myself will show you to your quarters.'

Thank you, I know the way – but thankfully she recognised the futility of protest and held her tongue. Then, as he led her out through a side door, she realised that of course she did not know the way; all that was certain was that she would not sleep tonight in the room that she was used to.

'My luggage, your grace . . .?'

He smiled, and patted her hand. 'Brothers have fetched it already, my dear, as they should also have prepared a bath by now. You have your woman to attend you' – and indeed Elisande was tailing them like a dog, a sour dog to judge by her sudden sniff – 'and I will send some supper to you both. Be patient; the young baron's men may seek to detain him, but I think he will come soon.'

Above all else she wanted one thing, one thought in her head, *let him come when he will, why should I care when he come or how, sober or drunk or reeling, vomiting, stinking with drink?* And she could not manage so much dishonesty, even in the privacy of her own mind, and she could have wept with frustration: to be enslaved to a boy – sold and seized and snared all three, by her father and his uncle and himself, and the last of those the only one that mattered – when she had so much to think about that was not Imber, so much on her mind that she could not share, so far to go where she could neither take him nor let him follow . . .

The preceptor took them out into the still, warm night, across a ward and so indoors again; and those were dried rushes that they walked on, that was a door she knew and a stranger, an Elessan on guard alert beside it, opening it, bowing them in when it should have been a brother.

'Your grace,' she said awkwardly, stammering almost, 'these are your own apartments . . .'

'My gift to you,' he said equably, and then with a wry smile, 'only for the night. It is no great sacrifice. The elder baron is insistent that you must away tomorrow. So I will sleep in the masters' tower as I used, and be very comfortable there. My audience-chamber you know; the bedchamber is here, and there is another room that connects to them both, my study, where a bed is made up for your companion,' with a gentle nod to Elisande, palliative, almost conspiratorial.

'Your grace, it's very kind, but—'

'But not enough, I know. Alas, these are the most fit quarters we can find, to entertain a baroness. And her husband. I'll bid you a good night, my lady, and a blessed wakening to follow.'

Was that the suspicion of a wink, as he bowed to her? No, surely not. The Preceptor of Roq de Rançon was surely above and far above innuendo.

The Preceptor of Roq de Rançon, she reminded herself bitterly, was a man; and like all men of noble birth, no doubt he'd hunted as a youth, before he took his vows. Like all men, noble or otherwise, he was no doubt pleased to see another hunt successful, another woman caught and brought to heel, brought to bed . . .

Bathed and fed, dressed in the most respectable nightwear that her baggage could produce, she sat in the bedchamber – on the bed itself, plain but comfortable and easily wide enough for two, though she was sure that it had never before entertained so many – and waited for Imber to come to her.

Elisande had played servant to the last, combing out Julianne's hair to a shining, glorious fall; playing along, Julianne had played mistress and dismissed her to her own makeshift bed, determined to wait out this time alone. She'd refused to talk, to plan, even to conjecture. Morning would come soon enough; tonight her thoughts seethed, she couldn't concentrate.

At last she heard footsteps, voices, two men talking; she heard quiet laughter – Karel's, that – and then a brusque goodnight, and a door firmly closed.

One man's booted feet; she watched the doorway and the hanging that closed it, and saw that slowly rise.

For a moment he stood there, tall and young and limned in light, his blond hair like a halo, bright, diffuse.

She rose to her feet as he stepped inside, and curtsied dutifully.

'My lord baron.'

'My lady baroness.' He raised her up with gentle hands, and touched her cheek; she gasped at the tingle, the thrill of his fingers on her skin.

He frowned, and stepped away. It was all she could do to suppress a groan. She wanted to cling to him, and would not.

'My lady Julianne,' he said slowly, effortfully, 'I regret deeply the pain that this required marriage has brought to you.'

'Imber, no . . .'

'We need not dissemble, with each other. Let us at least have honesty in private. You tried to flee; I wish I could be sorry that I found you. That I cannot, because truly I welcome this match. I am only sorry for the nature of it, my uncle's insistence that it be made so soon. I would have taken you to Elessi and given you time to accustom yourself to it, to learn I hope to love me.

'I will still hope for that. But I saw your reluctance in the ceremony, and I see what it costs you now, not to flinch from my touch. This much at least I am resolved upon, that I will not force my body on you while you are yet unwilling. My uncle need not know,' and for a moment he was all boy beneath his careful formality, *please don't tell my uncle*, and her heart surged in sympathy, 'but for tonight and for the future, until you are ready for me, let your companion sleep with you; I will take her bed.'

'Imber . . .'

Imber, no, but she couldn't say it. Better if he did think her estranged, distressed, even disgusted by his closeness; he'd stay further off, give her more time and privacy with Elisande, perhaps give them another chance to get away. Better for the turmoil in her soul also: she had both yearned for and dreaded his body in this her bed, his body and hers tight as a fist. So closely tangled with him, she thought she might never break free . . .

So no, she said nothing but his name; and he took that for what it was not, apology and gratitude both. He bowed and left her, by the other door; moments later, Elisande came hurrying through.

The door closed quietly, firmly, irrevocably behind her.

Julianne wouldn't speak; when Elisande tried to draw her out in whispers, 'What happened? What did he say, what did he do?' she only shook her head in miserable refusal.

The two girls climbed into the bed, and when Elisande reached to hold her, to offer silent sympathy and comfort, again Julianne shook her head, and pushed her away.

And lay all night on the far edge of the mattress, as alone as she could be, touching her friend nowhere; and not till she was certain that Elisande was sleeping did Julianne dare to let her tears, the first of many tears fall.

18

His Honour With His Clothes

Marron had had a difficult day.

He'd never expected nor looked for an easy life; he'd genuinely tried to be a good and dutiful brother Ransomer, and felt that his failure there had not been his own fault; he wanted to make as honest a commitment to his new position. But if a squire had to work hard sometimes to please his master, having only one good arm made the work harder. It was harder still when his fellow squires treated him with contempt and derision; and when that same one-armed squire had dangerous secrets to keep hidden, when his loyalties tugged in opposite directions, what was already so hard became almost impossible.

The long ride back to the Roq had been weary enough. When at last they'd made the final climb up to the castle and through into the stable-yard, he'd wanted no more than to fall from his mule and find a pallet somewhere to sleep on. But a wide dark stain on the cobbles had made a cruel reminder that there were no stable-boys any more, to care for his mount or his master's.

He'd struggled through the crush alone, first with Sieur Anton's great destrier, and then with his own little mule. He'd found stalls for them both, and fetched them feed and water; he'd cleaned saddles and harness as best he could one-handed, and his wounded arm had ached brutally before he was done, for all that it was bound so tightly against his chest that he'd had no use of it.

Finished at last, he'd drawn one more bucket of water and thrust his head into it, had come up gasping from the cold refreshing bite of it. As he'd pushed his fingers through his dripping hair, he'd heard a jeering laugh behind him. 'Oh look, little monkey's making himself pretty.'

'All washed and clean and ready for the night,' another voice had replied.

'The knight? Which knight?'

'Kind Sieur Anton, of course . . .'

Marron had stood up slowly, his fingers straying towards his belt, feeling for the hilt of his new knife; but he'd checked before they reached it, walked away without looking back. Didn't matter which lads it was that sneered at him, they were all one in this. And Sieur Anton would have been furious if he'd fought all or any one of them. Doubly furious if he'd died, no doubt. Which he would have, quite likely. One-handed and hurting, distracted and incensed, he'd have made easy meat for the skewer of another boy's blade. *Self-defence, my lords, your grace, Sieur Anton,* the other boys would have said, all in chorus. *Marron attacked him without cause, he was in peril of his life . . .*

So no, no fighting, only another scar on his soul and another derisive name they could call him, *scared little monkey.*

He'd made his way slowly through the castle's courts and passages, then taken an undutiful detour up onto the high walls, seeking answers where there were only views; he'd stood for a while gazing at the ancient stones of the Roq's hidden mystery, the Tower of the King's Daughter – *the Tower of the Ghost Walker*, Mustar had named it, and would not tell him why – and then he'd recollected himself, and hurried to Sieur Anton's room.

Where he'd been roundly scolded for his delay, and for his appearance, his tunic soaked and filthy: 'The bell will summon us to service any minute, and would you go before the God in such a state? On any night, let alone this night, when the lady Julianne is to be married to Baron Imber? Or had you forgotten that, in your dallying?'

He hadn't forgotten, because he hadn't known. He'd offered no excuse, had only struggled awkwardly out of his tunic when Sieur Anton threw a clean one at him. The knight had relented then, seeing what he himself had seem-ingly forgotten in his anger, Marron's injured arm in its bindings; had helped him dress, even asked forgiveness where none was due or needed. The bell had interrupted them before Marron could answer, and they'd hastened together down to the hall.

Marron had stood by the wall with the other squires, and even here before the God's altar their fingers had poked at him and their eyes suggested, making a lewdness of all that poking. More than anything Marron had wanted to poke back, with his dagger in his hand; instead he'd sidled along the smooth plain plaster until he stood more with the traders than the squires, and let people think what they would of his simple white against their gaudery.

He'd been sorry for the lady Julianne, when he saw her wed. She'd seemed so pale and reluctant, so stiff, leaning on her friend as though she couldn't do the simple things, the walking and standing and kneeling, without support. That marriage must be a dire thing to her, he'd thought, seeing how she fixed her stare on the God's sign above the altar, wouldn't even look at her husband in the making.

The God's sign was something to look at, he'd supposed, flaring with light chasing light. *Chased and caught*, he'd thought, and how bad could this wedding be, what reason did she have to dread it so much that she would run away, after having come so far in obedience? But the sign hadn't seemed so impressive to him tonight, only a trick; Rudel could do as much and more, and Rudel was a heretic. Did that mean that the light came not from the God, or did it mean that Rudel still stood in the God's grace regardless of the teachings of the Church, or Marshal Fulke?

Marron had no answers to such questions. Sieur Anton might know, but of course he couldn't ask him. Nor anyone, but especially not him. Sieur Anton was devout in a way that Marron had been, or at least had thought himself, when he first came to Outremer; but where Marshal Fulke's call for a great purifying holy war against Surayon only sickened Marron, even the words carrying the stench of slaughter with them, it seemed to inflame Sieur Anton as though he had never known carnage, had never said *these things happen here*, or else had said it with approval.

Wherever Rudel stood in the God's eyes – if God there were, and if the God were looking; both of which Marron was inclined to doubt, even here before His altar – the jongleur hadn't been standing there in the hall, unless he was still hidden among the dark ranks of the brothers. Even the traders' bird-bright clothes couldn't match Rudel's; if he'd been on the far side of the hall, in shadow and behind a pillar, Marron still couldn't have missed him.

Perhaps he and Redmond had after all slipped away in last night's rumpus, or else in the confusion of a breaking camp this morning. Perhaps they were far gone and luckier than the ladies, unsought-for, quite unmissed – though not for much longer, surely. How long could that poppet in the dungeon fool the guards? Or the questioners, next time they went to question? The girls had left others in their beds last night, it seemed, and cold daylight had shown them up for what they were, rags and rope and a man's death for believing in them . . .

If the Elessans would do that to one of their own, Marron had wondered just what they might have done to him, if their truth-speaker had actually forced him into telling true.

She'd been there in the hall, he'd seen her, easy to find with that face among the veils of the other women who rode in the Elessans' train: not whores, surely, in such a grim and righteous company, only servants. Cooks and launderers, if great lords travelled with such; he didn't know. Attendants to serve the lady Julianne, perhaps. She came of a great family, and travelled with none but Elisande, who was more friend than servant.

Come of one great family, she now belonged to another;

he'd seen Baron Imber claim her with a ring, possess her with a kiss. Marron was half-surprised that she didn't faint, she looked so pale and shaken; it had taken Elisande as well as her new husband to keep her on her feet as they'd backed away down the altar steps.

Marshal Fulke had preached for an hour, and said nothing new throughout; all that was new or surprising or unusual had been to look along the kneeling row of knights and see Sieur Anton one among them.

He'd been simple to pick out, because his head was bare. Not that he'd been alone in that. Fulke himself had come to every service unhooded, since that first sermon. The preceptor had taken no action, against him or his increasing number of adherents; there were knights who routinely came to worship uncovered, there were squires and men-at-arms, there were brothers who dared the anger of their confessors by coming before the God bare-headed. Even some of those same confessors were at it now; tonight, for the first time, Marron had looked towards the back of the hall and seen Fra' Piet's shaven head shining in the torch-light. Fra' Piet and half his troop: Marron couldn't be certain, but he thought he'd spotted Aldo's shock of brown hair among them.

When the service was over they'd all filed out in order, the squires almost last, as fitted their lowly station. The new-married baron and his lady had stayed behind, with their attendants and the preceptor; Marron had spared the lady Julianne one last glance as he left, trailing the other lads to avoid their jabbing fingers in his back. Brothers had been extinguishing torches, all down the hall; all he'd really seen of her was the gleaming hair and the line of one arm outstretched, one hand that Baron Imber had held imprisoned, *I have you now, I will not let you go.*

Marron had sent her a brief commiserating thought – an impertinent thought for sure from a squire to a lady, a new-made baroness; but she'd never know, and he did pity her – and then he'd turned to push his way through the mill of bodies outside the hall, looking for his master.

After the marriage, the marriage-feast: that was traditional, it was universal. Even here, in a castle of the grim religious that had been attacked and nearly taken three nights since, even after a match made in such haste and against such reluctance, there had to be a feast.

Not for the women, even had there been any women of rank present, besides the bride; that was not the custom of the house. The Order would welcome women guests because that was a duty laid upon it, so long as they kept decorously to their allotted quarters, where *here are the guests' rooms* meant *here are the women's rooms, safely in a tower apart*; it would shelter and feed, flatter where politic but it would not feast, it would not celebrate their being in the castle or the world.

Marron had expected nothing, then, like the marriage-feasts he'd known in long barn or village square: a riot of dancing and drunkenness, of fast feet and flashing skirts, fast hands and slapped faces; *licensed debauchery* the old priest used to call it, scowling momentously, though it was he who issued the licence and he who cried the musicians on, louder than any. One marriage in the endless summer of Marron's childhood had always seemed to lead to half a dozen more, and welcome so.

Here it must be different; he'd thought it would be dour, a required part of the wedding ritual and no more: the baron paying Master Cellarer as little as he might and then sitting sour and scowling with more intent and far more effect than the old priest ever had, turning the bread stale and the milk bad, driving the celebrants from table as soon as he could manage, later than he would like . . .

Well, no. Marron hadn't seriously thought they would be drinking milk. It would be the knights who feasted, after all, with perhaps a table also for the stranded traders, down at the foot of the hall. If the baron didn't supply them with wine enough, he'd thought they would send for their own.

He'd still thought it would be a dull affair, though. Elessans made famous fighters, but no one had ever woven a tale about their conviviality, their lightness of foot and touch or how quick they were to laugh, how slow to quarrel.

What Marron hadn't expected, who he had quite stopped looking for – hope triumphant over reason – was Rudel the jongleur.

Marron hadn't known there to be so many lewd songs in the canon; and yet he'd thought himself so wise, so experienced in the ways of wedding-feasts . . .

Rudel had wandered the hall at first – the lesser hall it was, knights' territory, neither brothers' nor the God's – drifting between the rowdy tables. He'd sung, he'd thrashed the strings of his mandora, he'd chivvied the young men into joining in where they knew the words, humming along where they did not, when he could keep them from exploding into raucous laughter that he had himself provoked.

Like any squire Marron had served his master, anticipating no time to listen to the singing. Except that Sieur Anton had eaten little – though the food was better and more plentiful than Marron had expected – and drunk less; so that after the first rush to see that the knight had trencher and meat, goblet and wine within it when every lad was fighting for the same and he had only the one hand to fight with, in fact Marron had found himself with time to stand behind his master's chair and indeed listen to the singing.

He'd never thought to hear such bawdy stuff here. Neither, apparently, had the Barons Imber. Elder and younger, they'd both seemed startled when Rudel was forced up onto a table and enough of a hush fell that the whole hall could hear him. Marron's eyes had moved instinctively to the top table, to look for trouble before it came; so he'd seen the new-wed baron's blush.

His uncle's face also had changed hue, darkened, turned a livid shade of red all across his shaven scalp. When Rudel had finished that one song and immediately begun another, to a shouted chorus and a rhythm of booted feet, the elder baron had had enough – but it had been he who'd stamped out of the hall, with his own retinue of friends and cronies following.

Sieur Anton had seemed to like the singing little more, no more than he liked the food or the wine. He'd stayed, though, so perforce Marron had stayed too. And had watched Rudel as they all did, and listened with less attention than most, and thought that there was a private message for him in this very public performance. *We're still here*, he'd thought Rudel was saying, *and I'm still a jongleur*. Which very likely meant that Redmond was again a prisoner, the man taking the place of the poppet and that whole escape brought to nothing. Undiscovered, which was good; unavailing and undone, which was not good at all.

And there was a second message too that Marron had read, one that he'd heard before and saw now in how Rudel never glanced his way for a moment, ignoring him as he was ignoring every squire else. *Your task is finished*, Marron had thought he was being told, *lead your life, serve your master, forget about us. I know where and how; I've put him back alone, I can lead him out alone next time.*

Rudel had sung on with gusto, what Marron most lacked. Soon his hand had found its own way onto the back of Sieur Anton's chair and he'd been leaning on it, only to hold himself upright. He'd snatched it away as soon as he'd realised, before his master could; but his legs had wobbled, his head had swum and he'd had to take a grip again to save shaming himself and Sieur Anton both.

Movement on the top table, ribald voices and laughter: he'd looked that way, focusing desperately against a sucking darkness, and had seen young Baron Imber on his feet. Blushing again, making his way out of the hall with a fixed expression on his face, followed by his grinning cousin Karel.

That was apparently what Sieur Anton had been staying for, his sense of duty not allowing him to leave before the guest of honour. As soon as the young men were gone, he'd pushed his chair back from the table.

And had felt the resistance of Marron's hand, jerked away too late; had glanced at his face and frowned, said, 'Lad, you look terrible. Is that arm paining you again?'

'No, sieur,' or *yes, sieur*, but no more than it had been half the day.

'I'm sorry,' again, the second time tonight. 'You need food, and rest. Bring that,' with a gesture at the bread and meat he'd barely touched, 'and follow me.'

They'd come to Sieur Anton's room, where Marron had been told to sit on the bed and eat, without arguing. For once, he'd practised instant obedience; and when he'd eaten all there was to eat and had drunk a glass of his master's wine, Sieur Anton said, 'Better?'

'Yes, sieur. Thank you . . .'

'Good. I keep forgetting, don't I?'

'Sieur . . .' *I keep failing you*, but he couldn't say that. Sieur Anton might ask how, and there was so much he daren't tell him, it was wiser far to curb his tongue and say nothing.

Knight sat beside his squire, laid a gentle hand on the back of his neck; said, 'They'll be making their jokes about us now, as well as about the baron and his bride. I can't prevent that, I'm afraid. Do the other lads give you trouble?'

'No, sieur.'

A little shake, from that strong hand. 'Truly, Marron?'

'Only a little, sieur. It doesn't matter.'

'Does it not? Boys can be cruel to each other. Worse than a bad master, sometimes.'

Marron shook his head, before Sieur Anton could do it for him. 'I'm used to it, sieur.'

'Are you?'

Oh yes, that was true enough. His uncle's workers had made a great mock of him and Aldo, for years before they'd taken their vows and joined the Order; nor had their fellow novices been kinder. The squires' sharp tongues provoked more memories than distress, though those memories brought their own distress, a friend lost where he had thought the two of them immune, immutable, eternal.

'Why are you used to it, Marron?'

Marron just looked at him. He knew, he must know; and Marron didn't have the words in any case. Even Sieur Anton couldn't play his confessor, for this.

The knight's hand moved gently on his neck, squeezing, teasing, promising more.

'You're worn out, lad. I should let you sleep.'

'No, sieur.'

'No? Are you sure?'

'Yes, sieur.'

'Your arm's bad, I don't want to hurt you . . .'

'You won't hurt me, sieur.'

'Well. Just cry out, if I do.'

He took his hand away and Marron wanted to cry out in protest, in hurt; but Sieur Anton only crossed his legs, seized his boot and wrenched it off, tossed it away across the room. Marron moved to help him with the other, but the hand came back for a moment, gripped his shoulder and, 'No, you sit still. I am able to undress myself. And you.'

And he did: stripping off his own clothes fast and carelessly and then helping Marron out of his, playing the squire almost, though a squire with impertinent, questing hands and a touch that made Marron alternately squirm and gasp.

Lastly, the bindings were unknotted and cast aside, so that the bandaged arm came free.

'Now, how shall we manage with this? We must put it out of the way. If you lie on the bed, thus, it should not trouble us. Good. Does that feel comfortable?'

'Yes, sieur. Do it again . . .'

That won him a chuckle, and a sharp slap. 'I meant the arm, fool. Well, I won't mind it, then, if you don't. I have some oil here' – a flask of it, Marron knew, scented with thyme and rosemary – 'which will ease things somewhat; but again, if I hurt you—'

'You won't hurt me, sieur.'

'You seem very sure of that.'

'Yes, sieur.'

'Marron, my name is Anton. Only for tonight, while we're alone, do you think you might manage to use it? Or at least not to call me sieur in every sentence?'

'No, sieur. I like it . . .'

A slow sigh, with a smile hidden in it; and then no more talking, only those fingers slowly working on him and inside him, sometimes rough and sometimes tender; the scent of the oil rising as it warmed, only to mingle with and be lost in sharper, hotter smells; Sieur Anton's long, lean body against him and about him, within him, encompassing him absolutely.

'You are not quite stranger to a man's body, are you, Marron?'

'No, sieur.' *Oh, Aldo . . .*

'Tell me.'

And so Sieur Anton did play confessor after all; what had been unthinkable before was possible now, as he was held close and warm and weary while the candles guttered and died in the room around them, that seemed suddenly so far away. Slowly, haltingly, Marron told of his friend: childhood friend and friend of his youth, more than friend when they'd played boys' games together that had become much more than games.

'Only the one?'

'Yes, sieur.' All that he'd wanted or needed or would ever need, he'd thought; and after they'd taken their vows they'd touched each other no more, despite what the other boys whispered. Their bodies given over with their souls to the God, they'd thought it would be a great sin. And there'd been no chance anyway, no possibility of succumbing to temptation in a novice's life or a brother's after.

'Sieur?'

'Yes, Marron?'

'Forgive me, but—'

'Nothing to forgive. How could there be? I leave my pride, my honour with my clothes; it's only you who insist on bringing it to bed. Boy,' caressingly. 'Come, ask your question. If I know an answer, you'll have it.'

'Sieur,' as bold as he could manage, then, even lifting his head so as not to mumble into his master's chest, 'you are the most devout man I know, more than any of the brothers, even. You say your prayers to the God, you serve the God, you gave your life to Him – and yet you do this too . . .'

'Ah. And do I leave my religion also with my clothes, you mean? I do not.'

'Does the God not forbid this?'

'The Church forbids it. And the Order, too; there, yes, I break my vows. But the God? I do not know, Marron. I know this, though, that I have done worse things. And will do worse again, and soon, I think. Marshal Fulke will lead us against Surayon, as soon as they break that man in the cells. They say he is the Red Earl, Redmond of Corbonne. Master Ricard will know; they fought together, under the King. He has refused to go down, thus far; he says it is dishonourable to torture a man so, and he will have no part of it. I think he will yield soon, though, I think he must. The preceptor will order him, on his obedience. And when we are certain, then the man will be broken. No one can hold out forever, under question.

'And then he will tell us the secret, how to enter Surayon; then we will march, and the God will wreak a terrible vengeance against that damned land. And yes, I will be there; and I will kill, and I will burn heretics, men and women and children. I will do it; and against that, what can this matter? If I am to be condemned, I do not think it will be because I lie down with men. Or boys,' and his calm, warm hands put an end to talking again.

For a while.

'Sieur?'

'What, again? Go to sleep.'

'Please?'

'Well. Once more, then. What is it this time?'

'Sieur, tell me what happened to your brother.'

A long silence, a stillness in him that made Marron tremble; then, 'I killed him.'

'But how?'

Wrong question. 'With my sword,' coldly.

'*Why*, sieur? What had he done? He must have done something dreadful, you loved him . . .'

'You have been gossiping about me, if someone told you that. I dislike being the subject of my squire's gossip, Marron.'

His throat was tight and dry, it was hard to speak; the words were gravel-sharp in his mouth. 'I wanted to know . . .'

'I'm sure you did. Know this, then – but do *not* noise it around, boy, do you understand me? This is for your ears only, and only because I'd sooner you believed the truth than some chatterer's invention. Yes?'

'Yes, sieur.'

'Very well. Yes, I loved my brother, and he me. Like me he was, as you say, devout; like the churchmen, like you, he thought it was a great sin for men to love each other with their bodies. There was talk about me, of course, then as now, but I suppose he shut it out, refused to listen. He never asked me for the truth of it.

'But he found me one day, in a field of maize, with another man. Charol carried Dard everywhere, I'd given it to him the month before, he was so proud of it; and I, I had Josette also, though why I can never remember, for a tryst in my own family's fields. The God orders these things, not us.

'Charol was mad, I think, with shock or anger. Disillusion, perhaps: he had admired me, worse, adored me. Worshipped me, almost. He drew his sword, and went to kill my friend; that man was older, he farmed on our land, Charol must have blamed him, I imagine, for corrupting his perfect brother.

'I tripped Charol, and told him the truth as he lay at my feet there; I stood over him quite naked and said that it was I who had first seduced my friend, that I had done the same with other men, and always would.

'Charol scrambled up and swung his sword at me. Mine was the first blood Dard tasted: here,' and his fingers guided Marron's to a thick seamed scar on his ribs. 'He saw me bleeding, and turned away – sane again, I thought, for a moment. But then he went after my friend, and what could I do? He would have killed him. So I snatched up my sword and called him back, called him a coward to run after an unarmed man.

'He came, and we fought. I think his madness infected me – or perhaps I simply lost my temper. You know I have a temper,' and this time his fingers touched the bandaged arm, and Marron remembered that long duel in sunlight, so long ago it seemed, the intense fury that had so nearly killed him; and the look on Sieur Anton's face that day as he'd flung his sword away, a look he understood now. *Not twice, not a second time . . .*

'I killed him,' Sieur Anton said again, and yet again. 'I killed him, and he died. And then I took his sword, because he had disgraced it, or I had, either one. In the end I came to the Order, I gave my life to the God to do what He would with it; and they sent me here. My father sent me money,' bitterly, 'to keep me from a brother's vows. He needn't have bothered. How could I ever be a brother again, anyone's, under any meaning? I can hardly bear to say the word . . .'

And then silence, painful and difficult: Marron lacked the insolence to break it. It was the great bell that did, Brother Whisperer's voice thudding into their bones. He stirred gratefully, tried to sit up, and was prevented; Sieur Anton's arm and his leg too held him down, comfortably pinioned between man and pallet and wall.

'I don't leave my religion with my clothes, Marron, but I think this once we will say the prayers as we are. Call it an affirmation, if you like.'

Some men, many men in this castle would call it heresy. Marron was far beyond knowing who was right and who was wrong, beyond even trying to guess. He knew Sieur Anton's weight across his body, he knew the young knight's strength, he guessed what might happen if he resisted; and he knew how good it felt to lie constrained like this, though his arm ached sharply and every other part of him was numb and heavy with exhaustion.

'Yes, sieur,' he said.

Prayers mumbled, almost whispered like love-talk to each other, like those times when no matter what is said, it's the whispering that counts. These were prayers, though, and for his master's sake, for his piety Marron tried to focus on the words; but they drifted, they were a string he lost all grasp upon, grabbed for in the darkness, couldn't find.

He thought probably he fell asleep before the prescribed finish, though Sieur Anton did not wake him nor tell him next morning, and certainly he did not ask.

*

What roused him was the bell again, striking deep; anything less massive could not have done it, so little, far too little sleep he'd had.

This time no lying-in, no muttering of blessings with their minds and bodies too distracted. Up and kneeling, naked as they were; Sieur Anton's voice was clear and firm, which seemed unfair.

Then into his clothes, with the knight's help to bind his arm against his chest once more; and that aside it was clearly to be the normal routine this morning, and why not? Little enough had changed, except that what everyone suspected had finally come to pass. They were still squire and master, nothing had altered that.

So he ran for his master's breakfast, and his own; endured the taunts of other boys on the same errand, thinking how little they knew, and how foolish they sounded; went back to the room where he was happiest, saw Sieur Anton eat and drink, waited for permission to do the same.

All that time there was something stirring in his gut, though, where it had worked its way down overnight from his head, where he had heard it. This was what tore at him, this dual life he tried to lead, servant and traitor. He must betray one man, or betray the other; and it wasn't really any choice at all, because one betrayal had the stink of inevitable death upon it, one death soon and many more to come. The other, who could tell? Not he. Only that it might forestall some people's dying . . .

So when Sieur Anton dismissed him – 'I want some swordplay, and not with you; I won't risk any more damage to that arm, and neither will you. You're to rest, Marron, do you hear me? Go sit in the sun and sleep an hour' – he used that licence to search for Rudel.

The castle had never seemed so crowded; there were men everywhere, and none of them the man he sought. The stable-yard was hectic with traders' wagons and their grumbling owners. None had seen the jongleur, nor had any patience with Marron's questions; Baron Imber had decreed that he and his party would leave that afternoon, and any traders who wanted their protection on the road must be ready. Which they would be, but resentfully: their animals needed rest after the long haul back yesterday, they themselves would have appreciated a day or two to recover from the wedding-feast, and why was this boy bothering them . . .?

He tried the great hall and the lesser hall, the kitchens and the dormitories, even the latrines, and had no joy. At last, thinking that Rudel must have left the castle altogether – with Redmond, perhaps, finding another way to smuggle the prisoner to freedom? – Marron went up high onto the walls, careful to keep some distance from the brothers who stood guard. Perhaps he would practise a little obedience after all, find some warm seclusion and let sleep wash over him.

But his feet took him almost without permission to the place where he had stood before, where he could overlook the tower that had no doors, the Tower of the King's Daughter; and there, when he had quite given up on his search, there he found Rudel.

Found Rudel standing as he had himself, gazing down on the squat and secretive tower; said, 'Sir?' and saw the man startle, saw him turn sharply, warily, and only slowly relax with a huff of breath and a hand scratching at his beard.

'Marron. What are you doing here?'

People were always asking him that, as if he had no right, no place in their mysteries. He stifled his first response, *and what are you? Sir?*, and said only, 'I was looking for you.'

'Why so? What you have done, I am grateful for; but you shouldn't—'

'Sir, I have to tell you. Did the Earl go back into his cell?'

'Yes, he did. He insisted, but he was right in any case. A simulacrum has a short life, only a day or two at most; it was wiser that the real man replace it for a time. A little longer, he can bear that. I have strengthened him, as much as I am able . . .'

'Forgive me, sir, but it won't be enough. My master tells me' – *and I betray his trust by telling you* – 'that Master Ricard can name Redmond.'

'We've always known that, Marron. Ricard has his own honour, though, he won't—'

'Sieur Anton says that he will now, he can't hold out any longer against Marshal Fulke and the preceptor. And when he does – it may be today, even, as soon as the Elessans have gone,' that was his own embroidery on what his master had said, but it was true enough, it might be today, tomorrow, any day, but soon, 'when he does, they will put fresh questions to the Earl,' use other of those machines, no doubt, 'and he won't be able to resist them then, my master says . . .'

'Your master is very probably right. Redmond is wiry, wily and tough; but they have been holding back somewhat,

I think, in case his accuser was simply mistaken. One old man can look pretty much like another, and it has been forty years. Once they're certain, though, they'll be implacable. And no, not even Redmond could resist them then. He would deny that, but every man breaks at last. Very well, this changes things. You were right to tell me, Marron, and thank you; we are in your debt again.'

'What will you do?'

'I'll take him out immediately, today. During midday prayers, I think; the brothers are more watchful now, but there'll still be many fewer eyes to see.'

'How will you escape the castle, though? You can't go disguised as brothers, not during prayers, the guards on the gate would stop you . . .'

'And they're too many for me to confound, I know that. But there is another way out of this place. I had hoped not to take Redmond that way, it's a dangerous path, especially for a wounded man. Necessity forces my hand, though. Redmond must endure the risk.'

'Another way, sir?' There was famously only one gate into and out of the Roq.

'A secret way, Marron, every castle has its private exit; and no, I will not tell you. We are in your debt, but what I said before still holds. You have your life, your own path to follow, and here it separates from ours. Take our gratitude, and be content with that.'

'Sir, I don't want—'

'It doesn't matter what you want. This is how it must be. Outremer is a land divided, and we find ourselves on opposite sides of that divide. How it will be resolved, I cannot see; as it stands now, we must pray that we never meet again. If we do, it will probably be on a battlefield. Go on, lad, leave me now. I need to prepare . . .'

He turned his back; Marron hesitated a moment, then left him.

Obedience had been drilled into Marron all his life; rebellion was a new condition, difficult to sustain. Doubly difficult, after last night. But last night had been a blade with two edges, each of them biting deep. He felt both bound and cut free, terribly torn; he also felt desperately curious, and determined not to be set aside so casually, to be granted no place in this story's ending.

Rudel might have rejected him, but he still had one way to turn. Obedient to no one, making his own choices at last, he went towards his master's room but not so far. Went instead into the buttery, where the knights' little luxuries were kept; put a bottle of good wine and a pair of goblets onto a tray and carried that awkwardly one-handed through the castle to the preceptor's own quarters, where gossip said the new Baroness Julianne had slept the night with her lord.

There was an Elessan guard at the door, to confirm the rumour. He frowned at Marron, and said, 'What's this?'

'A gift, from my master to your lady,' trying to sound like a squire on a tedious errand of courtesy, no more. 'He cannot come himself to bid her farewell, but he sends wine in token. May I go in?' For all the world as if he didn't care, he'd be just as glad if he were turned away.

The guard shrugged. 'Aye, boy, do.'

He even opened the door, to pass him through; Marron nodded his thanks, and went inside.

Julianne was there, with Elisande at her side. As soon as the door was closed, she lifted an eyebrow above her veil and said, 'Marron?'

'My lady, forgive me – but do you still want to leave?' *To run away* he meant but was too embarrassed to say, face to face with two young women, ladies of rank and one of them high rank, new-married, whom he was inviting to flee her husband. 'If you do, there may be a way . . .'

19

A Door and a Daughter

He couldn't have meant that, could he? What she'd just heard him say?

She stared at him and he'd never seemed younger, never more of a boy: his hair awry and his face flushed with nervousness above a worn and grubby squire's tunic that didn't fit, one sleeve hanging loose and empty while his injured arm made an unsightly bulge beneath. Almost her fingers reached out to tuck the sleeve into his belt, to smooth his hair and make him neater, while her mind reeled.

She couldn't answer him. She didn't know the answer.

Elisande it was who reached to touch him, but not to tidy him into some more fitting semblance of a knight's squire; she seized his arm, his one arm, and spoke sharply.

'What way?'

He only shook his head mutely, still gazing at Julianne and seeming to wait for her word. Elisande gave his shoulder a wrench that nearly spilled the wine from the tray he carried, forcing him to turn to her.

'What way?' again, more urgently.

'I don't know, my lady,' he said, looking around apparently, absurdly, for somewhere to set the tray down. Julianne recovered just enough of her wits to take it from him, and then stood as she had before, befuddled, only listening.

'You don't *know*?'

'No. But Rudel does. You know Rudel, and, and his friend,' in a mutter, with a quick glance towards the closed door and the man beyond who guarded it. 'You met them in the gully, you know who they are, don't you?'

'Yes, we know. Explain.'

'Rudel is taking him, his friend, away. Today, during midday prayers. He says he knows another way, a secret way, out of the castle. He didn't tell me how. But you could go with them, perhaps. He said it would be dangerous, but I thought, if it was important to you, my lady,' his eyes coming back to Julianne, 'if you wanted to . . .'

'What do you want, Marron?' she asked, again putting off his question, to which she could still find no answer.

'To see them safe, my lady.'

'For yourself, I meant.'

'I don't know, my lady . . .'

Well, there were two of them in that case, then. Not three: it was blazingly clear what Elisande wanted.

'I know what he means to try,' she said. 'We must go with him, Julianne. We *must*.'

'There is a guard on the door,' Julianne said, equivocating pointlessly.

'One guard. He is nothing. If we meet others I can maze them, or you can play the haughty baroness, you do that well. But we have to go. Remember your father, remember the djinni . . .'

This all felt increasingly familiar to Julianne: Elisande mysterious and insistent, Marron useless and herself so muddled and confused when all her life she'd been accustomed to knowing her own will and making her own choices, right or wrong but always certain.

If she slipped away again, if she even tried to, and was caught – she thought her new Uncle Imber would take her back to Elessi in chains. For sure she'd be disgraced, humiliated beyond recovery, mewed up for a lifetime and powerless in the land, which would destroy any point as well as any pleasure in this marriage her father had made for her.

If she stayed, if she held to Imber's hand and Imber's fortune, then her father would die. The djinni had said so; the djinn did not, could not lie.

Had it said so? Perhaps not. Great danger it had said, though; and her father was more important to Outremer than she was, baroness or no. For the land's sake, she should save him if she could.

Was her father more important to her than Imber? There again she felt her mind shy away from the question. She couldn't do that, she couldn't balance one against the other and see which weighed the more.

Which brought her back to reason and sound argument, and she was glad of that. She took a breath and said firmly, 'We'll go.' Good. That was a decision made, and never mind the consequences. 'What should we take with us?'

'Money, jewels, knives. Nothing more. We can't be seen walking through the castle with blankets and packs.'

'My lady, I could . . .'

'No, not even you, Marron.' He sighed softly; Julianne thought that perhaps he regretted the loss of an excuse, a reason to come that little further with them. Elisande read it otherwise, though. 'This time we daren't take risks, there's too much at stake.' *More than our lives*, she seemed to be implying. Well, Rudel's and Redmond's lives, for certain; but beyond that . . .? 'What we need, we can find on the road. Wherever that may lead us.' Again there was more in her voice than her words allowed; again Julianne bit back a challenge. They were putting themselves into Elisande's hands here, and it was poor policy not to trust your guide.

Still, 'Where are you taking us?' One was entitled to ask, after all.

'Truly, Julianne, I do not know.'

'You said . . .'

'Oh, I know where the road begins, I know how Rudel hopes to get away from the castle.'

'And how is that?'

'By, unh, a hidden gateway. I can't tell you more than that, I don't know much more. I know where to find it, but I don't know how it works.'

I couldn't make it work would seem to be the truth of that, or so it sounded. Julianne thought that this must be why Elisande had come to the Roq, to find and work that gateway; there was so much chagrin in her voice, in her face. Rudel could make it work, where she could not. Or thought he could, at least; and she must hope that he was right, as they all must if they were to get away. A bitter draught, clearly, for Elisande.

*

'What time is it?'

Elisande went to the window – narrow and tall, an arrow-slit knocked out, but not too far: the preceptor's suite of rooms was in one of the older parts of the castle, which had needs made its own defence – and twisted her head awkwardly sideways to see the sky, try to see the sun.

Just as she did so, Marron displayed a sweet sense of bad timing, saying, 'It's rising noon now, my lady. Half an hour, maybe; not more.'

'We'll be expected to go to service,' she said, over Elisande's snort of irritation. 'If we wait here, my Imber' – she could do that now, she could say *my Imber* in public that way, and let them all think she did it only to draw the distinction – 'will come to escort us.' With the grinning Karel, no doubt, and numerous others; not she thought with the louring uncle. He wouldn't dance attendance on her, not now she was married. Part of the family, submissive, safe. Why should he bother?

'Then we'd best go immediately, before we can't go at all.'

'Yes. My way, though, Elisande. At least we'll try it my way.' She hadn't forgotten the sight of that man crucified across a doorway, set to dwell in the house of his own pain until he died; she wanted no more men punished for seeing her where she was not, or for not seeing her where she was.

Quickly they collected up weapons and what small valuables they could – 'water would be better than half of this,' Elisande grumbled, 'but we've no skins to carry it, so we must just want for water' – and then Marron opened the door, and Julianne swept out.

When the guard moved to bar her way, she lifted one

caustic eyebrow and gave him the full benefit of her glare.

'We go to holy service, man. Would you prevent us?'

'I have orders, my lady . . .'

'Indeed? To keep us prisoner?'

'Not to let you wander without an escort. The castle is a confusing place,' he seemed to be reciting rather than speaking his own thoughts, 'and you might lose your way.'

'But we have an escort,' with a waft of her hand at Marron. 'This squire is a resident here, he knows every stair and every turning. There is no danger of our becoming lost. And I want some period of quiet contemplation at the God's altar, before the Order assembles for general service. You may be dismissed to rejoin your troop for prayers; there is no purpose in your standing guard over empty quarters. Is there?'

'Er, no, my lady. Thank you, my lady . . .'

He bowed and hurried away, ahead of them, even; so keen he seemed to be gone, she wondered if Elisande had after all leaned on his mind a little, to urge him into compliance. She didn't know if the girl could do that, and decided not to ask. The man might have to face his lord's anger, but she had reason to hope not, if he'd reported his orders accurately. A knight's squire ought to make an acceptable escort, to the military mind; Elessans were not famous for their imagination.

Elisande led them a way Julianne did not know, that took them nowhere near the great hall, but further into the dark and ancient heart of the castle. Walls climbed high on either side of them, the sky was a slender band of blue above; they met no one coming or going, heard only the silence of old stone and the whisper of wind against it, the rustle of their own clothes, their own soft footfalls and tight breaths.

They came into a small ward of cracked uneven flag-stones, where the body of the castle made two sides of the court and a wall the other two. That was unmanned, a simple wall with no walkway on its height. In the furthest corner stood a tower, squat and square; after a moment's puzzled gazing, she realised that its age-blackened stones held no visible door or window.

Behind her, she heard Marron suck in his breath, more in understanding than surprise.

'The Tower of the King's Daughter,' Elisande said, her voice little more than a whisper. 'This is where he will bring Redmond, this is his route out. And ours.'

'The Sharai call it the Tower of the Ghost Walker,' Marron murmured.

'Do they?' Elisande laughed shortly. 'They would.'

There were currents here, tugging at both, that Julianne could not read. She said simply, 'How do we get inside?'

'Well, that's the question. I don't know. I thought I did, but I was wrong. We must hope that Rudel is not.'

They lingered in the mouth of the narrow way, not venturing out into the clear space of the ward; Julianne peered up at small windows in massive walls, and said, 'Can they see us down here?'

'Those are the knights' rooms above, my lady,' Marron told her. 'There might be men and their servants up there now, changing for prayers; we should keep out of their sight. When the bell sounds, they will leave.' But his face changed even as he said that; he went on, 'Except for one.

Sieur Anton will pray alone, in his chamber. He won't be looking out of the window, though. Er, will you excuse me? Just for a minute?'

Having politely asked permission, he didn't wait for it, but turned and ran off regardless.

'Where's he going?' Elisande demanded.

'I don't know . . .'

'Maybe he needs the latrines in a hurry?'

'Don't joke, Elisande.'

'I'm not. I could half use a pot myself, I'm nervous.'

'Of what's in there? Marron said it could be dangerous . . .'

'More than he guesses. It could be fatal. But no, what I'm really nervous about is just what Rudel is going to say, when he finds us here waiting for him.'

Again it sounded like a joke; again, Julianne thought, it was not.

They waited in silence then. Shortly they heard light footsteps running towards them, and both girls stiffened; but it was only Marron returning, fumbling to buckle a sword one-handed to his belt as he ran. The scabbard gleamed, white and silver as sudden sunlight drove the shadows back.

'Marron?'

'My lady?'

'Is that your own sword? It seems very fine.'

'Yes, my lady,' though he flushed as he said it, and not she thought at her implication that it was not his, that it was too fine for a humble squire. 'Sieur Anton gave it me. He wasn't there,' *not quite*, his panting breath suggested, 'and Lady Elisande said we should go armed . . .'

'So we should; though blades will do us little good in the tower. Did anyone else see you?'

'Oh yes, my lady.' Julianne smiled, seeing how he struggled not to say *what of it?* with voice or gesture. He was right, though. A squire running in and out of his master's room, fetch and carry, in empty-handed and out with a sword: it was hardly remarkable.

Elisande acknowledged as much with a nod, a fraction late; then she said, 'I suppose you couldn't possibly call me by my name? Formal manners make me uncomfortable at any time; very soon now, they're going to sound ridiculous.'

Not in the tower, she quite clearly meant, but in the face of Rudel's anger. Marron smiled at her distantly, as though he were thinking of something entirely other; then he confirmed it by flinching visibly away from whatever stray thought or memory it was had caused that smile.

Elisande received no more answer than that. Just then the great bell beat out its first summons. Although no window overlooked them here in this narrow passageway, although they were so far hidden by thick stone that they couldn't hear the rush of sandalled or booted feet that would be sweeping like a breeze through every other part of the castle, still they pressed back warily against the wall, trying to squeeze themselves out of the sun that beat down almost vertically now to find them.

'Won't we be missed?' Elisande murmured, under a sudden doubt.

'Perhaps. Imber will have come to escort us, found us gone; but his place in hall is on the floor with the Ransomers, he did his year's service among the knights, all those Elessans do that. Didn't you see the badges on their clothing? Even if he looks, it's hard to see who's in the gallery from down below. I don't think we'll be missed. If he has doubts, what's he going to do? Stop the service, to send out search parties?'

'His uncle would.'

'His uncle won't even know to miss us, until afterwards.' *I hope.* 'And by then . . .'

By then Rudel and Redmond should have come, and they should all be inside the tower. She hoped.

The Tower of the King's Daughter, they'd called it; also the Tower of the Ghost Walker, which had made Elisande laugh as though it wasn't funny at all.

Perhaps they were both of them joke names. After all, one thing that was certain – one of the few certainties about that particular man – was that the King had no daughter . . .

'Why does the tower have those titles?' she asked.

'Can I tell you when we're inside? Please?'

Meaning that if they didn't get inside, it was safer or wiser or better if she still didn't know. Meaning that trust went only so far, even between friends who took such risks together.

Meaning that she could strangle the girl, actually. But she didn't, she only turned her head the other way to watch for Rudel's coming.

At last he came, they both came: Rudel in jongleur-garb and with a pack slung over his shoulder, his slow-shuffling companion once more in the black habit of a brother, probably not for disguise so much as necessity, the choice that or prisoner's rags, which meant that or nothing.

Surely, surely Elisande would not work her mind-tricks on this man, these two men, even if she could. Did magic work on magicians? Julianne didn't know; but Rudel must have been confident of not being followed or challenged, at this time and in these hidden alleys. His sword-arm gave his friend support, their heads were bent close together, Rudel watched Redmond's feet and neither one of them noticed the three who waited in the bare fall of shadow.

Not until Elisande spoke.

'Rudel, you won't go through the tower without me.'

She'd kept her voice deliberately soft, not to startle them, though her words were challenge enough and typical of the girl. Neither man did startle; for a long moment neither one so much as spoke, they only looked. Redmond looked, at least. Rudel glared.

His eyes moved from Elisande to Marron and back again, as though he couldn't decide which of the two of them more deserved a beating. If he'd had his hands free, Julianne thought, perhaps they might both have received one, justice swift and severe.

When he did speak, it was to her; he said, 'These two may make a game of what is deadly, but I am disappointed in you, Baroness.'

That stung; she hoped her face did not show how deeply, but was very afraid that it had.

Her voice was steady enough, though. 'No game, sir. Not for any one of us. I think we all wish to see you safe—'

'Then go back. You endanger us all, simply by being here. Do you not know how they will search for you?'

'We all wish to see you safe,' she said again, calm and even, as though she'd never been interrupted, 'and we also each of us have our own reasons for going with you, if you can truly show us a way out of this castle unobserved.'

'Lady,' and in his mouth that was no title of respect, not now, 'you clearly have no idea, no concept of what you are asking. I am looking to slip quietly away from here, with a day's grace before they realise that either one of us is gone. You will have the whole garrison turned out at our tail within an hour. That's assuming we survive the tower. Bad enough to go in there with one wise and crippled old man; with a gaggle of foolish children clinging to my belt – and one of those hiding a fresh wound beneath his tunic – I wouldn't put money on any one of us coming out of it whole.'

'You misunderstand me, Rudel,' Julianne replied. 'I am not asking anything from you. Except that you open some way into the tower, which you intend to do anyway. We will follow you through, wherever it may lead us; and once through, we will leave you and go our own way. I do not think you can prevent us, except by abandoning your own intentions. Again.'

'Oh, can I not?'

His eyes grew wide and bright suddenly, hawk-sharp and staring; and then his face was fuzzy and all her thoughts were blurred, her legs were uncertain beneath her, she couldn't quite remember where she was or who was with her, but she did very much want to sit down . . .

But there was a slap that sounded in her ears, and her mind cleared in a moment, although it was not she who had been slapped. Rudel's face was piebald, red and white: white fingermarks on his cheek and all red else, and Elisande looked much like him, her bones showing pale while her skin flushed in her fury.

'How dare you, how *dare* you? Trying to maze my friend? I should—'

'You should stop this. All of you.' That was Redmond, unexpectedly throwing his hood back and glowering around him. His voice was thin and drained, but sharp enough to silence Elisande. 'We haven't time for dispute. Rudel, there may be advantage in their coming with us. We don't know what we may meet, in the tower or afterwards; extra hands could be useful.'

'Of course we will be useful.' That was Elisande again, not crushed for long. 'You *know* that I should carry the Daughter, it's only sense . . .'

It sounded like nonsense to Julianne. Whoever or whatever the Daughter might be – the way she'd said the word, it definitely had a capital letter to its name – Elisande was the smallest of them all, the least likely porter. But after a moment Rudel nodded briefly, reluctance and anger and acceptance all contained within that one small gesture as he turned to walk without further argument across the small court towards the tower.

Marron and Elisande followed; Julianne delayed to offer her arm to Redmond, but he shook his head and smiled gently.

'Thank you, but I have taken enough strength from Rudel; this much I can manage.'

Even so she stayed at his side, matching his slow pace. It was perhaps an opportunity to ask questions – *what is the Daughter, how do we gain access to the tower, how will it lead us out of the castle?* – but she was tired of being given misleading answers. Time would reveal all.

Or not. When they caught up with the others, Rudel

was already frowning at the blank wall of the tower, frustration showing on his face and in his hands where he had laid them against the stone, as if he were trying to push his way inside.

'I *tried* that,' Elisande said, only poorly hiding her satisfaction.

'Then we must try something more.'

Julianne was still watching his hands; she saw them clench for a moment, fists to batter the wall or possibly Elisande, before unfolding again to trace invisible patterns on the age-worn stones.

He muttered a few words and phrases, each by the sound of them in a different tongue, each incomprehensible and each to no effect. No effect on the wall, at least; there was some noticeable deterioration in his temper, which was not improved by Elisande's steady, repetitive murmur, 'Tried that.'

'Elisande.' Julianne beckoned her over, and was a little surprised when she came; had to think fast, and said, 'Just how much magic do you people have?'

'This isn't magic,' was the quick reply, 'it's power.'

'There's a difference?'

'Well. Perhaps not; but it's not our magic. The power's in the wall, in the tower; say the right words and a door will open. Anyone could do it. You could, if you knew the words.'

As in the cave, when my finger was plenty, anyone's finger would have been enough . . . But she didn't want to think about the cave. 'And do I take it that neither of you two does know the words?'

'Ah. We thought we did.' The insouciance in her voice

was belied by an anxious glance at the sky, at the relentless sun; they were running out of time.

Rudel stepped away from the wall, shaking his head. 'My father said . . .'

'Your father,' Elisande rejoined instantly, 'does not know everything.'

That won her a glance, but no words; after a moment, he went back to the wall.

'Who is his father?' Julianne asked quietly.

'A sweet old man. You'd like him.'

Julianne reminded herself again not to ask questions.

Redmond shuffled slowly forward, to join Rudel. He laid his hands above the younger man's, and said, 'Together, now.'

They spoke slow words in chorus, and had a response at last: the wall seemed to groan, so deeply that Julianne didn't so much hear it as feel it in her ribs; she thought she saw flakes of light fall like cinders about the men.

Redmond breathed deeply, and wiped sweat from his face. 'There is a block.'

'I know that. If there were no block, we would be inside by now.'

'I mean a resistance, something works against us. The words are right. Elisande, stop your mocking and give us some help.'

Perhaps because it was he and not Rudel who asked – commanded, rather – or else because the urgency of their need overrode even her bitter tongue, Elisande stepped up immediately. She stood between the two men, and added her hands and her voice to theirs.

This time the groan was palpable, bone-shaking; the

wall faded for a moment, and light shone between or perhaps through the stones. Julianne saw it touch Marron's face, turning his skin a strange, sickly colour.

He gasped, as the light died. She moved quickly to his side, and reached to touch his wrist; it was chill, and slick with sweat.

'Don't be afraid,' she murmured, trying valiantly to suppress her own heart's rapid beating. 'Mystery is always unnerving, but only because it's unknown.' She was quoting her father, for her own comfort as much as the squire's; she added, 'They know what this is,' and only hoped that it was true.

'I'm not afraid,' Marron answered, thin-lipped. 'My arm hurts, that's all.'

Typical boy, hiding his fear behind a confession that didn't hurt his pride. She nodded easily, patted his shoulder and let him be.

'Once more,' Redmond said. 'Be confident. It has to comply; that is laid into its foundation.'

Again the same words, not shouted but spoken with force, three voices joined in determination. Julianne knew the syllables now, if not the sense; she could chant along with them, and would if it were necessary, if it would help.

No need, though. This time the stones seemed to cry their own word in response, and that light – it had a colour, but none she'd ever seen before, she didn't know how to call it – blazed out across the ward, from a doorway too bright to look upon.

No, not a doorway. A door. Redmond laid a hand against it, and maybe it was only because she was squinting but she thought she saw the light shine through his flesh, showing his twisted bones beneath; certainly she saw how his hand was stopped by it, how his fingers spread and pressed, how solid it was to him. She also heard the soft hiss of his breath, as a gauge of how much the contact hurt him.

'Not you,' Rudel said, grabbing his shoulder, pulling him away.

'Why not? It'll be no easier inside. If I can't bear it, better to learn now.'

'Don't play with me. You can bear anything, old man.'

'Well, then?'

'Well, be careful, then. It may be more than blocked, it may be guarded.'

'Yes.'

If Redmond did take any more care after the warning than before, Julianne couldn't see it. He only placed both hands on that door of light, and pushed. Not hard, he didn't have the bodily strength, but with determination, with strength of mind.

And as he pushed, so the door retreated. It didn't swing open, it wasn't hinged; but it drew slowly back from him and coloured smoke seethed around its edges, unless it was mist, unless it was light gone to liquid, like inks dropped into water.

Every step he took, it was as though Redmond stepped on and into pain, stronger and deeper, further than the step before. He hissed, gasped, cried aloud and kept on walking. The smoke, mist, whatever it was wreathed itself around him; Rudel fidgeted, suddenly snapped, 'Come, then,' and followed.

Elisande was only a pace, half a pace behind Rudel and hurrying to catch up, not to follow him.

Julianne felt briefly forgotten, almost abandoned: those three had overriding interests of their own in there. She glanced sideways at Marron, ready to give him a wry smile and a polite arm, to make nearly a joke of this; but he looked dreadful, his eyes glassy and all his skin shining with sweat although the whole ward was chilly now, despite the high bright sun. She reached for his hand instead, gripped trembling fingers and squeezed encouragingly. She must look like this, she thought, those times, those few and dreadful times she stood of necessity on a high place and gazed down: pale and feverish, shaking, terrified.

'They're leaving us behind,' she said, trying to sound cheerful and sounding only false to her own ears, an adult jollying a nervous child.

It was true, though, they were being left. That vivid door was only an opalescent glow now, lost behind clouds of colour; their companions were shadows within its frame, and fading.

She walked forward determinedly and Marron came with her, his hand locked painfully tight about hers. Tendrils of misty light seemed to reach towards them, wrapping around their legs and bodies, arms and faces, fogging her eyes so that she didn't notice when they passed through the tower's wall.

It was her feet that felt the change, from hard-edged broken stones to something softer and more resilient: like walking on water, she thought, startled, looking down instinctively and seeing nothing but roiling mist.

She dragged her eyes up again, with an effort; whatever it was that she stood on, it bore her weight and Marron's, they weren't sinking. And the others had come this way:

there they stood, three murky figures off to her right, beside the shining panel of that strange door.

And here came Rudel's voice, speaking snappishly to her, 'Hurry, we need to let this close . . .'

She tugged at Marron's hand and felt him come stumblingly after her, breathing in short hard gasps. Dizzy with fear she thought he was, totally dependent.

Close to, the figures resolved into Elisande and the two men, their faces only a little blurred by drifting mist. Redmond stood stiffly, leaning on her friend's shoulder, as though the effort of opening the door had exhausted him despite the help he'd had. It was Rudel who reached a hand out to touch the door, fiercely bright again at this little distance, who murmured other words to release it.

It had taken three to force it open; one was enough to undo that. Julianne expected to see it spring forward, to fit again into the wall before it vanished, but the light seemed simply to fray into the swirling fog. It dissipated in moments, and was gone. When she looked behind her, she could see no way back, no sign of the sunlit ward.

The fog carried its own light, though, or else was itself made of light, if these sad, unearthly colours could be lights. A floating veil that was neither blue nor green draped itself across Elisande's face; Julianne could still see her friend's features through it, though sickly shaded. As she watched, the veil stretched and curled itself into a rope, and twined around Elisande's throat and Redmond's, both at once. She thought she saw it tighten, and moved to snatch; but the rope parted before her fingers reached it, and was no more than threads of shifting colour among great wafts of the same.

'Where are we?' she whispered.

'In the Tower of the King's Daughter,' Elisande said, valiantly chuckling. Pity was, that the valour was so evident.

'Perhaps; but—'

'You stand on a bridge, Julianne.' Rudel's voice was pitched soft but not gentle, low and rumbling and forceful. 'A bridge between worlds, the one you know and another like it and yet quite unlike. I am sorry to have led you this way, because that other world is deadly; but mortals can walk within it, and we must. Follow me, and do not stray. All of you – and I mean you particularly, Elisande – mind what I say, and do as I tell you, and we may survive. But remember, one false step, one false word may be fatal. Now come. You two girls, help Redmond and Marron; they have been hurt, and this place is not easy for them.'

She could see the truth of that, though she did not understand it. Redmond stood cramped and awkward, head low, while the mists eddied around him, seeming to probe like clutching fingers beneath his robe; when she glanced at Marron she saw a skein wrapped all about him, pulsing to the ragged beat of his blood that she could feel against her fingers where he still clasped her hand.

She tugged at him and he followed slowly, dumbly. Elisande had put her arm round Redmond's waist and was murmuring to him softly as she led him forward; he moved like a man in terrible pain, and she thought Elisande wasted her words, she didn't think he was hearing anything outside himself.

The floor they walked on – smooth and yielding still, *smoke made solid* she thought, and then didn't want to think about that any more, for fear that it might be only faith or ignorance that kept it so – rose underfoot much like the arch of a bridge, though Rudel surely hadn't meant it so literally. A long bridge, a high bridge: unless this was all magic, all deceit, they couldn't possibly be still within the walls of that squat tower. There simply wasn't the space.

The higher they climbed, the harder it was on Marron; and on Redmond too. She could see him stumbling at every step, almost, needing all Elisande's strength to keep him upright and moving. Julianne was doing something of the same service for Marron, though that boy had a stubbornness to him that was helping also. She'd changed from leading to dragging and from dragging to hauling, her shoulder under his for extra support. He breathed raspingly in her ear, set his jaw and swallowed any noise else, though she could read so much into his sudden pauses and hard silences, he might as well have cried aloud each time the searing pain ran through him.

She'd been wrong before; it wasn't fear doing this to him, to both men, working on them so savagely. *They have been hurt*, Rudel had said, and that was surely true of Redmond. But Marron only had a cut on his arm, albeit a bad one and slow to heal; he'd been running round the castle an hour since, and now he couldn't walk without assistance, could barely breathe without pain . . .

'Elisande,' she called ahead at last, 'what's *wrong* with them?'

'It's the Daughter,' the reply came back. 'It's not a safe thing, not for men, even when they're healthy. When they're not – well, you can see. Coming this close costs them greatly.'

'What is the Daughter?'

'It's what I came here for,' and she was still being oblique, and Julianne was not going to accept that any more.

'I know that. But why, what *is* it?'

'To us, to Surayon it's a terrible danger. It could be the weapon that destroys us all. That's why I came, to take it, to keep it safe where Marshal Fulke and his kind couldn't find it . . .'

She'd heard all that before. Foolish to expect any straighter answer, or any answer at all if she went on asking straight; so she tried a little subtlety. 'Why is it called the Daughter, the King's Daughter?'

'Because the King thought it a great joke. I guess he thought it was funny to leave it here, too, where Fulke or someone like him could lay their hands on it. That's why—'

'That's why you disobeyed your father and your grand-father, to come here,' Rudel's voice joined in suddenly, from the mists ahead. 'It wasn't likely that Fulke would ever have found his way in here, though. That door needed more than knowledge: it needed more than a woman's strength, but it needed a woman's voice. Which is as good a lock as any, in a Ransomer castle. Nor would Fulke have known what he had, even if he'd laid hands on the Daughter.'

'Redmond would have told him, in the end. Wouldn't you?'

'I might have tried to show him, what he had. I'd have enjoyed that. Where is it?'

'Here,' Rudel said.

*

Very like a bridge, the slope they climbed had levelled at last; if it weren't a bridge it might as well be a hill. Artificial or otherwise, the top of it flattened by man or god, she couldn't see the ground to guess and wasn't going to stoop and feel with her fingers. She truly didn't want to touch that resilience her feet still reported, another state of smoke. She thought it was a construct, a spell-made thing woven from art and charm and little more, and she was glad the bright colours of the air hid it from her.

The drifting banks and swirls of coloured fog were less vivid up here, or more diffuse, as though they'd climbed above the thick of it. There was nothing but darkening, purpling shadow above their heads, there was still only the fog's own luminescence to see by and she still couldn't – thankfully – see her feet; but she could see further ahead than before.

She could see past Redmond and Elisande, where they had stopped walking and stood still, only looking now; she could see Rudel standing beside some kind of plinth, the first solid matter she had seen since they'd walked through what had previously seemed so very solid, the old weathered wall of the tower.

A plinth, a pedestal – it might have been a broken pillar if it weren't so neatly cut off at what was chest height to a big man like Rudel, what would be near enough chin height to Elisande. It was angular and a little tapered, but still easily broad enough at the top to have been a pillar, to have taken some massive load entirely alone.

Like the air she breathed – and felt in her lungs, damp and heavy, so different from the clean dry breezes in the castle or the hot dusty air of the road – like everything that belonged in this place it had a colour, its own colour that she couldn't give a name to. Somewhere between blue and grey, she thought vaguely; only as soon as she thought either 'blue' or 'grey' it didn't shift but her perspective did, whatever label she gave it she knew instantly that she was wrong, so it must be the other colour, only that it never was.

It was a colour she'd know again, though, if ever she saw it in that other world they'd come from; and the shape of the thing she would know also, if ever she saw something similarly cut. She wondered what artist had figured this so finely, its angles so perfect, and from what rock, if rock it was . . .?

The plinth was more impressive than what lay upon it. That seemed to be a ball, a hard and chitinous ball of red ochre, about the size of a man's head. She frowned: something strange there. Even having so little to make a judgement on she was sure that there was a judgement to be made, and that it mattered.

It took a moment for her own thoughts to catch up with her; but of course, again it was the colour. Whatever it might be, this thing had a colour she could see and name outright; which meant that it had no right of place here, it was a thing of her own world that had been set where it was for some deliberate reason. As a safeguard, she would have guessed, even if she'd known no more.

'Here it is,' Rudel said, and he reached to pick it up—

—and stopped, at Elisande's uninhibited shriek.

'Don't *touch* it!'

He stilled, turned his head to look at her with his hands still half-cupped, ready for their burden, poised a finger's length away on either side.

'Why should I not touch it, Elisande?'

'You know why, don't be so stupid! It isn't safe for you . . .'

'It isn't safe for any of us.'

'For me it is. Of course it is, why not?'

'I will carry it, if it must be carried.'

Julianne startled, they all stared: that was Marron making the offer, and the surprise was only partly at his speaking at all when he'd been so silent for so long, turned in on himself. It was his voice that was shocking, thin and racked, desolate almost, as though he felt so lost already that no further danger could touch him.

'*No!*' Elisande again, a moment ahead of Rudel's own refusal. 'Haven't you been listening? No man can touch it safely, and you least of all. You shouldn't even have come this close, neither you nor Redmond. This is my task, it's why I'm *here* . . .'

'And I'm here to prevent you,' Rudel said flatly. 'You're too young to handle this. You betray yourself, even by thinking that it's safe for you to take it. The Daughter is subtle, where you are not. You deceive yourself, it will deceive you, and that is peril for us all.'

'Age does not equate to wisdom,' she spat back. 'Are you so sure of yourself, Rudel? You have no scratch on your body, you won't so much as prick your finger on a thorn between here and Surayon?'

They glared at each other across the plinth; Rudel did draw his hands back, but then he moved deliberately to place his body between Elisande and the object they were both so wary of.

Julianne disentangled her fingers from Marron's, and

walked slowly forward to see it more clearly. Its skin was textured, smooth in places and elsewhere oddly ridged, with crevices so deep she thought she could force a finger into them. It seemed to have sunk a little into the glossy surface of the plinth – not stone after all, she thought, but some substance as strange as its colour was strange to her – as though it were monstrously heavier than it looked.

Her veil hung around her neck, long since pulled free of her face. A formal length of silk, intended to satisfy the strictest brother, hanging almost to her waist: she slipped it off, held it a moment in her hands, then reached to wrap it around the red ball on the plinth.

It was Redmond who noticed first, who whispered a warning to the others, 'Watch, she has it . . .!'

Too late by then: she had already lifted the veiled thing in her hands, and was hugging it against her. Not heavy at all, oddly light it felt, for something so momentous; she had to grip tightly to feel sure of it, as she watched the little dimple in the plinth's surface rise and vanish.

'Julianne, don't . . .'

'Why not?' she challenged Elisande, all of them. 'Someone has to, or we'll stand here bickering till the world ends. If it's safe for you, it's safe for me also; if not, let me run the risk of it.'

'You don't know its dangers.'

'So I'll be all the more careful. It might carry dangers that you don't know, that you wouldn't think of,' that was what Rudel had meant, she was sure, 'so better if I have it, because I'll never be complacent.'

She wanted to show Rudel that she could be subtle in

her thinking; he didn't look happy, but he nodded slowly.

'You carry it, then. For the moment. That may be the best solution; I need my eye on the path we take from here, and having the Daughter in my arms would distract me. Redmond, come; we've lingered too long already. I'll help you. Julianne, behind me, but not too closely, for his sake; Elisande, you bring Marron.'

With his dispositions made he led them on past the plinth, though the decision in his voice was belied by his constant glances back. Julianne nursed the Daughter in her arms and followed; at her back she could hear Elisande cursing under her breath.

Like a bridge, like a hill the floor she walked on fell away from its summit, smoothly but uncomfortably steep. It was hard to keep her balance, when she had both arms wrapped around the Daughter – what *was* it, this thing that her companions were so mysterious about, that felt both hard-shelled and hollow, like the blown egg of some monstrous bird, only not so securely shelled? – and the billowing mists played constant tricks on her eyes.

She leaned back against the tempting drag of the slope and kept her head down, focusing on the burden she carried; and so almost walked into Redmond's back, was only alerted by his sudden gasp of pain. She jerked to a halt and scuttled to the side, remembering Rudel's warning, not to come too close to the ailing man. Only then did she lift her head, to see what had brought the men to such an unexpected stop. Rudel was confronting a great wall of shadow, a darkness that loomed through the fog, rising far above them and stretching away both left and right, barring their way absolutely.

'What is it?' she asked at last, after Rudel had stood silent for a full minute.

'I do not know,' he answered her.

A futile question, but she asked it anyway: 'You don't have any words, like before, that could pass us through?'

'No. I was expecting a gateway, into that other world I spoke of; and for that, yes, I have the words. But this is something entirely other, and I will not waste my breath on it. Some power has closed this way to us.'

'The same that blocked the door before,' Redmond whispered, 'though that was only an echo of this. That we could force; this, not.'

One more question, then, and again she was sure that she knew the answer already. Someone had to ask it, though. 'What must we do?'

'I am afraid,' Rudel said, 'I am very afraid that we must go back.'

Back over this mystical bridge, and back into the castle, escape denied a second time; back to where she was undoubtedly being sought by now, to where their small party could not hope to avoid discovery, however cautiously they slipped from shadow to shadow.

'What of the Daughter?' Elisande's voice came from behind her, oddly tight and anxious. 'Should we leave it where it was?'

'We dare not, now. If they take us, we could not hide the truth.'

That was certain; Julianne knew that she at least could not withstand the Order's questioners. She lacked Redmond's courage.

'What, then?'

'I am afraid,' he said again, and this time he did indeed sound frightened, 'that we must use it.'

'Rudel, no!'

'How else?' he demanded, and Elisande could find no answer.

20

The Devil Runner

Marron stepped – or shuffled, rather – into the courtyard, Elisande his prop and motive, her springy body compelling his. There was nothing more he could do, nothing he wanted except perhaps to stop, to lie down and never move again; but he was so drained he lacked the will even to do that much, that little, while her arm and shoulder and purpose nudged him forward.

She gasped, as they passed from gauzy mists to clear air; he felt her sudden rigidity, saw how her head turned to look back, to look up. He couldn't manage so much curiosity, but his head moved none the less in echo of hers, all his body tuned to imitation.

Behind him he saw the pale lights and twisted colours of that place they had come from, of which he had only dim and confusing memories – his companions' voices and a few of the words they'd said, pain and sucking and being passed from one girl to the other for a reason he could not now remember – and he saw those lights not fade but disappear. First they shone, and then there was a wall like a curtain, through which they shone; and then the wall was stone, and lights won't shine through stone so of course they didn't, and Marron stood in darkness.

Near darkness. Above him stars, and starlight all there was to see by; and slow he might be, in this as in everything, but he understood Elisande's startlement now. It had been midday when they'd entered the tower. That was when his blurring nightmare had begun, and he had little sense of the passage of any time at all during that period of reeling dizzy horror, but even he was puzzled. They'd gone in and not gone through as they had meant to do, and so had turned and come back – bearing something with them, a trophy, they called it the Daughter and Julianne carried it, which was why Elisande was all but carrying him – and so brief a foray, it could surely not have taken half a day?

Half a day and half the night to follow, he thought, seeing how the sky glowed a little silver above one black-shadowed wall; the moon had passed that way already.

Not only he was puzzled. Julianne and Rudel were murmuring together, a few paces off. Odd that Elisande hadn't abandoned him to join them, so strident she was with her opinions: he glanced down, and saw her fingering his tunic, scowling.

'I didn't notice in there,' she said, 'with all those lights and strangeness, nothing looked right or felt right either – but this is soaked, I saw it before the light went, all this side looked black. It's blood, isn't it? Your arm's been bleeding, ever since we went in there . . .'

'Has it?' It had been hurting, worse than ever it had hurt before, pain run rampant; he hadn't thought about bleeding. She was right, though, now that he reached with the other hand to feel. His tunic was saturated. He lifted his damp hand towards his face, and his nostrils filled with the warm copper tang of fresh-drawn blood.

'Take it off,' Elisande ordered. When he glanced aside at the others, 'Whatever's happened, whatever they choose to do, it can wait a minute. All those windows up there are shuttered, no one's overlooking us; and if we've lost so much time already, a little more can't matter. If you've lost so much blood already, a little more might matter a lot. Take the tunic off, and let me see.'

He tried, but couldn't do it. His belt came off easily one-handed, but the tunic was wet and heavy, clinging to his skin; and his one good arm, that felt heavy also, too much so to lift above his shoulder. The effort only made his head swim and the ground buck unsteadily beneath him.

Elisande helped in the end, undoing the ties and then tugging the tunic over his head. While he was in that deeper darkness, he heard her voice, snappishly, 'He's hurt. *Look . . .*'

The tunic fell free of him, and now he saw how it was that the others might look: a little ball, a star of golden light hung in the air above them, softly shining. By that light he could look too, and see how not only the bindings that held his arm but all his ribs and stomach were sheeted with blood.

While Elisande fought with wet knots, Rudel said, 'Take your time, and see to him properly. Things have changed, and my first thought is not perhaps the wisest route to follow.'

'I *told* you that . . .'

'Things have *changed*, Elisande! Somehow we've lost touch with time, in that tower. Even assuming that this is the same day, or the night that follows that day, the situation is completely different now.'

'How so?'

'Foolish of me, I know – but I wish you would think sometimes, before you speak. Julianne will have been missed, immediately after the midday office. The castle will have been searched thoroughly, and she not found; so they must have assumed that she had slipped away somehow, past the guards on the gate. They will have been scouring the country, and perhaps they are still. The gates may be open, parties coming and going; if we can get to the stables unnoticed, then five more riding out in brothers' robes might not be stopped or questioned.'

'Ifs and maybes,' Elisande said, but she said it with more relief than criticism.

'Quite so. But we may be lucky; and the alternative—'

'No. There *is* no alternative. You mustn't.'

'I may have to.'

'*No!* Think of your father . . .'

He sighed, and said, 'See to Marron, Elisande. And pray that we'll be lucky.'

After a moment, she nodded; her fingers went back to picking at knots.

At last, the bindings came loose. She slid Marron's arm free, and glanced at him anxiously. 'Does it hurt?'

'No,' he told her, truthfully; it felt nothing but numb now, no part of him, only a stiff and useless weight joined somehow to his shoulder.

She looked disbelieving, but turned her attention to the

bandage on his arm. That needed her knife slipped beneath, to cut it away; she threw the sodden linen to the ground and probed gently at the wound, which had burst open around its stitching.

'It's a terrible mess, but it's not bleeding much, not any more. I can bind it up with these,' the wet lengths of bandage that had bound it to his chest before, 'only then there'll be no way to support it . . .'

'It doesn't matter,' he said, speaking true again, albeit with an effort. It was hard somehow to care. 'I can't feel it anyway.'

Elisande sighed, nodded reluctantly, and began.

He was just dressed again, with the dull dead weight of his arm tucked under his belt, the best they could manage, when the sudden call of Frater Susurrus startled them all. Three slow strokes, that brought a brief smile to Rudel's voice.

'Midnight. We may be lucky after all. We'll wait ten minutes, let the brothers go to pray . . .'

Not all would go, that was understood; but those left on guard should be looking outward, a lesson learned at cost. At least the way to the stables ought to be clear.

At the second sounding of the bell, Marron's gaze drifted upward, looking for one darkened window among many. Sieur Anton should be in his room by now, if he wasn't out hunting a runaway bride . . .

One window among many was suddenly aglow, softly shining around a man's shadow as the shutters were thrown back. Marron stared, and felt his stare returned.

'Elisande,' a tight whisper, not his own, 'the light . . .!'

The little star vanished, plunging them into darkness, too late.

'We'll go,' Rudel said sharply. 'Now.'

And they did. But they went first without Marron, who stood staring up at that window even after the figure it framed had wheeled away and was gone; stood staring until Elisande came to pluck at his elbow, to hook her arm through his and drag him away, hissing in his ear, 'Do you *want* to face the questioners, and betray us all? Come on . . .'

They hurried through the darkness, or tried to. Marron struggled against his exhaustion and his distraction both, but Sieur Anton filled his thoughts, overriding even his companions' urgency. What had the knight seen, what was he doing now? Saying his prayers and letting them go? Or snatching up his sword and running, crying the alert, racing to intercept them . . .?

Marron couldn't answer the questions, nor escape them. He wasn't even sure what answers he wanted. His feet stumbled on broken flags, and he thought that was a sign: he was consumed by temptation, he wanted to push Elisande away and stay, abandon the others, just wait for his master to find him.

It was only his indecision that kept him moving, that and Elisande's tugging hands. Even at his awkward pace, they caught up soon; there was a glimmer of gold ahead, another little ball of witchlight, and it showed them Redmond shuffling along with one arm against the wall for support, while the other two waited at a corner further on.

As they all came together, the older man wheezed, 'I can't rush, I'm sorry. You could go on, and leave me . . .'

'Not alive,' Rudel countered grimly. 'And I haven't gone through all this to kill you now, old friend. We'd be wise to tread slowly, in any case: slow and without light, once we get into the open wards where the guards might look down and see us. Take my arm, we'll go at your speed. If any of you believes in prayer, pray to be lucky . . .'

They'd been lucky once, to have emerged from the tower at such a time, with night blanketing the castle and the bulk of the Order going to prayer; perhaps that luck had been outmatched by Sieur Anton's opening his shutters just then. The God's path ran through light and darkness both, and Marron had been taught that men's lives reflected that path. If there were any truth in that teaching, he couldn't say. He only followed Rudel as they all did, prayed not at all nor hoped neither; escape or capture, he saw no real hope for himself in either one and was simply too weary and too distressed to gift his share of hope to his companions.

Luck or the God or something else, pure chance perhaps brought them all the way through the main body of the castle unchallenged. No stray brothers, no sight or sound of the knight's rousing the guard; down the long passage to the stable-yard they came, and though he had none himself Marron could hear the dawn of hope in the way Elisande breathed at his side, he could feel it in her fingers where they lay more lightly on his arm now, urging but no longer compelling him on.

Out into the open they came, and a light breeze touched

them as they crossed the cobbles, like a promise of freedom. Elisande, he thought, believed it; he saw her head lift, her eyes shine in the starlight. No doubt she smelled the horses, saw herself and all her friends saddling, riding, down to the gate and away.

All he smelled was his own blood, and all he saw was darkness.

'No torches,' Rudel murmured, echoing his own thought. 'If there is a search, it's long gone from here and they don't expect it back this hour. Still, the gates may be open, against its return; or if not, the three of us can perhaps maze the guards, between us . . .'

Three of them? Three Surayonnaise, but only if Redmond were fit to work magic, and if that magic worked. If not, there were only two fit to fight, and one of them a girl. He didn't count the lady Julianne; stubborn and determined she might be, but she was trained to a court life, a lady's life, she couldn't be a fighter. Besides, she had that thing they called the Daughter, that most precious thing, and no other weapon visible. The Daughter was a weapon, he remembered, someone had said that, but she wouldn't have the skill to use it even if she knew how.

Elisande at least had a blade, and a sharp one; he thought she could probably fight. He thought she was very little of a lady under her fine dress, and that was Julianne's.

He thought he himself would be less use than the ladies, and Redmond the same. If the gates weren't open or the guards not susceptible to magic, he thought they were doomed, dead, death by burning it would be in the end; and by report, by inference a whole land would burn and be dead beside them, if the Daughter were the key to Surayon.

Best hope or pray, then, and he could do neither . . .

Neither hope nor prayer would have saved him anyway, he thought later: hope had always been his undoing, and it was prayer – other people's prayer – that betrayed him now.

Rudel stepped lightly through one of the high arched doorways into the great stable complex – *room for a thousand mounts* was the boast, and Marron believed it – and beckoned them in after. He swung the great doors closed at their backs and then lit another ball of witchlight, so that they needn't fumble in darkness for harness and horse.

And there by its shine, a warm fire that burned nothing, Marron and all of them saw men: a troop of men rising from their knees in an empty stall. Where they must have been saying the midnight office silently, or else had fallen silent when they heard footsteps in the yard, because they might have been praying but they were still on guard. And they had their swords ready at their sides, and there were too many of them already; and forth from the midst of them strode Fra' Piet with his shaved head gleaming like a hairless skull and his polished axe-head glinting at his side, and he was too many on his own.

Behind him, none of the brothers was hooded any more than he was, although they must have been at prayer; among the boys and men who crowded at his back, Marron saw Aldo and Aldo and no one else but Aldo.

Rudel drew his sword, and stepped forward. Marron reached for Dard as Elisande left him, but stayed with his hand on the hilt. What was the point? There were two dozen men confronting them; they couldn't make a fight of this, it was hopeless. Rudel must know that too . . .

And perhaps he did, perhaps he only had surrender on his mind, some hope of protecting the ladies at whatever cost to himself and his people. But Fra' Piet scowled, shielded his eyes from the wickedness of the witchlight that shone down on them all, made the sign of the God with his finger and lifted his axe; cried, 'Heresy! For your souls' sake, lads, be at them . . .!'

And leaped at Rudel with his axe swinging.

Blade met haft, with a shock that resounded through the stables. Rudel grunted, heaved, sent Fra' Piet reeling back; and as he staggered the sword's point sliced across his face, opening a gash from nose to ear.

Blood ran. Fra' Piet roared and came back, axe-head scything, glinting in the light; and his men came boiling after.

The first to reach Redmond overlooked Elisande at the old man's side, and felt her knife in his ribs before his slashing sword could bite home. He slumped and fell, and those behind him checked. A moment bought, no more: just time enough for Marron to hear Julianne's gasp, to see her glancing desperately about her, her arms still wrapped around the veiled Daughter.

Here was something he could do, at least, for what little good it might be worth. He lurched towards her, reached and snatched one-handed. With that thing taken from her, he thought she could run, she could escape this madness and survive.

He groaned to see her reach instead into her gown and

pull out a knife, a pair of knives. With his one arm clutching the Daughter against his chest, he wrenched his dead other from his belt and tried to stretch it out, to bar her way to the fight—

—and felt it come to burning, agonising life just as his other arm burned to match it. Crying out, staring down, he saw brief flame flow like liquid spilt across the thing he carried; and where it ran it left flakes of ash that had been the dense silk veil.

Pale grey ash, dark red beneath – and what was red was stirring, shifting, opening . . .

It could be the weapon that destroys us all, he remembered that, someone had said it when they were inside the tower. If ever they had been, if that place could exist within those walls.

Whatever it was, this Daughter, it was surely destroying him. His right arm was singed and flinching, twitching as the thing grew hotter, as cracks in its shell split wide; but his other, his left arm was beating blood again, throbbing to an alien pulse and every pulse was pain.

Well. If it was a weapon, let it bite on others, not on him. He lifted his head and twisted his body, cocked his arm as best he could, ready to throw as far as he could manage. It was very light, but oh, he was hurting; he didn't expect to toss it any distance.

Didn't need to. There was stillness all about him, the swarming brothers had fallen back; even Fra' Piet and Rudel had stepped away from each other, snared first by his cry and now by what he held, what he was doing with it. Only one brother was moving, plunging right at him, and Marron tried to hurl the Daughter full into his face.

Tried, and failed. It uncurled in his hand even as he threw it, and though his fingers burned on the skin of it, somehow it still felt less solid than it had, as if that hard shell were dissolving; and inside it was nothing but smoke, red smoke that hung in the air and suggested something living, an animal, an insect, a monstrous breeding of the two.

Beyond it, the black-robed brother stood as still as any of them now, only staring.

It twisted in the air like smoke in a breeze, although there was none; it turned and changed, drifted back to Marron, wrapped itself around his dripping arm and seemed not to vanish but to slip through the sodden fabric of its bandaging, seek out his running wound and pour through into his body, against the current of his flowing blood.

Or so it seemed to Marron. He felt it as an alien heat, a wave; but as a creature too, mindless but sensate, a stranger making a habitation of his body. Its rhythms jarred with his as it hammered through his flesh, followed the paths of his bones, licked and learned him from his toes' ends to the inside of his skull. It curled around his heart, he thought, and for a moment, for an eyeblink it seemed to rest, almost to sleep.

Then it was living and moving again, stretching to all the limits of his skin; but this time pulsing to the beat of his own heart, strange still but no alien now, melded with him.

He gazed at the world with hot eyes and saw it smoky, shaded red.

And saw Aldo right there, the brother before him, stilled no longer; saw him raise his sword and swing it with a scream of disgust and horror and ultimate betrayal.

Too late to draw Dard, if he could even have managed to grip the hilt with his burned and blistering fingers, if he could have wielded the blade against a lifelong friend gone so suddenly to foe.

Really Marron wanted simply to stand and wait for the blow to fall; he had a moment to make his choice and that was it, to die here and now at Aldo's hand. It didn't seem so bad. Worse for Aldo, who must survive this and dwell on it later, have Marron's lingering ghost infest his soul, whispers of a bonding broken for such petty reasons . . .

But that was his mind's choice, and not his body's. Instinct flung his arm up against the blade, no more than that: a gesture that should have proved useless, a moment of further life bought with a scream.

He flung his arm up, and it was his left, his bandaged, blood-soaked arm; and from the dark dank mass of bandage came a thread, a wisp of crimson smoke that frayed and fell like a veil between him and the shining blade in its death-stroke.

Gossamer-thin it was, but he felt it like his own skin, almost, a new and further limit to his body. He felt when and where the sword met it; and there was no jar, no shock of contact – why would there be, when steel meets smoke? – but neither did the blade hew through to find and hack his own flesh. The haze sparkled and spat, Aldo shrieked and dropped the hilt of his sword, which clattered and spun on the floor between them; its blade was gone, shattered, and Aldo's face was a horror, glinting grey where a thousand splinters had pierced his skin.

Marron stared, saw the grey turn to red as blood began to ooze, saw Aldo lift trembling hands to his blinded eyes;

and was almost relieved when that veil of smoke moved to swathe his once-friend's head, seeming to thicken as it went, making a mask that hid the sight from him.

Almost relieved, he was, and only for a moment.

He couldn't see it, but he heard Aldo's choke, and had a sudden dreadful picture of what might be happening within the wreathing smoke, how it might be pouring down Aldo's throat and filtering through all those tiny punctures in his skin; for a heart's beat he thought he felt Aldo's racing heart beating against his, all out of time and desperate.

Then there was a soft implosive sound, and Aldo's black habit ripped itself to rags and what had been inside it, what had been Aldo was a dark wet mess, a spill of blood and shreds of flesh flecked white with shards of bone.

Marron sobbed, once, a deep tug of loss and guilt and love betrayed that tugged at his gut but was only a gasp in his throat, he had no voice to sound it; and then the madness took him.

The Daughter, the wraith of smoke that killed, hung in the air before him; all around, people were stiff and gaping. Perhaps predictably, Rudel recovered first. He took one swift step forward, made one swift thrust, withdrew his sword cleanly. Blood followed the blade, and Fra' Piet fell.

Blood was the token. Aldo's blood hung heavy in the air, was rank in Marron's nostrils, a spray across his face; he closed his eyes, took one hard breath, and howled.

His own blood surged like rampant fire in his veins. He burned, all weakness seared from him; he opened his eyes again, saw the brother nearest to Elisande – *Jubal*, his mind supplied the name and an image, a memory, Jubal on horseback with a mace, slaying and slaying – and he flung up his hand to point, to pick his target out.

The Daughter needed no such gesture; it was moving already, flying to engulf the hapless man. Jubal saw it coming, had just time enough to start a scream: a scream that was cut off suddenly, horribly, as the red skein cloaked him.

Again that quiet sound, again the slumping catastrophe of ruined flesh. Marron's eyes were already moving on, finding another face he knew, a name and some history his mind could supply; but his thoughts were all on death, and destruction followed his gaze.

Vaguely he was aware of sobs and pleading, of brothers on their knees hurling their swords away, of his own companions shouting his own name; but nothing reached him, nothing could touch him now. Blood was all he sought, and blood he found. The floor ran with it, soaking his boots and overflowing the drains and still there was not enough, there could never be enough blood to drown Aldo's voice or wash his face away.

It was Elisande who halted him at the last, who seized his shoulders, shook him, slapped his face.

'Marron, enough! Stop this, *stop* it, you've done too much already . . .'

He stared at her and felt the Daughter come, knew how it loomed behind him. She must have seen it; there was terror in her eyes, but she said his name again though her voice trembled against her control, said, 'Marron, it's finished now, the fight is over. Do you hear?'

Over? He didn't understand. There were still two, three brothers living, penned in a stall there, he had names for them all; Rudel stood before them with his sword drawn, but it was Marron he was facing, his back turned to the black-robed men, and he added his own voice now.

'Marron, call it back. It is no longer needed. Take it into your body again, your blood will draw it.'

Slowly, slowly he lifted his bleeding arm – no pain now and the muscles were his own again, but still the blood dripped endlessly from his fingers – and there was a swirl of hot red mist around it, a diminishing eddy to his eyes and a fierce flood within him, a doubled pulse that was all to the same beat, all one.

He watched his fingers, saw when the blood stopped coming.

'No horses. This whole block is empty.'

That was Redmond, stating what must have been obvious to anyone who could remember why they had come here. Horses would have been maddened by so much blood, kicking and screaming, filling the night with their terror.

Rudel looked round from where he knelt, tying the brothers throat to ankle, using their own girdles to do it. 'There must be parties out looking for us; be glad they took all their mounts from here. These brothers will have been left to watch, I suppose, and tend the horses when they returned. We'll try another stable. Though it'll need the three of us,' *us Surayonnaise* he must have meant, 'to settle them, with the stink of this work on us all. Julianne, can you bring Marron?'

'I don't want to—'

'You must; above all, we can't leave him after this. Be easy, girl, he'll not harm you. Look at him, he couldn't even harm himself just now, which is something new for that boy. Follow us, but don't let him near the horses.'

Marron needed no girl's arm to support him, all his body throbbed with power and his mind was racing; but there was a gulf somehow, a broken bridge between the two, his will was missing. His ears followed the talk, but his eyes were still fixed on his fingers and what had dyed them; he carried Aldo and half the troop else on his skin, and their killer inside it. The Daughter, himself, no difference . . .

So it did after all take Julianne's tentative touch on his elbow to make him move, her hoarse and tear-stained whisper, 'Marron, will you come?' to draw him to the doorway; where they found the others not gone ahead but strangely waiting, Rudel standing to one side, Redmond and Elisande the other.

The reason stood in the yard there, alone and deadly: Sieur Anton, sword in hand.

Rudel had snuffed out his witchlight before he opened the door, but the stars were enough to mark the knight, to name him. For Marron, one star would have been enough.

Julianne's fingers clenched on his arm, but no need. Whatever happened, he would not call the Daughter forth again, not this time. Not for this.

No more had Sieur Anton called the guard. If he knew what had happened in the stable, he gave no sign of it. He said only, 'Forgive me, my lady, but I cannot allow you to leave. With my squire, or without him. Marron, come to me.'

A moment of bitter hesitation, again a sense of irredeemable loss; then two soft words, the final disobedience. 'No, sieur.'

'Well. So be it. You, sir,' and the sword picked out Rudel, who still carried his own weapon drawn, 'will you lay down that blade?'

'I will not.'

'Then I must take it from you.'

'You must try, of course.'

'May I know your name, before we begin?'

'You know it already, Sieur Anton. My name is Rudel.'

'Truly?'

'Indeed. Shall we . . .?'

Those polite manners hid the truth of it, but this would be a fight to the death. Marron thought someone should cry a warning, but there was only him to do it and he didn't know which man to warn. Both, he knew, could be lethal; the death of either one would be unbearable. He supposed he should hope for Rudel's victory, for the others' safety if not his own, but that must mean the knight's life and he could not, could not wish for that . . .

Neither did he have to. The two men approached each other cautiously, touched swords – and Sieur Anton swayed where he stood, lowered his point, lifted a hand to his head and fell without a sound beyond his sword's clattering on the cobbles.

Marron wanted to cry foul, to rush over and tend to his master, mourn his master if that were all that remained; but his body was still only tentatively his own, and when he made choices he made mistakes, people died. All he did was call weakly, 'What have you done?'

'Not I, lad,' Rudel answered. 'Him,' with a nod toward Redmond.

'Dishonourable, wasn't it?' the older man confessed, with the suspicion of a smile in his voice. 'But we couldn't afford a duel, out here in the yard. There are guards on those walls, they'd have heard it and come running. Oh, don't worry, he's not dead. Not hurt, even. I could take him unawares, with his focus all on Rudel; he's little more than sleeping, though his dreams will be a sore puzzle to him.'

'Enough now. Leave the knight; we need horses, and we need to be gone. Marron, you stay with Julianne, and keep out of sight; Elisande, Redmond, with me. You two, wait for my whistle.'

They waited, he and Julianne, standing against the wall's darkness; he saw how she would not meet his eyes, how her own moved incessantly, irresistibly back to the black arch beyond which he'd practised his black art, slaying and slaying for Aldo's sake, all of Aldo's brethren to give him company before the God.

'Please,' he whispered, 'don't be afraid of me.'

'Of you? I'm not. I'm afraid of *that*,' with a nod towards and through the arch, meaning the Daughter. The same thing, Marron thought, only she didn't think so, or else she didn't understand. 'So should you be.'

Oh, I am, he thought, though it wasn't really true; how could he fear something that beat to the rhythm of his own heart, that shared his skin and his intent? He drew breath to say so anyway, *oh, I am*, just to comfort her, but she forestalled him.

'No, I'm wrong,' she said flatly, 'I am afraid of you. Ignorance is always frightening, ignorance married to power is terrifying; and you don't know what it is any more than I do. Do you? You don't know what it can do, or what you can do with it . . .'

No, of course he didn't. He had a stranger in his veins, a clamorous, calamitous stranger; and there was nothing he could say to comfort her, he thought perhaps there was no comfort left in the world.

They waited, and no one came. The guards must all have been watching the shadows on the plains, listening to the wind, the castle a surety at their back and the only danger outside the walls.

They waited, silent now, no more to be said; and at last they heard a soft, summoning whistle, and moved obediently at its command.

Another archway, with the faintest glimmer of witchlight within to guide them; they went through into another stable, this one warm with the presence, the smells and sounds of horses.

There was the usual double rank of stalls, with a wide aisle between. In the aisle Rudel stood with two horses ready, saddled and harnessed. He had a hand hooked into each bridle and was murmuring quietly, soothingly as the big animals stirred and stamped. Behind him, Elisande and Redmond had charge of one horse each.

'There are five of us,' Julianne said slowly.

'Marron cannot ride,' Rudel told her.

'Yes, he can. I've seen him . . .' There was almost a smile in her voice as she said it, but puzzlement too, *of course he can ride, why not?*

'Not now. No horse would carry him.'

Marron didn't understand any more than she did, but he saw how both Rudel's horses shifted, shying away from him even at this distance. He stepped back automatically into one of the empty stalls, to leave a clear path for them out of the stable; behind him, someone screamed.

He twisted round, startled, and saw a tiny creature cowering atop the wooden division of the stall, at the very extremity of its leash. Only a monkey, the trader's monkey that had loved him so much before: he chirruped at it, and it screamed the louder.

'It must be the smell of blood on you,' Julianne said uncertainly.

'No,' a voice came from the deeper shadows at the back of the stall. A woman's voice, thickly accented; straw rustled as she stood, and he recognised Baron Imber's truth-speaker as the light fell on her appalling face. 'He is the Ghost Walker. I knew.'

'What does that mean?' It was Julianne again who asked.

'It means fear and wonder, it means he is blessed and cursed; animals see it as I do, but they only see the cursing.' She shuffled forward and touched his hand, straw in her hair and her eyes wide and white. 'I knew,' she said again.

Marron nodded. At his back he heard the passage of horses, and then Rudel's voice.

'Come, we must hurry. Julianne, I think we have landed

lucky; this should be your own palfrey, by the harness we found with her.'

'She is.'

'Lead her, then, and follow me. I have mazed her, just a touch; the skill is effective on horses also. Marron, you must go in front. Woman, return to your dreams; you have not woken tonight, do you understand me?'

She snorted. 'I am the baron's truth; me he believes.' She turned and went back to her concealing shadows, pausing to touch the monkey into shivering stillness, its eyes dark pools still fixed on Marron. He sighed for another loss, and slipped away.

Down towards the gate they went, down the slope of the tunnel and the steps beyond. Rudel would allow no lights here, for fear of shadows flying ahead to warn any watchers at the gate; Marron had to grope along the wall in darkness, his only guide the rag-muffled sound of hooves behind him growing louder to say when he was going too slowly.

The steps were easier; there was at least a slit of sky above him, a hint of starlight. He found then that he could see better than he'd expected to; perhaps it was only the change from utter black, but it seemed to him that there was a red cast to the world, as if the Daughter were lending him better eyes than his own.

A gentle hiss stilled him, on the bottom step. The gate lay just ahead, around a corner; he heard the horses halt, and Rudel joined him.

'This is your task, I regret, if the gates are closed,' the man murmured in his ear. 'We will mount now, and follow you. If they are open, then just run through; if not, you must break them down. Try not to kill, but unleash the Daughter.'

'I don't know how . . .'

'I do. Give me your arm.'

Your left arm, he meant. Rudel gripped it, pushed back the blood-soaked sleeve and cut the bindings away to expose sodden leather stitches and raw flesh. 'I am sorry, Marron,' he said, 'I never meant that this should happen to you, but there is no escaping it now. I have you; I must use you.'

And with that he unpicked the stitches with the point of his knife and slid the edge of it into and across the wound, not deeply, just enough to make it bleed again. There was no pain.

Smoke seethed up around the blade; Rudel squeezed Marron's shoulder, and pushed him lightly on.

His good hand gripping stone, the Daughter fogging the air in the corner of his eye – and the world gone darker, that red light lost to him – Marron peered around the corner. He saw torches and shifting shadows on the wall above the gate, and moving figures, men on guard; light also in the window of the gatehouse.

The gates were closed.

He took a breath and stepped out, glad at last of so much stain on his white tunic, making him only a small dark figure against a deeper darkness. He gazed at the gates, attacked them with his eyes, thinking nothing of their great weight or the massive bar that held them.

Where his eyes and his will went, there went the Daughter. He saw that thin smoke flow forward, felt the contact when it laid itself against wood and iron; flinched from the sudden cracking, snapping noises and the shooting sparks, and then stood gaping foolishly at the absence where the gates had been, the clear road beyond.

Cries of shock, of fear; men running to and fro along the wall, all of them staring outward still, looking for danger where there was none.

At his back the rush of hooves, Rudel rounding the corner, his mount shying and screaming, almost throwing its rider as it backed in terror from Marron.

'Run, Marron! Run on . . .!'

And Marron ran. He plunged through the gate, just as a lone iron hinge fell with a crash from its shattered post; he sprinted down the hill, fearful of an arrow in the back, but none came. Only he thought he heard a voice cry his name, 'Marron . . .!' and at the bend he chanced one glance over his shoulder, thought he saw a man in white standing solitary on the wall, staring after him.

Marron ran.

At first he ran alone; but soon the Daughter caught him, flowed back into his arm, filled his body with its strength and fire, gave its light to his eyes. Then he ran like a demon, he thought, faster than any horse would dare on this winding, perilous slope.

He had run like this with Mustar, wildly behind their cart, and ended in disaster. But Mustar was dead and Marron had become a thing that boy had feared, a devil perhaps; for sure he had a devil's luck tonight. His every footfall was firm and certain, he tasted the breeze and outran it; at the foot of the hill he waited, but he could have run on till dawn and after. He was all flame and smoke, he had forgotten what weariness was.

He waited, and eventually horses came: four horses, he saw and counted them from his distance as they followed the twists of the road above him. They came with more caution than speed, one led by another rider, Julianne he thought by Elisande; too slowly for his liking but fast enough, he couldn't see any pursuit yet however high he looked.

'Well done!' Rudel called, drawing his horse up some little way away. Marron made no move to come closer. 'Now we must ride. North and east. Can you run?'

Marron ran.

Daylight found them resting in a gully below a cliff, where the horses had sniffed out water: a muddy pool fed by a spring hidden deep in the rock, where it could escape the season's drought.

Marron stood by the cleft that had given them entrance, gazing out over the baked land. He needed no rest, nor the warmth of their little fire; neither the warmth of their company.

He could hear their talk, though, his ears as sharp suddenly as his eyes were sharper; and he listened, because they were speaking about him.

'. . . Why are his eyes red?'

No answer. She knew the answer. They were not his eyes.

'What is the Daughter?' Julianne again, this time in a different voice: exhausted but determined she sounded, demanding true and clear answers.

'The Daughter is a key, and a door.' It was Redmond who replied, his voice faint but his spirit renewed by flight. 'It leads to that same other world to which the tower holds a bridge. The bridge may be barred, but nothing can bar the Daughter.'

'But, it destroys things, it killed all those men . . .'

'Used properly, used fully, it will tear open a doorway from world to world; used only partially or in ignorance, it simply tears where it touches. Marron knows nothing.'

'That's why you called it a weapon?'

'No. Used properly, used fully, it could bring a thousand, ten thousand men marching into Surayon. *That's* why we call it a weapon; that's why we dared not leave it where it was. There are voices all across the Kingdom, crying war on Surayon. Fulke is response, not cause; but how if Fulke had found it?'

'Is it alive?'

'Not truly, or not alone. It has some mockery of life; but it enters a man and melds with him, and then, yes, it has his life and purpose, as he has its strength and powers. Which is why we dare not let the Order have Marron now, why we must take him out of Outremer altogether. The King called it his daughter because it marries itself to a man, and he meant to make that marriage. A bad joke, but a good marriage: it cannot be broken until the man is dead. The Sharai call him the Ghost Walker; traditionally, he is very hard to kill.'

'We were going to the Sharai,' Elisande, muttering.

'As Marron must, I think,' Rudel, 'to learn what it is that he has now, what he has become. I cannot teach him. Why were you going to the Sharai, Elisande?'

'Because the djinni sent us.'

'What? What djinni?'

'Wait.' Julianne again, interrupting sharply. 'We will tell you, but I want to know one more thing first. Who *are* you? Both of you? Not your names, I believe your names, but I am tired of your secrets.'

'Very well, then,' Rudel answered her softly, just as Marron spotted a blur of dust at the limit of his sight and a darker shadow within it, someone coming this way, a single man afoot. 'I am the son of the Princip of Surayon.'

Marron could even hear Julianne's gasp, so acute his hearing was.

She recovered quickly, though. 'And you, Elisande?'

'I? Oh, I am the granddaughter of the Princip of Surayon. I told you, he's a lovely man, you must meet—'

'Stop. Wait. You the granddaughter, he the son? What are you two to each other?'

'He's my father,' said coldly, and with such bitterness to it.